...

SAVING
SOPHIE

...

D0204564

• • •

ALSO AVAILABLE FROM
RONALD H. BALSON

Once We Were Brothers

...

SAVING
SOPHIE

...

Ronald H. Balson

St. Martin's Griffin

New York

SAVING SOPHIE. Copyright © 2015 by Ronald H. Balson. All rights reserved. Printed in the United States of America. For information, address St. Martin's Press, 175 Fifth Avenue, New York, N.Y. 10010.

www.stmartins.com

The Library of Congress Cataloging-in-Publication Data is available upon request.

ISBN 978-1-250-06585-8 (trade paperback)
ISBN 978-1-250-08129-2 (hardcover)
ISBN 978-1-4668-7286-8 (e-book)

Our books may be purchased in bulk for promotional, educational, or business use. Please contact your local bookseller or the Macmillan Corporate and Premium Sales Department at (800) 221-7945, extension 5442, or by e-mail at MacmillanSpecialMarkets@macmillan.com.

First Edition: September 2015

10 9 8 7 6 5 4 3 2 1

To my wife, Monica,
My rudder and centerboard

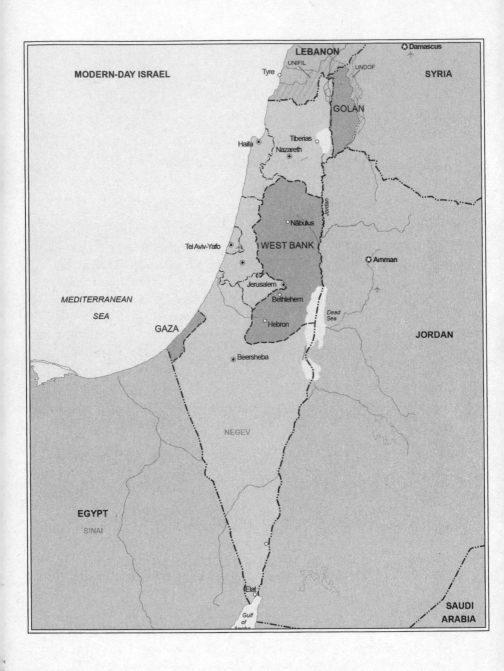

ONE

...

PELLETS OF RAIN AND snow, driven by bone-chilling February winds, splattered the windows of Chicago O'Hare's international terminal, occluding the view of those ticketed passengers trying to get a look at the tarmac. Intermittent gusts bowed the windows with an unsettling creak. Restless travelers paced the gate area, silently willing the gate agent to pick up her microphone and start the boarding process. After all, the flight from Chicago to Rio de Janeiro, from winter to summer, would take over twelve hours. Groans rumbled through the room as the beleaguered agent posted yet another delay. Sadly, she could offer no explanation other than "It's weather related."

A tall, thin man in a blue sport coat, white polo shirt, and cream-colored panama hat stood beside the Starbucks kiosk, a leather briefcase in one hand, his coffee cup in the other. He patiently scanned the crowd until his eyes finally settled on a young student seated cross-legged on the floor, an olive backpack by his side. An open laptop, plugged into the wall, rested on his legs. The man pulled out his cell phone and meandered toward the student.

"Yes, this is Dr. Sommers," the man said loudly into his phone, pausing directly before the student. "What's her heart rate? . . . Hmm. I see. Where's Dr. Goodman? Who's attending?" He nodded as he listened. "Has she been stabilized?"

Drawing an inquisitive stare from the student, the man continued in his high-decibel discourse. "I'm at O'Hare about to board a plane. . . . To Brazil, for Christ's sake. Isn't Dr. Withers available?" Pause. Then calmly, with a sense of resignation: "No, no, I understand completely. . . . Yes, I'll cancel the trip. I'll be there in an hour."

He ended his call, shook his head, and looked down into the face of the curious young man. "There goes my trip to Rio. I've been planning this for over a year, but when the congressman's wife has a heart attack, all bets are off."

The explanation drew a sympathetic response. "Sorry for you, man. Guess you'll have to go another time."

Sommers shrugged and gazed at the passengers who were finally lining up to board. "Want to fly first-class?" He held out his boarding pass. "You can have my seat. I sure as hell can't use it."

The young man shook his head. "They won't let me take your seat. I have a coach ticket."

"I purchased this seat, I don't see why it should go empty. We've already gone through security. We've shown our passports. The flight attendants don't know what I look like. Take my ticket. When you get on the plane, tell them you're John Sommers. Who would know the difference?"

The young man examined the boarding pass. Seat 4A. "Do you think I can? Do you think it'll work?"

"I don't know why not. Go for it."

"Hell yeah." The young man bounced to his feet, taking the boarding pass. "Thanks a lot, Doc." Sommers watched him scan the boarding pass and proceed down the first-class Jetway.

Sommers exited the international terminal and hailed a green-and-white taxi. The laminated license identified the driver as Delroy Johnson. Sommers set his hat, attaché, and overcoat on the seat beside him.

"Where to?" the cabbie said.

Sommers exhaled. "I'd like to go to the Milwaukee airport," he said quietly.

The cabbie nodded and put the car in gear. "Up on Milwaukee Avenue, you mean," he said over his shoulder. "Now they callin' it the Chicago Executive Airport. Used to be Palwaukee Airport. That's in Wheeling, you know, 'bout fifteen minutes, but you have to pay meter and a half."

"No, Delroy," Sommers answered as the cab pulled away from

the terminal. "I mean Milwaukee. The city of. General Mitchell International Airport."

Johnson slowed his cab and pulled to the side. "You serious? I don't go that far. I'm a Chicago cab. Shit, man, you at the airport. You could fly up there."

Sommers leaned forward. "Delroy, I just want a nice comfortable ride to Milwaukee. It's worth five hundred dollars to me. Will you take me?"

"Well . . . since you put it that way. You crazy, but for a five spot, just sit back and relax, and let Delroy do the driving."

Eighty minutes later, Delroy glided to a curbside stop at Mitchell International. His passenger, who had slept most of the way, handed him a roll of bills. "Thank you, Delroy. You have a nice day."

"Hey, thanks to you too, mister," Delroy called, leafing through the bills, but Sommers had disappeared into the terminal.

With boarding pass in hand, Sommers walked directly to the security line. He shuffled forward and handed a Kentucky driver's license and his boarding pass to the TSA agent, who examined them and smiled.

"You have a pleasant flight, Mr. Wilson," she said.

Sommers nodded, checked the departure board, and walked to his gate. His flight to LA was lightly booked. Sommers placed his leather case carefully into the overhead bin. It held a laptop, a trifold wallet filled with assorted credit and debit cards, and a change of clothes. On this day, at this fork in his road, that was everything he'd need. He took his seat by the window and watched the ground crew.

NINETY MILES SOUTH, IN the brick-and-steel canyons of Chicago's Loop, a group of businessmen and their attorneys gathered to celebrate the consummation of a business deal—Leland Industries had acquired the assets of Kelsen Manufacturing Company. The mood was ebullient. Champagne flowed. All of the tedious negotiations, the threats, the maneuvers, the posturing, were now history. The deal was sealed. The air was light.

Walter Jenkins, managing partner of Jenkins & Fairchild,

Attorneys at Law, stood by the conference-room windows with his client, Victor Kelsen. Jenkins was tall, in his midsixties, gray at the temples, and elegantly dressed. Kelsen, a few years younger, was stocky, with a workingman's physique. Plainly dressed in a suit from a department-store rack, Kelsen's understated appearance belied the wealth he had amassed in his business career.

The morning storm had lifted, and the setting sun painted long shadows in the federal plaza below. A visual metaphor, Jenkins thought—the end of days for Kelsen Manufacturing.

"Why, Victor, you're actually smiling," Jenkins said. "I haven't seen that in quite a while."

"Well, why shouldn't I? I got a good price for my company, and now some other sucker can worry about the packaging market." He gestured across the room at a group of young men, uniformly dressed in two-button shades of charcoal. "Look at them all, Walter. Clinking glasses, laughing and joking. All my high-priced executives. So pleased with themselves to receive bonuses on the sale of a company they had no part in building. And I ask you—how long will that bonus money last any of them? These guys just don't get it. Leland Industries doesn't need any of them and won't keep them past next Christmas. And soon they'll all be sending out résumés in our dandy economy."

"Oh, they're bright people, I'm sure they'll land on their feet," Jenkins said. "Anyway, are you taking Helen out to celebrate tonight?"

"Nope. The Deacons are playing Northern, and Helen hates basketball. But I haven't missed a home game in years and I'm certainly not going to start now, just because I sold my company."

"And cleared ninety-six million dollars." Jenkins reached across the table, grabbed a bottle of champagne, and offered to refill his client's glass, which Kelsen declined with a shake of his head.

"Ninety-six before taxes, Walter. Listen, I got to get out of here. I'm sick of looking at these guys. It took me thirty years to build my company. On my back. These MBA types think they bring something to the table. They bring nothing. It's guys like me who built this country, not a bunch of full-of-themselves finance majors with six-figure salaries."

Jenkins winced. "Yes . . . well . . . I get your point, Victor. But you won't have to put up with that any longer. What time's your game tonight?"

Kelsen checked his watch. "Seven thirty, but I usually go early." He retrieved his wool overcoat from a rack and Jenkins held it for him as he slipped his arms into the sleeves. "Most importantly, Walter, what time do I get my money tomorrow?"

"We expect the closing escrow to disburse about eleven A.M. I'll have Sommers over there first thing in the morning. I assume that Harrington will be there as well?"

"He'd better. That's why I pay him. That's another thing I won't miss. Paying my good money to a gloom-and-doom CFO."

Jenkins took a sip of his champagne. "Speaking of your CFO, I haven't seen Harrington at all this afternoon. Isn't he going to join the bunch for dinner?"

Kelsen shrugged. "As far as I know. I expected him to be here by now. It's not like him to miss a free meal. But since you mention it, I haven't seen your man Sommers either." He feigned a chuckle. "They're probably both sitting in a bar somewhere discussing balance sheets and tax write-offs."

Jenkins smiled and patted Kelsen on the shoulder. "It takes a lot of work to sell a three-hundred-million-dollar company, and they've been the men in charge. I'm sure they'll be here soon. Relax."

"I'll relax when the escrow closes and I get my money. See you at eleven tomorrow," Kelsen said, and left.

Two

...

SOMMERS AWOKE ABRUPTLY AS the plane's wheels bounced hard on the LAX runway. He shook the cobwebs from his head and checked the time. Barely an hour to make his connection to Honolulu. He lifted his carry-on from the overhead bin and stretched his cramped muscles. Emerging from the Jetway, his hat pulled low over his forehead, he paused to survey the people standing at the gate. What would he do if they were already here? The FBI. The LA police. Waiting to greet him. Not a thing, he supposed. Not a thing he could do.

He exhaled a sigh of relief when no one paid attention to him. Head down, avoiding eye contact with someone who might later say, "Oh, yes, Officer, I saw that man getting on the flight to Hawaii," he ambled slowly through the crowd and made his way from Terminal 4 to Terminal 6, stopping to buy a newspaper and a couple of bottles of water. Taking a seat in a back row at Gate 16, he slouched and buried his face in the financial section.

Boarding could not come soon enough for Sommers. He had read the same page over and over, never managing to digest a single word. When the flight was finally announced, he merged into line with a noisy tour group and smiled at the gate attendant as she took his ticket, though he failed to respond when she said, "Have a pleasant flight, Mr. Wilson."

A bittersweet memory stopped him as he stepped onto the Jetway. The last time he'd boarded a plane to Hawaii he was with Alina and Sophie. They were just beginning their first family vacation. Back then, he held hands with his giddy four-year-old, who bounced along, full of glee, bursting with joy. Back then, he and Alina had smiled so proudly as Sophie skipped along beside them. But that was back then.

His window seat was toward the rear of the plane, and for a brief time the adjoining seat was vacant. How fortunate, he thought, as he set his panama hat on the empty seat and took out one of his water bottles. But as the doors were closing, a young woman, the last to board, rushed down the aisle and stood before his row.

"I think that's my seat. Twenty-two B?"

Sommers nodded, rose, placed his hat on his attaché in the overhead, and slid back into his seat.

"Must be a pretty special hat," she said, smiling. "It almost had its own seat all the way to Hawaii."

Sommers returned the smile. He watched the belated traveler compose herself, organize her knicks and knacks, and settle into her seat. She was obviously of Polynesian lineage, with smooth, gentle features and rich, black hair. He judged her to be in her late twenties or so, maybe six or seven years younger than himself. Her skin was tanned, but her face was flushed and her forehead was slightly moist, which Sommers attributed to her dash to catch the plane.

"I almost didn't make this one," she said, still breathing hard. "Bad traffic on the 405." She slipped her magazine into the seat pocket, took a series of deep breaths, and eyed the bottle of water in Sommers's hand.

He caught the look. "I have an extra bottle, would you like it?"

"Oh, God, yes. You're a lifesaver."

"Are you all right?" Sommers said, handing the bottle to her.

She nodded. "Winded, that's all. I only had a few minutes."

Sommers thought of other things he could say to keep the conversation going, but decided against it. Perhaps at another time, in another part of his life, it would have been nice to start up a conversation with this pretty Hawaiian girl, pass some of the next four or five hours engaged in pleasant small talk and maybe even catch up with her on the island. But given the present circumstances, he thought it best to say little and retain his anonymity. It would be safer if she didn't remember him.

The preflight video started and the plane pushed back from the gate. Sommers let his eyes stray every now and then. She was leafing through her magazine when she caught him in the middle of one of his glances. "Malani," she said with a smile, and held out her hand.

"Jack," Sommers answered, shaking her hand and immediately sorry that he'd used his real name.

"First time to Hawaii?"

"Yes," he lied. "I'm looking forward to it."

"Well, you'll love it. I've lived there all my life."

Sommers buried his attention in a magazine. Malani took out her earbuds, untangled them, and was soon lost in her music.

Three

...

I N THE JUDEAN HILLS, south of Jerusalem, in the ancient city of Hebron, a group had gathered to celebrate a wedding. The mid-winter weather favored them with kind temperatures and soft desert breezes. Though a few of the men wore black coats and wide-brimmed Borselino hats, most were dressed in white, short-sleeve shirts and woven kippot. Women, young and old, surrounded the bride, whose train was carried by two young bridesmaids. A small group of musicians played traditional music as the joyful assembly danced its way up the stone pathway.

The celebrants were not a part of the small community of Jews who lived in the H2 sector of Hebron or the seventy-five hundred or so who resided in the adjacent West Bank town of Kiryat Arba. The wedding party had traveled from Jerusalem by tour bus to witness the exchange of vows at the Tomb of the Patriarchs, Ma'arat HaMachpelah, which Abraham purchased from the Hittites thirty-seven hundred years ago for four hundred silver shekels, and where he, along with Isaac, Jacob, Sarah, Rebecca, and Leah, are buried.

The young groom's eyes were locked upon his betrothed and a broad smile lit his youthful face. The nervous bride breathed deeply, unable to exhale, as she carefully stepped her way toward the flowered canopy. While the party wound its way toward the sand-colored walls of the holy shrine, a black sedan, its windows down, approached from the south. Suddenly, a clap was heard. Then another. The startled bride grabbed her side, her legs buckled, and she fell to the ground. Crimson slowly seeped through the fabric of her white lace dress as her stunned entourage hustled her to the shelter of the security hut.

More shots. Three men fell. Rivulets of blood filled the crevices of the large stone blocks on King Herod's walkway. Guards fired at the sedan as it sped up and disappeared around the corner. Shrieks and cries from the wedding party drew some of Hebron's residents to their windows.

The young bride, bleeding badly and suffering from shock, was carried to the tour bus and laid upon the seats. "She's losing too much blood," an elder said. "She won't make it back to Jerusalem."

A woman pleaded, "We need a doctor! Someone help us!"

One of the security guards spoke up. "I know of a doctor, but he's Palestinian. Dr. al-Zahani. He lives just north of here in the Arab sector. Not too far."

"Please," the woman cried.

The bus traveled several blocks, through the military checkpoint, to a large, walled compound in the north quadrant of the H1 sector. The guard jumped from the bus, ran to the gates, and pressed the buzzer several times. He was soon met by a powerfully built man whom he addressed as Bashir. After a short and excited discourse in Arabic, Bashir nodded and opened the mechanized gates. The bus pulled in and the unconscious bride was carried to the front door.

Dr. Arif al-Zahani, tall, slender, with a gray goatee and white hair, neatly trimmed, came to the entrance. "What is this, Bashir?"

"A girl has been shot, *Sayyid*," he said with deference, pointing to the bride, who was carried in the arms of her groom and two others.

Al-Zahani stared at the security guard and the group. His gaze was stern and unfriendly.

"Doctor, please help us," the groom pleaded. He spoke in Hebrew, but the urgent plea was unmistakable in any language.

Al-Zahani finally nodded. "I will treat the woman in the guest room," he said to Bashir. "Keep my grandchild in her bedroom."

He led them down the hall, where the men laid the bride gently down upon the bed. Al-Zahani surveyed the wound. "You must all wait outside."

Al-Zahani worked for over an hour. When he emerged from the

guest room, he spoke dispassionately, addressing his remarks in Arabic to the security guard. "She survives. But she has lost much blood and needs hospital care. You would be well advised to take her to an Israeli hospital."

The groom, his black coat splattered with blood and dirt, stuck out his hand. "Thank you so much, Doctor. God bless you. I will pay you whatever you wish, but no amount can ever repay the kindness that you have shown."

Al-Zahani declined the hand. "There is no charge," he said through the interpreter. "Take her now to the hospital. Do not delay."

When the group had left, al-Zahani turned to Bashir. "The sheets, the pillows, the bed itself. Dispose of it all."

FOUR

• • •

WALTER JENKINS SLAMMED THE handset onto the telephone cradle. He'd been trying to connect with Sommers since early afternoon. It wasn't as if this were an off day. Sommers, who was J&F's top transactional partner and the point man on a $300 million deal, was AWOL. He was seen at the title company all day yesterday, monitoring the escrow submissions and doing what needed to be done to transfer all of Kelsen's buildings, machinery, vehicles, and other assets to Leland. And then he doesn't show up at the office. He doesn't show up for cocktails. Now Jenkins was getting damn tired of hearing Sommers's voice-mail message.

Jenkins walked down to the fifteenth floor. "Where the hell's Sommers?" he said to a secretary who was getting ready to leave for the night.

"I don't know, sir, people have been trying to reach him all afternoon."

"Do you have any way of contacting him that I don't know about?"

"I have his cell phone number." She shook her head. "But I've tried it. No answer. No answer at his home either." She shrugged. "Sorry."

Jenkins sighed. "Well, I guess there's nothing else I can do. I'm sure we'll see him tomorrow morning when the escrow funds disburse. We'd better."

"He may be out with Mr. Harrington. Some of the Kelsen people have been calling and asking if Mr. Harrington was here."

Jenkins shook his head. "They can't find their guy either. Isn't that just peachy."

V ICTOR KELSEN ARRIVED AT St. Joseph's Arena as he customarily did, pulling up to the side entrance in his black Bentley sedan. His driver quickly jumped out of the car and circled around to open the back door. Deacon students in their coats and hoodies huddled on the sidewalk in the frigid evening air waiting for the arena doors to open.

The usher guarding the media entrance smiled. "Good evening, Mr. Kelsen." The usher stepped aside and handed Kelsen a program. A fixture at the arena, Kelsen could come and go as he pleased. Same center-court seat for the last fourteen years—two rows behind the Deacons's bench. Kelsen was the athletic department's most revered booster. He shook several hands on his way into the arena and arrived at courtside during warm-ups.

Deacon players in their blue satin cover-ups were spread around the hardwood for the pregame shootaround. A few players nodded or waved at Kelsen. Two stopped their practice shots to give him a fist bump. Kelsen wandered over to the baseline where Darius McCord was swishing corner jumpers. "Looking sweet, Darius." Kelsen said.

Darius smiled a little. "Yes, sir, Mr. Kelsen."

"I think I'm going to see quite a show tonight. Nobody at Northern can guard you."

Darius never lost his modest smile. "I don't know about that, Mr. Kelsen." He spun to his left, pushed off the floor as if he were weightless, and arced an eighteen-footer softly through the bottom of the net.

Kelsen made his way to his section as the arena doors opened and the students scrambled for their seats. The band fired up, the cheerleaders bounced on the sidelines, the JumboTron came to life, and the arena's energy level began its rocket climb.

A portly man in a Deacons sweatshirt sidled down the second row to the seat next to Kelsen. He set his cup of soda in the holder, took a flask out of his pocket, and dumped a shot or two into the cup. "Hey, Vic, whaddya know? Good one tonight, huh?"

"Mismatch."

"What's the line tonight?"

"Eleven, last time I looked, but that's a soft spread. No way Northern contains Darius. More like eighteen."

"Agreed."

THE FLIGHT WAS MIDWAY over the Pacific, dinner had been served, and the cabin lights were dimmed. Sommers had consumed three little bottles of airplane wine and was finally relaxed enough to nod off.

Alina was being coy. Her voice was soft and alluring, her dark eyes enchanting. Her singsong accent made him chuckle. *Zhock,* she called him. She rested her head gently on his shoulder, her silken, black hair smooth upon his face. A hint of her floral perfume filled his senses. "I love you so much," he said.

"Sshhh, you'll wake the baby," Alina said.

He leaned over to kiss her and she shifted her weight, jostling him a bit.

Sommers opened his eyes. Of course, it wasn't Alina. He would never hold Alina again. It was his tardy seatmate Malani, who had slumped to the side, over the armrest, her head settling softly on his shoulder, her hair brushing his neck. She was sound asleep. *And I almost kissed this stranger,* he thought. *That would've been challenging to explain.*

The two sat just that way for the next half hour, her head against his body, her breathing slow and deep. Though his muscles were beginning to cramp, Sommers sat very still. His legs were asking to be stretched, and a walk up and down the aisle would have done him good, but then, he'd have had to wake her up. For as long as it would last, he'd let this woman's physical closeness touch off pleasant memories of Alina. Pleasant but sad. Yet, it calmed him. Comforted him. He leaned his head back, shut his eyes, and gave himself to his memories.

Back then, they had been off to Hawaii on their daughter's first airplane trip. As the plane droned on, Alina and Sophie had busied themselves looking at pictures of the Hawaiian Islands in a magazine. Sophie's boundless and enchanting excitement drew the smiles of the neighboring passengers. "She is *so* cute," Jack heard one woman say, and he thought his chest would burst with pride. Soon, Sophie had dozed off. Alina snuggled next to Jack, and he put his arm around her shoulders and drew her close. Whatever Hawaii had in store, paradise could be no sweeter.

Now, suddenly, the intercom barked, "Ladies and gentlemen, the captain has turned on the seat-belt sign. There's some rough weather ahead. Please return to your seats and fasten your seat belts until the turbulence has passed."

Malani opened her eyes and took stock of where she was—her head on Jack's shoulder, his arm around her. She looked up at Jack and giggled.

"Oh, I'm so sorry," Jack said, quickly lifting his arm. "I . . . I was sleeping and dreaming and . . . I'm so embarrassed."

"I'm the one who should be embarrassed. I leaned on you. You should have awakened me or pushed me back in my seat."

From there, a conversation gained traction. He said he was traveling on business and was thinking about finding a place on the islands. She said her family was deeply rooted in the islands, they'd been there for generations. She was currently vice president for *Hawaii Magazine,* a periodical owned by her family. She handed a business card to Jack.

"Honolulu is quite a fascinating place to live," she said. "Hawaii has over a million residents and over eight million visitors every year—every color, size, and shape. It's the crossroads of the Pacific. No matter who you are, it's the ideal place to melt into the mosaic of humanity."

"Very poetic," Sommers said, as though the idea had not occurred to him.

She turned her attention back to her music, and Jack returned to his thoughts. The time passed slowly for him, and eventually the plane touched down. "I hope you find the right opportunity, Jack," Malani said as she walked down the Jetway. "It was nice meeting you. You have a comfortable shoulder."

"Thank you," said Sommers with a short laugh.

Evening rain splashed hard against the banana leaves as Sommers followed the covered walkway to the main terminal. Tired and hungry, his joints aching from his long journey, he merged into the crowd moving toward the baggage carousels. The fragrances of orchids and tropical foliage filled the hall but did little to calm his nerves.

Once again, Sommers scanned the baggage area for law enforcement: men with large chests and broad shoulders, in blue blazers, their hands clasped before them, their feet spread apart, eyeing the arriving passengers, waiting to spot Sommers and take him into custody. But there were no such men and Sommers exhaled another sigh of relief.

Hello again, Hawaii, he said to himself. *A place of happier times long ago. Now, you're just a spot for me to hide at the other end of the world.*

Without pausing, he walked past the baggage area, through the automatic doors, and directly to the taxi stand.

"Two sixty-four Kaiulani Avenue, please."

The cabdriver nodded and drove east in the direction of Waikiki.

I N HIS TRUMP TOWER condominium, Dan Gibson started worrying about his partner, Denny Harrington. It was 1:30 A.M. It wasn't like Denny to be late and not even call. He'd never done that before. Gibson got out of bed, slipped on his robe, and went to sit vigil by the living-room window, not that he could identify anyone from the fifty-third floor. He stared at the city lights below. Then he called Harrington's cell for the third time.

"Hi, this is Denny. I can't take your call right now, but . . ."

"Really, Denny," Gibson said aloud as he hung up. "I know you had a gigantic transaction and a celebration dinner, but do we have to be so inconsiderate?"

At two he called again. And at three. At four he called the police.

FIVE

...

"COME, MY PRECIOUS LITTLE one, it is time for madrassa."

"No, Jaddi, please. I'm not going, I hate the school," said the little girl, her arms defiantly folded across her chest. She stuck out her chin. "I want to go home."

Squatting before his granddaughter, his hands gently on her shoulders, he spoke softly. "Oh, my little *hafiida*, we have spoken of this so many times. This is now your home. Your Jadda and I love you very much." He smiled warmly and raised his eyebrows. "And you must go to school."

The little girl, with fair skin and light hair, stood before her caramel-skinned grandfather and tightened her lips. "This is not my home!" She stomped her foot. "And I'm never, never going to that school."

Dr. Arif al-Zahani stood and slowly shook his head. "You are six years old. All children go to school. They do not stay home. And we will not argue further."

Tears formed in her eyes. She lowered her head. "They make fun of me."

"Who makes fun of you?"

"Everybody. I don't know what they're saying, I can't speak Arabic. I don't know their games. They laugh at me. I hate them all."

"Bashir will talk to your teachers. We will see that no one makes fun of you. Now, get ready for school and Bashir will walk with you."

"I don't want to wear a hijab."

"Why not? It is just a scarf, and a very pretty one."

Tears streamed down her cheeks. "I want to go home, Jaddi. I want to see my daddy. I want to be in my own room."

Al-Zahani patted her on the head, turned, and walked out, leaving the little girl sitting on the marble floor, her head hanging low against her chest. She rocked back and forth, clutching tightly to her stuffed bear. The brown bear was dressed in a blue sweater with a large orange *C* in the middle. She sat on the floor, cheek to cheek with her bear, and sobbed. Her bear understood. He was the only one who cared.

In the next room, her grandfather called for Bashir. The solid, broad-shouldered man in his tan sport coat came into the room. His walk had purpose, his movement efficiency, his bearing befitting a calm, strong constitution. He was not a man to be trifled with. Bashir bowed slightly. *"Sayyid?"*

"Please walk my granddaughter to school. Speak to the headmistress. Tell her I am displeased with the little one's integration into the classroom. The children are unkind. She tells me they make fun of her. We must see that such conduct stops immediately."

Bashir nodded. "I will talk to the woman."

The large man walked quietly into the library and held his hand out for the little one. She slowly rose and put her tiny hand in his.

Bashir looked down at her and gently said, "We must leave the bear at home."

"His name is Sweetness," she said quietly.

He smiled and sat Sweetness on the shelf. Hand in hand, they left together.

JENKINS CUSTOMARILY ARRIVED AT his office early, but on this day, a day when his firm was in charge of closing the book on a $300 million sale, he was especially early. And he had an uneasy feeling. All his voice-mail messages to Sommers had gone unreturned. He paced the office and made a few more attempts to reach him.

"Damn it, Jack," he said to the ringing phone. "Get up. Answer the phone." Finally, at eight thirty, he summoned Gil Roberts, a junior partner.

"Gil, you were seconding Sommers on the Kelsen deal, right?"

"Somewhat, but Jack wanted to handle the deal himself. I prepared some papers for him, but that's about all. I know the deal pretty well, if you have a question."

"My question is, 'Where's Jack?' So far, I've been unable to reach him. In the event he's sick or something and doesn't come in, would you make yourself available to tie up any loose ends and make sure everything goes smoothly this morning?"

"Of course, Mr. Jenkins. All of the deposits have been made. It's pretty routine."

Gil went to Sommers's office to retrieve the file and prepare for the closing. Sommers's papers and files were neatly arranged in stacks. A few personal items were here and there: a paperweight made from a painted rock, a marble bookend, and a framed picture of Sommers standing on a beach, his left arm around the waist of his wife and his right arm resting on the shoulder of his curly-haired, lithesome child. He picked up the photograph. Sommers and his wife were in their swimsuits. Jack, a head taller than his wife, was still fit from his high school tennis days. Alina was lovely. She had smooth gentle curves, long dark hair, well past her shoulders and parted in the middle. A classic beauty. Dazzling in her two-piece suit. They made a handsome couple. Sophie, her nose scrunched up as she squinted in the sunshine, held a blue plastic bucket and shovel in her hands. *The perfect family*, thought Gil. *What a shame.*

Gil found the Kelsen closing papers stacked on the shelf over the credenza. He thumbed through them. Everything seemed to be in order. He picked out the unsigned copies of the two bank releases. Later that morning, when the title company received the signed originals, evidencing full payment of Kelsen's loans, the balance of the purchase price would be disbursed to Kelsen.

Midwestern Title, the escrow company selected to close the transaction, had wire-transferred funds to pay off each of the bank loans the previous day. When Midwestern received the signed releases, it would disburse $96 million to Victor Kelsen. All neat and simple. The parties estimated that the payoff would occur no later than 11:00 A.M. At 10:00 A.M., Gil called Jim Ellis at Midwestern to make sure everything was in place.

"Jim, it's Gil Roberts at Jenkins and Fairchild. Can I confirm that you are prepared to disburse Kelsen's proceeds?"

"I thought Jack Sommers was handling this deal."

"He is. I'm just helping out. Are we all set to disburse?"

"Not quite. I've got First Bank's release in front of me, but not the one from Exchange. They've yet to send over their signed release."

Gil knew that Exchange Bank was owed $88 million to pay off Kelsen's commercial loan and would sign the release as soon as they got the money.

"Do you know whether Exchange received its loan payoff?" Gil asked.

"I'm sure it did. I wired the money first thing yesterday morning, the same time I wired First Bank's, but we don't have the Exchange release of lien yet."

"Not good. Kelsen's money is supposed to be disbursed to him in an hour. Do you have any idea why there's a delay?"

"No. But I know they received the wire. I have the Fed confirmation number."

Gil ended the call, thumbed through the documents, and found the telephone number for the Exchange loan officer, Greta Dahmshultz.

"I have your release all set to go," Greta said, "but we haven't received our funds yet."

"Are you sure? I've been told the money was wired to you yesterday morning," Gil said. "Ellis told me he had the Fed number."

"I'm sorry, but the money hasn't been credited yet. Sometimes these Fed wires are slow. It'll probably be credited later today. Why don't you call me back at noon?"

Gil was frustrated but knew his hands were tied until the wire was received. He thanked her and went to talk to Jenkins.

"This is just dandy," Jenkins said, standing behind his desk, clenching his fists. "Kelsen'll be here in half an hour and he'll have my ass. I don't care what Dahmshultz says, call her back at eleven. Stay on her."

As he was told, Gil made the call at eleven, but heard the same dismissive answers, along with "I thought I told you to call me at *noon*." He buzzed Jenkins. "I'm sorry, sir, but Ms. Dahmshultz still maintains they didn't get the money."

"Gil, I'm sitting here with Mr. Kelsen right now," Jenkins replied in an irritated tone. "He's not happy about this. And neither am I. Would you please find out what the hell happened to the wire and the release? Do whatever you have to do." Jenkins set the phone down and forced a smile at Kelsen. "I'm sure this will clear itself up in a short while."

Gil looked at the telephone receiver in his hand. *Whatever I have to do? What does he think I can do?*

Kelsen shifted impatiently in his chair and looked around Jenkins's expansive corner office. Antique oak bookcases and side tables bordered one end of a nine-by-sixteen Oriental rug. A Tiffany lamp hung in the corner over a small marble conference table. The walls were covered with distressed-oak paneling, which Jenkins boasted was salvaged from the demolition of the old St. Aloysius Church on South Kildare.

Jenkins opened a walnut humidor, took out a large cigar, held it under his nose, and lifted his eyebrows. He offered it to Kelsen, who waved it off.

"It's a Cuban," Jenkins said, "but, of course, you'll have to wait until you get outside. Can't smoke in my own damn offices anymore."

Kelsen shook his head. "No, thanks. I just want to get my money and be on my way."

"I understand completely, Victor. I guess Murphy's Law is hard at work on this deal. You know, if something can go wrong, it will go wrong." Jenkins forced a nervous chuckle. "But don't worry, we'll clear it up."

"So, the bigger the deal, the bigger the fuckup, is that right? Is that what you're saying?" Kelsen snapped. "Who is this kid, this Roberts? What happened to Sommers? Why isn't he working on this? Didn't I pay you guys enough?"

Jenkins shrugged. "He must be ill. I can't reach him. What about your man Harrington? Does he have any idea why the wire is delayed?"

Kelsen took his glasses off and rubbed his eyes. "Fuck Harrington.

I can't find the prick. Of all the days to go missing, Harrington decides to be a no-show on the day the escrow closes. His partner called me earlier this morning and he doesn't know where Harrington is either. In fact, he called the cops."

"The cops?"

"Missing persons. Wants to file a report because Harrington didn't come home last night." Kelsen swiveled to look out the window.

Jenkins rocked back in his chair and raised his eyebrows. "Is this typical of Harrington?"

"Fuck no. You think I'd keep an irresponsible CFO? He was the most punctual, detailed, boring man I ever met. His partner says he's never done this before."

Kelsen and Jenkins locked eyes as the same thought entered both of their minds. Harrington and Sommers had been in charge of the entire transaction. Together. And now both were inexplicably missing. And so was the money. Jenkins shook his head to clear that thought. Not possible. He'd known Sommers for years. But, still.

"I want my money, Jenkins," said Kelsen, spitting out every word. "I hold your firm responsible." He popped his finger on his watch. "It's now twenty-five minutes overdue. I trusted you. I paid you a fortune. Now get me my money."

"I'm sure everything's okay. This is just a temporary snafu." Jenkins dialed Roberts again. "Gil, forget the phone calls. I want you to go over to Midwestern Title, sit at Jim Ellis's desk until this deal is closed, and make sure those proceeds are transferred to Mr. Kelsen. Call me every fifteen minutes."

Six

. . .

THE HONOLULU TAXI DROPPED Sommers at 264 Kai-ulani Avenue, a two-story, white stucco motel. The script above the office read THE CORAL REEF in aqua blue. A neon sign in the window informed the world of a VACANCY. A balcony ran along the perimeter of the second floor. All of the motel's rooms were accessed from the outside.

Sommers opened the office door and a small bell announced his entrance. A corpulent man in a loose Aloha shirt patterned with pastel coconut trees and hula dancers shuffled out of the back room. With his hands on the counter, he leaned forward and gave Sommers a once-over. "Ca'I help ya?"

"My name is Eugene Wilson. I spoke to you last week. I re-served a kitchenette. Sent you an eight-hundred-dollar deposit."

The clerk nodded and stuck out his right hand. It was soft and sweaty. "Glenn. I got your deposit. You're in room 212 on the second floor. Nicest one I got too. On the corner. I need eight hundred dollars."

"I already sent you eight hundred dollars in a money order," Sommers said. "We agreed on eight hundred dollars a month."

"Right. But the money order was a security deposit. I gotta have eight hundred dollars more, in advance."

Sommers huffed, reached in his bag, and took out his trifold wallet. The slot inside the cover held a picture of his daughter. He selected a MasterCard and slid it across the counter.

Glenn shook his head. "I don't take no credit cards. Cash only."

Sommers pursed his lips. "It's a debit card."

Glenn was unmoved.

"It takes the money directly from my bank account. Don't worry, it'll go through."

"I ain't worried, I just don't take no credit cards. Debit neither. This is a small, friendly operation."

"You didn't mention that on the phone."

Glenn shrugged. "You didn't ask. Is what it is."

Sommers leafed through the bills in his pocket and slid $800 across the counter. He looked at the balance of his cash. "I need directions. A place to eat and an ATM."

Glenn nodded and pointed his pudgy index finger. "Five blocks to Kalakaua. All the big-buck-o hotels are there. They got lots of ATMs and restaurants. But if you ask me, Cappy's Fish Shack round the corner got the best plates on the island." Glenn handed two brass keys to Sommers. "Check out Cappy's garlic shrimp. You won't be sorry."

Sommers opened the door to Room 212. The window air conditioner had been off and the air was stale. He flipped the switch and the fan came on with a rattle. He looked around. It was livable, minimally. The furniture had seen younger days, the woodwork had scratches and gouges, but the pieces were functional. The double bed had a chenille coverlet that had once been pink. A small, tube TV sat on a melamine desk. The kitchen had a greasy odor, but the stove worked. Through the dusty windows, Sommers had a view of an apartment complex across the street. Hip-hop music blasted from the bar on the corner.

Sommers took a five-by-seven, framed photograph from his case and set it gently on the bedside table. He kissed the picture of the little girl. *Soon we'll be together and we'll look for a new home,* he said to the picture. *But now we wait.*

T HE PHONE RANG ON Greta Dahmshultz's desk. She looked at the caller ID, shook her head, and pushed the speaker button. "If this is Gil Roberts, I still don't have your payoff."

Both Gil and Ellis hovered over Ellis's speakerphone at Elli's horseshoe desk. The Kelsen/Leland escrow file lay open on the desktop. "Greta, I'm with Jim. Can you give us an update on what's being done to resolve this problem, *please*?"

"What's being done by whom?" she said. "My task is to check to see if we've received your wire transfer. And we haven't. What are *you* doing to resolve this problem?"

Gil reached for the Fed wire confirmation. Holding it in his hand, he waved it as though Greta could plainly see it. "I have proof that the funds were wired to Exchange yesterday morning, Greta. Right here. I'm looking at the Fed confirmation. Maybe if you took a copy down to your wire-transfer department, they'd be able to acknowledge receipt and we could put this to bed. Let me scan it to you along with the wire instructions that *you* signed."

She agreed.

An hour later, the phone rang on Ellis's desk. The two men jumped to their feet and pushed the speaker button.

"Gil, this is Greta, and I'm here with Jennifer Server. I took the liberty of contacting Jennifer after I received and reviewed your e-mail. She's an attorney from our risk-management department. Gil, it looks like you do indeed have a problem."

Jennifer interrupted, "The account identified on your wire confirmation is not connected to this transaction. Midwestern wired the funds all right, but it wired them into the wrong account. The funds were credited to a private corporation's business account, not the Exchange loan account."

"What?" Ellis said. "How is that possible? Midwestern wired out eighty-eight million dollars to the account identified on the Exchange payoff letter that bears Greta's original signature. It's sitting right in front of me."

"When I first looked at the paper," Greta said, "I was also confused. I saw what *appears* to be my signature on your copy of the instructions. It initially fooled me too. But when I compared it to the payoff letter that *I prepared*, I saw the difference."

"What difference? What do you mean?" Ellis said.

Greta continued, "Your copy has a different bank account number, it's not even an account at our main branch in Chicago. And it reads, 'For the account of Loan Services, Co.' You wired the money to an account belonging to some private company called

Loan Services, Co. There is no division at Exchange called Loan Services."

"But the wire instructions you signed—"

"No way. Someone altered the instructions after I signed them."

"I don't have any idea how such a thing could happen," Ellis said. "Both Harrington and Sommers reviewed and approved the document. I followed the instructions exactly as written."

"Let's not argue about whose fault it is, let's reverse the wire," Gil said. Turning to Ellis, he said, "Get on the phone with the Fed and reverse the transfer. Get the money out of that Loan Services account and direct it to the correct Exchange account to pay off the loan." Leaning forward and talking loudly into the speakerphone, Gil continued, "Greta and Jennifer, would you please take whatever steps are necessary on your end to freeze that Loan Services account until we can straighten this out?"

The response was direct: "It's not in that account anymore."

"In which account?"

"In any account," Greta said. "It was withdrawn from the Loan Services account yesterday. After that, we don't know what happened to the money. We're looking into it. That's why I have our counsel here."

The line was silent for a moment.

"Greta," Gil finally said, "please scan all the relevant documents and e-mail them to me immediately. I'm going to seek an injunction to freeze that money."

"You just don't get it. There's nothing to freeze. It's gone. It was wired out ten minutes after it came in."

"I . . . I'm going back to the office," Gil said. "I have to confer with Mr. Jenkins. We'll call you later."

"Call Ms. Server. She's in charge now."

JENKINS'S DOOR WAS SHUT when Gil returned. "Is Mr. Jenkins in his office?" he said hurriedly to the secretary.

She nodded. "He's in there with Mr. Kelsen." She leaned forward and whispered, "In a real bad mood."

"Who is?"

"Both of them."

Gil quietly said, "Then would you buzz Mr. Jenkins and ask him to come out. Tell him I'm out here and I need to speak to him privately."

A moment later Jenkins came out. "Well?"

Gil shook his head. "Sir, this deal is screwed up beyond belief. No one knows where the money is."

"What are you talking about?"

He answered in a hushed tone. "I mean that the title company wired eighty-eight million dollars to a bogus account in New York, and the money was immediately withdrawn by some stranger and it's not there anymore."

"Where?"

"Anywhere."

Jenkins pulled Gil into an adjoining office where a young lawyer was busy researching. "Would you excuse us, please, Jerry," Jenkins snapped at the lawyer, and waved his hand at the door, shooing him out. "Please. Now!"

With the door closed, Jenkins said, "What are you talking about? What bogus account? What stranger? Explain this to me."

When Gil finished, Jenkins said, "Then Midwestern has to make it good. They're the escrow company. They have to send eighty-eight million dollars to Exchange, not to some phantom account. The missing money's their problem. If they wired it to the wrong account—"

"They're not taking responsibility, sir. Ellis says he precisely followed the Exchange payoff statement that was given to him. And he did. I mean he followed the written instructions that I saw."

"Then it's Exchange's fault."

"No, sir. Exchange denies that the instructions are genuine. They say it's an altered document. And what's worse is that both Harrington and Sommers signed off on it. Greta Dahmshultz insists that someone intentionally changed the numbers to redirect the funds. She had the bank's lawyer on the phone. No one will take ownership of this fuckup."

Jenkins stood dumbfounded, like a stuffed grizzly bear in the corner of a Northwoods tavern.

"Well, we need to inform the client. Let's go talk to Kelsen."

They rejoined him in Jenkins's office where Kelsen sat nervously swinging his leg and tapping his fingers.

"Victor, does Kelsen have a business account at Exchange's New York branch?" Jenkins said.

"What are you talking about?"

"Well, does it? Do you have an account called Loan Services?"

"No. Our accounts are all at Exchange in Chicago and at Evanston National on Davis Street. What's going on, Walter?"

"Mr. Jenkins, I think we need to get hold of Sommers or Harrington," Gil said. "They should have the answer. They're the ones who were present at the escrow with Ellis. They signed the disbursement statements. Right now, neither the bank nor the title company will do anything further. They both refer us to their legal departments."

"What's going on, Walter?" Kelsen said again.

"I can't reach Sommers," Jenkins said through clenched teeth. "But I'm sure there's an explanation to this debacle and a way to straighten it out. You can't lose eighty-eight million dollars."

"What do you mean *lose*?" screamed Kelsen.

"Hang on, Victor. Gil, go into Sommers's office, into the closing file, and bring me our copy of the payoff statement. The one from *our* files." Turning to Kelsen, Jenkins said, "Apparently, the funds were wired to some fuckin' account in New York called Loan Services and weren't applied to pay off your loan. From what I'm told, it was a private account and the funds were immediately withdrawn. This is crazy, but it's all the responsibility of Midwestern Title. They're the escrow company. They're charged with the responsibility of disbursing the funds into the proper accounts."

Gil double-timed it down the hall to Sommers's office and started thumbing through the papers. The sounds of breaking glass blasted out of Jenkins's office. "Get this fucking deal straightened out, you idiot!" Kelsen bellowed. Gil rushed back to Jenkins's office. Everything had been knocked off Jenkins's desk. Kelsen was storming out of the room, screaming, "I want that money in my account by tomorrow, you incompetent bastard!"

Jenkins, clearly shaken, looked at Gil. "Victor took his forearm and swept everything off my desk." Jenkins wiped his hand across his brow. "I would have called the police, except, if I were in his shoes, I probably would've done the same thing."

Gil bent down to pick up some of the items on the floor. "Don't bother," said Jenkins, "I'll have it cleaned up. Where are the payoff instructions? What did you find in Sommers's office?"

"Here, sir." Gil handed over the Exchange document. "The numbers are definitely different. But, sir, I also found this as well: a receipt for a ticket to Brazil. First-class seat on American. For a flight yesterday."

SEVEN

• • •

IN THE BACK ROOM of the Breadstone Bakery, in the narrow, winding streets just north of Hebron's Bab al-Zawiyah market, ten powerful men, each an influence in his own way, sat around a circular, mosaic table. A silver coffee urn with several small cups sat in the middle of the table.

"The coffee is good and strong tonight," said a thin, angular man, pouring a small amount into his cup, barely a sip.

Fakhir, the squat owner of the shop, nodded and chuckled. "Turkish. None of us would object, Ahmed, if you poured a little more into your cup. Then you wouldn't have to get up so often."

"Never fill a cup so much you cannot see the bottom," Ahmed said. "I was taught that by my mother. It's sociable."

"Who called for the assault on the wedding party?" said Dr. al-Zahani.

The men looked at one another and shrugged. "What difference does it make, Arif?" said Nizar Mohammed.

"How does it further our grand plan to shoot a young girl on her wedding day?"

"How does it help us to remain silent under subjugation and occupation?" Nizar said. "Everything doesn't have to stop because of our 'grand plan.' Are you going soft on us, Arif? Was this not warranted? The group was defiling the Al-Haram Al-Ibrahimi shrine with a Jewish ceremony and Jewish prayers. It's a Palestinian heritage site and Israel is in violation of its international commitments by promoting ceremonies at Palestinian holy sites. Israelis now advertise buses to take people to perform Jewish ceremonies at the Tomb of the Patriarchs."

"Maybe Nizar forgets it is precisely on those tour buses that we will carry out our operation. Or maybe Nizar would do it by camel train."

On a stuffed futon in the corner, Fa'iz Talib sat quietly, observing the banter. The eldest member of the group, he leaned his back against the wall. His head tilted forward and his wiry beard rested on his cream-colored kurta. From his knitted taqiyah to his laced sandals, his bearing bespoke composure and wisdom, affording him deference. "Vitriol among us does not further anybody's plans," he said. "What is your concern with the wedding incident, Arif? I, myself, authorized it."

"I care nothing for the wedding party or the people who were shot, including the bride, who, some of you know, was treated at my home. I care only about jeopardizing our operation. The public perception—the newspapers, CNN—they pick it up and use it in their campaign to portray us as barbarians."

"Maybe that's not so bad. Anything that creates fear in the hearts of our oppressors suits our purpose, no?"

"I don't dispute that. But the timing is bad. In the wake of our operation, it will focus attention on Hebron. It's bound to bring more IDF, more Israeli police. The IDF will now go door-to-door to dig up a suspect. For a tiny act of retribution, the swatting of a few mosquitoes in a wedding party, it increases the risk of our exposure."

The baker rubbed his grizzled beard and smiled. "But maybe they don't come back so soon for weddings, huh?"

The others laughed.

Fa'iz held up a hand. "What's done is done, let's talk about the bus. What is our progress, Rami?"

"We have converted and painted an identical tour bus. It has a false floor. Undetectable. It will be ready well before we need it. Aziz has already taken a job as a Jerusalem tour bus driver and is dispatched twice a week."

"And the bags, Arif?"

Al-Zahani nodded. "Coming along."

Fa'iz stood and the others followed suit. They joined hands in a circle around the table.

"From the river to the sea," Fa'iz said.

"From the Golan to the Gulf," the group responded. "Blessed be the Sons of Canaan."

EIGHT

...

JACK SOMMERS'S FIRST ORDER of business was to shop. He needed clothes, kitchen and bathroom essentials, and apartment furnishings. He had sufficient funds through his Panamanian debit cards, all issued in the name of Eugene Wilson. For a larger purchase, he knew he'd have to open an account at a local bank.

Sommers set out on Waikiki's main thoroughfare. Fragrances of orchid leis hanging from Kalakaua's sidewalk kiosks mingled with the ocean breezes. Palm trees lined the busy avenue, shading a stream of pedestrians from the morning sun. *A river of dawdlers in flip-flops,* he thought. Their slow progression would have irritated Jack at some earlier time, but not today. There were no deadlines, no appointments. Life was on temporary standstill.

Clothing stores were plentiful on Kalakaua, and Sommers needed clothes, but he was also wary of laying out too much money in any one store and becoming a conspicuous consumer who might stick out in some shopkeeper's memory. *Buy a little here, buy a little there,* he thought. *Never too much at one place. Nothing too extravagant. Try not to return to the same place too often. New rules to live by.*

Sommers needed to make Room 212 more livable. He bought an assortment of cleaning supplies and spent the afternoon scrubbing down the room. New bedding, new pillows, new pots and pans, and even a new window curtain helped to erase the gritty feeling he'd experienced when he first opened the door. He told Glenn that it would be unnecessary for the housekeeping staff to care for his room, that he would do it himself, thank you very much. Glenn responded, "You're talking to the housekeeping staff, and you're very welcome."

The Coral Reef had no Internet service, but the coffee shop around the corner had free Wi-Fi. The library down the block had free Wi-Fi. He could get by. For transportation, a four-year-old, blue Acura in excellent condition was available at a nearby dealership. Sommers purchased the car with funds wired from his Panamanian account and titled the car in the name of Eugene Wilson at his Kaiulani Avenue address. His vehicle registration provided him with yet another ID. Things were starting to come together for him, and he was sure it would not be too much longer. He expected to hear good news any day.

DAN GIBSON, A BUNDLE of nerves since Harrington went missing, received a call from CPD detective O'Herrin. "Did you locate Dennis Harrington?" Dan asked cautiously, fearing the worst.

"Not yet, but we found his car. It was parked at the North Avenue Beach."

"At the beach? Why would it be at the beach?"

O'Herrin paused. "We saw no indication of foul play. There may be all sorts of explanations. All we know is that his car was left in the lot at North Avenue. It was snow covered and locked. We had it towed to the pound at Randolph. I just thought I'd let you know. If you have a key, you can come and pick it up."

"Will you keep looking for Dan? Will you canvass the area?"

"The immediate area is a vacant, snow-covered beach. We did take a look around, but we didn't see anything. If you're talking about canvassing the people who live in the high-rises across Lake Shore Drive, no, sir, we do not intend to do that. But we'll keep his MP file open."

"Is it against the law for me to post signs in the area? You know, like, 'Call me if you have information.'"

"I don't see the harm, sir."

* * *

JENKINS HURRIEDLY ASSEMBLED HIS firm's executive board. The e-mail was short and to the point: *Emergency meeting in the conf. room. 2 pm. Serious situation. No excuses.*

"Who owns this Loan Services account?" a partner asked after Gil had narrated his story.

"We don't know yet," Gil said. "I've requested all of the information from Exchange. It should be here soon."

"Who's at fault here, Walter?" another partner said. "Is this our fuckup?"

Jenkins gestured for Gil to answer.

"I hate to keep saying this, Preston," Gil said, "but we don't know yet. There may be several explanations for the missing funds." He counted them off on his fingers. "One, the money may, in fact, be sitting at the bank and the bank is wrong, they'll find their error and straighten it out. Hell, it might be a firestorm over nothing. Two, there could be some glitch in the Internet transfer and the Fed wire was never completed. Maybe the money is still in transit, in limbo somewhere. It's happened before." Gil looked around the room. "Either one of these would solve the problem." He shrugged.

"Three, maybe it's Exchange's fault—maybe Greta signed more than one letter," Gil continued. "Or somewhere between Greta and Midwestern, the document was corrupted by a third party." He shrugged again. "Could be."

"I thought you said that Harrington and Sommers signed off on the letter," Preston said. "They both eyeballed and approved the goddamn letter."

Gil nodded. "That's true. I'm sorry, I guess we can forget about number three." He held up four fingers. "Still, someone at Midwestern Title could have changed the numbers after the letter was approved by Sommers. I doubt it was Ellis, I've known him for a few years, but I guess you can't exclude anyone. Also, it's possible someone got into his file cabinet. Maybe another officer at Midwestern.

"Five, Harrington could have changed the numbers and slipped it by Sommers at the closing. Six, I guess you all know what's coming. Sommers and Harrington could have jointly participated in a monstrous embezzlement. They're both missing." Gil looked around the room. "I recommend we notify our liability-insurance carrier immediately."

"What are the limits of our policy?" a partner asked.

"Fifty million," Jenkins said.

"So we could be holding the bag for thirty-eight million dollars?"

Jenkins nodded. "That's true. If we're found to be at fault, if it was stolen by one of our partners, or through the firm's negligence, this partnership and every partner here could be liable for thirty-eight million dollars."

"Shouldn't we also notify the FBI?"

Just then, Jenkins's secretary entered the room with an e-mail from Exchange and handed it to Jenkins. He read it and closed his eyes. He dropped the note on the table where Gil retrieved it and read it to the group:

"'Wire transfer for eighty-eight million dollars received yesterday by the New York branch of Exchange National to be credited to the account of Loan Services, Co. The account was opened by Richard Hudson, president of Loan Services, Co., on December twentieth with an initial deposit of one thousand dollars. At ten thirty A.M., within minutes of the receipt of yesterday's wire transfer, Mr. Hudson directed Exchange to immediately wire-transfer the entire balance to the First Republic Bank, Panama City, Republic of Panama, to be credited to the account of Capital Investment Funds, Inc., account no. 14-961245444. The transfer was completed at ten forty-five A.M. EST. The account was then closed. It appears that neither Mr. Hudson's telephone number nor his address is valid. Duplicate copies of the documentation to follow.'"

There was silence in the room. The partners looked around, hoping that someone would offer up an answer, a solution.

"Does anyone know anything about this bank in Panama?" Jenkins said.

"I've never dealt with the First Republic Bank, but I've done business with other Panama banks," a partner responded. "They have the second-largest international-banking center in the world, next to Switzerland. There are over a hundred international banks in Panama, with the tightest banking-secrecy laws in the world. Panama law prohibits bankers from disclosing any information about a private banking client to any person, including the United States government. Panama has enacted severe penalties for any violations.

"Accounts are easy to set up. You can do it from anywhere; you don't have to be in Panama. All you need is two financial reference letters from banks or brokerage houses, bearing a notary stamp, the kind that every secretary in our office has sitting in her desk drawer. You also need a passport, but they'll accept a photocopy. The documents are rarely, if ever, verified, especially if no credit is requested."

Jenkins stood. "Enough. Susan, contact our insurance carrier and put them on notice of a possible claim. Gil, contact Tom Tryon at the US Attorney's Office and schedule a meeting. I am going to contact a very good private investigator I know."

Everyone rose to leave. "I don't have to tell any of you," Jenkins said, "that none of this information leaves this room. If it hits the street, it could ruin us. As of this time, our position is, and will remain, that we have done absolutely nothing wrong."

SOMMERS TURNED IN EARLY. The last few days had frayed his nerves and he was exhausted, mentally and physically. He poured himself a small glass of Scotch from a bottle he kept within reach on the nightstand. Although he dozed off quickly, his sleep was fitful, beset by the same disturbing dreams. There he was, back again at Northwestern Memorial Hospital, standing by Alina. Her beautiful olive complexion had paled. She had lost so much weight. He stood frozen by her bedside. Everything he loved was slipping away and he could do nothing to stop it. Totally helpless. Totally useless.

Alina looked up from her bed and smiled weakly at him. "Take care of our little butterfly," she said in a whisper. "Promise me you'll take care of her, Jack. Don't let her forget me."

"Alina," he pleaded. "Stop. You're going to be fine. The doctors are treating you. They'll cure you. They said they're hopeful."

"I love you, Jack. I've loved you since the day I met you." She smiled and reached for his hand. "Remember that first day? I was playing the piano. You were wearing a tux. You were so handsome."

He tried to grasp her hand, to lean over the bed, but the rail kept rising, higher and higher, blocking him, separating him, keeping him back. Alina withdrew farther and farther from his reach.

"Jack, stay strong. For me. For Sophie. For yourself. Remember our wedding vows: 'So long as men can breathe or eyes can see, so long lives this and this gives life to thee.'" Then, in a whisper: "Jack, it's time. I have to go now."

"No. It's not time. Not yet. Stay with me, Alina. You know I can't . . . I don't want to be without you."

She raised her hand and smiled. "But you have to." He grabbed the bars of her bed rail. "Stay with me, please. Keep fighting. Sophie and I need you."

"I can't fight anymore, sweetheart. I've tried. Now I have to leave. From time to time, show Sophie my picture. Tell her that her mother loved her very much."

"Alina," he cried. "Wait. Let me call Dr. Stone." He frantically tried to dial the doctor's number, but the phone kept slipping from his hands. He looked down at Alina. She was fading in and out of focus.

"Take care of Sophie, she needs *you* now. You must stay strong for her. Good-bye, my love." Alina's eyes closed and the bed was suddenly empty.

He woke up in a sweat. "No!" he yelled. He reached for the Scotch, poured another shot, downed it, and flung the glass into the wall. *"Alina!"* he screamed.

It was 4:00 A.M., but Sommers needed to get out of the room. He grabbed a sweater and left the motel. The ocean breeze had cooled the night air. His walk was aimless, just one block and then the next, and soon he found himself back on Kalakaua, wiping away the tears that wouldn't stop.

The beachfront hotels were dark and quiet. Just past the Hyatt he came upon Kuhio Beach Park, where he took a seat on a wooden bench. The bright, gibbous moon reflected off the calm seas. Soon it would be dawn.

His dreams of Alina had shaken him to the core. They were a clarion reminder of his abject failures: he had failed to keep his promise, he had failed Alina, he had failed Sophie. Sommers felt as if every single internal organ was tied in a knot. He stared at the sea: calm, dark, peaceful. *Come join me,* it said. *I offer peace.*

He stood and let the vast sea reel him closer. *Alina, I'm so lost,* he said to himself. *I've made such a mess of things. I'm falling apart, honey. Sometimes it's even hard for me to take a breath.*

The water echoed, *Come join me.*

In numbing obedience, he walked slowly into the shallows and watched the waves softly lap over his sandals and splash against his knees. *Don't you see, Alina, I'm not as strong as you thought I was. I was only strong because of you. Can't you help me?*

The sudden, brash call of a seagull raised his eyes to the night sky. He took a deep breath and nodded. He looked back at the black water and gave it a swift kick. "I know, I know. Get a grip, Jack. There's a job to do."

Walking back to the motel, he took determined steps. *I can't continue to wallow in this sadness. It doesn't do any of us any good. Have faith in me, Alina, I made you a promise and I won't let you down. I've worked out a plan and I'm going to see it through. I'm sure word will come soon. I'm going to get her back, sweetheart, I promise you.*

NINE

• • •

LIAM TAGGART WALKED UP the steps of his fiancée's three-story brownstone in the Lincoln Park section of Chicago, put his key in the lock, and entered the foyer. He shook the snow from his coat and hat and brushed the slush from the cuffs of his trousers.

"Liam, you're getting snow all over my floor," Catherine said as she hurried to meet him in the hall. "Take your shoes off."

"I'm sorry. It's really coming down out there. You should see the Drive."

"I know. I just got in myself." She took his coat and hung it on the foyer rack. Almost as tall as Liam, Catherine Lockhart brushed her blond hair back from her face and leaned over to give him a kiss. She was comfortably dressed in her jeans and a blue cable-knit sweater.

"I'll clean it up," Liam said. "I don't want your aunt Edna getting mad at me."

Catherine handed him a towel. "I talked to Aunt Edna today. She says it's eighty-four degrees in West Palm."

"Oh, that's unkind. Tell her to come home, we'll trade places."

"I don't think she's ever coming back. She loves it down there. She said she wants to give me this house."

"Whoa. That's quite a gift."

She shook her head. "I can't accept it. It's worth a million dollars or more. I told her that."

Liam finished wiping the floor and carried the towel back to the laundry room. "And what did she say?"

"She said it would be a good place to raise my family."

Liam raised his eyebrows. "Does she know something I don't know?"

"Very funny." Catherine turned and walked to the refrigerator and took out two beers. "She says I'm not getting any younger." Catherine handed a bottle to Liam. "She's right, you know. Next month I'll be thirty-seven. It's getting late to start a family."

"Is that a proposal?"

"Is that what you think?" Catherine put her hands on her hips. "Let me tell you, I'd be a lot more romantic than that if *I* were going to propose. When the time is right, I want it done with ceremony. Pomp and circumstance. Not some off-the-cuff remark."

"Excuse me. I'll remember that when the time is right."

She turned and walked back to the kitchen, repeating *when the time is right* under her breath.

"Cat? Is something wrong?"

"No."

"Cat?"

"Don't worry about it. Tell me about your day."

"Extraordinary. You'll never guess who came to see me today."

She shrugged. "I give up."

"Walter Jenkins, of all people. He called for an appointment and came right over before I could tell him no. He wants to hire me."

"I hope you told him to get lost."

Liam smiled and bit his bottom lip. "I didn't. I listened to his story and it was a whopper."

"Another problem with one of his precious insurance clients?"

Still smiling, Liam opened his eyes widely and shook his head. "Nope. A disaster of nuclear proportions. He told me I could share it with you; he thinks he may want to hire you as well."

Catherine pursed her lips. "Hire me? The unprincipled bastard fired me last year and then tried to bribe me to drop my client." She put her hands on her hips. "I wouldn't work for him under any circumstances. Not if he ran the last law firm in Chicago."

Liam smiled. "He regrets his conduct."

"Only because it now suits his convenience. He wants to hire my boyfriend. Are you seriously going to take this assignment? He's a pompous, self-absorbed, unethical bastard."

"Calm down. I told him I'd think about it and discuss it with you. If you said it would make you uncomfortable, I'd have to decline. He was okay with that. That's why he told me that it was all right to disclose the case to you, but you'd have to swear an oath of secrecy." He raised his eyebrows. "It's a whopper, Cat. He'll give me a fifty-thousand-dollar retainer."

Catherine whistled. "Fifty grand from Mr. Tightwad?"

Liam took a seat in the overstuffed chair by the fireplace. Catherine curled up on the corner of the couch and tucked her feet under her like a young girl. Liam smiled lovingly at her. Her ability to enchant him had been unwavering for twenty years.

"Regale me," she said.

Liam repeated the information Jenkins had laid out earlier in the day.

"And he wants you to find Sommers?" Catherine said.

"He wants me to find the money. He's not sure Sommers has it."

"I barely knew Sommers when I was at the firm. I remember him as a sad and troubled man, but not the kind who would steal eighty million dollars."

"Eighty-eight," Liam corrected. "What do you know about Sommers?"

"Not much. He was a transactional attorney who handled purchases and sales of businesses: asset purchases, stock purchases, mergers, acquisitions. He was kind of lanky, not bad looking, with a lot of brown hair. A nice guy. Quiet. Unassuming. Everyone seemed to get along with him. He was married to a very sweet woman. She was Middle Eastern, I think. He was completely devoted to her. They had one child, a cute little girl. A couple of years ago, his wife contracted a fatal illness that took her very rapidly. He was devastated."

Liam nodded his head slowly. "I can see why you say he was sad and troubled."

"There was more. A custody dispute with his wife's parents or something. I really don't know the details. That was about the time I left the firm."

"So, what do you think?" Liam said. "About the assignment?"

"It's a whopper, all right. And I'm not going to tell you to pass up a fifty-thousand-dollar retainer, but what makes him want to involve me?"

"Unless the money turns up immediately, he's sure that Kelsen will file suit. He needs a good lawyer."

"He has a firm full of lawyers, good ones. And his malpractice insurance company will provide lawyers."

"He's got to have an independent lawyer. He can't assign any lawyers from his firm when they could all wind up being defendants in a suit for the deficiency. He has to have private counsel in addition to the insurance lawyers. He told me that you're the best attorney he knows." Liam spread his hands. "He thinks it's logical to have us work together, like we did with Ben Solomon. He was really impressed."

"Yeah, he was so impressed, he fired me."

"Seriously, he spent several minutes reminiscing about Ben's case. He stands there, punctuating with his index finger, and says, 'She takes up the case of an old man, a pensioner, with no money, and sues the wealthiest man in Chicago. Not only does she sue him, but she accuses him of being a Nazi. A Nazi, for chrissake.' Then he walks around the room shaking his head. 'I thought she was nuts. Elliot Rosenzweig, a Nazi? He's the biggest Jewish benefactor in the city. The lawsuit almost puts me out of business. I beg her to drop it. I even offer her a financial motivation, but she tells me to stuff it and walks out. Then she proceeds to litigate the case on her own, out of her house. With your help, naturally. Jesus, Liam, that's got to be the best lawyering Chicago's ever seen.'"

Catherine smiles. "Financial motivation. That's funny. Most of us would call it a bribe. What about this Loan Services, Co.? What did they find out?"

"It's a Delaware corporation owned entirely by a man named Robert Hudson and formed seven weeks ago. Victor Kelsen says he never heard of it. Or anyone named Hudson. It's probably a shell company formed to accomplish the theft."

"Will Jenkins hire you even if I refuse to accept his offer?"

Liam nodded. "He said he would understand if you didn't want to represent him, but he would hire me anyway."

"Then tell him I said, 'Piss off.'"

TEN

• • •

ANOTHER AFTERNOON AND ANOTHER check of his secret e-mail address results in further disappointment for Sommers. Days come and days go and still there is no word. No new messages. He posts, *How are the plans progressing? When can I expect to hear something? I am anxiously awaiting your response.* He clicks SEND and stares at the computer screen. He commands the screen to answer him, but it doesn't respond.

His entire life is on hold. The inactivity is becoming insufferable. Sommers closes his computer and walks slowly back to the Coral Reef. *I can't face another afternoon in this motel room,* he thinks. *I've got to get out. I got to do something or I'll go mad.*

A page in a Hawaii travel brochure provides a suggestion: "Take a Scenic Drive to Oahu's Friendly North Shore." A picture of a restaurant looks appealing. It's a long ride, but Sommers thinks it might take his mind off his gridlock.

With the sunroof open and the windows down, Sommers heads west on Interstate H1, past Pearl Harbor, Hickam Field, and Aloha Stadium. It is the archetypal Hawaiian day with temperatures in the mideighties. Trade winds carry a mélange of tropical fragrances through the open windows.

He motors north onto H2 toward Wahiawa, the North Shore, and the travel brochure's destination: the artsy town of Hale'iwa. He glides past pineapple plantations and sugarcane fields, but his mind predictably wanders back to Alina, Sophie, and happier times.

He had just walked in the door and Alina was calling to him

from the living room. "Jack," she said excitedly, "Sophie has some-thing special to show you." She took his hand and pointed to So-phie, who sat poised at the piano. The little four-year-old, a pink ribbon tied in her blond curls, sat on a booster seat that Alina had strapped to the piano bench. A big smile stretched across Sophie's face in anticipation.

Alina nodded to Sophie. Sophie stretched her fingers the way she had seen her mother do so many times and lit into a lively rondo. She attacked the keys with astonishing maturity. Jack clapped loudly and urged her to repeat the selection. And then again. "How can a four-year-old play that well?" he said.

Sophie giggled.

"She's special, Jack," Alina whispered to him. "I know you'll say I'm biased, but I've been around the other kids. Sophie has extraor-dinary talent. Someday she'll change the world."

Jack laughed. "Alina, she's only four."

"You mark my words; with Sophie, the sky's the limit."

Turning onto Highway 99 and lost in his memories, Jack's rev-erie was shattered by the lights of a highway patrol car. A knot formed in the pit of his stomach and sweat beaded on the band of his panama hat.

He checked his speed. Seventy-three. *Damn. What a fool I am. This is the last thing I need. What if this cop figures out I'm not Eugene? What if there's an interstate warrant. If he arrests me, I'll have come all this way only to fail again. All because of a damn speeding ticket.*

The uniformed officer stepped out of his squad car and slowly walked up behind the Acura. He looked at the LICENSE APPLIED FOR sticker in the back window.

"May I see your license and registration, please?"

With a shaking hand, Sommers reached into his wallet, took out the driver's license, and handed it to the patrolman with a copy of the receipt for his new vehicle registration. He thought the beat-ing of his heart would break his ribs.

"Was I speeding, Officer?"

"Oh, yeah. I clocked you at seventy-two in a fifty-five."

"I'm sorry. I wasn't paying attention to my speed." Sommers hoped the officer would just write the ticket and not investigate beyond the plates.

The patrolman carefully looked over the interior of the car. "Visiting from Kentucky, Mr. Wilson?"

"Actually, I'm here for an extended time, doing work for a client." He swallowed hard, fearing the worst—a trip to the police station.

The officer shook his head and grinned. "I know it's pretty quiet out here today, Mr. Wilson, but you never know, one of these farmers'll drive out of a little gravel road. You wouldn't see 'em until it was too late. Take it easy, huh?" The officer handed back the license and registration. "Have a nice day."

Sommers was flabbergasted. "You're giving me a warning? You're not going to give me a ticket?"

"Not unless you want one." The officer tipped the brim of his cap and turned back to his car. "We'll chalk it up to the aloha spirit."

"Thank you very much," Sommers called after him.

The officer smiled and nodded.

Sommers, his heart still beating loudly, sat in his car and waved as the officer drove past him. "I'm sorry, Alina. It won't happen again."

He drove slowly the rest of the way to Hale'iwa and pulled into the parking lot of McDuffy's-by-the-Sea, a rustic wooden restaurant with a large outdoor patio, sheltered by two banyan trees. Sommers walked straight past the outdoor tables, up the steps, and directly to the bar. Sitting on a stool, he ordered a double and drank it quickly. He took deep breaths.

"You okay?" the bartender said.

"Now I am."

Wooden blades of the overhead fans circulated the heavy sea air. Sommers ordered another drink. He was beginning to relax.

Suddenly, a woman's voice startled him. "Jack? Jack Sommers? What the hell?"

He spun around, looked directly into a familiar face and breathed a sigh of relief. "Marcy! What a surprise."

Marcy greeted Jack with a hug. She was dressed for a day in the sun—khaki shorts, a sleeveless shirt, and leather sandals. Jack had always thought that Providence had a tomboy in mind when she put Marcy Grant together, giving her more straight lines than curves on her small, athletic body. But there was no denying her fair and gentle face, softly framed by rich auburn hair. A blue cotton overshirt was tied around her shoulders. Her thick hair, streaked by the sun, was pulled back in a loose ponytail. A Nikon SLR digital camera hung from a strap around her neck. She placed her camera on the bar and took a seat on the adjoining stool.

"What are you doing out in Hawaii?" she said.

"It's just a stopover. Only for a day or so. I'm on a business trip."

"Why didn't you call me?"

"To tell you the truth, I totally forgot you were out here."

She feigned a pout. "Oh, thanks a lot."

"I'm sorry. It's been a crazy few months."

She smiled and gave him another spontaneous hug. "I'm so happy to see you. I think about you and Alina all the time. Is your business here on the North Shore?"

"No, it's in Honolulu. But I've been under a lot of stress, so I decided to take the afternoon off and go for a relaxing ride. It didn't work."

"Why not? You couldn't ask for a prettier day, and you came to the best side of the island."

"So I've heard, but I got pulled over by the highway patrol."

Marcy laughed heartily.

Sommers chuckled as well. "But he let me go." Sommers laughed a little harder. "He gave me a warning. Tipped his cap. Called it the aloha spirit!"

"That's never happened to me. They never do that. You're as lucky as a Menehune."

It occurred to Sommers that he had just laughed, and he tried to think of the last time he thought anything was funny. "I cannot remember," he said aloud to himself.

Marcy was puzzled. "Remember what?"

He shook his head. "Never mind. It was really nice to see you, Marcy."

"That's it? It was nice to see you? Not even a 'Do you have time for a drink?'"

"I'm sorry. My mind is somewhere else. Of course, I'd love to have a drink." He signaled to the bartender.

"Gosh." She swiveled on her chair. "Jack Sommers. I haven't

seen you since . . . Jesus, since the funeral. How have you been getting along?"

Sommers tilted his head this way and that. "Not so good, Marcy. It's been real hard. Listen, can I ask you for a big favor? Can we keep my trip out here just between the two of us? Would you mind not telling anyone that you've seen me? You know, don't text anyone, call anyone. Please don't put it on Facebook. Okay? What I'm doing here is pretty private. Really, I don't want anyone to know."

She bit her bottom lip in a conspiratorial smile. "Are you back with the State Department?"

Sommers smiled and patted her on the leg. "I can't even tell you that. I shouldn't even be socializing."

"Oh, what bullshit. We've known each other for ten years. Ever since Alina and I met at the Shakespeare Theater. Stay for dinner, the food's great here. I'm buying." She called the bartender over. "Derrick, another round for my Chicago friend and a mug of my usual."

Jack had another tumbler of vodka, which Derrick poured generously. Marcy had a Tangerine Wheat beer in a frosted mug.

"So, what are *you* doing out on this side of the island with a camera around your neck?" Jack said.

"I live out here, in Hale'iwa. You remember, after Ted and I split, I had to leave Chicago. He wouldn't let me alone. He was stalking me, for chrissake. Alina must have filled you in."

Jack acknowledged the memory with a nod.

"So, I came out here to start a photography career."

"Right, I remember you were into photography. How's it going?"

She laughed. "Shitty. I can't get my pictures into the magazines. That's where the money is. It's a real homeboy network in Hawaii. I can't get past the front door. But I'm selling pictures at the hotels and in art shows, and that pays the bills most of the time. It's a real change in lifestyle."

"Well, you don't look any worse for the wear."

"Thanks. You look pretty good yourself. So, did you come out here with Sophie? How is my little darling?"

Jack smiled with tightly closed lips and nodded. "She's great. Debbie's watching her while I'm here on my assignment."

"Oh, I'm sorry you didn't bring her. I'd have watched her. I've loved that little imp since the day she was born. You tell her that her aunt Marcy misses her a bunch and wants to give her a big hug."

Sommers's eyes misted and he turned his head.

"What's wrong, Jack?"

He shook his head. "Just memories, Marcy."

She reached over and put her arm around his shoulder. "Let's get a bite to eat."

They waited for a table on the lanai and ordered another cocktail. Conversation centered on better days back in Chicago and the escapades of their social group. By the time dinner was served, Jack was starting to lose his equilibrium. He finished his mahimahi, ordered dessert and an after-dinner cordial. Beyond that, he would have no memory of the balance of the evening.

Jack awoke the next morning on a double bed, in white cotton sheets with embroidered edges and feather pillows, clothed only in his boxers. The windows were open to the sea air, and the smell of coffee permeated the bedroom. He sat up, his head thick and heavy, a painful reminder of the night before.

What the hell did I do?

He stood, balanced himself, and located his pants, which were lying in a rumpled heap on the floor next to his shirt and socks. On unsteady legs, he followed the aroma of fresh-brewed coffee to the kitchen. He found cups in a cabinet and began to pour, then spotted a copy of a lawsuit lying on the counter, *Pacific Properties, Inc. v. Marcy Grant.* He picked it up, read through it, shook his head, and placed it back where he found it. Then he refilled his cup and walked out to the porch.

In a T-shirt and running shorts, crossed-legged on a cushioned glider, Marcy sat holding a mug of coffee and reading the morning paper. Bougainvilleas in reds, pinks, and purples splashed their colors on trellises around her patio. Gentle morning breezes, precursors to the afternoon trade winds, carried sweet, floral fragrances. Music played softly on a stereo.

"Very pretty," he said, smiling. "What smells so nice?"

"Plumeria." She pointed to a five-petaled flower. "Its fragrance peaks in the morning. It's the scent most people associate with Hawaii."

He pulled up a patio chair. "Marcy, I'm really sorry about last night. I didn't . . ."

"No, you didn't. No matter what you were going to say. You didn't do anything other than have a few too many. I certainly couldn't let you drive. You passed out as soon as we got in the door."

As he tried again to stumble through an apology, she held up her hand to cut him off. "Why don't you finish your coffee and I'll drive you to your car."

Jack sensed the change in her demeanor, a sudden chill. He looked quizzically at her. "Did I say something wrong last night? Did I do something wrong? Offend you in some way?"

She shrugged. "You paid the check with Gene Wilson's credit card. You're out here masquerading as your brother-in-law? What are you doing with Gene's identification and credit cards? I'm sure it's not State Department policy to use a family member's IDs. And you don't want me to tell anyone you're here. This isn't just some stopover. What's going on? If I called Debbie, what would she say?"

"Listen, Marcy, you can't call Debbie. You can't call anyone. You promised. Please trust me. If you ever loved Alina and me . . ."

"What do you mean *ever loved*?" Marcy snapped. "What kind of thing is that to say?"

"I'm sorry. I didn't mean it like that. I just need for you to believe I'm doing the right thing and honor my request. Please."

Marcy pursed her lips and gave a couple of shakes of her head. "I won't tell anybody, Jack, but . . ."

"I need for you to believe in me. Someday you'll understand. Please?"

She nodded.

"I should leave now. I don't think it's a good idea for us to hang out."

"I don't like this, Jack, whatever you're up to. For your sake and Sophie's, and because of my love for Alina, I won't tell anyone I've seen you, but if you need something, if you're in trouble, you can call me. Maybe I can help."

Jack hung his head. "I'm sorry, Marcy. Not this time. It's for your own good."

She set the paper down and grabbed her car keys. "You know

I'd have done anything for Alina. That was the saddest day of my life, Jack. And I'd do anything for you and Sophie. Call me when you need me."

Jack swallowed hard and walked with her to the car. "I want you to know that before I made a fool of myself last night, I was having a nice time, a really good time. For the first time in many months. Like the old days."

"Thanks, sweetie. Me too."

As she pulled into the lot, he started to say something else, then stopped. "Good-bye, Marcy."

ELEVEN

· · ·

Y ET ANOTHER BASKETBALL GAME on the road to the NCAA tournament, and the Deacons led Midland State by fourteen at the half. The Saturday-afternoon game was just weeks before Selection Sunday. Kelsen turned to the man beside him and said, "No contest, George. I thought it'd be closer, but I guess those Vegas guys know what they're talking about, setting a twenty-one-point spread."

"I stayed away from this game, Vic. Laying twenty-one points against a ranked team is suicide. Did you lay the points?"

Kelsen smiled and shrugged.

George laughed. "As always, the inscrutable Mr. Kelsen never discloses his positions."

"Right."

The second half saw the Deacons's comfortable lead teeter between eighteen and twenty-two points. With the clock running down and the Deacons ahead by twenty, Marcus Fields stole the inbounds pass from Midland State and broke toward the basket all alone. His attempt at a two-handed slam hit hard off the back of the rim and bounded out to midcourt. Midland's point guard grabbed it and laid it in as the buzzer sounded. Final score: St. Joe's 87, Midland State 69.

"What the hell?" George said. "That was an easy bucket for Fields. He was unguarded. Woulda won by twenty-two. Totally blew the point spread. How the hell does he slam it off the iron?"

Vic stood and put on his coat. "Overly excited, I guess. What's the difference, they won big."

"Big is right, if you took the points." George gave Kelsen an inquisitive smile. "Didja, Vic?"

"G'night, George."

SOPHIE STOOD BY HERSELF in the corner of the playground, as she did each recess. She watched as the other children played on the equipment. A line was forming to go on the slide, but she did not move. One swing was empty and Sophie liked to swing, but she didn't stray from her corner. One game looked like tag, but the children were yelling words that Sophie couldn't understand. So she watched, as she did each day.

"My name is Jamila," said a voice behind her.

Sophie turned and saw a girl just about her size, smiling at her. Sophie timidly returned the smile.

"My mother is from India, so I can talk in English. Did you just move to Hebron?"

Sophie nodded.

"Do you have friends?"

Sophie shook her head slowly.

"I could be your friend."

Sophie smiled.

"Teacher said your name is Safiya?"

Sophie giggled. "It's Sophie. Safiya is my aunt."

"I love to paint. Do you like to paint?"

Sophie nodded enthusiastically.

"Would you like to come to my house after school someday? I can ask my mother."

The smile broadened on Sophie's face. "I would."

CATHERINE FINISHED THE LAST of her scheduled appointments at 4:00 P.M. She walked with her client, an elderly man in a tweed sport coat, into her small reception area. In stark contrast to the posh surroundings she used to enjoy at Jenkins & Fairchild, she now ran her solo practice from a small storefront on Clark Street, north of Diversey. Small, but cozy. Much to her satisfaction.

"Remember to bring your estate-planning questionnaire with you when you come next time," she said to her client, who sat on a chair putting on his rubber boots. "Be sure to list all your assets, name all your heirs, and write out any special bequests."

The old man smiled as he reached for the doorknob and said, "Where there's a will, there's a way."

Catherine smiled, picked up her phone messages, and returned to her office.

Shortly thereafter, a smartly dressed man stepped out of a taxi. His camel cashmere coat covered a blue Armani suit, complemented with a purple Brioni tie and contrasting pocket square. He was careful to keep his Italian shoes away from the curbside slush. After pausing for a moment to look at the door, which read OFFICES OF CATHERINE LOCKHART, ATTORNEY AT LAW, he entered and asked the secretary if Catherine was available.

"Do you have an appointment, sir? I don't have anyone else scheduled to see her this afternoon," said the young woman.

"No, I don't. But would you please ask her if she could spare a few minutes for Walter Jenkins?"

The secretary walked back to Catherine's office. "Cat, you'll never guess who's in the waiting room."

Catherine looked up from her work, brushed her hair from the side of her face, and shrugged. "I give up, Gladys."

The secretary put her hands on her hips and wiggled in a snooty manner. "Mr. Walter Jenkins, Esquire, that's who. I do believe he was your old boss? And now he asks, ever so politely, if you could spare him a few minutes." Gladys raised her eyebrows. "How about them apples? Should I shoo him away or show him in?"

Catherine leaned back in her chair. "Jenkins came down to my office?"

Gladys nodded sharply. "Yep. In the snow. What do you suppose he wants?"

"I have an idea. Bring him in."

Gladys took Jenkins's coat, offered him a glass of water, and walked him from the reception room back to Catherine's office. Catherine came around her desk to shake his hand. "How have you been, Walter?"

"So-so." Jenkins took a moment to survey her office. He smiled. "Same old Catherine. Papers everywhere. Empty coffee cups." He nodded. "You're looking good, Catherine."

"Thanks. Things are going well." Catherine motioned for him to have a seat and returned to her desk chair.

"I guess you've heard. We've been scammed. Someone embezzled eighty-eight million dollars from a corporate deal we were handling. J and F is on the hook for almost forty of it. Never saw it coming from these guys."

"Do you know where the money is, who took it?"

Jenkins shook his head. "No proof how it was done or who did it. Sommers was the man in charge. They tell me that the money's now in Panama in some untouchable bank."

"Why didn't you call before you came over here? I would have told you—"

"You would have told me not to bother. You would have told me you're not interested. You would have told me that you have no experience in matters like this. You would have told me there's no way you would work for an asshole like Walter Jenkins."

"That's exactly what I would have said to you, except I would have had the civility not call you an asshole."

Jenkins sat back in his chair, smoothed his trousers, and crossed his legs. He looked calm and in control, but at the same time sad and embarrassed. He spoke quietly. "I need you, Catherine. I realize we ended badly, but I have to go outside the firm, and you're the best lawyer I know."

"Let's be honest. You're here because you don't want to hire any of the prominent firms in the city. You can't afford to air your dirty laundry. You don't want your competitors snooping around inside your office. You certainly don't want to give them on-the-street gossip material. You're afraid they'll raid your client base, fragment your firm, and J and F will fold like Montague, Post and Evans did last year. You're looking for a strong litigator outside the Loop establishment."

Jenkins bit his lip and nodded slowly. "For argument's sake, let's say you're correct. Can I hire you?"

"No. I'd never work for an asshole like Walter Jenkins."

He sat up straight and furrowed his brow. "Seriously?"

Catherine smiled. "Sorry, I couldn't resist. I've been waiting to say that to you for more than a year. Has suit been filed?"

"Not yet, but it's coming. No doubt about it. Kelsen won't return my calls." Jenkins shook his head. "I guess you know we hired Liam. You two work so well together, I just think it's a natural package. I get a great lawyer and a great PI. Will you at least consider it? Please?"

"I'll think about it. Call me after you get served with the lawsuit. No promises, but I'll take a look at the case." Catherine stood. "If I do decide to represent J and F, I'd want full cooperation and full access to the system, all of the partners and the J-and-F staff. No restrictions. Nothing held back. I'd need support: secretarial, paralegal, and a good associate, someone like Rob Hemmer. And I'd want senior-partner rates—seven hundred and fifty dollars an hour."

Jenkins stood and held out his hand. "You can have Hemmer, anything you need. Money will not be an issue. You'll have our full cooperation."

"I'll think about it. Let me know when you get served."

TWELVE

• • •

SOMMERS MERGED INTO THE noontime stream of pedestrians walking along Kalakaua. Waikiki's arterial vein was
full of midday energy. The breeze was light and the sun beamed
hot upon his skin. Dressed in sandals, shorts, a light blue golf shirt,
dark sunglasses, and a U-of-H cap, he felt more secure walking in
public without fear of recognition. As Malani had described it, he
was "melting" into the population.

At Lewers Street, Sommers took a turn onto Kalia Road. He
knew where he had to go and what he had to face. Since arriving
in Honolulu, he had stayed away, but his yesterdays were beckoning to him and he wanted to know what they had to say. At the
end of Kalia, he reached the Hilton Hawaiian Village and its shops,
pools, and expansive crescent beach.

Bittersweet memories carried him along the winding pathway,
past the kidney-shaped pool, past the sunbathers and the children
squealing in the water. Next to the beach was an outdoor café, where
Sommers took a seat. He shut his eyes and allowed the sounds and
smells to take him back to earlier times when life was sweet. Before
his world imploded. He prayed that when he opened his eyes, it would
be three years ago. Alina would step out of the pool, grab a towel,
and come to him, her brilliant smile lighting up all of Waikiki.

"Can I get you something, sir?" the waitress said, wresting him
from his daydream. She set a glass of ice water on the table.

"There are three of us," he said with a knot in his throat. "Please
bring us two mai tais and a fruit juice, and they all must have purple umbrellas."

She nodded and left to fill the order.

Damn, I'm a prisoner in the present. I don't want to be here. I don't have the strength to be here. I want to open my eyes and find out that the last two years were nothing but a bad dream.

Without waiting for the drinks, he stood, left money on the table, and walked past the Rainbow Tower to the beach. He stared intently at a spot where the ocean met the sand. Again, he saw only his memories. Sandals in hand, he walked across the hot sand to stand in the shallow water. He looked down at Sophie, sitting with her plastic bucket and shovel. He looked back to the sand to see Alina on a beach chair reading her magazine. Images that quickly dissolved. Tears rolled down his cheeks.

God, his mind shouted, *are you listening to me? Because it's time for you and me to have it out. Right now, right here! Why did you do this to us? C'mon, I want answers! Alina always told me that everything happened for a reason, there was purpose in the universe. Okay, what's the purpose? What possible reason could you have for destroying my family? What's your grand plan? You took my wife, you've stolen my daughter, you've reduced me to a common thief. I've lost everything I had, including my self-respect. Are you happy now? Does this suit your grand plan? And my little daughter, she's just a baby, why would you do this to her?*

He dropped to his knees in the surf and wept convulsively.

Please, please, God, help me get my daughter back. She doesn't deserve this. I need your help.

A man came up to him and bent over. "Are you all right, fella? Do you need me to call someone, get you some assistance?"

Sommers splashed water on his face and stood. "No, no, I'm okay, thanks. Really, I'll be all right." He walked out of the surf toward the hotel lobby.

Thirteen

• • •

CATHERINE HURRIED TO MEET Liam at Café Sorrento, but she was almost an hour late. She found him sitting at the bar watching the Bulls and the Lakers. His cocktail glass was nearly empty.

"Sorry," she said as she set her purse on the bar and slid onto a stool. "The pretrial conference lasted all afternoon." Turning to the bartender, she said, "I'll have a light beer, please."

Liam tapped his glass for a refill. "You could've called."

"I'm sorry. I was in chambers. I came as soon as I could. Anyway, how was your day?"

"Depressing. I spent the whole day looking into the bedeviled life of John Sommers. One tragedy after another. I talked to a couple partners in the transactional group and his deceased wife's friend and neighbor Sharon Oberman. He has a sister, Deborah, but she hasn't returned my calls."

The bartender brought the two drinks and Liam took a sip of his cocktail.

"So, you left a message for Deborah Sommers?"

"No. Now she's Deborah Wilson. Married to Eugene Wilson. They live in Louisville."

"What did you learn about Sommers?"

"Everyone I talked to likes him, and everyone feels sorry for him. And no one is surprised that he left his job. They worry about him."

"Do they think he took the money?"

"I didn't raise that issue with everyone. It's not common

knowledge. Yet. Walter asked me to keep quiet about the money, at least until the lawsuit is filed and it hits the papers."

Catherine took a sip of her beer. "Does anyone have any idea where he went?"

Liam nodded solemnly. "The general consensus is Brazil. Walter found a receipt for a plane ticket, and the FBI confirmed that Sommers was issued a boarding pass for Rio a few hours after the closing."

"Why Brazil? Does he have a connection there?"

"Not that anyone knows of. There's a picture of Sommers, his wife, and daughter on a beach that sits on Sommers's desk. Could be Brazil. But Walter thinks it's most likely about Brazil's extradition policy. It's almost impossible to get someone extradited from there, so the ticket might make sense. Brazil amended its constitution in 1988 to state, 'No Brazilian shall be extradited.' If he planned all this and applied for Brazilian citizenship, who knows?" Liam shook his head. "But I don't think that's it. I think it's more likely the ticket was a diversionary tactic, a misdirection. He might not have gone there at all, but even if he did, he could have gone on to someplace else."

Catherine grabbed her beer and her purse. "I'm starving, let's get a table."

The owner led them to a corner table covered with a red-and-white-checkered tablecloth. In the center, a straw-covered bottle of Chianti had been converted into a candleholder. They waved off the menus. "We'll both have the cannelloni special, Tony," Liam said. "Sausage and peppers to start."

Catherine took another sip of her beer. "So, tell me about your depressing day."

"I started at your old firm. Walter introduced me to Chuck Henderson, who seemed to know John Sommers well. They were both transactional attorneys, ate lunch together, sometimes socialized. Sommers headed up J and F's business group—he was the practice-group chairman."

"I knew Jack was a group chairman, he was appointed to the position before I left. But he worked on a different floor and we didn't cross paths very often. I also remember Chuck. A little overweight, a little thin on top? Fighting that middle-age battle?"

Liam nodded. "Middle age is a formidable opponent. Chuck's losing the war. To quote Charles Barkley, 'Father Time is undefeated.'" Liam tore off a piece of garlic bread and placed it on his plate. "Anyway, Chuck's a nice fellow who was close to Sommers and had a lot of information to tell. As far as Jack's service to the firm, he was a diligent, hard worker. There was never an issue with his professional responsibility or his work product. He was never accused of mismanaging a file or neglecting a matter. He was entirely trustworthy, and Chuck cannot believe he misappropriated any money."

"But?"

Liam shrugged. "He's gone and the money's gone. As Chuck reluctantly admitted, 'The inference is compelling.' It makes him very sad. He says it's 'just the cliff at the end of Jack's road.'"

"What does that mean?"

"It means Jack was in a tailspin. The events in his personal life had devastated him."

"His wife?"

Liam nodded. "Sharon was a close friend and gave me the Sommers family history at her kitchen table. It's a long story."

Catherine opened her hands and raised her eyebrows. "And?"

"Jack met Alina overseas about ten years ago. He was a junior Foreign Service specialist on assignment for the State Department in Amman, Jordan. She was pursuing an advanced degree in psychology at the University of Jordan. She was also an accomplished pianist, and that's how Jack came to meet her.

"Alina was performing at the embassy one night with a classical trio. It was a cocktail party for some dignitaries, and Jack was in attendance. According to Sharon, he couldn't take his eyes off her. He was smitten. Sharon showed me pictures, and I don't blame him, Alina was striking. Dark hair, perfect complexion. A Middle Eastern beauty. They were a good-looking couple." Liam paused. "She wasn't Jordanian." He wrinkled his brow. "Palestinian, I think. Sharon said her family lived in one of the West Bank cities.

"Anyway, Jack takes a liking to her and hangs around after the concert to ask her out, which according to Sharon was a giant step because Jack's a very shy person. He's a Jew, she's an Arab. He's an American, she's a—I don't know—a Palestinian. This is a relationship that's never going to work. But, like Sharon says, he's smitten, so he musters up his courage and asks her if he can call on her. Customs being what they are over there, she won't go out without a chaperone. She's staying with her aunt Safiya, who lives in Amman, and so the three of them take a walk. Then they go to dinner. And then another dinner. And, you get the picture."

"I like this story," Catherine said.

"I would too, if it didn't end so tragically." Liam reached over and took a healthy share of sausage and peppers off the serving plate. "They dated solidly for the better part of a year. Safiya was their cover. She liked Jack and delighted in the intrigue. Then in the spring, things began to change. Alina graduated and Jack was informed that the Foreign Service was going to send him to Turkey. At that crossroads, they decide to get married. Neither of them wanted to move to Turkey, so they decide to move back to the States."

"Uh-oh."

"Right. Alina hadn't told her parents about Jack. They didn't know she had been dating anyone, let alone an American Jew. And Jack, he wanted to do the right thing. He told Alina he was going to ask her father for her hand in marriage. So the two of them travel to Alina's home to see the father. Naïve as can be. Surprise. It did not go well."

Liam offered the sausage-and-peppers plate to Catherine. She took a single green pepper and cut it into small bites. Liam shook his head.

"What does Sharon know about Alina's father?" Catherine asked.

"We didn't talk too much about the father's background. Supposedly he comes from a very old and respected Arab family. He's a doctor. A prominent man in his community. Alina's family is well-to-do and lives in a large home in some West Bank city."

"It must have taken enormous courage for Jack to petition her father."

"Without a doubt. But he shows up at the front door with Alina. A manservant shuttles them into this fancy library with marble floors and Oriental rugs. A few minutes later, Alina's father comes into the room and asks them to sit down. Not wanting to be rude,

Jack waits to be recognized before he starts speaking. The silence is deafening. Finally, Alina's father nods and gestures with his fingers in a rolling motion, as if he's saying, 'You may begin.' Jack stumbles with an introduction, tells him how much he loves his daughter, tells him that he and Alina are very much in love and would like to make a life together. He would like his blessings for their marriage.

"The father nods his understanding. 'You are Muslim?' he asks. 'No,' Jack says, 'actually I'm Jewish, but I have great respect for your religion and I would support Alina in the practice of her faith.'

"The father nods again. 'Where do you think you will live?'

"'In Chicago, sir,' Jack says. 'But I promise that Alina will visit you often. As often as she wants. Or, as you want.'

"Her father listens politely, rests his chin on his hand, nods, pauses, and then calmly announces that Jack is to leave, not only the house but the city. He is never to see Alina again. Alina is forbidden from ever contacting him. Jack tries to reason with him: they are adults, they are entitled to make decisions about their lives, they love each other." Liam shook his head. "No dice. In comes the father's manservant, like out of *Arabian Nights*, and takes Jack by the elbow and walks him out to the street. He says to Jack, 'If I see you here again, it will not be good for you. Forget Alina.'"

"But he didn't, did he?" Catherine said.

"Nope. He goes back to Amman in hopes that Alina's aunt can intercede. Safiya says she has no chance of changing her brother's mind, but Safiya is a romantic. She will contact the family and try to bring Alina to Amman, where they can see each other again. Weeks go by. Safiya says Alina is being watched and is confined to her home. Finally, Jack is informed that Alina is coming to visit Amman, but she will be chaperoned."

Liam paused. "Are you sure you don't want any more of the sausage and peppers? You're missing out here."

"No, Liam. Tell me what happens next."

"Alina arrives at Safiya's, but, as expected, she is watched very closely. Jack dares not show his face or Alina will be whisked away. But, as Sharon said with a devilish glint in her eye, Safiya is a romantic and a schemer. She arranges a secret rendezvous for them at the market. The reconnection is stronger than ever, and Jack and Alina vow to be together. There is a recital at the university and a plot is hatched. Safiya buys tickets for everyone. In the midst of the performance, Alina excuses herself to go to the ladies' room. She dashes out the front door, meets Jack in a taxi, and the two of them hightail it to the airport, where they catch a flight to Rome and then to Chicago."

"That's so exciting," Catherine said with a broad smile. "I almost don't want to hear the tragic part."

The cannelloni was served and the two ate in silence for a while, commenting only on the superb quality of the pasta.

FOURTEEN

· · ·

SOMMERS WALKED SLOWLY FROM the sand toward the hotel lobby. He was spent. Drawn to the Hilton to visit with his memories, he had underestimated the pain. He would not come again. As he approached the lobby, he noticed a sign on the kiosk.

Hawaii—A Photographic Essay
An Island Journey Captured Through the Lens
Marcy Grant, Artist
Rainbow Tower Lobby
Pictures Available for Purchase
10–5

The lobby was crowded. The show appeared to be running successfully. Several framed prints rested on easels; others were propped against the walls. Unframed prints, covered with acetate, were arranged in plastic crates. Marcy sat behind a table, cheerfully chatting with tourists who were busily thumbing through the prints. With his hands clasped behind his back, Sommers meandered around the room, admiring the photos. Memories made him pause and stare at a picture of the Pali Lookout.

"Are you going to buy that one, Jack?" Marcy said from behind him.

"You do very nice work."

"Thank you. The one you're looking at with the frame is only two hundred and fifty dollars."

"If I buy the picture, will you have a cup of coffee with me?"

"No. You should buy a picture because you like it, not because you want me to have a cup of coffee with you. Besides, I won't let you buy the picture, I'll give it to you."

"I'd like to make amends for the other night."

"With a cup of coffee? Pretty cheap amends. I thought you said it was better for us not to be seen together."

"That's probably true, but I've had a real bad day. Besides, I'm still ashamed of myself. The other night was totally out of character for me."

Marcy laughed hard. "Not entirely. I seem to remember the six of us sitting in your living room getting quite shitfaced when you closed your first merger."

Jack smiled. "Everyone except Alina."

"That's right, of course. She didn't drink. But I was sure drunk enough for the two of us. You have nothing to apologize for."

A woman's loud laughter and the sound of broken wood quickly grabbed Marcy's attention. She spun around to see a large man in a bathing suit and a tank top lying on top of framed pictures and broken easels. His tropical drink had spilled all over his shirt and Marcy's pictures. He was trying to control his amusement.

"Whoops," he slurred. "Guess I didn't see that stop sign, Officer." He and his girlfriend broke into sloppy belly laughter. He wiped his nose with the back of his hand. "Y'know, lady," he said to Marcy, "you shouldn't have all those fuckin' pichurs lying around the floor for people to trip on. Y'know? Iz a fuckin' hazard."

"You're right, Randy," his girlfriend said. "We should sue this stupid hotel."

"Right, baby." Then to Marcy, he said, "You owe me fourteen bucks for a tequila sunrise. It was practically full. I only had a sip or two."

"Owe you?" Marcy said angrily. "You broke four of my framed sixteen-by-twenties. At four hundred and fifty dollars apiece. That's eighteen hundred dollars."

Randy stood and puffed out his chest. "I wouldn't pay eighteen cents for this shit. I want fourteen bucks for my drink or I'll take it out of your cash box." He pushed Marcy aside and moved toward the table. Jack blocked his advance and, without thinking, nailed him flush with a hard right cross. Randy stumbled backward, falling onto the stairs.

"Down goes Randy," his girlfriend said, laughing.

Randy scrambled to his feet and bull-rushed Jack, forcing him back through the doors of the lobby and onto the floor, where two security guards finally separated them.

"Fuckin' guy cheap-shotted me," Randy said, rubbing his jaw.

"This is the second time we've had a problem with you, Mr. Webster. You need to find another hotel. Now!" The security guards walked him out to the front desk, one on each side.

Jack returned to the lobby, where Marcy was salvaging what remained of the broken pictures. The hotel staff was picking up broken glass. The lobby had been cleared of customers.

"Are you okay, Jack?" Marcy pointed to his chest. "Your shirt is ripped."

Jack shrugged. "I guess so."

"What were you doing? Are you crazy? That guy was twice your size."

"He was a jerk. And he picked the wrong day to fuck with me." Jack looked down at the mess, shook his head, and bent down to pick up a couple of pictures.

Marcy leaned over and gave Jack a simple kiss on the cheek. "If you wait a few minutes while I pack up, I'll have that cup of coffee with you."

Jack smiled, and when he did, he grimaced at the mouse growing under his right eye.

As they wheeled the cart with her stacked pictures toward the parking lot, Marcy looked at Jack and liltingly mimicked, "Down goes Randy."

They laughed.

"Actually, Jack, I'd prefer something stronger than a cup of coffee."

"I wasn't going to suggest that, for obvious reasons."

"It's okay. Let's put these away and go back to the Tiki Bar."

Jack shook his head. "I don't want to stay here. I've had enough of the Hilton for today. Can we go somewhere else?"

FIFTEEN

. . .

THE DINNER PLATES WERE cleared and the dessert cart appeared. Catherine shook her head and ordered coffee. "Tell me the rest of the story," she said to Liam.

Liam pointed at the cart. "What about the cannoli? Aren't you going to have cannoli? Sorrento's makes the best."

"You have it. I want to hear the story."

"Two cannoli, please," Liam said to the server.

"I don't want cannoli," Catherine said.

"We always have them. You might change your mind."

"No, I won't. You always order two cannoli and I never eat mine."

"Okay, so then we'll take it home. But you might change your mind."

"The story."

"Okay. Jack and Alina fly to Chicago, Jack's hometown. They rent a place on Roscoe while Jack interviews for an attorney's position. In a few weeks, he lands a job at J and F in their transactional department. Meanwhile, Alina finds work teaching piano while she takes classes to be a social worker. All in all, Sharon describes quite the love story. Sommers is totally devoted to Alina, and she to him.

"Although Alina had never been to the US, she's very social. She finds things for them to do together. She's a musician, so of course they attend concerts. They subscribe to the Lyric Opera. And she gets Jack involved in the Chicago Shakespeare Theater."

"Shakespeare? They're actors?"

Liam shook his head. "Nah, they just like Shakespeare. Apparently, that was Alina's passion; she studied it in college. In Jordan. Go figure. In fact, they had a plaque hanging on their living-room wall with a Shakespeare quote. She told Sharon it defined the moment that she and Jack decided to take the plunge."

"Really? What was on the plaque?"

Liam shook his head. "A quote from *Julius Caesar*. About the 'tide in the affairs of men.'"

Catherine smiled. "Of course! It would define the moment they decided to disobey the father and run away. If I'm not mistaken, it goes, 'There is a tide in the affairs of men, which, taken at the flood, leads on to fortune. Omitted, all the voyage of their life is bound in shallows and in miseries.' I think I'm getting a pretty good idea of who Alina was."

"You know that quote? Word for word?"

"You're too easily impressed. It's not obscure. Tell me the rest of the story."

"Well, Alina was looking for ways to build a social life in Chicago and came across the Chicago Shakespeare Theater. That was something they could do together and meet people. She became a board member."

Catherine shook her head. "I've never been to Chicago Shakespeare Theater. And I've lived here all my life. She comes from Jordan and within weeks she ends up on the board. That's pretty cool."

"You think that's cool? Every year, Jack and Alina would hold a Shakespeare-themed party. All the board members would come dressed as their favorite characters. Sharon described one of their parties where Alina was Cleopatra and Jack was Marc Antony. Sharon dressed up as Brutus, which was pretty funny if you saw Sharon, a skinny, little redhead. Sharon said it was so cute how they were always quoting Shakespeare.

"Anyway, back to the important stuff. Jack and Alina bought a little brick bungalow up in Logan Square, and six years ago they had a little girl. They named her Sophie."

"After Safiya?"

"Could be. Makes sense." Liam took a small picture out of his pocket and handed it to Catherine. "This is a copy of a picture that sits on Sommers's desk. Alina and Sophie are standing with him on a beach."

"What a pretty family. She's lovely and the child is precious. Look at that smile. Where are they, in Brazil?"

"Could be, but I don't think so. I don't think he ever went to Brazil, then or now, and I'll tell you why in a few minutes."

"You're getting to the sad part, aren't you?"

Liam nodded. "Until a couple years ago, everything went fine. Sharon says they were the 'quintessential American family.' Her words. Wonderful friends and neighbors. She described a very close neighborhood group of friends.

"Then, about a year and a half ago, Alina got word from Safiya that her mother had suffered a heart attack. She was in critical condition and was scheduled for open-heart surgery. Alina tells Jack, 'I've got to go back.'"

"Had Alina been in touch with her parents during any of this time?" Catherine said.

"Only with her mother. But secretly. Her father had disowned her. When she snuck out of Jordan with Jack, he washed his hands of her. To him, she didn't exist anymore. Alina would send letters and pictures, especially of Sophie, but her father never acknowledged them. Her mother would send private notes to Safiya, who would forward them to Alina. Her father never knew."

Catherine shook her head. "I can't imagine. How does a man disown his daughter? And how does a daughter deal with that pain?"

"Sharon could tell you. She spent many a night consoling Alina, who loved her father and suffered through tremendous guilt. She begged him in her letters to acccpt her family and reestablish a relationship. But he never answered. Safiya said that he forbade Alina's name from being spoken in the home."

"Defies comprehension."

Liam nodded. "So, Alina goes back to Amman. Jack stays behind with Sophie."

"Wasn't Alina afraid to return? I mean, her father kept her prisoner. How could she risk going back?"

"She had to chance it. Alina leaves in June, a year and a half ago. She's gone a month. First to Amman, where the surgery takes place, and then back to her parents' home in the West Bank to help her mother recover. She stays with her mother until July, and only returns to Chicago when her mother is up and about."

"What about the father?"

"Her father was distant to her, but not *imperious*. Again, Sharon's words. He spoke to her from a distance. He'd look at her and shake his head in disapproval. He never asked about Jack or Sophie. Any conversations between the two of them focused on Alina's mother and the care she needed. But Alina told Sharon that toward the end of the visit she thought his demeanor was softening. Right before she left, Alina saw a framed picture of Sophie sitting on the mantel. She looked at her father, right into his eyes, and he acknowledged her. He nodded with a little bit of a smile. Alina thought that was a big break in the ice."

"So then Alina returned home to Jack?"

Liam nodded. "But she was not well. Sharon told me that, when Alina returned, she looked a little thin and sickly, which was unusual for Alina. She was a healthy woman, very fit. Sharon figured Alina was exhausted, but that wasn't it. Apparently, she had picked up something on her trip. In her weakened condition, she began to run a fever and she couldn't shake it. One afternoon, Sharon called Jack at the office and told him to come home. 'Alina needs to see a doctor right away,' Sharon said. 'She can't hold her food down.'

"Jack took her to Northwestern Memorial, where she was admitted and seen by a team of specialists. They pumped her full of antibiotics and fluids and sent vials of her blood to infectious-disease centers, but the disease was very aggressive. Despite their care, she just wasn't getting any better. Jack practically moved into the hospital. Sophie stayed with Sharon.

"The doctors tried everything, but Sharon said it was like trying to hold a handful of water. No matter what they did, she just kept slipping through their fingers. Too much damage had been done. Then she started bleeding internally. Five weeks after she returned home, Alina died.

"Jack was overwhelmed with the suddenness of the loss. In a moment, his life had changed. Nevertheless, he and Sophie did their best to carry on. They were great for each other. At Sharon's urging, Jack and Sophie attended some therapy sessions. That helped somewhat. Then he went back to work and Sophie went back to preschool, and that helped as well. By Christmas, Jack was on his feet. It seemed like he and Sophie were standing on a stable platform. And then the second wave hit him."

Catherine sat mesmerized. "What second wave?"

"Alina's parents came to Chicago and hired Fenton and Gibbs."

"The divorce firm?"

"Right. They sued for guardianship, claiming that Jack was unfit, that Sophie's life was in danger, and that the best interests of Sophie would be served by a change of custody to the grandparents."

"Was that true? Was Sophie's life endangered?"

"Not according to Sharon. She says Jack and Sophie were as close as any father-daughter she'd ever known. They went everywhere together. Sophie was very well adjusted and doing well in school."

Catherine gestured for the waiter to bring another cup of coffee.

"Cat, I paid the bill," said Liam. "Don't you want to go home?"

"Not until you've finished. What about Jack's parents? Were they still alive?"

"No. But Jack was not about to give up custody of Sophie to anyone. He hired Harold Fine."

Catherine nodded. "Good hire."

"The case lasted for months and was a nightmare of a legal battle, but in the end, Jack won. The grandparents's petition for guardianship was denied, and Jack retained sole custody of Sophie. The judge gave Alina's parents limited weekend visitation within the Chicago city limits. And that ended up being the problem. One weekend they came, took the child, and never returned.

"Jack called their hotel and was told they had checked out. He called the police, the FBI, there was an Amber Alert." Liam shook his head and shrugged his shoulders. "Gone."

Catherine leaned forward. "Did anybody find out what happened?"

"Nope. Speculation only. I think it's a safe bet they're back in the Middle East."

"Can't the State Department get her back?"

"Not from where they are. I know there's some law on international child abduction, but I doubt that the Palestinian Authority is a signatory. You would know better than I. Jack made several inquiries through diplomatic channels with no success. Anyway, all of this happened a couple months ago. Then this Kelsen deal came up, and now both Jack and the eighty-eight million dollars are gone."

"And you don't think Jack's in Brazil?"

"Could be, but it doesn't make a lot of sense. Jack wants his daughter. He needs to mount a plan to get her back. How does he do that from exile in Brazil? By himself? I don't know, it doesn't fit the story."

"What fits the story?"

Liam raised a finger. "The Taggart hypothesis? Brazil's a clever diversion. I think he wants us to believe he's in Brazil, but he's really somewhere else. He's got the money and he's planning to use it to finance Sophie's rescue."

"If he's not in Brazil, then where is he?"

"I don't have a clue. Someplace where he can hide out and raise Sophie. Maybe he's still in Chicago."

Catherine stood. "What's the next step?"

Liam helped her with her coat. "Keep asking questions, keep poking around. Something will come up. It always does."

SIXTEEN

• • •

SOPHIE SAT AT HER desk and stared out the window of her
bedroom. Her chin was cradled in her palm. The outbuilding
to the side of the house was going through its shift change.
Three times a day, workers would come and go from the building.
Sophie wondered what was in the building. Why was there so much
activity? But Jaddi would not let her go there. "You are forbidden,"
he told her sternly.

She ambled over to her closet. It was full of strange new clothes
that Jadda had hung there. She didn't like them. She wanted to
wear the clothes that she and her mother had picked out together.
Colorful, fun clothes. It was warm most days in Hebron, but there
were no short sets, no T-shirts, no pink Nikes. There were white
blouses with sleeves that buttoned at the wrist, which she had to
wear with ankle-length skirts. And long dresses from the neck to
the shin. And the long, heavy coats that Jadda called jilbabs. Those
were the uniforms for madrassa. She didn't belong in those clothes.
She didn't belong in this bedroom. She belonged in her own house.
Why couldn't she go there?

"Come here, my little one. Come," al-Zahani called from the
other room. He sat in his large wingback chair and patted his lap.
"Come sit and have a cup of chocolate."

Sophie, her head lowered slightly, walked to her grandfather and
stood beside him. He reached down and lifted her onto his lap.
"And how was school today?"

Sophie slowly shook her head from side to side.

"I am told that one of the little girls, Jamila, has invited you to play at her home tomorrow. Yes?"

Sophie nodded. "We're going to paint pictures."

"That is good. You will have many friends here in Hebron. I promise you." Al-Zahani turned to his side table, lifted his silver-filigreed pitcher, and poured warm chocolate into a demitasse cup. He offered it to Sophie, who took it with both hands.

"Thank you, Jaddi," she said softly.

"You know, my precious one, we have many friends in our city. We are a proud family here. We are known here for many, many years. I can trace my ancestors, my great-great-great-grandfathers, all the way back to the land of Canaan. Do you know of Canaan?"

Sophie raised her eyes from her cup. She shook her head.

"I will tell you, because they are your great-great-great-grandfathers as well." Al-Zahani smiled and kissed her on the forehead. "Many, many years ago, thousands of years ago, our ancestors lived peacefully in the valleys of Canaan in the middle of Palestine. In this very area, here in the mountains of Hebron, lived the people known as Hittites. They were descended from Heth, the second son of Canaan. And you know what? So am I, and so are you. We are also descendants of the great warrior Heth. And do you know how I know this?"

With wide-eyed curiosity, Sophie shook her head.

"Because when I was just a small boy, no older than you, my blessed grandfather Ibrahim sat me on his lap with a cup of chocolate, the same as you and I are today, and told me of the glories of our ancestors. We are proud Canaanites, Sophie. Do not ever forget that. Once there were seven nations of Canaan. And they all dwelt peacefully in these lands. Until"—he stopped and pointed his finger—"until the Israelites were sent to wipe them out."

"Who sent them?" Sophie said.

"Ah, child, it's all in the Bible. No doubt you are too young to have studied the Bible, but it is in the book of Deuteronomy, chapter seven. The Israelites are commanded to smite all the people in the seven tribes of Canaan. They say that God commanded them and said to them, 'Thou shall have no pity upon them.' But, I ask you, what good and loving God would command such a thing?"

Sophie shrugged.

"It was at that time that one of the spies of Moses . . . do you know of Moses?" Sophie nodded. "Oh, of course, your father must have told you the Jewish stories of Moses. Well, Moses sent one of his spies, Joshua, to explore the lands of Canaan. After Moses died, Joshua became the leader of a massive army, and with thousands and thousands of Israelites, he invaded the lands of the Jordan Valley to settle his people. The peaceful people of Ammon were not fighters. They did not have the weapons of Joshua's army. But they were proud and told Joshua he could not have their land. They tried to defend their homes, but Joshua conquered them and showed no mercy.

"After conquering Ammon and leaving no person alive, Joshua and his people did not even settle there. No, they went north to conquer more of Canaan. Again, my precious, the peaceful people of Canaan had attacked no one. They threatened no one. They only wished to be left alone to live on their land. But the Israelites and their ruthless armies marched north to fight against them."

"Why, Jaddi? Why did the Israelites want to fight?"

"They say in their Bible that God commanded them, but in truth, that is their way. They are conquerors and occupiers of other people's houses and lands. Even today. Just the same. Did you ever hear the simple song 'Joshua Fit the Battle of Jericho'?"

Sophie's eyes brightened. "'And the walls came tumbling down.'"

"Just so. Only, the song is a fable. We are not told the real story. Do you want to know?"

Sophie nodded.

"Jericho, the oldest city in the world, was a peaceful little village in Canaan. It was small, but it had a large wall around the city to protect the people. Jericho didn't have very many soldiers. Only about five hundred. Joshua had a huge army of eight thousand Israelites, some on horses, some on foot, but all with weapons. There were four times as many men in Joshua's army as there were all the people in the town of Jericho. But the people had built a wall, six feet thick and twenty-six feet high, so they felt safe."

"Like the wall around your house, Jaddi?"

Al-Zahani laughed. "Maybe. Only a little bigger than mine, no?"

"How did the walls come tumbling down?"

"That is only a fairy story. The truth is that Joshua and his army encircled the city and for six days marched around making terrible noise and blowing loud horns. Then a woman named Rahab, a very evil woman who thought only of herself, made a secret deal with Joshua. In exchange for her safety, she snuck Joshua's soldiers into the town and they opened the gates for the army. What happened next is too terrible to tell. The Canaanites who lived in Jericho were brave and honorable, but no match for such a large army. After Joshua finished fighting them, he set the whole town on fire. Then he marched on to fight other towns in Canaan."

"And our family comes from Canaan, Jaddi?"

Al-Zahani nodded. "For thousands of years. Even though their lands were taken and they were left to wander without a home, they struggled against their oppressors and resisted the unlawful occupation then, as we do now."

"Did you ever have to leave your home?"

"Yes, I did. My whole family, my friends, and everyone I knew had to flee from the bombs. I was just about your age. We lived in Haifa, by the ocean."

"Did you have a home like mine?"

"Well, I've never been inside your home, but I think they were probably very much alike. I had my own bedroom."

"Why did you leave your home?"

"Because a war was about to start. Because far, far away from us, in New York City, a group of other countries decided to split up the land of Palestine and take our part away from us and give it to the Jews for a new country called Israel. So that we could keep our family safe from the war, we had to flee from our home. And we could never come back."

"That's not fair."

"You are right, little one, it is not fair."

Al-Zahani lifted Sophie from his lap and kissed her on the forehead. "And now it is time for bed."

SEVENTEEN

...

LARGE SNOWFLAKES, ILLUMINATED BY the head-
lights of Kelsen's black Bentley, gave the illusion of space
travel as it motored through the streets of a quiet subdivi-
sion north of Chicago. The Bentley turned into a driveway at the
end of a cul-de-sac and flashed its high beams against the side of
the house. A figure soon emerged, dressed in a black, hooded parka.
He sloshed through the snow to the back of the Bentley and a
window was lowered.

The man leaned in. He spoke with a Russian accent. "Is it all
arranged?"

"Yes," Kelsen said.

"You are sure? Dmitri will be playing large. This must be
assured. Nothing can go wrong." The man wagged his finger side
to side.

"Nothing is assured, Evgeniy. It's a basketball game. Things can
go wrong. Tell Dmitri to lay off if he's worried."

"Dmitri want to know, are you in?"

"Big-time."

"Okay. Okay. Then I give you this. You better be right." Evgeniy
passed an envelope through the window.

Kelsen held the envelope by the window. "Don't give me any of
that 'better be right' crap. I did what I had to do. Either he wants
this money played or he doesn't."

"He wants it played."

Kelsen counted the bills. He nodded and raised the window.

* * *

D AN GIBSON RECEIVED A call just after dinner. The door-
man in the Trump lobby informed him that two policemen
wanted to come up and talk to him. Gibson opened the door when
they arrived.

Detective O'Herrin spoke, his head lowered slightly. "I'm afraid
I have bad news for you, sir. Mr. Harrington's body was found this
evening at the Fullerton breakwater."

Gibson's legs went wobbly and he sat down on the couch. "What
happened?"

"Well, sir, it . . . it looks like there's been foul play. There was a
bullet wound. His body was taken to the medical examiner's. You
can see him there, sir, if you want to. Are you okay?"

"No, I'm not okay. Would you be okay?" Gibson's chin quivered.
"Where was the wound?"

O'Herrin hesitated. "In his right temple."

Gibson grabbed his face with both hands and cried.

O'Herrin pulled a small writing pad from his back pocket. "Can
we ask a few questions?"

Gibson swallowed hard. "Can we do this tomorrow?"

"Sure. That'd be all right. We'll call you tomorrow, but can I
ask just one question? Just one or two?"

Gibson nodded.

O'Herrin pulled up a chair opposite the couch and sat on the
edge. "Was Mr. Harrington depressed recently? Were there
any . . . what they call suicidal ideations? Would he take his own
life?"

Gibson sobbed. "No. Never. We were so happy. His company
was just sold and we were going to take a vacation. Denny's idea—a
cruise through the Panama Canal." Gibson grabbed a tissue. "Did
you find a gun?"

O'Herrin shook his head and penciled a few notes. "If his company was sold, where was he going to work?"

"We have some savings. Denny can easily get another job if he
wants one. He's very good at what he does." Gibson caught himself. "At what he did."

"I'm truly sorry, sir. Do you know whether he had money troubles? Was he indebted to anyone?"

"I told you, we have savings," Gibson snapped. "And besides, he told me he was getting a substantial bonus on the sale of the company."

"Excuse me for asking this, sir, but with him dead and all, would he still get that bonus?"

Gibson shook his head. "I don't know. It's not something we ever discussed. Would you leave now, please?"

"Of course." O'Herrin stood and took a step toward the door, then stopped. "Just one more question, please. Did he have any enemies?"

Gibson shook his head.

"Anybody who would want to do him harm?"

Gibson shook his head.

"Excuse me for asking this, but did he have any other relationships? You know, other guys who would, um, would be jealous enough to be violent?"

"That's insulting. Now please leave."

"Very sorry, sir. Can we call you tomorrow?"

Gibson nodded and showed them out.

EIGHTEEN

• • •

MARCY SMILED OVER THE rim of her wineglass. They sat side by side at a plank table on the veranda of Paca's Seaside Sushi Shack. Her elbows rested on the table and she wrapped her hands around the glass. "You were so gallant."

"That was not my intent. I assure you it was all knee-jerk." Jack gazed out at the Pacific. The stars and the horizon were both discernible in the minutes following the sun's dip beneath the edge of the earth, known to sailors as nautical twilight. The sea moved in shadows. Swells and whitecaps.

"'Twas gallantry nonetheless. I choose to believe my version of the story. Reasonable minds can differ. Isn't that what you lawyers say?" Marcy took a deep, relaxing breath and stared at the ocean. "This reminds me of that weekend at Grand Haven. Remember? We were all sitting at a picnic table on the beach. It must have been midnight, but Sophie wasn't the least bit sleepy. She kept running through the sand, chasing fireflies." Marcy chuckled. "What a sight. Alina chasing after her, trying to slow her down. They had quite a bond, those two."

Sommers was silent. His lips quivered.

"Jack, I'm sorry. Should I not bring up the past? They were such good times."

He nodded. "I'm okay. Let's talk about you."

"Oh, now there's an interesting subject. Struggling photographer trying to make ends meet in one of the country's most expensive locations. I used to think Ted did me a favor, chasing me out of Chicago, but now I think I bit off more than I can chew. I'm not even sure where I'll be living next week."

"Pacific Properties?"

"How do you know about that?"

"The summons and complaint were sitting on the counter beside your coffeemaker."

"So you read them? Nosy!" She shook her head. "I'm getting evicted. Mr. Nakamura wants me out of the house and he's been looking for an excuse. I was out of town on the first when the rent was due. I took it over to him on the third but he wouldn't accept it."

"Two days late? Did he serve you with any notices?"

She shook her head. "He showed me a section of the lease that said that if the rent wasn't paid on time, he would have the right to cancel the lease. It's right there in black and white."

"How much time is left on the lease?"

"Eighteen months, but it looks like I'll have to find another place pretty quick. The court date is next Tuesday."

"Have you talked to his lawyer?"

"He doesn't have one. He's a real estate man. He filed the papers by himself."

Jack nodded and smiled.

"Jack," she said quietly. "A few minutes ago, I didn't mean to upset you. You should cherish those memories of the good times. They're yours to keep. They're ours to keep. And to share with Sophie."

"I know." He turned his head away to look at the ocean.

"Jack, I'm worried about you. Alina's death was a heartbreaker for all of us, but most of all, you need to hold it together. You've got Sophie to raise. She needs you."

Jack stood suddenly. "Thanks, Marcy. I have to go. I'm sorry."

He put a $100 bill on the table and walked away.

HELLO, MR. JENKINS," CATHERINE'S receptionist said. She took his coat and offered a cup of coffee, which Jenkins accepted. He carried a large manila envelope. Moments later, she showed Jenkins into Catherine's office.

"Here's the lawsuit." He placed the envelope on her desk.

She took out the pleading and skimmed through it while Jenkins sat quietly with his coffee. When she was finished reading, she said, "Who's your malpractice carrier and what's the coverage?"

"LNA. And it's fifty million dollars, inclusive of defense costs."

She nodded. "That leaves thirty-eight million dollars uninsured. Who did LNA hire to defend you?"

"Alan Beaverton."

Catherine raised her eyebrows. "High-priced talent. Are you any closer to finding out what happened?"

Jenkins set his cup down and sat back in his chair. "Well, it's pretty obvious. Someone engineered a theft of eighty-eight million bucks from the closing escrow and siphoned the money off to Panama—and from there, who knows where? Harrington and Sommers both signed the wire instructions and both are missing. Hard for me to believe that Sommers did this to me. The firm was so good to him after his wife died."

"And you feel you need an attorney for the deficiency?"

"Of course. Besides, and I know you don't believe me, but I've always thought you have extraordinary litigation skills. Your approach is incisive. Intuitive. You see things that others do not. I've known that since the day we hired you. Please, Catherine, we're in a fix and I need the best. You can name your initial retainer, but I'm prepared to give you a check for fifty thousand dollars this afternoon."

Catherine stared into Jenkins's eyes. "All right, Walter. I'll take it on. I'd like a satellite office at J and F that I can use for this case."

Jenkins breathed a sigh of relief. "Done. And we've assigned Rob Hemmer to assist you. Anything you need."

"I'll want access to Sommers's personnel file and any other files he maintained at J and F."

"We've already pulled them. He has a file for the purchase of his house and a file, quite thick, for the custody dispute. There's really nothing in his personnel file, but I'll set the three files in your office. Then, of course, there's the Kelsen file."

Catherine stood. "I'll come in tomorrow."

NINETEEN

...

THE GROUP OF TEN, the self-styled Sons of Canaan, met again in the back of the Breadstone Bakery. A short man, in a black-on-green Palestinian keffiyeh, rushed in, out of breath, agitated.

"You are late, Rami."

"I think I was being followed. I diverted my route and came through the rear of the butcher shop. I ran two blocks behind the square. I didn't see her again, but I can't be sure."

"How do you know you were followed?"

"A woman was waiting when I left my building. She pretended to be texting on her cell phone, but when I started walking . . ."

"What did she look like?"

"What did she look like? She looked like any other woman in a burka. But she held her cell phone sideways, like she was taking a picture. I spotted her and she turned her back."

Fakhir, the bakery owner, lowered his head and put his hands on top of his knitted taqiyah. "The IDF. They've discovered us. And *my* bakery. We have to abandon our project."

"Stop panicking, Fakhir. Rami is a frightened squirrel. There's no evidence that anything has been discovered," Nizar said. "Who ever heard of IDF spies running around in burkas?"

"Nevertheless, I don't want to meet in my bakery again. We should meet at Arif's. He has privacy, a house with a wall around it."

"Out of the question," al-Zahani said. "I want no attention drawn to my laboratories. There are to be no meetings at my home. Beside, my granddaughter is living with me."

"The granddaughter, the granddaughter, we hear too much of this American Jewess," said Nizar.

Al-Zahani jumped to his feet and took a step in Nizar's direction. "She is my blood, you cocksucker. The lineage of my ancestors runs through her bones. She traces her descent from the ancient Canaanites. You live in Hebron because my father liberated it. My father and my grandfather are icons to our people. They died for us. Can you say the same of your pig family?"

Fa'iz interrupted. "Stop. What are you accomplishing? You insult his granddaughter? And you call his family pigs? Are you both out of your minds?"

"Did he not bring her from America? Is she not a Jew?"

"We will have no more of this," Fa'iz said. "We will not abandon our glorious plan. We will continue to meet. Fakhir does not want us to meet here, then we will meet somewhere else. We have much to do in the coming weeks. There is an empty apartment not far from here. I will arrange for Rami to rent it."

"Maybe we should put off our meetings for a while," said Ahmed. "If the IDF is looking for us, it jeopardizes the entire operation."

"The IDF is not here. The Palestinian police patrol this area; the Israeli police are only in the H2. The IDF knows nothing of what we do," Nizar said. "If we put off our meetings, then the entire operation is scuttled. Our target date is only two months away."

"And we still do not have sufficient quantities," al-Zahani said. "We will need every bit of two months."

"Then we meet at the apartment on Monday."

TWENTY

• • •

LD, FAMILIAR TERRITORY FOR Catherine as she
walked the hallways of Jenkins & Fairchild. Bittersweet.
It looked the same. Not much had changed. Two years ago,
she had considered it a secure, comfortable place to be, only to
abruptly learn that the firm valued pandering to clients more than
moral imperatives, forcing her to tender her resignation. But she felt
no regrets. Quite the opposite. Her present practice was far more
satisfying. No intrafirm politics. No pandering to influential clients.

Staff members smiled and welcomed her back as she made her
way to her assigned satellite office, a large, windowed room overlooking the federal plaza on Adams Street. Several expandable folders were sitting on a credenza, the largest, by far, being the matter
labeled "In Re: The Guardianship of Sophie Sommers." She would
save that for last.

She picked up Sommers's personnel file and thumbed through
the contents: application for employment, tax forms, health insurance
forms, and yearly self-evaluation letters written to the J&F Compensation Committee. The first several letters were unremarkable. They
recited his successful handling of certain mergers and acquisitions. As
the years progressed, he assumed more of the responsibilities in the
business and transactional group. Four years ago, he was elevated to
practice group chairman.

In the last couple years, since his wife's death, the file reflected
long absences and multiple requests for medical and family leave.
Yet, as Walter said, the firm was good to him. His compensation
was not reduced. His most recent self-evaluations were short and

apologetic. He was sorry for his inattention to the practice. He vowed to do better.

The last few pages in the personnel file referenced loans from his pension and profit-sharing accounts. These coincided with the period when Sommers was defending the guardianship petition. From the size of the custody file alone, Catherine could surmise the enormity of the financial drain. Loans from the retirement account would have netted him $150,000.

Sommers's house-purchase file held little of interest. The home was purchased six years ago for $325,000. It was titled to "John Sommers and Alina Sommers, husband and wife, as tenants by the entirety." There was a second mortgage and a refinance for a total of $415,000 fifteen months ago, during and after the custody battle.

The guardianship file consisted of four folders, each four or five inches thick. Catherine poured herself a cup of coffee and started at the beginning. "Petition for Guardianship of Sophie Sommers, a Minor." She spent the rest of the day perusing the file, occasionally setting papers to the side for further review and copying.

The al-Zahanis's guardianship petition was aggressive. It accused Jack of dangerously neglecting Sophie. It asserted that Jack had become so depressed over the death of Alina that he was unable to make day-to-day decisions or properly care for Sophie. "The minor's residence has become a dark and unhealthy tomb of despair," read the petition. "Continued residence in the home would be dangerous to the child's physical and mental well-being.

"On the other hand, the Petitioners, Arif and Lubannah al-Zahani, are kind and loving grandparents who are capable of nourishing and providing for the care of the child. They have a warm and comfortable home. The best interests of the child would be served by granting guardianship to the al-Zahanis."

At the inception of the case, the al-Zahanis filed an emergency motion for an immediate change of custody. It was supported by the affidavits of two private investigators with a picture of Sommers sitting on his front porch, a beer bottle by his side, dabbing his eyes with a tissue. The motion accused Sommers of "diving into alcohol and drugs." It was obvious the petitioners were pulling out all the stops.

The affidavits stated that women were coming and going into the home at all hours of the day and night. Grainy pictures were attached showing women entering the front door, time-stamped 1:00 A.M. and 2:30 A.M. The motion continued, "On one occasion, when staying in rustic, temporary quarters because his electricity was shut off, Sommers left the child all alone in the middle of the night without any adult supervision."

Judge Karr set the emergency motion for an immediate hearing, acknowledging "serious allegations." Sommers's attorney, Harold Fine, asked the court for a short continuance to take discovery and investigate the charges, but the request was denied and a hearing was set for the very next day. A transcript of the hearing was in the file.

Though it was not a lengthy hearing, to Catherine it clearly indicated how much dirt the al-Zahanis were willing to throw and how far they were willing to bend the truth to win their case. The first witness was the private investigator who had followed Jack surreptitiously for several weeks. He attested to the photographs and his statement that the child had been left alone at some rustic, wooden dwelling. He also testified that Sophie was at home when the "various female subjects were coming and going into the home at all hours of the night."

The direct testimony was damaging, and Jack's attorney needed a strong cross-examination to rebut the inferences of neglect. He began his cross by asking the investigator exactly when he was hired by the al-Zahanis.

"Nine weeks ago," he answered.

"And all during that time," Fine said, "as you were hired to do, would you take careful note of any activities you thought might be important to your clients in their custody case?"

"Basically."

"If you saw something you thought was not in the best interest of the child, you would write it down, wouldn't you?"

"Yes."

"Or take a picture?"

"Yes."

"Like the pictures you attached to your affidavits?"

"That's right."

"Anything you thought was wrong."

"Correct."

"And you took this picture because you thought it was wrong to be drinking a beer on the porch?"

"I thought it was wrong for the man to be drunk when his child was at home."

"Did you talk to Mr. Sommers?"

"Of course not. We were doing covert surveillance."

"So you didn't know if he was slurring his speech or not?"

"I couldn't hear him, counsel."

"Did you take any pictures of him falling down?"

"I'm not sure. Not that I recall at this time."

"Not that you recall? Hmmm. You mean you might have taken a picture of him falling-down drunk, a picture that would be very important to your clients in this case, but it might have slipped your mind? Maybe you forgot to bring it with you today?"

"No. I don't think I saw him fall down."

"How far away were you when you took this picture?"

"We were on the next block. We have a high-powered telephoto lens."

"How many pictures did you take of Mr. Sommers and a beer bottle?"

"Not certain. But I sure took that one."

"In nine weeks?"

"Yeah. So?"

"Well, I thought you told me you were going to take pictures every time you saw him do something wrong."

"Yeah?"

"And that's the only one with alcohol?"

"That's the only one I brought to court."

"Are there others?"

"Maybe. I can't remember."

Fine grabbed a court-stamped document. "I'm going to show you a document entitled 'Petitioners's Response to Request for Production of Documents.' I direct your attention to page two, in paragraph five. There is a list of all the pictures that the al-Zahanis or their attorneys have. Would you take a look at it?"

The investigator looked at the paper, shrugged, and laid it down.

"Okay. So I guess there are no other pictures of him holding alcohol."

"Let's talk about the various female subjects. How many pictures of women coming and going from Mr. Sommers's home did you produce out of your nine weeks of covert surveillance?"

"Six."

"Who were the women?"

"How would I know? Why don't you ask your client?"

"Thank you. That's an excellent idea, and I will do that just as soon as we're finished. But getting back to my question, when you signed your affidavit, did you have any idea who any of these women were?"

"At two or three in the morning? What's the difference? Are you going to tell me that's a babysitter?"

"No, I'm going to tell you that's his sister."

"There are different female subjects, counselor."

"How many different women, sir? Take a look at your pictures."

"It appears that there are at least two."

"At least?"

"There are two."

"So, in your nine weeks of *covert surveillance*, you took six pictures of two different women going into Mr. Sommers's home."

"In the middle of the night."

"On how many different nights?"

"Two."

"And in nine weeks of *covert surveillance*, that's all you've got, right? Six pictures taken on two nights."

"And the beer bottle, counsel."

Fine held up a pointed figure and smiled. "And the beer bottle, thank you for reminding me. So that's all that Dr. al-Zahani got out of the nine weeks of covert surveillance?"

"No, counsel. When the subject's electricity was shut off, he went to a one-room dwelling and left his daughter alone at eleven at night."

"You're absolutely right. I forgot about the *dwelling*. The electricity was turned off, you say? Did he forget to pay his bill?"

"No idea, counsel."

"Had there been a storm?"

SAVING SOPHIE : 91

"I don't remember."

"Was the electricity out in the neighborhood that night?"

"I don't work for the electric company." The investigator must have chuckled at his smart remark, Catherine thought, because Judge Karr interjected, "The court will admonish the witness. There is no cause for levity here."

"This one-room dwelling that Mr. Sommers and his daughter went to, was it a cabin up in the Wisconsin Dells?"

"Yep."

"Is that a water-park vacation area about four hours away?"

"Correct."

"And you went all the way up there to take pictures?"

"That was my assignment."

"Twenty-four hours a day?"

"Practically. Me or Frankie."

"When he left Sophie alone in the cabin, where did he go?"

"How should I know?"

"You mean you didn't follow him?"

"No."

"You noted the time he left; did you note the time he returned?"

"No."

"How long was he gone?"

"Not exactly sure."

"You didn't see him return, did you?"

"No,"

"Did you fall asleep?"

"It's possible. I can't recall."

"Was Dr. al-Zahani paying you by the hour?"

"Yeah."

"In nine weeks of work, how many hours did you log?"

"Four hundred eighty-three."

"How much were you paid per hour?"

"Hundred and a quarter."

Fine jotted down a couple of figures. "So, for his 60,375 dollars, Dr. al-Zahani got these seven pictures?"

"I guess you could say that."

"Nothing further."

Catherine smiled. Fine's cross was thorough and precise. He had not only damaged the investigator's credibility, but he had deftly created a platform for Sommers to explain the accusations. Sommers then testified that one of the women was indeed his sister, and the other was his wife's best friend, Sharon, who had been over for dinner, left her purse, and had come back to retrieve it at twelve forty-five. Sophie and Jack had gone to the Wisconsin Dells when a storm had knocked out the neighborhood's electricity. Sommers's momentary absence was due to a noisy toilet in the cabin. He thought he would wake Sophie, so he stepped outside behind the cabin to relieve himself. He was gone for less than five minutes. As to the remaining picture, Sommers admitted to sitting on his front porch having a beer. Sophie was at a friend's.

At the conclusion of the testimony, the judge denied the al-Zahanis's emergency motion, but expressed his concern for the welfare of the child. He appointed an attorney to represent Sophie. He also appointed a social service agency to do a home study, and he scheduled the case for trial.

After many other pretrial hearings, interrogatories, and depositions, ultimately at trial both sides offered testimony from psychiatrists and child-care experts. Home visits had been made, including a report from a social agency in Hebron. Catherine estimated Sommers's fees probably ran upward of $200,000. The transcripts of the trial were lengthy, and she copied them and headed for home.

TWENTY-ONE

• • •

AL-ZAHANI KNOCKED SOFTLY ON Sophie's bedroom door and opened it without waiting for a response. Sophie was at her desk; a schoolbook was open and she was practicing her writing.

"Jaddi, I can't learn Arabic. It's too hard. The letters are too hard to make."

"They were hard for me too, when I was your age. They are hard for everyone. But we all learn."

"Jaddi, I don't want to learn. I want to go home."

"Jadda said you played at Jamila's house today. Did you have fun?"

Sophie nodded. "She's nice."

"Her father is also a doctor and her older sister will be married later this year. Jadda says that you and Jamila can play here next week. Maybe you can play the piano for her."

Sophie shook her head. "Jamila's nice and her mother's nice to me, but I miss my home in Chicago. I miss my daddy. Why can't I go home?"

Al-Zahani sat on the bed and patted the quilt. "Come sit here, my precious, and I will tell you why."

Sophie climbed up on her bed and crossed her legs.

"This will be hard for you to hear. I did not want to tell you. It might make you sad, but I will tell you because I think you should know. You cannot go home, little one, because there is no home for you in Chicago anymore. My people back in Chicago have told me that your daddy has gone. No one knows where he went."

"No," Sophie cried, "he would not leave without me. You're lying. He would never leave me. I know where my home is. It's at 3814 Logan Boulevard. There is a redbrick house there with a wooden chair on the front porch. It's *my* home."

"There is no one *in* the home. Your father has left you and everyone else, and no one knows where he is."

"You're lying," she cried. She beat her fists upon his chest. "I want my daddy. I want to call him."

Al-Zahani gently held her wrists. "Sophie, I would never lie to you. Your Jaddi would never lie to you. Come with me and I will prove it to you."

He led her by the hand down the hall to a room he used as an office. He lifted her onto a desk chair and moved the telephone close to her. "Do you know your home phone number?"

Sophie nodded. Through her sniffles, she said, "It's 1-312-555-3799."

Al-Zahani pushed the speaker button and dialed the number. It rang and the recorded message said, "The number you have dialed has been disconnected. No further information is available."

"I'm sorry," al-Zahani said quietly.

Sophie hung her head and sobbed.

"You remember when we were all in court and you talked to the judge?"

Sophie nodded.

"Jadda and I told the judge we did not think your father would be able to take care of you. We wanted you to come here and live with us. And we were right. Your father did not take care of you. Now he has disappeared. He has no home. He has no phone. He's run off and no one knows where he is. And, Sophie, he has never even called to ask about you. I'm so sorry."

"That's not true." She stuck out her chin. "He's a famous lawyer. I could call him at his office."

"Do you know the number, Sophie?"

"Yes, I do."

Al-Zahani slid the phone over and dialed the country code. "Go ahead, Sophie. Call his office."

"Jenkins and Fairchild," said the receptionist.

"Can I talk to my dad?" Sophie said.

"Who's your dad, sweetie?"

"John Sommers."

"Oh, I'm sorry, he's not here. He doesn't work here anymore."

"Where is he?" Sophie said through convulsive breaths.

"I don't know, honey. He didn't tell me."

Sophie dropped the phone and ran out of the office to her bedroom. She slammed the door.

TWENTY-TWO

• • •

S OMMERS WENT ONLINE YET again. He should have had a response to his last message by now. It was understood by all that the plan would take some time, but something should be happening by now. It shouldn't be taking so damn long! Back in Chicago, he'd put everything he had on the table. All in for one last deal. Things should be moving forward. If he didn't see something positive in the e-mail account soon, then he'd have no choice but to go back and confront them.

Back in his hotel room, he faced another lonely day. Just him and Glenlivet. He poured a drink and studied the amber liquid. Another day in oblivion. But first he decided to make a couple of calls to help out an old friend who deserved better than his rude behavior. He dialed Pacific Properties and asked for Mr. Nakamura.

"Hello," said a tinny voice. "This is Nakamura."

"Mr. Nakamura," Jack said, "this is Oliver Everett of the firm of Gladstone and Finchley. We represent Marcy Grant."

"Oh, good. You get her out, I waive the penalty."

"Quite the contrary, sir. If you withdraw the suit immediately, we won't seek fees and costs against you, and we won't report you to the Department of the Prosecuting Attorney for the City and County of Honolulu."

"What are you talking about?"

"I'm talking about filing a suit for summary possession without the statutory five-day notice. The suit is defective and you know it."

"She didn't pay rent on time. The lease says pay on the first."

"And Hawaii Revised Statutes, section 521-68, requires a landlord to serve a five-day written notice of nonpayment, during which time the tenant may pay the rent or move. Filing suit without serving notice is considered an unfair and deceptive trade practice. Besides, Ms. Grant tendered the rent to you on February third."

"Maybe she did and maybe she didn't. Can you prove it?"

"Are you an attorney?"

"No. I am the president of Pacific Properties, Inc. We own the house."

"Hmmm. Now that raises another illegal situation. Are you aware that a corporation cannot act on its own behalf in court? Since a corporation is a noncorporeal entity, it can only speak through its human representatives. It can't represent itself. It must have a spokesperson. And in a courtroom, that spokesperson must be a licensed attorney. By filing the suit and signing the complaint, you have violated Hawaii Revised Statute section 605-14: engaging in the unauthorized practice of law."

"Wait, no. What?"

"I'm afraid I will have to contact the Department of the Prosecuting Attorney. Two serious offenses here: engaging in a deceptive trade practice and the unauthorized practice of law. Very serious, indeed, Mr. Nakamura."

"Wait, no. We could, ah . . . you know, we could work something out. You tell her, I'll let her stay this time. I'll tear up the papers, she doesn't have to come to court."

"That's not good enough, Mr. Nakamura. The continued existence of this unjustified lawsuit is a blemish on her fine reputation. I want you to go directly to the courthouse and nonsuit this case. Obtain an immediate order of dismissal. Then I want you to take a copy of that order and deliver it to Ms. Grant's residence this afternoon. Unless she calls me by five P.M. and tells me that the case is dismissed, well, I will have to do what I have to do. Understand?"

"Yeah, yeah, yeah. I'll do it."

"There's something else. I charge six hundred dollars an hour and I've spent two hours so far on this matter. What should we do about that?"

"She don't have to pay the rent this month."

"Nice talking to you, Mr. Nakamura."

Jack smiled. "One down." He took a card out of his pocket and dialed another number.

"*Hawaii Magazine,* this is Malani Chen."

"Hello, Malani. This is Jack Montgomery. You sat next to me on the plane."

She giggled. "The man with the soft shoulder. How are you enjoying Hawaii?"

"Very well. I may even decide to live here. I wonder if I may be so bold as to impose upon you for a small favor?"

"Well, you didn't mind being bold on the airplane." She laughed. "What do you need?"

"I ran into an old friend of mine yesterday. She's a wonderful freelance photographer who moved to Hawaii several months ago. I wonder if you'd take a look at some of her work. No promises, you don't have to like any of it. But she can't even get in the door of any of the local publications. It would mean a lot to her just to have someone look."

"Absolutely. Have her call me. She's right about not getting in the door, it's a very close-knit circle out here. Very tough to break in. But I'm always looking for a good freelancer."

"Thanks a million, Malani. You can use my shoulder anytime."

She laughed. "Jack, a few of us are getting together after work today at Roland's. If you're free, why don't you drop by?"

"I have a meeting this afternoon, but if I can break away, I will. Thanks a lot, Malani."

Sommers set the phone down and returned to his solitude. He sat by the window watching a deliveryman wheel a dolly of beer into the corner bar. He felt good about giving Marcy a hand, helping her out. Back in Chicago, Marcy had been a good friend. More than a good friend. She'd been there at the end.

His thoughts reeled him back to that last day—to the poignancy, the sweetness, the profound sadness, that would forever change all of their lives—back to the hospital room. Alina, her voice weak, almost a whisper, beckoned Jack closer to her pillow. "Ask Marcy to bring me my makeup. Tell her that I would ask one more favor of her. I would like her to come in here, clean me up, and make me look the best she can. I need to say good-bye to Sophie, and I don't want her to remember me like this."

"Don't talk like that," Jack protested, but Alina waved him off.

"We both know what's going on here, Jack. The doctors told us that my liver, my kidneys, have all but shut down. They've stopped working. I'm in a lot of pain, sweetheart, and I'm only alive because of that machine, and who knows for how much longer. Please let me say good-bye to my daughter in the right way. Just the two of us. Do that for me."

He nodded and bent over to give her a kiss. His throat tightened. "Oh, honey. I'm going to miss you so much."

"And I'll miss you too. But Sophie, she's a part of each of us, our little butterfly, part me and part you. All of the love we shared will live on in Sophie." Alina patted his hand. "Go to Marcy."

Marcy rose to the task magnificently, with all the skill and love she could muster. When she had finished, she returned to the hall and nodded to Jack. He led Sophie into the room where Alina lay propped up on her bed. Though thin and drawn, she looked radiant. Her hair was styled; there was color in her cheeks. Marcy had worked magic. Jack lifted Sophie onto the bed and left the room, closing the door behind him, leaving the two of them lying there, locked in a hug.

After a while, Sophie pushed the door open and walked into the hall. Her eyes were red, but she was composed. She walked straight to Jack, who knelt on the floor. "Mommy's going to live with God," she said. "She can't live with us anymore."

They cried together.

Later that day, Jack honored Alina's wish to turn off the machines. He lay beside her, holding tightly to her as she left. "'And flights of angels sing thee to thy rest,'" he'd whispered in her ear. Soon, the doctor came into the room. "May I have just a few minutes more?"

The doctor nodded sympathetically. "Take all the time you want."

He'd said his good-byes and made his promises. What Alina and Sophie had discussed was private and special to them, but Alina told him that she felt confident, secure in her belief that she could leave and the two of them would carry on, that they'd be just fine. Jack could count on Sophie to weather the storm. "Be strong for each other," Alina had said.

Then his thoughts returned to Hawaii, to the present and his insufferable dilemma. He looked at his glass of Scotch. He shook his head. *I can't do this again today. I'm not doing myself any good. I can't give in to another day of self-pity. Alina would be ashamed of me. "Be strong," she'd say. "Get out of your damn quagmire," she'd say. And I know what she'd tell me to do.* He picked up the phone.

"Are you busy?"

"It's raining, Jack."

"Does that mean you're busy?"

"Sure does. There are rainbows all over the island. This is a photographer's canvas. I might even find the pot of gold."

"Do you want company, Marcy? I'm not doing anything."

Silence for a moment. "You'd have to stand in the rain," she finally said. "Why don't we make it some other time?"

"I don't mind the rain."

"I don't know, Jack. The other night ended kind of rough for me. You know, cab fare on the table."

"I know. I'm really sorry. Again. But I'm a very good rainbow spotter."

"Every bone in my body tells me there are insurmountable issues here."

"There are. So, can I see you?"

"Well, if that's what you want. I'm all the way over at Kahana Bay on the windward coast. Do you know how to get here?"

"I'll find it. Kahana Bay."

"If you're serious about coming, bring hiking shoes. I'll meet you on the beach."

He laid the phone down and wondered if it was a mistake. She was good medicine for his melancholy, but when she brought up the memories, it was heartrending. And he felt himself leaning on Marcy. He feared another dependency. He was determined not to get close to anyone until Sophie was returned, but truth be told, he craved Marcy's company. They had a mutual foundation of affection. A history. They had a bond.

Sommers parked his car in the lot near the beach. A warm and gentle rain continued to fill the air. From time to time, the bright sun would peek through breaks in the clouds and send shafts of light sideways to the hills and vertically into the sea. Kahana Bay's crescent-shaped beach was bordered by steep hills, foothills to the Ko'olau Range, painted dark green by the ironwood trees. He found Marcy standing in the sand, pointing her camera at rainbows forming over the Ko'olaus.

"Those are your hiking shoes?" She pointed to his sandals.

He shrugged.

"Well, follow me and be careful not to slip." She stuffed her equipment into her backpack and headed to a trail that disappeared into the rain forest and up the mountainside.

Jack scrambled after her. The trail bordered the Kahana creek and serpentined its way up several hundred feet above the bay. Soon they arrived at the base of a waterfall that splashed into a clear pool. Marcy pointed. "At the top of that waterfall, there's another freshwater pool fed by yet another waterfall. One to another, like a Slinky, all the way from the top."

They resumed their climb up the slippery, mossy trail, but Jack's sandals couldn't hold a grip and slid out from under him. He fell belly-first onto the muddy trail.

Marcy tried to muffle a burst of laughter. "Would you get mad if I said, 'Down goes Randy'?"

Jack had to admit it was funny and realized he had made the right decision when he'd called her. No doubt, Marcy brought the right medicine to brighten his day, a prepackaged effervescence, and coming out from under clouds of depression could only help him think more clearly.

"You're better off barefoot. You can't climb in those sandals."

A few hundred feet more and they stopped to survey the scene. Broad philodendron leaves bordered the lush forest. Bushy ferns, three to four feet high, were abundant. Small flowers popped out of the forest floor.

Marcy knelt in a clearing and snapped close-ups of orange canna flowers. Then she stood and pointed down at the bay, where the clear, turquoise waters lapped against the white-sand beach.

"Right here is a shot I've taken many times. It looks like a scene from *Mutiny on the Bounty* or *Pirates of the Caribbean*, doesn't it? It's as pretty a picture as there is in Hawaii, but I can't sell the prints."

"Why not?"

"Do you see anyone on the beach?"

"No."

"Exactly. As beautiful as it is—serene, idyllic—tourists don't come here. It's a long ride from Waikiki, and the tour buses don't bring them out here. There are no concession stands, no souvenir shops. No commercial kickbacks to the tour-bus drivers. Tourists like to buy pictures of places they've been. They don't come here, so they don't buy my Kahana Bay pictures."

Down at the bottom, back at the beach, Sommers said, "Are you hungry? Can I take you to lunch?"

She nodded. "I'm starved and there's a place out here that I love. But look at your shirt, Jack, it's all full of mud."

He pulled his shirt off, soaked it in the ocean, and wrung it out. "Am I okay now? Do I look presentable enough to accompany a pretty photographer to lunch?"

She smiled. "Follow me."

Jack drove south along Kamehameha Highway and then onto a red-gravel road bordered by fields of grapevines on trellises. At the end of the road sat a small chalet with chalk plaster walls and a red-tile roof, reminiscent of the Italian countryside and clearly out of its architectural element on Oahu. The hand-painted sign above the door read IL TROVATORE.

"Italian?" Jack said, outside the door. "Really, Marcy? I come all the way from Chicago and you're taking me for Polynesian-style Veal Parmesan?"

"Give me your critic's review when you've finished. As far as I'm concerned, it's fabulous, and Giovanni's got his own vineyard."

Inside the entrance, on the foyer walls, were several framed photographs, including one that Jack immediately recognized. "Kahana Bay. I thought you said you couldn't sell these."

"We have a barter arrangement."

A red-cheeked man with a hearty smile came out of the kitchen, wiping his hands on his stained apron. "Marcitta, *benvenuto*." He wrapped his arms around her.

"Gio, this is Jack, a friend from the mainland."

Gio's handshake was happy, warm, and exaggerated. "Come in, come in."

"I thought maybe your name might be Manrico," Jack said.

Giovanni raised his eyebrows. "Ahh. The troubadour. You know the opera?"

"I do."

Giovanni put his arm around Marcy. "And you are a suitor of my precious Leonora?"

Jack furrowed his brow. "Aha, Count di Luna, my rival, I challenge you to a duel for the love of Leonora."

Giovanni laughed. "'The fire of jealous love.' You are truly a devotee, and the wine today is a gift of the house."

Giovanni brought out two bottles of his estate-grown wine. A Grenache gris for starters and a sweeter muscat of Alexandria. He set five glasses on the table.

"Of all the varietals I've tried, these two are my only successes. It's too hot and too wet for anything but southern-Mediterranean wines."

He poured three glasses of Grenache gris, held one up to the light, admired the ruby color, swirled it, and smiled proudly. Then he waited while Jack and Marcy tasted the offering and bestowed their approbations. He shrugged. *"Libiamo."*

During lunch, Jack nodded to Marcy. "Pretty damn tasty. Right up there with Taylor Street."

She smiled.

"I have something for you." Jack pulled out Malani's business card. "Give this woman a call tomorrow. She'd like to see some of your work."

"Seriously? *Hawaii Magazine?* Son of a bitch. How did you do that?"

He shrugged. "I met her on the plane and called her earlier today. Simple as that. But when you call her, you have to tell her you're a friend of Jack Montgomery."

"Jack Montgomery? Is that the name you gave her?"

"Right."

She had a look of consternation. "Jack, what's going on?"

"I can't tell you."

Marcy shook her head. "There's a virtual wall between us, Jack, and given our past, it makes me very uncomfortable. You've set all these artificial limits to our conversation, and I don't like them. We have too much history, you and I. Besides, given the way you ditched me at the bar the other night, can I ask, why the hell did you call me today?"

"I called you because you're my friend. Because I'm in a tough spot. Today was rough, like every other goddamn day, but even more so. And as much as I need to be invisible, I need a friend more. I don't have anyone else to turn to."

"Wow." Marcy took a drink of wine. "As long as we're being honest, I'm a little worried about getting too close to you. You've obviously got some scary things going on. I have the feeling you're not out here on business. And, Jack, as your good friend, I'm worried about you. Why aren't you home with Sophie?"

Jack leaned across the table. "Hold on to yourself, Marcy. I'm not home with Sophie because she's gone."

Marcy's face froze in shock. Her eyes opened wide. "Oh my God."

"No, it's not like that. She's alive. But she's been taken from me. She's been kidnapped."

Tears formed in Marcy's eyes. "By whom? When?"

"A few months ago. By Arif."

"Arif? Alina's father has her? Is she in Hebron?"

Jack nodded. "I don't know for sure, but that's my best guess. Now you know why I'm so mysterious. I'm working on a plan to get her back, and I need to be real careful. Before coming out here, I had to do some things. Cross some lines. I had to associate with people who may not be doing things aboveboard. So, I had to drop out of sight. You don't want to get involved in this mess. Let's keep it that way."

"You called me today, not the other way around."

"I know. Sometimes need trumps wisdom."

"What does Arif say? Did you call him?"

"He changed his numbers. I can't reach him."

"If Sophie's in the Middle East and you know where she is, why are you going through mobsters? Why don't you go get her yourself? Hell, I'll go with you."

"Well, first of all, who said they were mobsters? They're just some guys with connections. And as to going into Hebron and rescuing Sophie myself, that's a near-impossible task and a last-ditch effort. Hebron's a violent, dangerous city. It's a Palestinian stronghold and Arif's well protected. It would be a risk not only to me but to Sophie as well. I'm not saying I won't do it as a last resort, but right now my plans call for me to wait here while others do their part. One day I'll tell you all the details."

"One day, my ass. You're talking to Aunt Marcy." She stood. "You can't leave off in the middle of the story. I want to know these details." She turned and waved at Giovanni. "Let's see if I can talk Gio into giving us another bottle of Grenache. We'll take it back to my place. At least I can say it's my place for a few more days."

TWENTY-THREE

...

CATHERINE SAT AT HER dining-room table. Stacked before her were twenty-four hundred pages of trial transcripts from *In Re: the Guardianship of Sophie Sommers.* The trial, which began in August 2012, lasted six days. They started with reports from the agencies. Jack took the stand on the afternoon of the third day and faced grilling cross-examination from al-Zahani's lawyer. Catherine flagged certain pages of his testimony:

(By Jerome Gibbs) "Mr. Sommers, after your daughter, Sophie, was born, did your wife continue to work?"

(John Sommers) "Not as a social worker. After Sophie was three or four months old, she returned to teaching piano."

"In the home?"

"That's right."

"In the five years of Sophie's life, did your wife ever have a job outside the home?"

"What's your point?"

"I'll ask the questions, sir, if you don't mind. Did she work outside the home at any time after Sophie was born?"

"No."

"And you, sir, am I correct that you have been an attorney at the firm of Jenkins and Fairchild the entire time that Sophie's been alive?"

"That's correct."

"How many hours did you bill last year?"

"Billable? Just about two thousand."

"Is that in line with what Jenkins and Fairchild requires of its attorneys?"

"Pretty much."

"Are you also required to log nonbillable hours?"

"Yes. Client development, community involvement, bar association activities."

"And don't you have to spend several hours in continuing legal education to keep your license?"

"Yes. About twenty a year."

"Altogether, Mr. Sommers, how many total hours did you report to Jenkins and Fairchild last year?"

"I'm not sure. About 2,400."

"Oh, I think it was 2,714, wasn't it?"

"That could be right."

"Now if my math is correct, that amounts to 226 hours per month, correct?"

"If you say so."

"And taking away the holidays and vacation time, that would be about fifty hours per week, am I right?"

"If you say so. I haven't done the math."

"And would you agree with me, sir, that some of the hours that you spend at the office in a day just aren't billable or recordable at all? I mean, you have lunch, right? Occasionally get a cup of coffee?"

(Witness is silent)

"Sir?"

"That's right."

"Oh, and let's not forget commuting. How long does it take you to get to work?"

"Half hour."

"So, we're really talking about sixty or more hours a week that you're away from the home, right?"

"I guess so."

"And that's pretty much been your habit for the last five years, hasn't it?"

(Witness nods)

"During the time that Sophie was growing up, and you were

putting in your sixty or more hours per week, who was caring for the child?"

"My wife."

"Exactly. Did she make her breakfast?"

"Yes."

"Get her off to school?"

"Yes."

"Make her lunch and dinner?"

"Yes."

"Bought her clothes, took her to the park, read her the bedtime stories?"

(By Judge Karr) "Counsel, we get the idea. Move on."

(By Mr. Gibbs) "Mr. Sommers, are you still working at Jenkins and Fairchild?"

"Yes."

"Now that you don't have a wife to assume the entire responsibility of raising your child, are you still putting in your sixty hours a week?"

"No, I work fewer hours."

"Well, I have your report for the last thirty days. May we mark this as an exhibit, please?"

(Exhibit is marked)

"Did you log 220 hours last month?"

"Yes, but it was—"

"How many Saturdays did you work?"

"That's not fair. I had a large transaction to close and—"

"How many, Mr. Sommers?"

"Two."

"And two Sundays?"

"Yes, but—"

"That's a sufficient answer, sir. Did you enroll Sophie in day care?"

"Preschool. I did."

"Does she go every day?"

"Weekdays."

"Isn't it true that for weeks and weeks Sophie cried hysterically when you dropped her off at day care?"

(Witness is silent)

"Mr. Sommers?"

"There were some adjustment problems we had to work through."

"She clung to you at the door and begged you not to leave her, didn't she?"

"Damn you, Gibbs, her mother had died. She was only five."

(Whereupon a break was called)

(By Mr. Gibbs) "Getting back to the day care, did the director of the facility recommend that Sophie seek professional help?"

"I was already bringing her to a child psychologist."

"A five-year-old girl in psychotherapy?"

"Her mother had died, you bastard."

(By Judge Karr) "Settle down, Mr. Sommers."

(By Mr. Gibbs) "Are you in therapy as well?"

"Yes."

"Let's move on to a different subject, Mr. Sommers. Let's talk about your wife. Was she in therapy?"

"No, never."

"Would you say she was well-adjusted?"

"Absolutely."

"Kind, loving?"

"Absolutely."

"Would you describe her as a happy woman?"

"Yes, I would, and so would everyone that knew her."

"Was she a good mother?"

"Yes."

"Was she a good wife to you?"

"The . . . the best."

(By Judge Karr) "Would you like some water, Mr. Sommers?"

(Whereupon a break was called)

"Did your wife possess all the skills necessary to make a happy home for you and your daughter?"

"Without question."

"In fact, isn't it true that you would love for Sophie to grow up to be just like her mother?"

"Yes, I would."

"Would you agree with me that Dr. and Mrs. al Zahani did a first-rate job raising Alina al-Zahani?"

"Alina was a wonderful woman."

"No further questions."

CATHERINE'S CONCENTRATION WAS BROKEN as Liam walked into the room.

"How do you like working for Walter Jenkins again, Cat?" he said as he slipped off his coat.

Catherine gave him an angry squint. "I don't work for him. J and F has engaged my professional services. I work for Catherine Lockhart, Attorney at Law."

Liam smiled. "Take it easy. I didn't mean to rile you up. I know you went by the office today. I'm only asking how it was."

"Weird. To tell you the truth, I did not like being there. It brought back all the bad memories of my separation two years ago. I could see Walter sitting in my office, ordering me to withdraw from Ben's case because suing Elliot Rosenzweig was too offensive to his big insurance clients. I remembered the day I came to pack up my office and he arrogantly barged in and tried to pay me off—a huge bonus if I dropped Ben's case."

"So why are you back there?"

"If you recall, I wasn't going to. Then you told me the story about Jack and Alina, and it brought back my memories of Jack Sommers. I didn't know him well, but from what I knew, I just can't believe that he stole that money. And then, when Walter sat in my office, and begged me to take the case, I don't know, I had a lot of friends back at J and F. They're personally on the hook for thirty-eight million dollars. I thought I could help."

Liam patted the couch. "Sit down, I have some information for you. I spent the afternoon with Jeff Miller at the FBI office. Miller is the agent assigned to the case."

Catherine headed toward the kitchen. "Would you like a beer?"

"I'll never say no to that." Liam raised his voice to be heard in the kitchen. "Miller told me that Sommers never went to Brazil. He checked in at O'Hare, went though security, he even scanned his boarding pass, but he never went through immigration in Rio. There are no records of his passport being swiped."

Catherine came back into the room with a bottle of Blue Moon for Liam and a frosted glass of Corona for herself. She set them on the coffee table and curled her feet underneath her on the corner of the couch next to Liam. "Maybe Sommers had a fake passport, or a forged passport, in someone else's name?"

"Nope. They checked the videos around the time the Chicago flight arrived. He didn't enter the country."

"Does Miller have any idea where he went?"

"If he does, he's not telling me."

"Israel?"

Liam shook his head. "Tel Aviv airport security has facial recognition software. They're pretty sure he hasn't landed in Israel."

"Maybe he could change his looks, false papers?"

"Cat, this guy is a transactional lawyer, he's not Jason Bourne."

"Do they think he has the money?"

"They're not sure he does, but they think he's involved. And they're positive there must be others. After all, at least one of the direct participants is dead. Harrington went missing the day after the theft and his body was fished out of the lake."

"Could Sommers be dead as well?"

"Possibly. But again, his body hasn't turned up, so who knows? Given Sommers's profile, the FBI doesn't think he's a murderer. Miller is convinced that Sommers was an enabler and that someone else was pulling his strings."

"What else did he tell you?"

"That's all he would say. They have more going on, but it's all secretive. He wants to set a meeting for us at J and F tomorrow. He has someone for us to meet."

"So that's why Walter called me," she said.

"Right. Ten A.M. tomorrow. It'll be you, me, Walter, Miller, and the other guy he's bringing."

"Who's he bringing?"

"He wouldn't say. But he doesn't want me to talk to anyone else until after the meeting."

Catherine shrugged. "Well, I guess we'll find out tomorrow." She took a sip of her beer.

Liam turned to face her. He leaned over to put his arm around her and give her a kiss.

Catherine looked at him as though something was on her mind.

"Liam, I've been thinking a lot about our talk the other night at Café Sorrento, and you know what I can't get out of my head? That quote from *Julius Caesar*, the one that hung on Alina's wall. About the tide. Do you suppose there's always such a moment in relationships?"

Liam took a gulp of beer. "You mean for you and me—for our relationship? Are you talking about when we were in college, that we should have run off together? Like Jack and Alina did? That maybe I should have grabbed the moment?"

"I suppose that could have been what I was thinking, but it wasn't. That's ancient history. I was really thinking about more current times."

"But we did, didn't we? I mean we took it at the flood, we got together again after all these years."

"Well, we did, but . . ."

"And we're doing great. Aren't you happy with the way things are?"

"I'm not unhappy, Liam, that's not the point. It's about more than just 'doing great.' I mean, is this the way you want to keep things? Just being together?"

Liam shrugged. "Why not?"

She stood, turned her back, and walked to the kitchen.

"Catherine? Did I say something wrong?" Liam rose from the couch and followed her. "Wait a minute, okay? I get it. We're not getting any younger, the talk about families, the talk about relationships, about you and me. Am I right? Work with me here, you know I'm a little dense. You wanted to talk about things, I can talk. We can talk."

Catherine shook her head. "Jesus, Liam. Never mind."

"C'mon, Cat. I didn't mean to be flip." Liam walked behind her into the kitchen. "I just didn't want to push things, you know. You had a bad marriage and maybe . . ."

"Maybe what? That I'd never want to marry someone ever again?"

Liam put his palm on his forehead. "I'm not going to get out of this in one piece. I just didn't want to push it, that's all. Things are going well, so I didn't want to upset the applecart."

"Look, my marriage to Peter was a failure because I let him and his fast, jet-set style change me. Not because I can't carry off a marriage. I let the most shallow of indulgences—possessions, parties, social circles—become important in my life. I wasn't myself then, Liam. That's why my marriage failed."

"Your marriage failed because Peter was a crook and a philanderer."

"It wasn't just that. I had lost my moral compass."

"But I'm me, Cat. And we're good for each other. We can talk about getting married anytime you want to."

"Thanks for the reassurance. What do you want for dinner?"

"Was that your pocket veto?"

She shook her head in exasperation. "Dinner, Liam. What do you want to do about it?"

"I don't care." Liam left the room to finish his beer. After a while, he brought the empty bottle back into the kitchen and flipped it into the recycle can. "Before the meeting came up, I was planning on going down to Louisville tomorrow."

"Is it Derby time already?"

Liam smiled. "Not for three months. I was going to go down to pay a visit to Sommers's sister."

"Did you make an appointment?"

Liam shook his head. "She refused to talk to the FBI. She told Miller that she knew her rights and she didn't have to talk to him and he better not come back to her house without a court order. I didn't think she'd want to talk to me either."

"But you're planning on going down there?"

"Right. I might catch her off guard. Put on me Ulster charm. No woman can resist."

Catherine smiled. "It always works on me." She walked over and gave him a kiss. "I do love you, you know."

TWENTY-FOUR

• • •

L UBANNAH WALKED QUIETLY INTO the living room.
"She's finally asleep, Arif. I sang to her. Every lullaby I know.
She's very unhappy."

"She'll get over it."

"Earlier tonight, I asked her again to play the piano. I took her downstairs, put a pillow on the bench, just like we used to do for Alina. I showed her the music that Alina played. It even had hearts on the page that Alina drew when she was six. It only made her sadder. Sophie says she will only play her own piano. At her own home in Chicago. And then she cries because she misses her mother and her father. It's so sad."

"She'll get over it."

"I do not mean to question your wisdom, Arif, but I worry that we have done the wrong thing, taking her away from her home. She begs me to go home. 'Talk to Jaddi,' she says, 'and tell him to take me back to my daddy.' She cries and cries and clings so tightly to her stuffed bear."

"You do not mean to question my wisdom, but you question my wisdom. She'll get over it. And that bear, I think we should remove it. The bear reminds her of her life in America. It is too strong a connection."

Lubannah put her hands on her hips. "Now I draw the line. If you throw away her bear, she will be inconsolable. What are you trying to do, drive her to hysteria?"

"No, I'm trying to raise Sophie as I would have raised Alina. Alina was lost to me, my only child, my only descendant. Sophie is the only one left of our bloodline, Lubannah. Does that mean nothing to you? Are the al-Zahanis merely to disappear from the earth? No, Lubannah, she will become what Alina would have been. What Alina should have been."

"She is not Alina, Arif. Alina is—"

"Stop, woman. I will not have this argument. Sophie will be raised in our home as our daughter. Out of respect for you, I will not destroy her bear. At this time."

Al-Zahani stood and walked toward the door. "I have a meeting. I'll be back late. Do not wait up."

T HE GROUP OF TEN met at the apartment. By previous agreement, they arrived several minutes apart and from different directions. When they were finally assembled, Nizar said, "So, were you followed this time, Rami?"

"Not that I am aware. I did not see the woman, but who knows with the IDF?"

"We have seven weeks left," Fa'iz said. "Is the warehouse secure?"

"It is ideal. One of a thousand identical warehouses in Jerusalem, but with a locked cold-storage vault and an inside garage," Ahmed said.

"And what about the bags, what is our progress?"

"On schedule," al-Zahani answered. "That will not be our problem. The bus and the deliveries. Those are our only problems."

"What about the tour bus?"

"A beauty to behold. Safe in the garage. It needs only stenciling. Undetectable from the Israeli tour bus. But we still have plenty of time before we switch them," Rami said.

"What about a practice run?" Nizar said.

"There will be no practice run," Fa'iz said. "The bus, the bags, they will go out as scheduled."

TWENTY-FIVE

...

S ELECTION SUNDAY IS ONLY two weeks away, Victor,"
George said, trying to keep his voice loud enough to be heard
in the noisy arena. "Where do you think we'll be slotted?"

Kelsen shrugged. "Maybe Midwest. I think the Deacs will
probably be a second or third seed. Tough one tonight, though.
MSU is on an eleven-game winning streak."

They stood as the color guard carried the flags to center court
for the national anthem and the arena grew silent. George removed
his blue Deacons cap and placed it over his heart. He leaned over
and whispered to Kelsen, "You think we'll cover three points tonight?"

Kelsen smiled and shrugged. "Giving us three on our home
court is a pick 'em. I stayed away, George."

"Even from the over-and-under?"

Kelsen smiled again. "That's a different story."

A FTER DINNER, CATHERINE SAT at the table and resumed
reading the trial transcript. On the fourth day, al-Zahani took
the stand to testify on behalf of Lubannah and himself. Once again,
Catherine flagged certain sections of the testimony.

(Direct Examination by Petitioners's Attorney Jerome Gibbs) "Doctor, please say your name for the court record."

"Dr. Arif al-Zahani."

"What is your profession, sir?"

"I am a doctor of medicine and a research physician. I have a private practice in Hebron in general medicine. I am on staff at Al-Alia Hospital in Hebron, a teaching hospital, the government hospital."

"Am I correct, sir, that you were formerly chief of staff at your hospital?"

"That is correct, although we did not call it that."

"Have you practiced at any other hospital?"

"I have practiced at the Islamic Charitable Hospital in Jerusalem and for a while at the Augusta Victoria Hospital in Jerusalem. But no longer."

"And your wife, Lubannah, what is her profession?"

"Lubannah was a nurse many years ago. She stopped working when we had our only child, Alina. She stayed at home, raising our daughter, making her dinners, teaching her, nurturing her. She was an excellent mother."

"Calling your attention, Doctor, to October 2011, did you have occasion to hire a private investigation firm?"

"Yes. I became concerned for my granddaughter's welfare. When I was in Chicago for my daughter's funeral, I could see that John Sommers was emotionally disturbed, and I was worried about Sophie's safety."

(By Harold Fine) "Objection to the witness rendering an opinion on the mental condition of my client."

(Witness) "Do not question my credentials, sir, I am a licensed doctor and I have completed a rotation in psychiatry."

(Judge Karr) "I'm assuming it's not offered as an expert opinion, but as a predicate for what happens next, is that right?"

(By Jerome Gibbs) "Correct, Your Honor."

(Judge Karr) "Then it's overruled on that basis. Move on."

(By Jerome Gibbs) "What were your instructions to the private detective?"

(Witness) "Just to keep an eye on Mr. Sommers and Sophie and report to me. I was really hoping that everything would be okay, that Mr. Sommers would get himself together, that we would not have to intervene, but the reports came back very bad. Drugs, alcohol, depression, hysteria. I knew I had to act quickly to protect our granddaughter."

(By Harold Fine) "Objection."

(*By Judge Karr*). "Sustained. Move on."

(*Witness*) "But, Your Honor, the reports told me that Mr. Sommers was in psychotherapy, was on psychotropic medication, was suffering from depression, and as a grandfather, I—"

(*By Harold Fine*) "Objection, objection. This man cannot be allowed to ramble on with hearsay testimony."

(*Witness*) "I have to protect my grandchild. What is hearsay? I get reports. I get pictures. I know it's true."

(*By Harold Fine*) "Objection, Your Honor."

(*Judge Karr*) "Sustained. Doctor, wait until there is a question asked before you speak. And you cannot testify about what someone else said. That's hearsay. You can only testify to what you've seen and heard. Now, Mr. Fine, please sit down. I hear your objections. I understand the hearsay rule. I think I know what's evidentiary and what's not—what I can consider and what I shouldn't. Mr. Gibbs, let's get on with the testimony."

(*By Jerome Gibbs*) "Doctor, without saying what was in the reports or what you were told, how many reports did you receive?"

(*Witness*) "One each week for about eight or nine weeks. I also talked to my investigators on the phone. And Sommers wasn't getting any better. Maybe worse."

(*By Harold Fine*) "Objection, Your Honor."

(*Judge Karr*) "The objection will be sustained."

(*By Jerome Gibbs*) "After reading these reports and talking to the investigators, what did you do?"

"I contacted you. I want to take Sophie to my home, where she will be well cared for."

CATHERINE STRETCHED HER LEGS, poured a cup of tea, and then moved ahead to the part where al-Zahani was cross-examined by Jack's attorney.

(*By Harold Fine*) "Dr. al-Zahani, on direct you described a warm and loving home in Hebron. Are you a warm and loving person?"

"I guess you would have to ask others about that."

"No, sir, I'm asking you. Are you a warm and loving person? Tell the judge."

"Yes, of course I am."

"I mean, you are asking this court to award guardianship of a young, five-year-old girl to you and your wife, six thousand miles away from her home and her father. Are you truly capable of providing a warm and nourishing relationship?"

"Absolutely."

"Do you expect that you will care for Sophie as warmly and lovingly as you would care for your very own child?"

(*Witness does not answer*)

"Dr. al-Zahani?"

"Of course."

"As warmly and lovingly, for example, as you treated your daughter, Alina?"

"It is different."

"Answer the question please."

"Yes."

"Just as warmly?"

"I said yes."

"Did either you or your wife attend Alina's wedding?"

"Regretfully, no. I was too busy with my practice to leave the country."

"Was your wife busy with her practice as well?"

"She does not have a practice. She cannot travel without me."

"You mean you wouldn't let her?"

"It is not proper."

"Since the wedding, how many times have you visited Alina?"

"I have not."

"Well, all right then. After your daughter had her baby, your grandchild, how many times did you visit?"

"I did not."

"Busy again?"

(*Witness nods*)

"For five years?"

"You have no idea. There are not many doctors in Hebron. I have a very busy practice."

"Do you have a telephone, Doctor?"

"Of course."

"How often did you speak to your daughter over the past eight years?"

"I don't know."

"Isn't it true, sir, that before your wife had her heart attack, you did not see or speak to Alina since she left Palestine eight years ago?"

"My wife was writing to her."

"And you, sir?"

"I let my wife write, I was very busy."

(Respondent identifies Exhibit #1)

"I show you a letter we have marked as Respondent's Exhibit One. Do you recognize the handwriting?"

"It is Lubannah's."

"And is that her signature?"

(Witness nods)

"The letter is in Arabic. Would you please read and translate into English the first three sentences."

(Witness is silent)

(By Harold Fine) "Your Honor, would you please instruct the witness to answer my question?"

(Judge Karr) "Dr. al-Zahani, please read and translate the first three sentences as requested."

(Witness) "My dearest Alina. I have your letter and I am pleased to learn that you and Sophie are doing so well. I have shown your letters to your father, but he will not read them and will not speak of you in our home."

(By Harold Fine) "Go on, Doctor. Read the next sentence."

"Maybe in time he will change his mind, but for now he says he has no daughter."

"Did you disown your very own daughter?"

(Witness is silent)

"Did you disown your daughter, Alina?"

(Witness is silent)

"Mr. Warm-and-Loving, did you kick your daughter out of your life? Was she dead to you eight years before she died? Is that how warm and loving—"

(By Jerome Gibbs) "Objection. Objection."

(Judge Karr) "Counsel, sit down. The objection is overruled."

(By Harold Fine) "—you will be to Sophie, just as warm and loving? Doctor, are you asking this court to grant you custody so

that you can disown Sophie six thousand miles away from her home if she crosses you?"

(Witness) "You do not understand. Alina had turned from us. She had rejected us and her Islamic faith. In marrying this man, she had dishonored her mother and me. We raised her—gave her everything—she was a beautiful pianist, she was a brilliant psychologist, a lovely Muslim woman—who ran off with an American who was, who . . ."

"Was a Jew?"

"A Jew. An American. What does it matter, he was not of our community. Notwithstanding, I remained devoted to Alina, she was my precious one, but I could not act like nothing happened. When she came to Hebron last summer, when she was back in the house, I tried, we talked, but I knew she had become the wife . . . I was not mean to her. I was trying, but . . ."

"You were distant?"

"Perhaps."

"You didn't change your mind?"

"I did not."

"You had no daughter."

(Witness is silent)

"No further questions."

CATHERINE SHUT THE TRANSCRIPT binder. "Case over," she said to herself.

TWENTY-SIX

• • •

CATHERINE AND LIAM WERE the last to arrive when they walked into J&F's conference room at 10:00 A.M. Walter Jenkins and three other people were already seated around the oval conference table, and they stood as Catherine and Liam entered.

Walter made the introductions. "I think you know Jeff Miller from the FBI. This is Harry Foster from Washington and Kayla Cummings, his associate."

"Washington? What agency?" Liam said as he shook their hands.

"Well, more precisely, you might say we're intelligence analysts," Foster said. His handshake was firm. His gray hair was thinning, but neatly cut. He stood tall in a light gray suit with a dark blue tie.

"Langley?"

Foster shrugged and gave a nod. "Middle East desk, Mr. Taggart."

"Liam. Just Liam."

Walter gestured for everyone to sit. Liam pointed across the table to Kayla Cummings, who sat posture-perfect in a dark blue suit, lavender blouse, and tricolored scarf, neatly tucked at the neckline, her hands folded on the table before her. She was exquisite, with dark eyes and warm olive skin. Gold hoop earrings glistened against her black hair.

"And may I ask who Ms. Cummings works for?" Liam said.

"I am assigned to the assistant secretary of state for Near Eastern Affairs, Mr. Taggart. I advise the assistant secretary and the undersecretary on policy issues, specifically with regard to Iraq, Iran, Israel, and the territories administered by the Palestinian Authority."

Liam tilted his head at Catherine. "The spooks are here." Then, leaning forward on his elbows, he asked Foster, "What brings the CIA and the State Department to Chicago on a theft of corporate funds?"

"Well, the simple answer to that question is Kayla," Foster said. "She believes there is a connection between the kidnapping of the Sommers child, the missing money, and certain activities she's been following in the Middle East. Although purely theoretical at this stage, there's enough substance to her theories to persuade me to come and talk to you."

"I don't understand," Liam said. "The theft of the escrow funds is a local issue. How are the Middle East desk and the Department for Near Eastern Affairs involved?"

"We're here because your corporate embezzlement in Chicago may be earmarked to fund the activities of a group I've been monitoring," Kayla said.

Foster angled his head in Kayla's direction. "Kayla's been trying to build a book on a group of Palestinians and has convinced me, maybe prematurely, that there's a reason for all of us to get together." He slid a group of papers across the table to Liam. "But before we go any further, we have to do the formalities. What we discuss here today must be held in the strictest confidence as a matter of national security. Our entire discussion, and any information that flows from our discussion, is classified and must remain confidential. Do we have an understanding in that regard?"

Catherine and Liam looked at each other and then nodded their agreement. Foster pointed to the confidentiality agreements. Catherine and Liam each signed them and slid them back across the table.

"Let's begin with Arif al-Zahani, a prominent doctor in the West Bank city of Hebron," Foster said. "His family has been well-known to us and our British cousins for more than ninety years. Indeed, Arif's grandfather Ibrahim al-Zahani was an adjutant to Amin al-Husseini, the mufti of Jerusalem, one of the most belligerent and dangerous men the area has ever produced, a man responsible for countless uprisings and murders. During their tenure, Ibrahim and Amin caused the deaths of dozens of British soldiers and countless civilians, both Jews and Arabs. Arif's father, Hamid al-Zahani, was an officer in the Jordanian army in the 1948 and 1967 wars and was the commandant of the Hebron garrison for twenty years."

"Arif operates at a much lower altitude," added Kayla, "though I believe he's no less sinister. He's a learned man. A medical doctor and a scientist. He has the respect of his community and others in his profession, even in Jerusalem, where he has lectured on his specialty. He has influence among his people. And he's very wealthy."

"How did he obtain his wealth?" Liam asked.

"He didn't get it practicing medicine," she said. "Even now, he works in a very poor community hospital. Those of us who have been following him believe he's been funded by Hamas out of Gaza, though it may be one of the other extremist groups. There are several operating in Hebron."

"Do you have any proof that he's involved in the theft of the escrow funds or that he's planning to use that money?"

"Not yet."

"You said he has influence among his people. What does that mean? Who are his people?" Liam said.

"Let me emphasize this," Foster said. "We have no solid evidence that he's engaged in any terrorist movements. That's why the Agency has thus far refused to devote any assets to him." He shrugged. "But then, Kayla—"

Kayla broke in. "He's far too clever to lose his professional persona, but I assure you he's waist deep in terrorism. First of all, he's a lineal descendant of mass murderers. It's in his DNA. His father and his grandfather before him were sworn enemies of peace in the region. For close to fifty years, they were at the core of violent insurrection. Secondly, Arif meets regularly with what I believe is an extremist cell in Hebron. Until recently, some of these men were in Gaza. Others are outspoken Palestinian hard-liners. Their activity level indicates that they are planning something. Of that, I'm certain."

"And now al-Zahani has Sophie Sommers," Liam said.

"Correct," Kayla said.

"And we're trying to find her father."

Foster nodded. "Correct again."

"Do you believe that John Sommers is going to use eighty-eight million dollars to buy his daughter back?" Catherine asked.

Kayla shrugged and spread her hands. "That's the jackpot question, isn't it? Is it possible? Sure. If that's what it takes to get his daughter back, why not?"

Walter slapped the table. "Never saw it coming. I knew his daughter was reported missing after the grandparents failed to return her. I knew he was using diplomatic channels to try to get her back, but I never suspected he would steal a client's money to pay a ransom. If I thought it was a possibility . . ."

Foster shook his head. "It isn't something you could have anticipated."

"Yeah? Tell that to the judge. We're being sued for malpractice because we failed to supervise our attorneys and allowed one of them to steal eighty-eight million dollars from a client. All based on the principle of foreseeability."

"Let's not jump to conclusions," Foster said. "We've uncovered no evidence of a ransom demand. And we don't know for sure that there's a plan to transfer eighty-eight million, or any sum at all, to Palestinian hard-liners. Again, those are merely working hypotheses. But if there is such a plan in the works, it isn't something we can permit."

"Didn't Sommers contact the State Department when Sophie was taken?" Catherine said.

"Yes, he did." Foster gestured for Kayla to answer.

"At the time, the State Department did everything it could. Not just through our agency but also involving the Department of Homeland Security. DHS immediately put out an alert for all airlines serving the Middle East referencing a passport bearing Sophie's name or photographic likeness. A Yellow Notice was issued by Interpol in Paris, but once again, that's only distributed to countries that are Hague Convention signatories. None of the Middle Eastern countries, with the exception of Israel, are signatories."

"I seem to remember, somewhere in the back of my mind," Catherine said, "that there's a parental abduction statute that applies to grandparents as well. Isn't it enforceable internationally?"

"There is a statute and it does apply to grandparents," Kayla said. "It's called the International Parental Kidnapping Act, IPKA. It's a federal crime and punishable in the United States. Outside our borders, we have to depend on treaties and to a great extent on our treaty partners. Some countries will send the children back because they recognize the Hague Convention on International Child Abduction, but there are many that will not. There's a long list of countries that will not comply with the Hague Convention. And Sophie is not even in a recognized country. The West Bank, the Palestinian Territories, the disputed land, whatever you call it, is not a country. It's not a legitimate sovereignty."

"I suppose it's a stupid question, but what about our embassy? Couldn't it do anything about getting Sophie returned?" Catherine said.

Kayla shook her head. "Our embassy is in Tel Aviv. Hebron, at least the part where al-Zahani lives, is administered by the Palestinian Authority. The US has no diplomatic relations with the PA. In fact, a couple years ago we sent a diplomatic delegation to the West Bank and it was attacked by Palestinian protesters. So, it's not a US embassy matter. Since the PA is not a Hague signatory and is noncompliant with the Hague Convention, Sommers would have to go through the Hebron courts. In our experience, non-Muslim parents stand very little chance of succeeding in a child-custody dispute in the Islamic courts of the Middle East."

"Did Sophie's passport turn up?" Liam asked.

"That's the strange thing," Foster answered. "At the time, Sommers told us that Sophie didn't have a passport. He never applied for one. And he's right. There are no records of a passport issued to Sophie Sommers."

"So how did she travel internationally?"

"It's a mystery."

Liam folded his arms and rocked back in his chair. "But you're not here because of Sophie's abduction."

"Well, indirectly, Mr. Taggart," Kayla said. "We're concerned about terrorists getting their hands on eighty-eight million dollars. I've noticed increased activity in Dr. al-Zahani's group. It's like a little beehive. Clandestine meetings in bakeries and empty apartments. They never use cell phones. No e-mails. The IDF monitors them, but at a distance."

"IDF?" Walter said.

"Israel Defense Forces. Israeli soldiers. They report suspicious activities to Shin Bet, the Israeli Internal Security Agency, and to the Mossad."

"What is the beehive planning?"

"I don't know," Kayla said. "But you can bet al-Zahani knows."

"Like I said before," added Foster, "this is Kayla's baby. We haven't yet developed any clear evidence that al-Zahani is engaged in any terrorist activity. Nothing we can move on. The Agency won't staff this operation unless Kayla comes up with something more concrete. But Kayla is so damn passionate and so obsessed with this guy that . . . well, that's good enough for me, at least for now. She's been right in the past. So, even if she can't get the Agency's formal attention, she's got mine. Enough to let her investigate it further."

"Let me see if I understand our respective positions," Catherine said. "While our purpose is to locate Sommers, recover the money, and protect the law firm from bankruptcy, your agenda is to make sure Sommers doesn't turn the money over to terrorists."

"Precisely," Kayla said.

"Where is the money?" Liam asked.

Foster shook his head. "Panama? We don't know any more than you do."

"And Sommers?"

"No idea."

"The CIA and all its agents can't find a transactional lawyer and some stolen money?" Walter said.

"You watch too many movies."

"So tell me, Harry," said Catherine, "why are we all meeting here today?"

"Well, partly it's about your Mr. Taggart. As I'm sure you know, Liam's worked for us before." Foster nodded at Liam.

Liam shrugged. "A long time ago."

"We'd like to work together again," Foster said. "You have the perfect cover. You're a private investigator hired to find a little girl. In that role, you'll be asking a lot of questions. You'll have access to people, become privy to important information, and we'd like to be included."

Liam shook his head. "I haven't been hired to find a little girl. I'm searching for stolen money."

"They have a common nucleus."

"Well, so far I've learned very little. I was planning on talking with Sommers's sister in Louisville."

"She won't talk to you," Miller said. "She practically threw me out of her house. Told me to get a court order."

Catherine wagged her finger. "Ah, but Liam has his Irish charm. Just ask him."

"'Tis true."

"In any event," Foster continued, "a private investigator looking for a missing six-year-old daughter has a valid reason to ask a lot of questions, maybe even get close to al-Zahani. People are sympathetic about a missing child. That activity isn't likely to arouse suspicion. There are places you can go and people you can talk to that we can't."

"I'm not looking for his daughter."

"Maybe the money is."

"Maybe. So far, I haven't uncovered any proof that Sommers has the money or even took the money."

"We think he did," Foster said.

"I thought you said you didn't know where the money was," Jenkins said.

"Oh, we don't. But we know that Sommers went to Panama a couple months ago. We traced the missing funds from the escrow account to the First Republic Bank, but the money's not there anymore. First Republic transferred the money to Pacifico Bank. And we've since learned that the money's not there anymore either. That's about all we know."

Walter stood. His face was red. "You people knew all this and said nothing? You knew he went to Panama? My firm is on the brink of collapse and we're fighting to stay alive. Fuck you. You're the government. You're supposed to work for me."

"Calm down, Mr. Jenkins," Foster said. "We're trying to get the money back just like you are, and we don't know where the money is any more than you do."

"How did you learn about the money transfers?" Catherine said. "I thought Panama banking was clothed in secrecy, that even our government couldn't get information."

"I can't comment on that."

"But you want to use me?" Liam said. "Have *me* ask questions and give *you* the answers?"

"We use civilian assets all the time, Liam. Just like we did when you were in Ulster. If your world-renowned Irish charm opens a few doors, gives you a lead, all the better. People will talk to a guy trying to find a little girl."

"Why do you keep saying 'trying to find'? We all know where she is. If the government is so concerned that money will be paid to ransom Sophie Sommers, why don't you just go to al-Zahani's house and get her?"

Foster had an exasperated look. "We don't send the Navy SEALs into a foreign jurisdiction to snatch children in a custody dispute."

"Well, Israel does."

"Perhaps. But, there's more. Right now Undersecretary Whiting is quietly in Cairo meeting with PA officials. It's an important step in the peace process. We may actually be making some headway after all these years. As you know, the president is planning to travel to the Mideast in a few months. Maybe even to make a bold announcement." Foster smiled patronizingly. "We can't have a terrorist act derailing the peace process."

Liam leaned back. He tapped his fingers on the table. "So, it's really not about the girl. You don't want her rescued, do you, Kayla? If she were back home, you wouldn't have a reason to poke around. You want to use Sophie as a cover to get close to al-Zahani and learn more about his little beehive. You hope my snooping around will flush out a terrorist plot."

"I don't deny we'd love to have your help," Kayla said, "flush out those terrorists, as you say, but we're not that hard-hearted. If you could bring Sophie home, that would suit us just fine."

"Bullshit. Anyway, that's not why Mr. Jenkins is paying me."

Walter stared hard at Foster. "Are you telling me that if we help get the girl back, you'll help us get the money back?"

"They're joined at the hip, Mr. Jenkins. If the money is earmarked to ransom the girl, then the money and the girl converge on the same corner. But let me be candid. We don't know that Sommers still has possession of the money. And, despite Kayla's theories, we don't know for certain there's any deal in the works, we only suspect it. Or should I say, Kayla suspects it. But we would agree to assist you in recovering the money. After all, wire fraud is a federal crime."

"Wait a minute," Walter said. "Taggart doesn't come cheap. Why should I finance the search and rescue of the daughter of a man who stole eighty-eight million dollars from me? The United States government has a lot more money than I do. Why don't you pay Taggart?"

"If that embezzled money is paid to terrorists, there are a lot of daughters whose lives will be at risk," Kayla said.

"I'm not that humanitarian," Walter said.

"Well, let me put it another way," Foster said. "We'll supply intelligence. You supply the Irish guy. You're looking for your client's funds, and you're looking to save your law firm. It can't hurt to have the blessing, not to mention the intelligence resources, of the United States government."

Walter looked at Liam and nodded. "I guess your assignment is officially modified."

"Look, if Kayla's right," Foster said, "if there is a deal in the works, then Sommers is in more trouble than he knows. He's in way over his head. If he's trying to trade eighty-eight million dollars to the Palestinians for his daughter's return, he's more likely to lose the money and get himself and his daughter killed. After you go to Louisville and talk to his sister, I'd like to meet with you again."

"She won't talk to him," Miller said.

"Call me when you get back from Louisville," Foster said.

TWENTY-SEVEN

• • •

LIAM WALKED UP THE front steps of a red brick home in
the Asbury Park section of Louisville. The house was a traditional two-story colonial on a wooded lot, with white trim
and shutters. A smattering of blue crocuses poked through the
ground on either side of the front stoop.

Liam knocked and the door was opened by a boy with a Play-
Station controller in his hand. Standing in his white socks, he kept
a cautionary hand on the doorknob, allowing the door to open just
a sliver. "Are you looking for my mom?"

"Yep. I'm a friend of your uncle's."

"Uncle Jack?" A smile brightened his face. "Well, Mom's not
home yet. She's picking up my sister at school."

Liam gestured at the controller. "What are you playing?"

"Black Ops II ."

Liam shook his head. "I can't play that game. I always die. Now,
if you had *Madden Thirteen,* I could whip your butt."

"No, you couldn't."

"Yes, I surely could. I'd eat your lunch."

The boy laughed. "No, you wouldn't."

"In my sleep. That'll be the day I lose to a fourteen-year-old."

"I'm twelve and I'm a pro at *Madden Thirteen.* No one beats me."

"That's 'cause you haven't played me. Course, if you're chicken . . ."

With that, the boy swung the door open, turned, and walked
confidently through the foyer. "It's in the other room. Prepare to
be humbled."

Liam followed him through the hallway, past the kitchen, and into a paneled den. A large flatscreen was mounted on the center wall. The picture was frozen on a scene from *Black Ops II:* a smoky, bombed-out neighborhood in a nondescript Eastern European locale.

"My name's Liam." He held out his hand.

"Sean," the boy said, putting a controller in Liam's hand and ejecting the war game from the console. "Just don't cry too loud when I beat you."

Sean's gaming skills far exceeded Liam's, and Sean laughed heartily every time he scored or Liam fumbled. "I thought you said you were good."

"I'm just getting warmed up. You have home-field advantage."

"A controller is a controller, Liam. There's no home field."

Just then, a woman, car keys in her hand, entered the room and stopped short. "Who is this, Sean?"

"His name is Liam. He's a friend of Uncle Jack's."

Liam stood. "Sorry to barge in, Mrs. Wilson, but—"

"Just barge right out. You have no business here. How dare you come into my house uninvited? Get out or I'm calling the police."

"I invited him, Mom. He's a friend of Uncle Jack's and he knows how to play *Madden Thirteen*. But he sucks."

"Get out."

Liam stood and handed the controller back to Sean. "You're right. You're a pro. You kicked my butt." Turning to Sean's mother, Liam said, "Would you just give me five minutes. Five minutes. I'm trying to help your brother. I think he's in danger."

Her stiff arm and pointed finger directed him toward the door. "Out. Out. You've got no business here."

"Deborah, listen to me, I may be one of the few people that can actually help your brother."

She stood at the front door and flicked a backhand. "You stand out on the stoop. I stand in the doorway. You have two minutes to tell me why I should listen to you." She turned around and pointed at her son. "Sean, you go and start your homework."

"Mom . . ."

"Go."

As directed, Liam stood just outside the doorway.

As her son had, Deborah stood with one hand on the doorknob, holding the door partially closed. "I told the FBI that I have nothing to say. I don't know anything and I haven't spoken to Jack in weeks. And you can be damned sure I don't have that missing money."

"I'm not the FBI, Deborah." Liam held his palms out like a stop sign. "I'm a private investigator and I'm working for Jack's law firm. I know that Jack is a good man. I know he wouldn't hurt anyone. I know that he didn't have anything to do with the murder."

Deborah's eyes widened. Her lips quivered. "What murder?"

"Can I come in? Can we talk for a few minutes?"

"We can talk right here."

"Last month, eighty-eight million dollars went missing from a business deal and was diverted to a Panama bank. The written instructions to the title company, directing them where to wire the money, came from an escrow controlled by your brother and a man named Harrington. Harrington was found in Lake Michigan with a bullet in his brain. That leaves your brother as a witness to the transaction. Whoever is behind these crimes is motivated to—"

"Who's behind this?"

Liam shook his head. "I don't know yet. But I don't think Jack was the centerpiece of this crime."

"Why not?"

"I've been working on this case for the better part of a month. I've talked to several people who were close to Jack. I'm working with a lawyer who has been studying the trial transcripts of the custody hearing. All in all, I think I've come to know what Jack was like, and that he was a good man. A smart lawyer. Desperate? Yes. But a criminal mastermind? No. Deborah, you have to believe me, right now he's in real danger."

"How do I know I can trust you? Who are you?"

"Just an investigator from Chicago." He handed her a business card. "I was hired by Jenkins and Fairchild, which, along with your brother, has been sued for eighty-eight million dollars."

"Why don't you think my brother is involved?"

Liam hesitated. "I'm not saying he's not involved. And he may have that money. But unless you think he killed Dennis Harrington by shooting him in the head, he's not the only one involved. We've also been looking into Sophie's disappearance."

"Kidnapping."

Liam nodded. "Kidnapping. We know that Jack would do almost anything to get Sophie back. And that money . . . who knows? But really, do you think Jack is capable of engineering an exchange of millions of dollars to Palestinians for the release of his kidnapped daughter all by himself?"

Deborah backed away from the door and motioned for Liam to come in. They sat across from each other on wingback chairs in the front room. On a little end table sat a silver-framed picture of Deborah with her arm around her husband.

Liam gestured toward the picture. "Your husband looks a lot like Jack."

Deborah smiled. "Yes, he did. With their hair cut short, their features were very similar. Eugene died last year."

"I'm sorry," Liam said quietly. He leaned forward. "Where's Jack?"

She shook her head. "If I knew, I wouldn't tell you, but I don't know."

"You're making a mistake. I need to talk to him. If the bad guys find him, and they will, they'll kill him. He's just a loose end to them. A liability—dangerous and disposable. You need to help me find him."

"I'm not stupid. Whatever I tell you goes straight to the FBI. They'll find Jack and they'll lock him up. I'm not helping you put my brother in jail. Then Sophie'll be lost forever."

"It doesn't serve my purpose to put Jack in jail. I want to help Jack and I want to help Sophie."

"Oh, please. You want to find the money."

"Yes, I do, but those ends are not incompatible. Let's be practical. Do you think he can rescue Sophie by himself? Halfway around the world in some West Bank town? Is he going to take a shopping bag full of money? Deborah, the whole world's looking for him. The CIA, the Mossad, they're not going to let him deliver that money. Wherever he is, he can't even get on a plane. How's he going to get Sophie back? You know as well as I that he has to involve other people—operatives that exist in a community way above his pay grade. He's a pigeon out there. He needs help, Deborah."

She took a deep breath and sat back in her chair. "Really, I don't know where he went. He wouldn't tell me."

"But . . . ?"

"I may have a way to reach him."

Liam stood. "My contact info is on my card. I'll do it all on his terms." He started for the door and stopped. "Be careful how you try to reach him. Your phone, your computer, your best friend's computer, the library computer—they're not safe."

"Understood."

TWENTY-EIGHT

• • •

S O, AT THE END of the trial, the judge awarded you sole custody?" Marcy said as she poured Giovanni's Grenache into two wineglasses, handed one to Jack, and sat beside him on her cushioned glider. The trade winds were settling down in the late afternoon, and light breezes were gently rustling the bougainvilleas bordering Marcy's veranda.

"It was after each side had rested," he said. "I thought we'd get the decision right then and there in open court, but the judge said he was going to take the case under advisement and rule in a week."

"The delay must have been torture."

"That was the longest week of my life. My lawyer remained confident and kept telling me not to worry, that we had won the case, but every time I looked at Sophie, I wanted to wrap my arms around her, hold her tight, and protect her from all those people who were trying to take her from me. I kept having visions of social workers prying my screaming child from my arms and carrying her off to their car. What if Judge Karr ruled for the al-Zahanis? Anything can happen in a court.

"Finally, one week after the evidence closed, we returned to the courtroom. My knees were shaking as I stood alongside the al-Zahanis in front of the judge's bench. Judge Karr came out of his chambers and read from a prepared decision. I could tell from the minute he started that we had won. He said that although he had concern for my emotional health, he had no doubt of my ability to nurture and care for Sophie. Uprooting her from her home and her father and moving her to Palestine was not in her best interests, he said. There's a strong presumption in favor of a parent and a heavy burden to overcome that presumption. The al-Zahanis had not met that burden. 'Far from it,' he said."

"But you told me the judge granted them visitation," Marcy said.

"Not at first. He denied them any rights at all. He said that throughout the trial he had observed bitterness and intolerance in the heart of Dr. al-Zahani. Visitation at this time would only permit the grandparents to drive a wedge between a father and his daughter. He said that sometime in the future, when and if their anger subsided, they could re-petition the court and maybe he would consider supervised visitation."

The sound of Marcy's doorbell interrupted Jack's narrative, and she excused herself to answer the door. When she returned, she had a paper in her hand and a shocked look on her face.

"Look at this," she said, holding out the paper. "It's an order from the Honolulu Circuit Court dismissing the eviction case against me." She pointed at the door. "Mr. Nakamura delivered it himself. He told me I was to call Mr. Everett right away and tell him the case was dismissed. And he told me I didn't have to pay this month's rent. Then he turned and hurried back to his car."

"That's great."

"But, here's the thing, I don't know any Mr. Everett." She shook her head. "I don't know what he's talking about."

Jack chuckled.

"You! Did you have something to do with this?"

Jack shrugged. "I don't think he'll hassle you anymore."

She leaned over and kissed him on the cheek. "I don't know how you did it, but I don't care, you're awesome."

"It's no big deal."

"Yes, it is, I don't have to move." She poured another round of wine. "Damn, how did you do it?"

"Skill and cunning."

She kissed him again and sat down on the glider. "You were telling me that the al-Zahanis were denied visitation. So, how did they get it? Did they re-petition the court?"

Jack shook his head. "When the judge finished reading his decision, Lubannah broke into tears. She ran up to the bench and begged the judge to allow her to see Sophie. The deputies had to restrain her. I thought she'd collapse right on the courtroom floor. As bitter as the case had been, I couldn't help but feel sorry for her. I'd never seen anybody so upset, so disheartened.

"But Judge Karr was resolute. 'I've made my decision,' he said. 'That'll be the order.' Lubannah wailed inconsolably. And then I made the biggest mistake of my life."

Marcy knew what was coming. She reached over and took his hands and waited for the rest.

"I told the judge I would agree to visitation. Please put it in the court order so they know and Sophie knows I'm not trying to keep them out of her life. Give them one weekend a month and restrict it to Chicago. If they choose to exercise it, fine. If they don't, well, that's up to them. But Sophie should know her grandparents. Sophie should know the people who raised her mother." Jack shook his head. "And that's how I lost her."

"You blame yourself for that decision?"

"It *was* my decision."

"Yes, but for all the right reasons. You were trying to do what's best for Sophie. After what the al-Zahanis had put you through, trying to take your daughter from you, for you to act so generously, I know I wouldn't have been so noble. You're a good man, Jack."

"Good, but stupid. The bottom line is I failed to protect my daughter. I'm her father and I failed her. The judge was wise. He saw right through them. If I had listened to him, she'd be here right now."

Marcy put her arm around his shoulders. Her touch was comforting. "I will never believe that was a mistake on your part. It ended up badly, but only because of the deceitful acts of the grandparents, not because of the goodness in your heart."

"Thank you for that, Marcy, but it doesn't matter."

"When you offered to give the al-Zahanis weekend visitation, what did they say?"

"At that moment, Lubannah dropped to her knees and thanked me. It was all in Arabic, and I'm sure the judge had no idea what she was saying, but the import was obvious. Arif, who had refused to even make eye contact with me during the entire trial, shook my hand and nodded. He never did speak to me, but I felt that the wall of ice that existed between us was starting to melt a little.

During the trial, he had seemed sincere, so caring where Sophie was concerned, and in some ways I tried to understand his despair at Alina's decision to leave Hebron. The fact that she died so many miles away from him. You know, he's a doctor. Maybe he thought if she got sick in Hebron, he could've cured her. Wouldn't I have felt the same way? I felt good about giving them visitation, but I underestimated what a deceitful son of a bitch al-Zahani was."

Jack picked up his glass. "At that time, I really believed we could connect, that Alina would have wanted it that way. I tried to believe that, deep down, Arif was a good man."

"So, how did they take her?"

"Visitation went smoothly two times last fall. The first weekend, they flew in and visited with Sophie in my living room. I left the house. Our friend Sharon was there to observe in case it didn't go well or Sophie was upset. But, apparently it was okay.

"The next visit, I let them take Sophie to a movie and dinner on Saturday. They picked her up in a limousine and brought her back in the evening. Sunday, they took her to the museum and to lunch at their hotel, the Ritz-Carlton.

"In December, they asked if Sophie could spend Saturday night with them at the hotel. They were going to take her to the evening presentation of ZooLights at the Lincoln Park Zoo. I agreed. It seemed so innocent and proper. She was to return after lunch on Sunday.

"When they didn't show up by two P.M., I started to get concerned. I was pacing by the front window. At three P.M., I called Lubannah's cell phone but only got through to her voice mail. Then I called the hotel. There was no answer in their room, and of course, the hotel wouldn't tell me anything about a guest. So I called the police and showed them the court order. They were able to verify that the al-Zahanis had checked out of the hotel in the morning.

"The police urged me to wait on any actions, that they might just be stuck in traffic somewhere, but when they didn't bring her back by eight P.M., they put out an Amber Alert. The airlines were put on alert for their passports. Their return reservations were booked to Amman through Zurich, but they never checked in. They just disappeared." Jack took another drink and rocked back on the swing.

Marcy slowly shook her head. "How could you know? You did what you thought was right for Sophie. We all have to trust our instincts, that's all we've got. None of us have a crystal ball."

"Everyone tells me that, but I still bear the responsibility for what happened to my daughter. I thought al-Zahani was a decent man. I thought the same thing when Alina introduced us. And even when he kicked me out of her house, I thought, 'He'll get past it. He's just a dad afraid of losing his daughter. We'll wind up being a close family.' But in the end, I gave him my daughter."

"No, you didn't. You gave Sophie a chance to know her grandparents under secure conditions."

"I guess they weren't very secure. I didn't protect her. That's the bottom line."

"What about the State Department? You used to work there."

"Well, I was in the diplomatic corps, but I did know some pretty well placed people and I called them all."

"And?"

Jack shook his head. "You have to understand the Israeli-Palestinian flash pot, they said. It's an explosion waiting to happen. A tinderbox. They won't send Israeli soldiers into a secure private residence to grab a child in a Palestinian-controlled area. Certainly not one as violent as Hebron. They have to do it through diplomatic channels, if at all. When it comes to the PA's autonomy in its West Bank cities, Israel is extremely sensitive to world opinion. They don't want to risk an incident with the Palestinians, and breaking into al-Zahani's compound in the middle of Hebron would likely cause an incident.

"Hebron is basically a Palestinian city with almost two hundred thousand Arabs. Except for a small section, it's a Zone A city, meaning that the Palestinian Authority is in administrative command of the city. Israel has agreed not to interfere and doesn't want to interfere in Hebron's affairs. That's the political reality. Israel has withdrawn its police forces and won't risk an incident by muscling its way in there to get my child."

"But you could go."

"By myself? With no backup or political support? It would be nearly impossible and perilous for both of us. Hebron is a very hostile city, especially for outsiders. There are shootings and murders all the time. And, Arif is a power in that town. He lives in a house with a large stone wall around it. Gated entrance. Plenty of security guards. There are checkpoints all around the city. Even if I got in and grabbed Sophie, I'd have a hell of a time getting out." Jack shook his head.

"I understand."

"Still, when the government wouldn't help me, I bought a ticket to Tel Aviv. My Arabic's a little rusty, but I figured I could get by."

"What were you going to do?"

"I didn't really have a plan. I was going to go over there, hang out in Hebron, try to catch Sophie alone outside the compound, maybe at school, a friend's house, or maybe she'd only have one chaperone."

"And do what? Shoot the chaperone? That sounds like a dumb plan, Jack."

He shrugged. "It was, but I wasn't about to give up. Then, before I could leave, an opportunity arose. I met people who said they could get the job done."

"What people?"

Jack shook his head. "I can't."

"So, now you're in Hawaii. Why? Why are you out here using your brother-in-law's ID?"

"All the things I had to do, the deal I had to make to rescue my daughter, required me to leave Chicago. Go underground. Disappear at least for a while. I had good memories of Hawaii and I thought it would be a nice place for Sophie and me to live when she came back."

Marcy whistled softly. "These people, what makes you think they can get Sophie out of Hebron?"

"I can't tell you. I just know they can."

She lifted her wineglass. "Here's to Sophie's rescue, whatever it takes."

"Whatever it takes. Thanks, Marcy."

She picked up the bottle of wine and held it up to the light. "I think we've dominated this muscat. Will you have another drink with me? I'll see what I can find."

Jack watched her walk into the house. Reconnecting with Marcy was a stroke of luck. Having someone to help him think through his problems was a plus, and he knew he could trust her.

He strolled to the edge of the patio, where the sea was visible. In the twilight he could just make out the surf. The waters were rough on the North Shore. Twenty-foot breakers, at least. A challenge to stability. Like the storms that were battering Jack's emotional centerboard. Swirling riptides. Hard to stay on course.

Jack thought about the secret e-mail address. He trusted that person too. Was that another bad decision? "You bastard," he said softly. "Why don't you post a damn reply? Why don't you answer me? If I don't hear soon, I'm coming after you."

Marcy returned with a bottle and a plate of cheese. "Fumé Blanc. It'll have to do."

She poured two glasses, handed one to Jack, and sat back down beside him. They rocked in silence for a moment on the small glider.

"Thank you for sharing all the details," she said. "I know it wasn't easy."

"It's painful to relive. All of it. But I've got to get through it. Thanks for your support."

As they rocked together on the glider, a gentle island mist began to fall. Jack stood. "I've had too much to drink. I'm going to call a cab."

Marcy put her hand on his shoulder. "You can stay out here, I . . ."

"I don't know, Marcy. . . ."

"No, Jack. It's fine. I have a guest room. You already slept in it once. I'll get a blanket."

K ELSEN'S BENTLEY TURNED THE corner at Belden, near the field house, and pulled to a stop at the curb. A few minutes later, two tall, thin men wearing gray hoodies slipped into the backseat and shut the door.

"Darius, we play Western Alabama in the first round," Kelsen said. "The opening line is seventeen. It could slide. I need us to win by no more than fourteen."

"I don't know, Mr. Kelsen, the team is fired up over this one. The game's at the Garden. We could blow 'em out."

"Fourteen, Darius. Do you agree, Marcus?"

The other young man nodded. "We try, sir, but we don't control Thomas. He could score thirty."

"Not if he doesn't get the ball," Kelsen said brusquely. "Why do you think I'm paying a fuckin' point guard?"

"Maybe we should talk to Thomas?" Darius said.

"How sure are we of Thomas?" Kelsen said.

"I don't know. He got a future. He thinks he could go late in the second round. I don't know if he wants to risk it."

"Then leave him out. You two will have to handle it." Kelsen slipped a sealed envelope to each of the players. "Make it happen, boys."

TWENTY-NINE

...

"S HE TOLD YOU SHE could get in touch with him?" Foster said.

Liam nodded. He sat across the table from Foster and Kayla Cummings in the State Department's office on the twenty-first floor of Chicago's Metcalfe Federal Building. In the March deep freeze, a few flurries blew around outside the windows trying to make their way down to Jackson Boulevard. Down on the streets, the wind-battered pedestrians pulled their coat collars as high as they would go and leaned into the powerful gusts as they walked.

"Deborah told me she didn't know where he was," Liam said.

"And you believed her?"

"I don't know. Doesn't matter. She's not going to give him up, but I think she'll get a message to him and maybe he'll talk to me."

"Kayla believes something's going down within the next few months."

"Why?" Liam asked.

"Al-Zahani's group is busier than usual," she said. "I've been watching them. More frequent meetings. Whatever their plans are, there's a good chance they'll want to use that money soon. Especially if they believe the peace process is gaining momentum. If there's a ransom payoff in the works, we need to get after it. Intercept it."

"What do you want me to do?" Liam asked.

"Ideally, we'd like to insert you as the go-between. If Sommers is planning on ransoming his daughter, we want you to be the one to make the swap," Foster said.

"I've never even been in that part of the world. I'm the wrong guy to do this."

Foster shook his head. "It's the perfect setup. You've got his sister's confidence. She'll talk to Sommers. Sommers'll trust you. The Arabs have no book on you. Nobody's ears'll perk up while you're poking around, there's no reason to think—"

Liam shook his head. "I don't have anyone's confidence. His sister hasn't reached out to me since I saw her. Besides, you told Jenkins you didn't know if Sommers even had the money."

Foster rocked back in his big leather chair. "He took the money. A perfectly responsible man who's never stepped outside the lines all of a sudden decides to throw away his career, the trust that everyone's shown in him, and steal a fortune from a client? Could there be any reason other than ransoming his daughter?"

"No."

"And now his accomplices turn up dead. Harrington was shot through the head, and the only other guy we know about, the escrow officer, was killed last week in a hit-and-run up on Lincoln Avenue. There's no one left but Sommers and whoever else might be involved."

"Ellis is dead?"

Foster nodded. "Crossing Lincoln at Fullerton with a bag of groceries. Witnesses said a white van tore around the corner, flattened him, and kept on going. No license plates, of course."

"So, who else is involved?"

Foster shook his head and pursed his lips. "We don't know. Just figure there must be others. People keep turning up dead."

"And you think the money is earmarked for terrorists?"

Foster looked at Kayla, slowly turned his head back to Liam, raised his eyebrows, and nodded. "You can bet that the money, or some of it at least, is earmarked for al-Zahani. Is he a terrorist? Kayla thinks so."

Liam looked at Kayla. "And this doctor, this rich doctor that there's no evidence on, you're sure he's a terrorist?"

"Positive," Kayla said. "He may be a rich doctor, but terrorism, it's a family tradition."

"We want you to go over there, let you get a feel for the landscape," Foster said. "Talk to whomever you can. Then come back, contact his sister, and tell Sommers you can make the exchange happen."

"Why don't you pick some guy who's familiar with the landscape? I don't know anything about that side of the world."

"No, you're the perfect guy. Sommers has to be thinking that whatever deal he made, it's starting to come apart," Foster said. "Two of the players are dead. If he hasn't already, Sommers is going to realize he's in over his head. He'll talk to his sister and she likes you. That's when you can step in. He'll trust you."

Liam shook his head. "I stopped working for the Agency years ago. I'm private now. Back when I was assigned to Northern Ireland, I knew about the landscape, the Provisional IRA, Sinn Féin. I could give you hours on Irish history. But the Middle East? I don't know shit about it or the Palestinians. I don't talk their talk. And I certainly don't know anything about the evil doctor."

"That's just a social studies lesson. Kayla can fill you in. She'll tell you everything we know about the al-Zahanis. And she'll go with you every step of the way." Foster paused and took a sip of coffee.

"When I was in Derry," Liam reminisced, "I could walk the streets. I had family there. I was one of them. I knew all about the war of national liberation and I knew all the players. And, hell, that was fifteen years ago. In today's world, I'm irrelevant. I don't know anything about the Arab-Israeli conflict. I don't know why people live on either side of a wall. I don't know this doctor's mind-set. What does he want?"

"He wants to be the grand cartographer. He wants to redraw the map of the Middle East," Kayla said.

"It's just education, Liam," Foster said. "Kayla can teach you everything you need to know. Middle East 101. She'll answer all your questions. You two can start tomorrow. Are you in?"

Liam shook his head, looked around the room, and then nodded. "Probably a big mistake. But, yeah."

THIRTY

• • •

"WHEN YOU GET TO the Hebron Archaeological Museum, take her to the back, to the Canaanite room," al-Zahani said to Bashir. "Let her see and touch the stones of her ancestors. Show her the discoveries dating back to the Iron Age, the age of King David. Even to the Bronze Age, when Moses sent his spies to Hebron. Let her see the evidence that Hebron was once the great capital of all of Canaan. Show her that Canaanites dwelled and farmed the land from the Jordan River to the sea. Let her see why it all belongs to us and not to the Europeans who now occupy our land."

"She is in her room, *Sayyid*," Bashir said. "She does not want to come out."

The doctor shook his head. "This has got to stop. Tell her if she does not come out immediately, I will throw the stuffed bear away."

Bashir spoke quietly. "Perhaps it is better if we let her take the bear on a trip to the museum. Then I can show the history of Hebron to the little one and her Sweetness."

Al-Zahani stood. "Fine. Do it your way."

Bashir nodded his agreement. "I will make sure she sees all of the historical treasures, *Sayyid*."

Bashir knocked and quietly entered Sophie's bedroom. She had pulled her chair to the window and was wistfully staring at the mountains far beyond. Her bear sat on her lap.

"Little one, would you like to take a walk with me?"

She shook her head. "I told Jaddi I don't want to go to the museum."

"But it is exciting and full of treasures. And we can take Sweetness on a bold adventure. To show him things of three thousand years ago. I think he might like to see the caves where teddy bears lived long before there were houses. And clay bowls where teddy bears kept their honey. Maybe afterwards, we can talk Sweetness into joining us for a dish of ice cream at the sweet store. Should we take him?"

Sophie smiled and nodded. "He likes chocolate."

A few moments later, Bashir and Sophie walked into the library, hand in hand.

"It's a wonderful museum," al-Zahani said. "A place where you can appreciate the deep history of your people. Bashir, make sure she sees the cyclopean stones from the great tower of Hebron. Do you know, Sophie, the tower was so high that when Moses sent his spies, they thought that giants must live in Hebron?"

He bent over and kissed his granddaughter on the top of her head. When Sophie left, al-Zahani drove across town to the group's small apartment. A teenager in a gray sweatshirt and soccer shorts stood by the back door. His arms were folded across his chest and he leaned against the brick wall. Al-Zahani ruffled his hair. "You're a good lookout, Dani. Is everyone here?"

The boy nodded. Al-Zahani opened the door and ascended the stairs to the musty apartment.

"You're finally here, praise be to Allah. The great doctor has arrived," said Nizar.

Al-Zahani responded with an angry glance and took a step toward Nizar but was halted by Fa'iz's calm command: "Stop. You are like children. We have serious work to do. We are four weeks from our destiny. How is the bus conversion progressing?"

"Almost completed," Aziz said. "I think we will begin our transports next week."

"I am pleased. And Sami? Who has heard from him?"

"I'm in contact with Sami," Ahmed said. "He has been working at the distribution center for eight months, one of only three drivers. He has a regular route that will include all of our targets. More importantly, at the beginning of each week he is given a printout of the quantities ordered at each location."

"Excellent. Have we solved the problem with the plastic bags?"

Al-Zahani answered tentatively, "Finally, we did. We received a shipment two days ago that meets our standards. They are being imprinted with the appropriate graphics and we will soon be filling them."

"What does *soon* mean, Arif?" Fa'iz said, rubbing his long, wiry beard, dark gray along the edges, light gray in the middle, like a mottled skunk. "We have deadlines."

"I need more time, I can't be rushed. We are still replicating the organisms. Filling the bags is a slow process."

Nizar shouted, "Four weeks is all we have. Can't you understand that? Your delay will be the ruin of our entire operation. We wait and wait for you, and all we hear is, 'I need more time.' Everybody else has done his job, Arif. Maybe you can spend a little less time with your American Jew-child."

Al-Zahani flew at Nizar and knocked him off his chair. He grabbed him around the throat, squeezing until his knuckles were white. "You say one more word about my granddaughter . . ."

The others pulled al-Zahani away. Nizar lay on the floor coughing.

Fa'iz shook his head slowly. "What he said was wrong, Arif. But choking him . . ."

"Fuck him. He can die."

"No, he can't. He is our brother and indispensable to our operation."

"No, Fa'iz, with much respect, I am indispensable to the operation. Nizar is a street thug. My father and grandfather were heroes, icons to our people. The al-Zahani bloodlines are royalty. My father commanded his army division, conquered this city, and ruled it for twenty years."

"Your father was a common foot soldier," Nizar said, his voice rough. "Everyone knows when he was a commandant in the Hebron garrison, he was a drunk and a womanizer."

Al-Zahani threw a cup of tea at Nizar, who blinked his eyes and yelled, "You putrid son of a whore, you're no better than anyone else. Your father and grandfather were murderers."

"Enough! There will be no more of this," Fa'iz demanded. "No more talk of Arif's grandchild. No more insults. Hamid and Ibrahim were honored soldiers in our cause. No more violence among us. Save it for the Israelis. If all goes well next month, we will repeat the operation this summer in Tel Aviv. Samir has a brother who is now employed as an orderly. What a glorious year this will be. We will meet again Tuesday. Be mindful of our mission."

THIRTY-ONE

• • •

L IAM KNOCKED ON THE door of the small state department office midmorning, carrying a cup of coffee.

"Come in please," Kayla said, rising from her desk chair.

"I brought a couple of cinnamon scones." Liam held up a paper
bag and shook it from side to side. "My old friend Ben Solomon
used to start his meetings like this. I guess it's become a habit."

"That's very thoughtful, but no thank you." Liam got the message: her wool suit jacket and skirt were fitted neatly around a trim
figure that didn't indulge in empty calories. "But you go right
ahead," she said. "I prepared some materials for you on the computer to go along with our discussion." She pulled an extra chair
over to her desk and angled the monitor to face the two chairs. The
tiny office was barely more than a cubicle, and the chairs were
squeezed into a small space. She gestured for Liam to take a seat.

Liam stared at the tight quarters. "Cozy."

"It's what they gave me." Kayla smiled and patted the side chair.
"Come on, sit down. You need to see the monitor. I prepared some
slides. I won't bite you, I promise."

Liam nodded and took his seat beside her, close enough that her
cologne was discernible, and the proximity of this attractive government official made Liam feel a little self-conscious. It occurred
to him that he was glad he'd brushed his teeth.

"We have a lot to cover this morning," Kayla said. "I'll do my
best to answer all your questions."

"To be honest, I don't know what questions to ask. I'm really
unschooled when it comes to the Middle East. I only know what I

read in the paper, and I don't read that much. You think that al-Zahani is a Palestinian terrorist; I don't know even what a Palestinian is. Exactly where is Palestine? What lands do the Palestinians claim and what is the legitimacy of their claims? Why do they refuse to recognize Israel?" He shrugged his shoulders. "And, most importantly, what's the Agency's dossier on al-Zahani?"

"Well, those are a lot of very good questions, Liam. Shall we begin?"

"Fire away."

Kayla smiled. "You ask, 'Exactly where is Palestine?' 'What's a Palestinian?' Those are good starting points, but perhaps there are no good answers right now. As to the al-Zahani family, we know quite a bit. In fact, tracing the genealogy of the al-Zahani family is a good way to follow the historical development of the modern Middle East.

"What is Palestine? A form of the word Palestine is found in ancient Egyptian hieroglyphics, apparently to refer to the land between Egypt and Phoenicia. The Greeks later used it in another form. The Romans referred to the land as Syria Palaestina, again to describe the land that lay east of the Mediterranean Sea. At present, there is no de facto or de jure country known as Palestine, nor are there any recognized borders for a state of Palestine. The last time there was an area of land officially referred to as Palestine was during the period of the British Mandate, from 1920 to 1948. Today there is no specific area of land called Palestine, though many people refer to the Palestinian presence in the West Bank as the Palestinian Territories.

"Who are the Palestinians? There are approximately 4.5 million people who call themselves Palestinians; 2.7 in the West Bank and 1.8 in Gaza. They are generally Arab, but not entirely. They are young, mostly under thirty-five, they are predominantly Muslim, more Sunni than Shia, and they are comparatively well educated.

"As I have mentioned to you, for the last ninety years, the al-Zahanis have been militants, extremists, and promoters of violence in the Middle East. They have always espoused the radical Arab causes, rejecting the right of Jews to live anywhere in the area and denying the existence of the State of Israel. Their violent struggle, their *état de guerre,* really begins during the British Man-datory period, so that is where we will start."

Kayla tapped the keyboard, and a map of the Middle East under Ottoman rule appeared on the monitor. "The Ottoman Empire ruled the Middle East for four hundred years. With a few minor interruptions, the inhabitants—Muslims, Jews, Christians, pagans—all lived under the reign of the Ottoman Turks. Arif's grandfather, Ibrahim al-Zahani, was born in 1892 in the city of Hebron, shown here on the map, which was then a part of the empire.

"By the time of the First World War in 1914, the Ottoman Empire was in decline, but still a global power. In August 1914, the empire declared jihad against Britain, France, and the Allies and entered the war on the side of Germany, Prussia, and the Central Powers.

"It was during the war, in anticipation of victory, that Britain and France began to discuss how to carve up the Middle East. In May 1916, there were secret meetings between British colonel Mark Sykes and French diplomat François Georges-Picot. The sole purpose of these meetings was to map out a division of the Otto-man Empire for Britain and France to share after the war was over.

"Sykes and Georges-Picot literally sat down, in secret, and drew lines on a map. We'll give this part to England, this part to France. And, oh, yes, Asia Minor we'll give to the Russians. They spelled out their agreement in a written letter dated May 9, 1916, to Sir Edward Grey, the British foreign secretary. It came to be known as the Sykes-Picot Agreement, and that became the blueprint for the next thirty years—the Mandatory Period."

Kayla moved to the next slide. "This is what they drew." The map depicted the Middle East and the lands apportioned for France, Britain, and Russia.

"France was given direct control over coastal Syria, Lebanon, and the area from Acre to the Sea of Galilee. East of that, in interior Syria, the French were given a mandate, that is to say, a governing power.

"Britain was to have direct control over Iraq and interior por-tions of Arabia. The British Mandate included the lands east and west of the Jordan River all the way into the Arabian Peninsula. It included what we know today as Israel and the West Bank territories. Jerusalem was the exception. The Holy City was to be under the international control of Britain, France, and Russia.

"In 1917, another concept began to gain momentum, that of setting aside a portion of the British Mandate for a Jewish homeland. Now, you might ask, why was Britain so prone to support this concept? Why declare it to be the official policy of Great Britain to favor a Jewish homeland in Palestine during the middle of the First World War?"

In the cramped quarters, Kayla turned to face Liam to listen to his answer. Her face was inches from his. He reacted to the awkward juxtaposition by unconsciously leaning back as Kayla spoke. "I'm sure you'll tell me."

"Are you uncomfortable? I can get us another office."

"No." He smiled. "We're fine."

"Okay. Why should Britain discuss devoting part of the land for a Jewish homeland? Several reasons. Partially, it was the war. Chaim Weizmann, a staunch Zionist, brought strategic military support, a process to synthesize acetone for cordite explosives, and Winston Churchill ordered thirty thousand tons of the stuff. Rothschild came to the table with Jewish financial support. America entered the war in 1917, and Americans supported Zionism. Then there was Russia, with its significant Jewish population. One British official noted that there was already 'widespread sympathy with the idea of restoring the Hebrew people to their land.'"

"I assume that Britain's intention was not so well received by Arab countries?" Liam said.

"True, generally speaking. Some opposed the declaration, some did not. But, what's important to us at this point is the emergence of the al-Zahanis. Ibrahim al-Zahani became a radical opponent of Zionism and the return of Jews to their homeland. The moment the declaration was issued, Ibrahim found an ally and aligned himself with the Mufti Haj Mohammed Effendi Amin al-Husseini. Have you heard that name before?"

Liam shook his head.

"He would emerge as the region's biggest troublemaker and a harbinger of what was to become years of violence. When the First World War ended, the Sykes-Picot Agreement was put into effect, and Britain, France, and Russia were given their mandates. The British, through Herbert Samuel, the high commissioner of Palestine, appointed al-Husseini as the grand mufti of Jerusalem, a puzzling choice because Amin was anti-British and had fought with the Ottomans against Britain in the war. Samuel, a Jew and a Zionist, believed that al-Husseini would bridge the divide between Arabs and Jews. He was dead wrong. Amin did just the opposite.

"Amin turned out to be anti-Mandate, anti-British, anti-Zionist, anti-Jewish, and anti any group that didn't agree with him. He was a violent, intolerant man who incited murders, not only of Jews, but of any Arab he considered to be a traitor. He despised the members of the Arab middle class who worked within the Mandate. And here's the thing: Amin's adjutant and constant companion was Ibrahim al-Zahani, Arif's grandfather.

"For sixteen years Amin served as the grand mufti of Jerusalem with Ibrahim right by his side. To be close to the mufti's cabinet, Ibrahim moved to east Jerusalem with his wife. It was there in 1921 that she gave birth to Hamid al-Zahani, Arif's father. Ibrahim later bought a house in Haifa at the foot of the Carmel Mountains, which became the family home for twenty years.

"While acting as mufti and the head of the Arab Higher Command, Amin fomented chaos whenever and wherever he could, all designed to rid the land of foreign settlers, especially Jews. He demanded a cessation of all Jewish immigration to Palestine, no further land sales to Jews, and international recognition of Arab control over all the land, with him as its supreme leader, of course.

"Throughout the era, Amin and Ibrahim provoked armed revolts, violent uprisings, and labor strikes, especially in 1929 and 1936, which were exceptionally bloody years. Finally, in 1936, the British forced the AHC to dissolve and declared it to be illegal. Arrest warrants were soon issued for Amin, Ibrahim, and the other militant leaders.

"With the British police closing in, Amin and Ibrahim snuck off in the middle of the night dressed as bedouin women and made their way into French Mandatory Lebanon to set up base in Beirut. From there, they supplied arms, plotted attacks, and organized uprisings against the British. From time to time, Ibrahim would bring his family from Haifa to join him. It was during one of those sojourns that Hamid met Mariam. When the family returned to Haifa, Mariam accompanied them and soon thereafter married Hamid. Together they had two children: Arif and Safiya. Arif was born in Haifa in 1944."

Kayla turned and smiled. "Liam, would you mind if we take a break? I have a conference call in ten minutes. Can we continue after lunch?"

"Sure." He stood and stretched his legs. "How about two o'clock?"

THIRTY-TWO

• • •

SOMMERS AWOKE BEFORE SUNRISE in Marcy's guest room and strongly considered a quiet exit and an early-morning drive back to Waikiki. Several thoughts were going through his mind, and they all seemed to be arguing with each other.

What am I doing here at Marcy's house drinking wine? I need to concentrate on rescuing Sophie and not hanging out with Marcy. Still, she's been good medicine for me and for that I'm grateful. She's a distraction and probably a liability. Truth be told, I'd be smart to get in the car and leave before she gets up. But, how do I do that without insulting her again? It would be wrong to disrespect her, she's a good person.

He fumbled about the kitchen trying to set a pot for coffee, but grimaced when all he could find was a bag of whole beans. The grinding would be sure to wake her up. He'd just have to sit outside on the swing until she got up.

In the predawn hours, the breeze was light. The only sounds came from the rolling surf, sounds that came to him in patterned intervals, like slow breathing rhythms. Sommers rocked on the swing and contemplated his options. To say that he was frustrated by the inactivity on the e-mail account and the failure of any progress was a gross understatement. The only responses to his e-mails had read *Be patient* and *Working on it*. Now it was becoming painfully obvious that no one was working on it. The delay in implementing Sophie's rescue was making his blood boil. Something had to be done.

Suddenly his cell phone chimed with a text message: *Please call me when you can. It's important.* It was Deborah—no one else had his number. He checked his watch. It was noon in Louisville.

"Hello, Jack," she said.

"Deb, are you okay? Sean okay?"

"We're great. I'm worried about you."

"You don't need to worry, I'm all right."

"Jack, I got a visit from a private detective."

"Tell me you didn't say anything."

"He showed up at the house and warned me that your life was in danger. He scared me, Jack. He said a man named Harrington had been killed, shot in the head. And then yesterday he called and told me that a man named Ellis was killed by a hit-and-run driver. He said that would mean something to you, that you would know them both."

"Shit."

"Jack, he also said you could be next, that you were a loose end. He said there were probably people looking for you. He told me to contact you right away."

"Deb, this is a trap. What do you know about this guy? How do you know any of that's true? He could be working for the wrong people. Christ, he could have some fancy electronic equipment on you right now. Hang up."

"I'm at a friend's in Newburg, Jack. No one's followed me. The investigator left two days ago."

"Hang up, Deb, and go home."

"Jack, the man said he wanted to help you get Sophie. He said he would deal with you on your own terms."

"You know we can't trust anybody. Especially somebody who just shows up at your house looking for a job. Did this guy give you his name?"

"Liam Taggart"

"Taggart? Big Irish guy?"

"Right."

"I know him. I've met Taggart at the office. He does contract work for J and F. He doesn't want to help me, Deb, he's been hired by Jenkins to find the money."

"He admits that. But he said you were a good man, and if he could, he would help us get Sophie back. I trust him, Jack. I don't know why, but I do. He's got kind eyes."

"Oh, Christ, Deb. Kind eyes?"

"Yes, he does. He says he wants to talk to you, that he can help."

"I doubt that Jenkins's PI wants to do anything to help us. He's being paid to catch me. What else did he say?"

"He said that you couldn't get Sophie back by yourself and that he could help. Is he right?"

"Maybe. I don't know. I really don't know what to do. I'm running out of options. The people I'm counting on continue to put me off. They've all but disappeared. Half the time they won't return my messages. Other times they tell me to be patient. I'm thinking I should come back to Chicago."

"No, Jack, don't. Taggart said it's way too dangerous."

"Taggart doesn't want me back in Chicago? That's odd. He's the one who's looking for me."

"That's what he said. If you come back to Chicago, you could get killed."

"Of course. If I get killed, he never finds the money. Right. I need to know how Taggart thinks he can help me, Deb. What does he think he can do to get Sophie back?"

"He didn't say. He just said he'd do it on your terms. Do you want to talk to him?"

"Maybe, but I'll have to figure out how. I can't talk to him on the phone, they can trace the call. Will Taggart meet with you again in person?"

"I don't know. He gave me his card. Do you want me to meet with him and find out what he can do?"

"I'm not sure what I want you to do yet. Deb, you better get off the phone. Can we talk tomorrow?"

"Sure. Same time?"

"Okay, same time. Be careful. I love you."

"Love you too."

Jack went back to the swing. More complications. More shoals to navigate.

Marcy walked out to the veranda with two cups of coffee. The hem of her light cotton robe, belted at the waist, fluttered softly in the morning breeze. "Were you just talking to someone?"

Sommers nodded. "My sister."

"Everything okay?"

"Not really."

Marcy sat beside him on the swing. "I'm sorry, Jack, isn't there something I can do?"

"I wish there were."

"What's the problem?"

"There's a person I'd like to talk to, but I can't figure out how to do it."

"Can't use the phone?"

He shook his head.

"Who do you need to talk to?"

"There's a guy back in Chicago who thinks he can help me, who may have some information, but I can't figure out a way to safely communicate with him. The only way seems to be in person, but that's out of the question."

"What about me? I can go to Chicago."

Sommers shook his head. "It's not an option. The last thing I want to do is get you mixed up in this."

"I feel like I'm already mixed up, like I'm living in a spy novel."

Sommers reached for her hand as she sat with him on the swing. "You're not. But I am. And sooner or later it's bound to catch up with me. I was a fool to think this would go smoothly."

"Hit a roadblock?"

Sommers nodded. "The people I told you about, the ones with connections, I thought I could count on them. I did what I promised to do. Now they've abandoned me or betrayed me. Whichever. They're not keeping up their end of the bargain. When I left the city, they were supposed to e-mail me, give me progress reports on what they were doing, their half of the deal, which was to bring Sophie back to the US. I've been checking my computer every day. I've sent dozens of e-mails." Sommers opened his hands. "There's been little or no response. I can only assume that nothing's being done. And I'm totally frustrated. I'm treading water. It doesn't matter if the sea is calm or angry, I can't make progress in any direction. I can't go forward, I can't go backward. All I can do is wait for these people."

"You want me to go talk with them?"

"Absolutely not. People who talk to them don't seem to live much longer."

"I suppose the police are out of the question?"

"The police, Marcy? Seriously?"

"Then who's the person you need to talk to?"

"He's a private investigator who came to see my sister. I know him. I met him once. He says he'll help me get Sophie if I help him get the missing money."

"Missing money?"

Sommers grimaced and nodded. "There's a lot of money missing."

"And you've got it?"

He tilted his head from side to side. "Not exactly."

Marcy stood. "Wow. Missing money, kidnapped children, dangerous criminals, private detectives, and a friend from my past sleeping at my house. I'm on the set of an international spy thriller."

"I'm sorry, Marcy. I'm a big mistake for you, right now." He stood to leave. "I need to get back to the city."

"Wait. That was a joke." She gave him a peck on the cheek. "You're not a mistake. Don't say that. I want to help. Sit down."

"You need to stay out of this. For me, it's just a matter of time. Maybe in a month, maybe a few months. I only hope for enough time to rescue my daughter, spend a little time with her, make sure she's okay, and get her to Deborah. It's only a matter of time and it's not going to end well for me. You don't want to be involved."

"Maybe you're not the final authority on what I need to do. I think I should decide what's good for me, and right now I think I want to be the person to help. For Alina, for Sophie. For you, Jack. Give me a chance to do something that I can feel good about. I'll be careful."

"You have no idea what you'd be getting yourself into."

"So, tell me and let me decide. Like Paul Harvey says, 'And now the rest of the story.'"

Sitting on the porch swing, finishing their second cup of coffee, tears rolling down both their cheeks, Sommers finished telling his story. He left nothing out. Now his sister had called with the news that an investigator working for the law firm had proposed a meeting. Did Taggart have the wherewithal to recover Sophie? Would he do it? Could he set up the exchange, make the payoff? Bring Sophie back to him? Could Jack trust him? Kind eyes?

"I can go meet with the investigator." Marcy said. "He doesn't know me or where I live. I'll meet him in some neutral, safe place, like LA."

"I'd be the biggest coward of all time if I let you go instead of me. I need to go myself."

"Coward? You may be a lot of things, but you're no coward. Nothing scares you. Trust me on that. Down went Randy."

He squeezed her hand gently. "You're wrong. I've been scared since the moment they took Sophie. Scared that I'll fail her again. I know she's counting on me and I can't let her down. I'm her father, Marcy; I'm all she's got in this world."

"Maybe you're not all she's got. I'll go meet with Taggart. I'll meet him in LA in a busy restaurant. How risky can that be?"

Sommers looked into her eyes and smiled. "You're a great friend. You shouldn't be doing this, but thank you. I'll tell Deb to set it up. I want you to be very careful. Strict parameters."

Marcy nodded.

"Of all the bad decisions that I've made lately," Jack said, "deciding to take a ride out to McDuffy's wasn't one of them. How lucky was I to have stumbled across you in the middle of nowhere? Pure dumb luck."

"Maybe not. Maybe things happen for a reason."

"That's what Alina used to say." He put his arm around Marcy. "I love you for what you're doing. You know, you'll be sticking your neck out?"

"I'll be careful."

She got up from the glider to refill the coffee cups. As she bent to pick up Jack's cup, her robe fell open. In a moment of unintended intimacy, her nightclothes and her midriff were exposed.

Jack sat mesmerized.

Marcy felt his stare but didn't move. She looked into Jack's eyes. The moment froze and then the moment moved on. She rebelted her robe and walked toward the kitchen. "We'll get her back, Jack. Together, we'll get her back."

THIRTY-THREE

• • •

LUBANNAH STOOD DEFIANT, HER hands on her hips, her jaw high and pointed at her husband. "You will not mutilate that little girl, do you understand me, Arif?"

Al-Zahani put down his newspaper. He spoke calmly, like a professor. "Circumcision is sunna. It is part of the *fitra*. Would a hajj have her as a wife if she were not circumcised?"

"A hajj? A hajj? What are you talking about? It's barbarism and you will not do it. This is the twenty-first century. You will not cut my granddaughter."

"Woman, do not tell me what I will do."

"It is banned by all enlightened society; the mufti himself has banned it."

"The mufti in Egypt."

"He is my mufti."

"Look, Lubannah, I am a doctor. It is a simple clitoridectomy. There is no danger to her health. I would do nothing to harm our precious little girl. It's for her own good. It will stabilize her libido. She will not be sexually reckless."

"You're only saying this because of Alina, because she married a man you did not approve of. She was in love, Arif, and—"

"Do not speak of her in my house!" Al-Zahani stood. "If you hadn't interfered with me when she was a child, she never would've run off with the first man she met. Do not tell me what to do."

Lubannah shook with emotion. "I will tell you this. If you mutilate that child, I will never respect you again. For the rest of your life I will curse you."

"Aaah! You and your threats. You are a foolish woman. We will talk of this again next month after my business is concluded. But I have to tell you, it will be done this summer, so you'd better get used to it."

Al-Zahani stormed from the room. "Bashir, get my car."

Al-Zahani parked three blocks from the group's apartment and took an indirect route to the back door, where he was once again greeted by the teenager in the soccer shorts.

"Am I the last to arrive, Dani?"

"Everyone is upstairs."

"Thank you, Dani, you're a good boy." Al-Zahani took one last look around, opened the door, and climbed the steps to the apartment.

"Once again the famous doctor keeps us all waiting because he is so much more important than we are, so indispensable to the operation," Nizar said with exaggerated facial expressions.

Al-Zahani spun around sharply.

Fa'iz spoke softly, "Stop. When will you stop acting like children? April sixteenth is rapidly approaching. What remains to be done?"

"The strain is slow to replicate," al-Zahani said. "Although the required concentration per IV bag is small, we have only fifteen hundred sixty bags under refrigeration. We are working day and night at the lab."

"Fifteen hundred?" said Nizar. "We are going through all this to infect maybe a few hundred people? We might as well throw firecrackers at them."

"Soon there will be more. We are going faster now. We can make forty a day. Before long, maybe fifty."

"Everyone here knows I have lost all patience with you, Arif," Nizar said. "But I ask this question sincerely: How do we know your solution will work?"

"I've tested it. It's virulent and unstoppable. It's a superbug, resistant to all known antibiotics. What's more, because of the incubation period, the pathogen is undetectable for several days, and when the victim does become sick, it's too late. The bacteria have done their work. Hemorrhagic fevers. Internal organs are damaged beyond repair. It is the most terrorizing weapon ever developed because people waste away before their loved ones' eyes. They are the walking dead. It will strike such fear, such panic, such horror, in the hearts of the public that they will bow to our wishes. I call it Canaan's One-State Solution."

"Is it like Ebola?"

Al-Zahani shrugged. "Ebola is a virus. Our strain is bacterial and will be injected directly into the body through an IV in a hospital. It's not airborne and must enter the body through injection. But the effects are similar. Backaches, headaches, nausea in the beginning. Then bleeding from the nose, eyes, and rectum. Coma. Shock." He shrugged again. "Similar."

Nizar held up his index finger. "But you have tested it on lab animals, right? Rats?"

Al-Zahani nodded. "Yes, several different subjects. The results are all the same."

"But, rats. Not humans. How do we know it will work, and how fast it will work?"

"There is no reason to suspect it will not perform just the same."

Nizar stood and faced the group. "There are many variables to consider. The level of concentration necessary per subject, the weight and age of the subjects, and the fact that humans, even Israelis, are not rats, am I right?"

Al-Zahani nodded. "I have considered those criteria and more."

Nizar looked to the elder. "Fa'iz, we are foolish not to do a trial run on a human subject. The success of our whole operation depends on it."

"Nizar is right," Fakhir said. "Myself, I would like to see how it works."

"This is not a new cell phone, Fakhir," said Ahmed, leaning against the wall. "To see how it works you must kill someone."

Al-Zahani agreed. "First, why waste a perfectly prepared IV? We only have fifteen hundred sixty. Second, it's medically immoral to use a human subject as a guinea pig."

Al-Zahani's comment brought laughter to several among the group. "Immoral to kill one, but perfectly acceptable to kill a thousand?"

"An operation this globally significant cannot end in embarrassment because we failed to properly test the solution," Nizar said.

"Maybe you'd like to volunteer?" al-Zahani replied.

Fakhir chuckled. "Why did I know that was coming?"

Fa'iz held up his hands. "Nizar is right. The solution must be tested. We must find a martyr."

"What about old Jabir? He is dedicated to jihad."

"He is the perfect subject," Rami said. "We have no doubt of his commitment, and he is old, weak, and suffering from cancer. He will die soon anyway. It will be a blessing for him to give his life to the cause."

"For those reasons, he would not be a proper subject," Nizar said. "If you're going to run a test, you need to run it on someone young and healthy. Am I right, Arif?"

Al-Zahani nodded. "I'm afraid so. Jabir would succumb too readily."

"If you infect one of our brothers, won't you start an outbreak here in Hebron?" asked Ahmed.

Al-Zahani shook his head. "I told you, it has to enter through injection. Essentially, it is not contagious."

Nizar spoke softly. "What about Dani?"

Fa'iz looked directly at al-Zahani, who nodded. Fa'iz raised his finger and gave a sharp nod. "Of course, Dani is a perfect subject. He is young, he is strong. He is one of us. Dani, it is."

THIRTY-FOUR

• • •

LIAM AND FOSTER SAT at a corner booth at Portillo's. Liam had talked Foster into an Italian beef-and-sausage combo with sweet and hot peppers. Large bag of fries. Several paper napkins.

"You eat this stuff very often?" Foster said, wiping his mouth. The crown of his head was sweating from the hot peppers.

"Every chance I get."

"How did the morning session go?"

"Dizzying."

"You mean the volume of the information?"

"Well, that, and she was practically sitting on my lap in that little office."

"You're a lucky man. Lot of guys in the department would pay big money for that privilege."

Liam smiled and nodded. "Kayla's an impressive woman in a lot of ways. She certainly knows her history. She's telling me more than I can absorb, but I'm also getting a good background on the al-Zahanis."

"We know a lot more about his father and grandfather than we know about Arif. His profile is scant. Kayla says he consorts with Fa'iz Talib, who's an Agency watch-list favorite, but we're not sure exactly how extensive this Sons of Canaan group is and where they operate. They're careful about where and how they meet. So far we haven't been able to infiltrate their organization. That's why we're hoping you might pick up some information, not only who the members are, but what they're up to. Obviously, that's why she wants you to go over there."

"I figured it was broader than the ransom exchange, but I don't know if I'm comfortable being Kayla's operative."

"Well, *operative*'s a little strong. Right now, we just want you to learn whatever you can."

"And you'll give me names, starting points? People to contact?"

Foster nodded. "Kayla knows people. Jamal Abu Hammad, for one. He's an old-timer who owns an antiquities shop in the Muslim Quarter of Jerusalem. For a long time he lived in Hebron, and his grandchildren are still there. If something's going on in Hebron, Abu Hammad is likely to know about it. His family is said to have ties to the al-Zahanis. But Abu Hammad won't talk to anyone from the Agency. Not even Kayla. That's why your cover is perfect."

"It's not perfect. If Sommers already has a deal in the works, then why would he send me over there to find out about the deal?"

Foster shrugged. "To find out about his daughter? To make sure the deal has no snafus?"

Liam shook his head. "And what about the language barrier?"

"That old fox speaks perfect English when he wants to. As to anyone else you need to talk to, Kayla will go with you. She knows her way around."

"She speaks Arabic?"

"Perfectly. Also Hebrew, Farsi, and Kurdish, and she can get by on Jordanian Levantine. But I think you'll find that most people will talk to you in English, if they choose to talk at all."

"Getting back to my 'perfect' cover, what reason would I have to talk to Abu Hammad?"

"You'll figure something out."

Liam checked his watch. "I better leave. Professor Cummings will give me a detention if I'm tardy."

Foster blotted his mouth with his sixth napkin. "Quite a sandwich."

"Around here, we call it a *sammich*."

They shook hands, and Liam left to make his way back to the Federal Building. As he walked down Clark Street, his phone rang. He looked at the screen: 502 area code.

"Hello, Deborah."

"Mr. Taggart, I want to talk to you again, but not on the phone."

"All right. Can you see me first thing tomorrow morning?"

"Make it ten. I want to be sure Sean's not at home."

Kayla was seated at her desk when Liam returned. "How was your lunch? You'll have to take me to Portillo's one day."

"How do you know where we ate?"

"I'm a spy. We have satellite surveillance."

"What?"

Kayla laughed. "I just got off the phone with Harry. We were coordinating my travel to Israel next week."

Liam smiled. "You might actually have a sense of humor."

"Oh, you'd be surprised." Kayla turned her attention to the monitor and showed the afternoon's first slide. "Do you remember Mufti Haj Mohammed Effendi Amin al-Husseini from this morning?"

Liam nodded and shoehorned himself into his seat beside Kayla. "The mufti of Jerusalem, fomenter of riots and strikes. Bad dude, snuck off to Lebanon in drag. Joined there by his henchman Grandfather Ibrahim."

Kayla raised her eyebrows. "You did listen!"

"Believe it or not."

"As I told you this morning, Amin and Ibrahim went into exile in Lebanon, but they used it as a base to incite further riots. It didn't take long for the French to issue an arrest warrant, and the two troublemakers were forced to escape from Lebanon into Iraq. They stayed there for two years. In 1941, Amin sponsored a pro-Nazi coup and tried to overthrow the British-run government. When Britain restored order, Amin and Ibrahim fled to Tehran, where they were welcomed by the pro-Nazi shah."

"So, they became Nazis?"

"Dyed-in-the-wool. It suited their purpose. British agents nearly caught up with Amin and Ibrahim in Iran, and once again they had to flee, this time to Italy. Because they were constantly on the move, Ibrahim kept his family—Hamid, Mariam, Arif, and Safiya—back at their home in Haifa, and that's where Arif al-Zahani grew up.

"While in Italy, Amin courted Mussolini. His purpose was to

convince Il Duce to support the creation of an Arab state in Palestine, with Amin in charge, naturally. In return, he promised to supply Arab military support for the Axis. Mussolini was open to the idea, but wasn't in a position to make it happen. So, Amin and Ibrahim then traveled north and sought out the world's number one anti-Semite."

"Hitler."

"Correct. Amin and Ibrahim traveled to Berlin. There they met and ingratiated themselves with Hitler, trying to get his backing for a Palestinian state, again with Amin as supreme leader. Hitler admired Amin's blue eyes and told him he must have Aryan blood." She tapped the keyboard for a picture of Hitler and al-Husseini sitting together in animated conversation.

"'The Arabs are Germany's natural friends,' Amin said to Hitler, and he offered to train Muslim armies for the Reich. In exchange, Hitler told Amin exactly what he wanted to hear: once Germany defeated Russia, the next step would be the destruction of the 'Jewish element residing in the Arab sphere under the protection of British power.' In fact, Hitler told him, 'The Jews are yours.'

"Amin and Ibrahim found an apartment in Berlin. Between 1942 and 1944 they assisted Hitler by recruiting Arabs for the Waffen-SS, and training Bosnian Muslims for the Nazi infantry. Amin's Bosnian Muslims were responsible for the death of ninety percent of Bosnia's Jewish community. Amin and Ibrahim met often with Himmler and Ribbentrop, and there's a strong basis for believing they toured the death camps with Eichmann, who treated Amin as a close friend. Al-Husseini's name was mentioned often at the Nuremberg trials, but by then he had escaped to Egypt, where he was welcomed by King Farouk.

"After the war, Amin and Ibrahim ended up in Gaza, once again heading up a group of militants. This time it was the al-Jihad al-Muqaddas, the Army of the Holy War. We know that group today as the Muslim Brotherhood. And it didn't take long for Amin and Ibrahim to latch onto another cause. By the end of 1945, there were a quarter million Jews living in displaced persons camps throughout Germany, Austria, and Italy. They were the survivors of the Holocaust. They called themselves Sh'erit ha-Pletah, the 'surviving remnant.'

"Overwhelmingly, the displaced persons, the DPs, wanted to emigrate to British Mandatory Palestine, but Britain had strict immigration quotas forged by Neville Chamberlain's 1939 White Paper. Quotas in the US, Britain, and Canada essentially closed all those doors, as well.

"Everyone knew that the existence of the British and French Mandates were temporary and unsustainable. But, no matter what Britain envisioned for the postwar division of its territory, it was always rejected by Amin and the Arab leaders. They would have no part of sharing the land. They wanted it all. As a result, postwar Palestine was a cauldron of violence—from Amin and the Arabs, from Zionist paramilitary groups like the Irgun and the Haganah who wanted open immigration, and from the British soldiers themselves.

"In the midst of the growing anarchy, Britain turned to the fledgling UN to work out the solution. An eleven-nation committee was established and known as UNSCOP, the United Nations Special Committee on Palestine. The members traveled to Palestine and concluded, not surprisingly, that the Arab objectives and the Jewish objectives could not be reconciled. But nonetheless, they proposed a division of the land.

"On November twenty-ninth, 1947, the UN General Assembly voted and approved the Plan for Partition. The first portion dealt with the termination of the British Mandate and withdrawal of the British troops. The second part was the establishment of borders for two separate states—an Arab state and a Jewish state. The exception was Jerusalem, which was to remain under international control. Here is a map of what they devised." A map of the partitioned territory appeared on Kayla's monitor.

"The UN's division, though it appeared to resemble a jigsaw puzzle, was based almost entirely upon ethnic demography. There were Jews living in the Arab portions and Arabs in the Jewish portions, but the lines were drawn to reflect the predominant culture. But Amin, the Arab League, and all of the surrounding Arab countries flatly rejected the UN Partition Plan and would not accept borders for either a Jewish state or an Arab state, no matter what the borders were.

"Ibrahim saw the future and it was violent. He knew that a

partition would never be peacefully implemented, and he quickly acted to position his family for an upcoming war. He sent Hamid to Jordan and, using his contacts, had him enlist in the Jordanian Army as an officer. Given Ibrahim's influence, Hamid rose rapidly in the ranks and soon became a squad leader. By the time of the 1948 war, he was commanding a company.

"On May thirteen, 1948, the British pulled out of the mandate, and the next day, May fourteenth, David Ben-Gurion took to the airwaves and proclaimed the Declaration of the Establishment of the State of Israel in the territories granted by the UN Partition Plan. The very next day, May fifteenth, the combined armies of the six Arab League States commenced a coordinated military invasion of Israel.

"Israel was attacked from all directions. Egypt from the south and Syria from the north. From the east, Jordan marched its army across the Jordan River and occupied the entire West Bank including the eastern half of the city of Jerusalem. Hamid al-Zahani was in command of the Jordanian company that took Hebron. The territories captured by Jordan were referred to as the West Bank of the Hashemite Kingdom of Jordan and remained that way until 1967. By the way, it was never referred to as Palestine. Use of the term Palestine was forbidden by the king of Jordan.

"A cease-fire was negotiated and an armistice was signed in April 1949. Not a peace treaty, mind you, just an armistice—they agreed to stop fighting, leaving the armies where they were. Jerusalem, which was originally intended to be international, was split down the middle for the first time in its history, Jordan on the east, Israel on the west. As it had in ancient times, Israel declared Jerusalem to be its capital."

"What became of the al-Zahanis after the 1948 war?" Liam asked.

"Well, I told you Hamid was an officer in the battalion that captured Hebron. The Arab population there hailed Hamid as a hero, and he stayed there to make his home. Ibrahim had him appointed commander of the Jordanian Army garrison in Hebron. Hamid built the house that Arif occupies today."

Kayla looked at her watch. "It's getting late and I want to finish. We'll jump ahead to the sixties because that was the era that launched the Palestinian movement. In 1964, the Arab League founded the Palestine Liberation Organization, which once again sought eradication of the Jews and the state of Israel. Ibrahim was a member of the inner circle from the very beginning.

"For the PLO, its credo was armed violence. Since terrorism, shootings, and bombings were Ibrahim's stock-in-trade, he was a valuable soldier in the cause. But his terrorist activities proved to be his undoing. When he attempted to bomb a Tel Aviv restaurant in 1965, a single shot from an IDF rifle hit the explosives in Ibrahim's arms and he was blown to bits. There wasn't enough to bury. Hamid, enraged at his father's death, led a party of Arab regulars into West Jerusalem in a late-night attack, killing fourteen civilians at a movie theater. From then on there was a price on Hamid's head.

"The sixties was also a period of military buildup, thanks to the Soviets, who supplied arms to the Arab countries. As a result, Arab aggression against Israel increased, and it all came to a head in 1967. On May fifteenth, Egypt massed its troops and told the UN to remove its peacekeepers from Gaza and the Sinai, declaring, 'Our basic objective will be the destruction of Israel. The Arab people want to fight.' Jordan, Syria, and Lebanon lined up beside Egypt.

"Israel looked to the US, but deeply engaged in Vietnam and in a cold war with the Soviets, Johnson told Israel to stand down. Do not fire the first shot. Israel realized it was going to go it alone, that it was only a matter of days before Nasser and the Arab League would attack. Greatly overmatched in troop size, weapons, tanks, and air power, Israel also feared the use of poison gas, which Nasser had used before. So, on June fifth, 1967, the entire Israeli Air Force took off in a surprise move at the breakfast hour and bombed the Egyptian airfields. Then the IAF flew north and destroyed the Syrian airfields. Jordan, which had been warned not to enter the fray, honored its pact with Egypt and announced, 'The hour of revenge has come.' Jordan began shelling Jerusalem.

"The battle for Jerusalem was fierce. Hamid brought his Hebron battalion north and attacked Jerusalem from the southern flank. But his aggression, like his father's, was to be his undoing. On June seventh, in a furious battle in the Kidron Valley, just south of the Temple Mount, Hamid was shot and killed. Arif would have been twenty-three years old at the time. Now he had lost his grandfather and his father to Israeli gunfire.

"Later that same day, the Israeli army gained control of East Jerusalem and the Western Wall. Moshe Dayan declared, 'We've reunited the city, the capital of Israel, never to part it again.' The 1967 War was over in six days. Israeli ground troops forced the Jordanian Army all the way back across the river into Jordan, capturing all of the West Bank territory Jordan had seized in 1948. Israel remains in control of the area."

"So, who does the land belong to? Who has the legitimate claim to the territories?" Liam said.

Kayla spread her hands. "Britain? It captured it from the Ottomans in 1920. Jordan? It captured it in 1948. Israel? It captured it in 1967. The UN Security Council took up the issue after the war and adopted Resolution 242. But it's a complicated resolution with unclear meanings and intentionally vague provisions; 242 provided that Israel should withdraw from 'occupied territories' to 'secure and recognized boundaries' when there was a 'just and lasting peace.' But it didn't specify which occupied territories, what recognized boundaries, or what would constitute a just and lasting peace. Furthermore, 242 didn't specify who would be entitled to occupy the territories after the withdrawal. The Palestinians are not mentioned at all in Resolution 242."

"And Israel has yet to withdraw from any occupied territories?"

"Not true. Sinai was given back to the Egyptians after Camp David in 1978, and Gaza was given up to the Palestinian Authority in 2005. That amounts to over ninety percent of the land Israel captured in 1967.

"But what about the rest—the so-called disputed West Bank? Why do you say the resolution was intentionally vague?"

"Resolution 242 didn't say that Israel should withdraw from '*all the* occupied territories' or even '*the* occupied territories.' At the time it was being drafted, Arab states insisted that the resolution say *all the territories,* but the Security Council rejected the language. The withdrawal was purposefully left vague for future negotiation. So, to this date, negotiations continue. Even now, almost fifty years later.

"There are 2.7 million Palestinians living in West Bank cities, under Israeli military authority, but Palestinian civil control. In 1995, at the end of the Oslo Peace Process, the West Bank was divided into three administrative divisions or 'zones.' The Palestinian Authority was created to provide a government for certain West Bank towns and Gaza. Palestinian cities with no Israeli settlements were designated Zone A. The Palestinian Authority was given complete civil and police autonomy over Zone A cities. Israeli citizens and military are forbidden from entering without permission, although the IDF does enter when necessary on security or emergency missions. Jericho, Ramallah, and Nablus are examples of such cities.

"Zone B areas have joint Palestinian and Israeli control. There is an IDF presence, generally due to Israeli citizens living in the area. Zone C has full Israeli control, both civil and security, and consists of Israeli settlements in Samaria and Judea. What Oslo did *not* do was to recognize a Palestinian state or restrict settlement expansion."

Liam nodded his understanding. "The two lingering issues. Arif al-Zahani lives in Hebron. What zone is that?"

Kayla clicked on a slide of Hebron. "It's a hybrid—part Zone A and part Zone C. Zone A is designated H1, with two hundred thousand Arabs, and this little part here"—she pointed to a shaded corner of the city—"is H2, which is a Zone C settlement with ninety Jewish families. H1 and H2 are separated by conflicting ideologies and a flimsy Cyclone fence. Hebron is one of the most dangerous cities in the world."

"And that's where Sophie is?"

"We think so."

THIRTY-FIVE

. . .

L UBANNAH ENTERED SOPHIE'S ROOM and found her
as she did most of the time—staring out the window and
talking to Sweetness. She gently placed her hands on the
child's shoulders.

"You did not eat much dinner tonight, Sophie."

She shrugged.

"How come?"

"I didn't like it."

"It was *maqluba*, what didn't you like?"

"It was yucky."

"It's just a casserole with rice, eggplant, and lamb. Some cau-
liflower, carrots. It's very good. What would you like instead?"

"A cheeseburger. I want to go to McDonald's."

Lubannah laughed. "There are no McDonald's in Hebron."

Sophie turned back to the window. "Jadda, I never see butterflies outside my window. Where are all the butterflies in Hebron?"

"I don't know, sweetie. I'm sure there must be butterflies in Hebron."

"In the summer, in my mother's garden, there are always lots of
butterflies. Blue and brown ones. Purple ones. Little yellow ones.
But monarchs are the prettiest of all." Sophie looked up at her
grandmother. "Mommy says you have to plant milkweed in your
garden for the butterflies. That's where they lay their eggs."

Lubannah smiled. "Your mother loved to garden. Even when
she was a very little girl. We would garden together." She shrugged.
"Since she left, I don't garden anymore."

Sophie nodded and turned back to the window. The outbuilding was going through its shift change.

"What are those people doing, Jadda?" Sophie pointed at workers carrying satchels and backpacks from the outbuilding and putting them into the trunks of their cars.

"I'm not sure, dear, I've never been in that building. Your Jaddi insists that we stay out. He tells me that they are preparing food and supplies for the poor people of Hebron. Because they are wrapping food and medical supplies, the building must be kept sterile."

"Where does the food go?"

"I am told that it goes to a food bank in the poorer sections of our city. Why do you spend so much time looking out the window?"

Sophie turned in her chair and reached for Lubannah's wrists. "I'm looking for my home, Jadda. I want to go home. Can't you talk to Jaddi and tell him that I don't want to live here?"

Tears formed in Lubannah's eyes. "Why, child? Am I not good to you? I love you so much."

"I love you too, Jadda, but this is not my home. These are not my clothes. I miss my daddy, I miss my friends." Sophie's requests gave way to sobs. "I just want to go home. Please tell Jaddi."

Lubannah stood. "I cannot. Even if I wanted to, Jaddi will not change his mind. You must accept that this is now your home." She turned to leave. "Jamila will be here soon and we will all bake cookies. Do you want to do that?"

Sophie nodded and sniffled.

"Try to be happy. There are lots of people here that love you."

THIRTY-SIX

· · ·

S O YOU'RE GOING TO Louisville again tomorrow?" Catherine said, bringing dinner to the table.

Liam nodded and took a sip of wine. "Six o'clock out of O'Hare. I'll be back in the afternoon."

"Oh, great. That means you'll be getting up at four in the morning and rustling through the closet."

"I can sleep at my apartment, or in the guest room."

"The hell you will. Pass the pasta, please. I'll get up, make you coffee, and go back to bed when you leave. How did your session with the demure Miss Cummings go?"

"Fact intensive, but I have a better appreciation of the Arab/Israeli conflict. Kayla's very knowledgeable."

"Oh, it's Kayla, is it?"

Liam smiled. "NORAD has detected a blip of hostile jealousy on the horizon."

"She's gorgeous."

"Then I guess you're not going to be thrilled to hear that she's going with me when I travel to Israel next week."

"Liam!"

Liam shrugged. "She's a woman of many talents."

"Is that right? Many talents? Well, maybe you *should* sleep at your apartment."

"Cat, I'm only teasing you."

"Well, I don't like it. She's very pretty and she's probably got her eyes on you."

Liam leaned over and gave Catherine a kiss. "Stop being jealous."

"Well, she seems very flirtatious. You told me she had you sit right next to her at her computer. For three hours. I mean, c'mon. Now with the two of you traveling around the world . . ."

"Cat, stop. It was a tiny, little office. She's been nothing but all-business. You're being unreasonable. I shouldn't have made the comment about many talents. I was trying to be funny. That was a mistake."

"Well, I don't have to like it."

"You've got nothing to worry about."

"I've got talents, too, Liam." Catherine smiled seductively.

"Aye, that you do."

"And don't you forget it."

L IAM ARRIVED PRECISELY AT 10:00 A.M. Deborah stood in the doorway for a moment scanning the street.

"No one followed me, Deborah."

She nodded and stepped back. "Would you like a cup of coffee?"

"I don't mean to rattle you, but it's better for us not to talk in your home. Let's just take a walk."

"Are you serious?" She looked around her entry hall. "They bugged my house?"

"I don't know that, but there are definitely people looking for your brother. On both sides of the law. Why take the chance?"

She stepped back into the foyer. "Let me get my coat."

As they strolled around the corner, Deborah said, "I can't tell you much about what's happening lately. He doesn't want to involve me. But whatever plans he's made, they're not working out. They've stalled. He's not sure he can count on the help he was expecting. He says he'd like to talk to you. He wants to know what kind of help you can give him."

"Is he planning on paying al-Zahani money for Sophie's release?"

"I don't know anything more than I just told you."

"Where is he?"

Deborah shook her head.

"How am I supposed to talk to him? Did he give you a phone number?"

"He doesn't want to talk to you on the phone. He's worried that the call can be traced and his location'll be discovered. He said he wants an in-person meeting in a busy restaurant."

"Okay. I'll do that. Where and when?"

"In Santa Monica. Friday at one o'clock. He said if you double-cross him, you'll never learn where the money is. I told him that you would not betray him."

"Oh, you did?"

"It's in your eyes, Mr. Taggart. You have honest eyes. I'm a very good judge of people. I told Jack I trust you—that sooner or later we have to trust someone."

"Thank you. You're right about having to trust someone; he can't manage this plan by himself. And frankly, you're right about me. I don't know about the eyes, but I'm an honest person. Santa Monica's a big place. Where am I supposed to meet him?"

"Belmonte's on Wilshire near Fifth. Friday at one. He said to please come alone. The reservation will be in your name."

"Agreed."

Deborah reached over and squeezed Liam's arm. "Please help him."

"I'll try. I promise. How are you communicating with him?"

"We each have safe, prepaid cell phones, purchased by other people. Untraceable."

"Nothing is untraceable. Make your calls quick. No more than thirty seconds."

THE DEACONS LED WESTERN Alabama by twenty-one points. Thomas was on fire. With eight minutes remaining in the game, he already had a double-double: twenty-six points and twelve rebounds. Marcus whispered to Darius during a time-out, "We got seven points too much. Mr. Kelsen said fourteen, make it less than fourteen."

"Can't help it," Darius said. "Thomas is a stud in the post. He's dominating their bigs."

"We gotta do something. Let 'em steal a couple passes at mid-court. Two, three fast breaks, they'll catch up."

Darius looked at the packed stands. Madison Square Garden. Second round of the East Regional. TV cameras everywhere. NBA scouts. Notepads. Every errant pass would be slow-mo'd. "I ain't fuckin' up my future."

The whistle blew and Marcus brought the ball up for the Deacons. He stood between the circles, passed up a clean look at Thomas and telegraphed a pass to the corner. Western's point guard snatched it midair and took it down for an easy layup. On the next play, Darius got a ball screen from Marcus and drained a jumper, but Marcus was whistled for an illegal screen and the basket was waved off. That was his fourth foul and he was called to the bench. As he walked by Darius, he said, "Spread's at nineteen. It's up to you now."

Western made both free throws and trailed by seventeen. Darius took the inbounds pass and fed Oliver, who missed a three. Western quickly responded on transition and scored on a three-point play. The spread sat at fourteen, but on the next play Darius saw an opening, spun to his left, and scored on a reverse layup. Highlight stuff.

"What the fuck?" mouthed Marcus as Darius ran by the bench.

Time out was called with two minutes left and the score at 81–65. "Sixteen, man. We still need to drop two more," Marcus whispered in Darius's ear.

The horn blew and Marcus reentered the game. At half-court, he lost his dribble. Western's guard scooped it up and scored on the breakaway. Marcus breathed a sigh of relief. Fourteen points. A minute forty-five to go. Just have to keep it there.

The spread remained at fourteen as each side missed a shot, but with twelve seconds left, Thomas grabbed a rebound and flipped the outlet pass to Darius, who took it coast-to-coast, finishing with a windmill that brought the Garden to its feet. Final score: 83–67.

In the locker room, Marcus pulled Darius aside. "What're you gonna tell Mr. Kelsen now, Darius? What're we gonna do? He told us fourteen. He told us not to give the ball to Thomas."

"Ain't my fault. Thomas had thirty-one."

"And the move at the end? With only twelve seconds? Was that

Thomas, or was that you hotdoggin' it for the highlight reels? You shoulda just held the ball. Twelve fuckin' seconds. Even Coach was pissed at you for piling on. Mr. Kelsen paid us and you fucked us."

Darius shoved Marcus back into the lockers. "Look, asshole, did you see all those NBA scouts? The whole country's watching the tourney. Tonight they seen Darius. They seen the best. I ain't gonna dribble it off my knee like you did. I'm goin' in the first round, maybe lottery. You think I'm gonna tank my career for some rich fuck in a Bentley? I be havin' ten Bentleys."

"He ain't gonna like it. He paid us."

THIRTY-SEVEN

• • •

LIAM WALKED INTO BELMONTE's promptly at 1:00
P.M. and approached the hostess stand. The restaurant, a sea-
food concept with white tablecloths and upbeat music,
was busy, serving its lunch crowd. The waitstaff, men and women
alike, were young and wore white shirts with large, Pacific-blue
neckties, patterned with splashes of colorful sea creatures.

"Do you have a reservation for Taggart?"

The young lady smiled. "Yes, we do, and your party's already
here. Let me show you to your table." She led him toward a crescent booth where a pretty, young woman in a coral sundress was
seated with a glass of wine, examining the menu.

Liam stopped. "I don't think this is the right table."

The woman looked up. "Please sit down, Mr. Taggart." She held
out her hand. "My name's Marcy."

"Okay." Liam nodded and turned to the hostess. "I'll have a Macallan 18 on a single piece of ice." He settled into the booth.
"Where's Jack?"

"Safe and sound."

"I need to speak directly to him, not through a go-between."

She shook her head. "I'm afraid you're stuck with the go-
between."

"I've come a long way. On a short turnaround. And I'm not in
the mood for a game."

"No games, Mr. Taggart. I'm here as a proxy, of sorts. I know
his situation and I have my instructions."

Liam sighed and took a sip of his Scotch. "It's Liam. Where does Sommers's deal stand with al-Zahani?"

"He doesn't know. He's beginning to doubt there's a deal in place."

"Why?"

Marcy tilted her head in a shrug. "He has a private e-mail account that was set up for communication with the people who were in charge of handling the transaction. He's not getting any meaningful responses, just an occasional 'Be patient.' He's come to believe they've abandoned him."

"Where's the money?"

"It's in a safe place."

"Then they haven't abandoned him. You can be sure they're looking for him."

"He's considered that possibility, but they don't know where he is."

The waitress returned to the table. They picked up their menus, studied them briefly, and ordered.

"Whoever they are, they know that sooner or later Jack has to show himself," Liam said. "There's a focal point."

"Sophie."

"Correct. What can you tell me about the deal, Marcy? How was it made and why does he think it's stalled?"

Marcy swiveled to face Liam and spoke softly. "After Sophie was kidnapped, Jack was approached with a proposition. He was working on a large business deal that was set to close through an escrow. Jack was to arrange for the escrow money to be sent to a sham account. He was assured that part of the money would be used for Sophie's return."

"Who gave this assurance?"

"Jack doesn't want me to disclose any names to you at this point."

"The person who approached Jack, what do we know about him and his connection to al-Zahani?"

"I'm sorry. I was instructed not to talk about the person. Jack was told that this person had made the arrangements to buy Sophie's return out of Hebron. What ultimately happens to the rest of the money is not Jack's concern. He doesn't want any of it."

"Did Jack ever have confirmation of this arrangement from al-Zahani?"

"No. He hasn't had any contact with the al-Zahanis since they picked up Sophie at his house."

Liam grimaced. "The *person*. Hmm. The entire scenario rests on the credibility of the *person*. Did Jack ever consider the possibility that this *person* may be running a number on Jack and may have never contacted al-Zahani at all?"

"Of course. Jack may be desperate, but he's not stupid. To Jack, the *person* was a godsend. Jack had tried all the legal avenues: the US government, the Israeli government. He just kept running into stone walls. Then along comes this businessman who has powerful contacts in the Middle East and can make it all happen. As far as Jack knew, millions of dollars, maybe tens of millions, would be more than enough to finance Sophie's return. Whether it's a payoff to al-Zahani or otherwise, doesn't really matter to Jack. The escrow money went to a Panamanian account that Jack set up."

Liam shook his head. "It's so foolish. You know two of the other accomplices are dead?"

"We heard that. Jack doesn't know if it's true."

"It's true. They're dead."

"Well, it took all three to complete the theft. Jack couldn't have misdirected the wire without them. They were recruited by . . ." She shrugged.

"I know. The *person*. Why doesn't Jack want me to know who this person is?"

"I guess he still holds out the possibility that the man will do what he said—rescue Sophie. There's a lot of money in that account. If the person actually made contact with al-Zahani, and if there's any truth to what he said, then there are millions of reasons that Sophie can be brought back to the U.S."

The waitress returned and set the lunch plates on the table.

"You're very brave to come here," Liam said. "Do you understand you're putting yourself in the line of fire? Why are you doing this?"

"I like spy novels."

Liam took a bite of his "sautéed mahimahi sandwich with zesty basil butter and garden sprouts." He made a face.

"And I'm very fond of Jack. You told Deborah you could help us. What can you do?"

"To be honest with you, Marcy, I'm not sure. I can tell you that I'll go to the Palestinian territories and try to open the channels. I'll try to find out if there is, or ever was, a deal. If I can facilitate Sophie's return, I will. But I'm not going to lie to you, I can't hand over the escrow money in exchange for Sophie. There's no way the government will let al-Zahani get his hands on that money. He's a suspected terrorist."

"I don't think Jack believes that al-Zahani is a terrorist. But if you're not sure what you can do, and you won't let al-Zahani have any money, why did you tell Deborah you could help? You don't have an alternative plan. You don't have anything. Why did you lie to her? Did you think we'd be so stupid as to let Jack come here and be grabbed by you at this restaurant?" She stood to leave.

"Wait, Marcy. Sit down. I didn't lie to anyone. I told her I would try to help, and I will do everything I can. I'll be on the ground over there. I'm going next week and I should be able to find out something, at least more than Jack presently knows. And I've got the support of the State Department."

"What do you mean, the State Department? They know about the money?"

"They know about the money—hell, everyone knows about the money—but they also suspect that al-Zahani may want to use this money for some kind of terrorist activity. And that may, in fact, be why al-Zahani took Sophie in the first place. They want me to get as much information as I can, and they think that by using me, a private investigator hired by Jack's family to find Sophie, people will open up to me. Maybe I can get close enough to al-Zahani to find out what's really going on. If there's a deal, they want to put me in the middle of it. If there is no deal, they want me to make the offer. It's our best shot."

"You'd get in the middle of this with a terrorist?"

Liam shrugged.

"That's very brave. What about the money?"

Liam shook his head. "It's gotta go back to the escrow. To the guy who owns the company. Not to a terrorist."

"I just don't think Jack believes that al-Zahani is a terrorist. A deceitful, manipulative bastard, yes. But a terrorist? Jack wouldn't give money to a terrorist. Jack tells me al-Zahani's a man who maintains a very high standard of living and probably requires a lot of cash. Jack figures he might be overextended. After all, it's hard for a doctor to pull down that kind of money practicing in a Palestinian town. He may need the money badly."

Liam nodded. "I understand. But I've heard the doctor is quite wealthy."

"Have you counted his cash?"

Liam smiled. "Fair enough. No, I haven't."

"Jack also believes that the *person* might need to use the money to finance a rescue. It might mean hiring people. It might mean paying off local governmental people. Jack doesn't care who gets paid off, all he cares about is bringing Sophie home. So why shouldn't he stick with the *person*?"

"You and Jack already know the answer or you wouldn't be here. So what are Jack's options? Is he going to go to Palestine himself with a bag of money? Is he going to hire another *person*? Is he going to recruit an army of mercenaries, soldiers of fortune, to sneak arms into Israel and firestorm their way in and out of the country? Don't you think that's a little out of Jack's element?

"And bear in mind, Marcy, someone has already killed two people. Jack would be in the crosshairs if they knew where he was. As you've described the embezzlement scheme to me, there were three active participants, and two of them are now dead."

Liam took another bite of his sandwich and wrinkled his nose. "Ugh! Give me a good Chicago sammich anytime."

"What do you want me to tell Jack?"

"Why don't you get him on the phone and let me talk to him myself?"

She shook her head. "I can't. I have to follow his wishes. I can talk to him privately. What do you want me to tell him?"

"Tell him to keep his head down. Tell him to stay out of sight. And tell him to set up a communication channel with me."

She pulled a cell phone out of her pocket. "I'll be right back." She walked outside to make the call.

Liam signaled for the waitress. "I'll have another Macallan. And you can take this sandwich. What's the possibility I can get a jumbo char-dog with relish, hot peppers, tomatoes, and a pickle?"

The waitress put a plastic smile on her face. "I'm sorry. That's not on the menu, sir. May I interest you in something else? Our avocado whitefish burger is very popular."

Liam sadly shook his head. She smiled and left to fill the order.

Marcy returned and slid into the booth. "He says he's grateful for your help. He urges you to do what you can. If you can set up an exchange or get the Israelis or the Palestinian Authority involved, he'll do everything he can to help you, including supplying details about the money and the other participants. He'll do whatever he has to do to get Sophie back. If you want him to trust you, you have to trust him and respect his need to stay out of sight."

A moment later the waitress returned with Liam's drink and the check. Liam reached into his pocket for cash. Marcy stopped him. "I'm on an expense account. Jack told me that I was to treat." She dug into her purse and pulled out her wallet.

"Marcy, how does Jack propose to raise Sophie when she returns? He's facing twenty years or more."

She nodded slightly. "I know, but that's Jack's business."

"Are you prepared to harbor a fugitive?"

"Look, I'm only trying to help Jack get his daughter back. She's being held captive in a violent city. What I do is my business."

Liam smiled. "All right, how do I stay in contact? I don't want to come back to Santa Monica. I don't care for fish sandwiches."

She wrote down a cell phone number. "Here. This is how you reach us. You leave a text message." Liam looked at the paper. It was Deborah's number.

THIRTY-EIGHT

• • •

DARIUS LEFT THE PRACTICE facility at 9:00 P.M. and started walking across the quad toward his dorm. The frozen grass crunched beneath his shoes. Coach's game plan for the third round kept playing out in his mind. So did his stellar performance against Western Alabama in the second round, clips of which were being shown hourly on *SportsCenter*. So far, it had been a great tournament for him, and he was the topic of every sports-talk panel. "Anti-gravity," they said. He walked through the brisk night with a spring in his step.

The familiar black Bentley pulled up alongside the curb. Darius pretended not to see the car and kept walking with his head down.

Kelsen's chauffeur dashed around the car and blocked his path. "Mr. Kelsen wants a word with you." He put a strong grip on Darius's arm, led him back to the car, opened the back door, and rudely pushed him in. Darius was placed in the middle of the backseat with Kelsen on one side and a large man in a gray wool coat on the other.

"Haven't I been good to you, Darius? Am I not like a father to you?"

"Look, Mr. Kelsen, I'm sorry about the other night, but I had to make a good showing if I want to be a high pick."

"High pick? You're only a sophomore, Darius. You've got another two years of eligibility."

"No, sir. I'm going to declare this year. Coach says I gotta good shot at bein' a lottery pick. That's why I had to play real good."

"I said fourteen, Darius." Then Kelsen's voice rose. "Fourteen! Not sixteen, you little punk."

"Hey, look, man, I said I was sorry. And I don't wanna do this no more. I'm out. I gotta worry about my future. I don't want your money no more."

"Money? Do you know how much money you cost me Tuesday, you and your future?"

"No, sir."

"Show him, Evgeniy."

Evgeniy's fist slammed hard into Darius's stomach. It knocked the wind out of him. He couldn't catch his breath.

"Show Mr. Anti-Gravity how much money his high-flyin' showboat cost me against Western Alabama," Kelsen said calmly.

Evgeniy, a smile on his face, took a police baton from the seat beside him and swung it hard, striking Darius on the shin. He screamed in agony. "Aaahh, my leg. You broke my leg."

"Let's see how high you can fly now."

Darius doubled up on the seat, his arms around his knee. The chauffeur walked around and opened the back door.

"Too bad about your leg," Kelsen said. "Accidents will happen. Tough break for the Deacons, though. Thought they might go all the way. But, you know, the good news is, broken legs can heal. Come next year, after your rehab, you'll be back, maybe not quite as quick, but you'll play. And you and I will talk."

Darius was thrown from the car onto the parkway. "Don't ever cross me again," Kelsen said. "You give me two more years. You owe me. You belong to me."

The Bentley pulled away, leaving Darius in the parkway. He lay on the grass, crying, shaking from the incident and unable to walk.

Several minutes later a young woman spotted him and cautiously approached. She set her backpack down beside him. "Hey, are you okay? Do you need help?"

"I been mugged. I think my leg is busted."

"I'll get someone here." She dialed 911 on her cell. She smiled encouragingly. "They're coming right over." Then she looked closer. "Are you Darius McCord?"

Shortly thereafter, an ambulance arrived and transported him to Memorial Hospital. While he was waiting to be x-rayed, Darius's mother rushed into the emergency room.

"Oh, my baby, what'd they do to you?"

"Mama, they busted up my leg. Took my money."

"Who did this to you?"

"I don't know. I didn't see 'em comin'. They got me from behind. Knocked me down and hit me with a ball bat. Then they ran off. There was two or three of 'em. Mama, I didn't have a chance."

THIRTY-NINE
...

CATHERINE SLID HER PILLOW over and snuggled up to Liam. "Are you awake?"

"I've been up for a while. I didn't want to move, you were sleeping so soundly."

"It's three A.M. Are you thinking about Sommers and where he might be?"

"I got a pretty good idea where he is. He's in Hawaii."

Catherine propped herself up on her elbow. "Did Marcy tell you that?"

"No. When she pulled out her wallet to pay the check, I saw a debit card from the Bank of Hawaii. So that's my best guess."

"Did you get her last name?"

He nodded.

Catherine laid her head on Liam's arm. With her fingernail, she drew little circles on his chest. "Sounds like you and I need to go to Hawaii."

Liam smiled. "We'll just go sit on the beach and wait for Sommers to walk by."

"I had something a little more romantic in mind."

Liam rolled over and kissed her on the neck. "I bet you do, you always do."

THE MORNING SUN BEGAN to peek through the draperies and Catherine was still lying on Liam's arm. "Many, many talents," he said with a purr.

"You better remember that when you go to Israel next week with Miss Gorgeous."

"You want me all to yourself?"

"Damn right I do."

Liam got out of bed, took a few steps toward the bathroom and stopped. "You know, Cat, I don't think he has the money."

"Seriously? Why?"

"Just a feeling. It might be in an account that he controls. But maybe not."

"Then who has it?"

"Good question. Maybe the *person*, who may have never talked to al-Zahani or ever made a deal. Who may just be working Jack. And if so, when he gets Jack to show his face, there'll be a third fatality."

Catherine looked at the clock. "Shit, I got to get going. I've got court at nine thirty. *Kelsen v. Jenkins & Fairchild* is up on the status call."

COURTROOM 1506 WAS BUSY, especially on status days, which were known as Sherwin's Cattle Call. Judge Sherwin, trying to move his lengthy docket, allowed only a few minutes to each group of lawyers, just enough time for them to inform him of their progress. When her case was called, Catherine and two other attorneys quickly approached the bench. Kelsen's attorney informed the judge that discovery was moving along well and that several depositions had been scheduled. The judge then ordered all non-expert fact discovery to be completed within 120 days.

"I'm going to set a preliminary trial date for next January," Judge Sherwin said. "Final pretrial orders to be completed by January fifth. Pretrial conference on January eighth. Trial to begin January seventeenth."

"What? January seventeenth?" Kelsen shouted from the back of the courtroom. "What the hell?"

The judge looked over and beckoned Kelsen forward with his index finger. "Come up here, sir."

Kelsen approached the bench with a determined walk. "Why do I have to wait until January? They stole my money. I want a trial right now. Isn't there a speedy-trial act or something?"

Judge Sherwin looked down at the attorneys. "Who is this man?"

"That's Mr. Kelsen," said the plaintiff's attorney. "He owns the company."

"Mr. Kelsen," Judge Sherwin said, "you have a lawyer. Your lawyer will address this court. Don't ever shout in my courtroom again. He'll talk for you."

"Well, he's not talking. I want a speedy trial."

"He's doing just fine. January, if we can hold to it, would be an early setting on my calendar. I don't want any more outbursts in my courtroom. Do you understand?"

"Your Honor, they stole eighty-eight million from me, those lawyers. I trusted them and they screwed me over. I want my money. I don't want to wait until January."

"I'm not getting through to you, am I?"

"No. Not if you want to stall this case until January. I want my money. Maybe I'm not getting through to *you*."

"Mr. Kelsen, do you understand the phrase *contempt of court*?"

"Of course."

"Well, you're in it. Do you need my deputies to take you into custody so you can better appreciate courtroom decorum?"

"No."

"One more word and you're going to spend the next week in the Cook County jail. Now am I getting through to you?"

Kelsen nodded.

"The court will take a short recess." Judge Sherwin pointed to Kelsen's attorney. "Talk to your client."

"We're very sorry, Your Honor," Kelsen's lawyer said. "Mr. Kelsen is obviously quite upset about the theft of eighty-eight million dollars."

"That's understandable."

FORTY

• • •

BECAUSE THERE WERE NO direct flights from Chicago O'Hare to Ben Gurion International, the trip to Tel Aviv would take fifteen hours. Liam tried to sleep, but the cramped coach seats were increasingly uncomfortable. In contrast, Kayla sat tall and composed, reading, shuffling department papers, making notes.

"How do you do that? It seems like we've been in these seats for days."

She shrugged and smiled.

"Kayla Cummings, that's a pretty name. Are you married?"

"I was. My husband died."

"Oh, I'm sorry. Do you have any children?"

She shook her head and went back to her reading.

"Where did you grow up?" Liam said after a minute.

She smiled and put down her papers. "You're just full of personal questions, aren't you?"

"Occupational hazard, I suppose. I'm a PI. And I'd like to know more about the person I'm working with."

Kayla shifted in her seat. "What about you? Are you married, engaged?"

Liam smiled. "No, but I'm working on it."

"The attorney, Ms. Lockhart?"

"Good guess."

"Not really a guess. It's pretty obvious. So, what does 'working on it' mean? That's an odd way of phrasing it. What's standing in your way?"

"Oh? Now look who's asking the personal questions."

Kayla smiled. "Ah, you're avoiding my question. How come the two of you haven't taken the next step?"

Liam shrugged. "I can't give you a reason. Maybe it just hasn't been the right time. Do you have a boyfriend?"

Kayla laughed. "You're right. This is getting too personal. We should keep it on a professional basis. We're headed to Israel to find out what we can about al-Zahani and his group. Is there a deal in play? If not, can we put one in play? Hopefully, you'll be able to sniff out some information, maybe even make contact with Arif. I know the land, the people, the culture. And I know about the evil doctor. I'll help you in any way I can. It's probably best for us to leave the personal doors closed."

Kayla went back to her reading, and Liam wrestled with the stiff, little El Al pillow, trying to give sleep another chance. He folded it, he stuffed it between his shoulder and his neck, he placed it against the window, and he even laid it on the tray table. Kayla watched in amusement.

"Why aren't you tired? How can you just sit there looking comfortable?"

Kayla smiled. "It helps to be half your size."

"Tell me something. Why are you so certain that al-Zahani is a terrorist?"

Kayla paused for a moment. "Earlier this year, there was a wedding in Hebron. At Ma'arat HaMachpelah, the Tomb of the Patriarchs. A car full of terrorists opened fire on the wedding party and then drove away. Four innocent people were killed and others were injured. A week later, they caught one of the shooters. I interviewed him briefly at the hospital. He was dying, almost too weak to talk. But he told me that Fa'iz Talib and Nizar Mohammed had sent them on the attack. I've since discovered that al-Zahani is associated with those men."

"That's it? He's associated?"

"There's more. We'll save it for a later time."

"And now he's got Sophie."

"Right. And he seeks to trade her for millions of dollars. It makes perfect sense. Millions of dollars to fund another terrorist plot. We can't let it happen."

The plane started its descent, and Liam stared out the window at Tel Aviv, its beaches, green parks, and span of high-rise hotels. "Beautiful."

Kayla nodded. "When Mark Twain visited here in 1867, he called the land desolate and unlovely. There's a famous quote from him: 'Even the olive and cactus, those fast friends of a worthless soil, had almost deserted the country.' He was right, you know. And it stayed that way for close to a hundred years, until it became the state of Israel. What you're seeing is Israeli development."

BEN GURION INTERNATIONAL WAS humming when they arrived. "Follow me," Kayla said, bypassing security, opening a side door, and shepherding Liam through immigration control and into a waiting car. As they settled into the backseat, Kayla said to the driver, "Twenty-three David HaMelech."

"Yes, ma'am," the driver replied, "the YMCA."

"What? The YMCA?" Liam said. "Are you serious? They're putting me up at a YMCA? All the time I spent in Northern Ireland, the CIA never put me at a YMCA. Is this how the Agency operates now?"

The driver threw his arms into the air and started singing the familiar song.

"Really?" Liam said. "The YMCA?"

The driver snorted through his bursts of laughter.

"The YMCA is across the street from the King David Hotel, where we'll be staying in Jerusalem," Kayla said between giggles.

"Oh, Jesus." Liam shook his head. "Are you guys having a real good time picking on the poor Irish chump?"

"Well, now that you mention it," she said, smiling. She pointed at the horizon. "The airport is southeast of Tel Aviv. Our route to Jerusalem parallels the 1949 Armistice Agreement line—the Green Line—east, then south, and finally around to the east again, from one side of Israel to the other on a winding highway. If one traveled straight across the country, the distance from Tel Aviv to the West Bank, from the Mediterranean to Samaria, is as short as eleven miles."

"Not very far for a rocket to travel," Liam observed.

"You're not the first to come to that conclusion."

Once into the countryside, Kayla pointed at the hills, lush with foliage, pine trees, vegetable farms, flowers, and greenhouses. "Israel in the spring. Verdant and plentiful."

"The land of milk and honey?"

"That's an interesting biblical phrase. The referenced honey doesn't come from bees. It comes from crushed dates. They grow on date palms in the valleys of the desert."

The car dropped them at the King David just before noon. Liam's room was on a top floor with a balcony overlooking the walls of Jerusalem's Old City. It was a ten-minute walk to the Jaffa Gate and from there to the Via Dolorosa, the crowded market passageway where Liam planned to make the acquaintance of Jamal Abu Hammad. After a ninety-minute nap, Liam met Kayla for a snack in the King's Garden Restaurant.

"What can you tell me about Abu Hammad?" Liam said.

"Well, he's an Arab and he currently lives in East Jerusalem. Before that, he lived in Hebron. His family and the al-Zahanis go back a long time. To Haifa. He knows Arif and he has his ear to the ground in Hebron. He owns a shop in the Muslim quarter of the Old City. He used to be a resource for us, but there was an incident several years ago and he will no longer knowingly be an asset. That's why you're so valuable in this matter."

"Why would he cooperate with me? I'm an American and we're underwriting the occupation of his homeland. Aren't we the great Satan?"

"Although we're mincing words here, Liam, Palestine was never considered the Arab *homeland*. Arabia is their homeland, over a million square miles of the Arabian Peninsula. The holy cities of Mecca and Medina. Saudi Arabia, Yemen, Oman, Qatar, Kuwait, Jordan. Those are Arab homelands. The West Bank was never considered the Arab homeland."

"Does Abu Hammad live in a Zone A city?"

"No, Abu Hammad lives in East Jerusalem. Sixty-six years ago, he lived in Haifa. When the 1948 war began, Abu Hammad's family followed the Arab commands, left Haifa, and fled to Jordan. After the 1948 war, they moved to Hebron. Later, Jamal moved to East Jerusalem when it was still under Jordanian occupation.

"The Old City, where you'll be going today, was captured by Jordan in 1948 and was off-limits to Israelis until 1967. All the holy sites—the Temple Mount, the Western Wall, al-Aqsa Mosque, the Dome of the Rock, and Church of the Holy Sepulchre, shrines for all three Abrahamic religions—were blocked off by barbed wire. The square that now sits in front of the Western Wall was a slum. Today, under Israeli law, everyone is allowed access. The Old City has four quarters: Muslim, Jewish, Christian, and Armenian. Abu Hammad's shop is in the Muslim Quarter, accessible easily through the Jaffa Gate."

Liam stood, put his folded napkin on the table. "Then I'm off to the Old City to pay Mr. Abu Hammad a visit."

FORTY-ONE

• • •

THE SKY WAS DODGER blue as Liam left the hotel lobby. A breeze rolled down from the hills and rustled the trees in the parks, carrying the scent of spring wildflowers. Liam stopped for a brief moment in a park. With his hands in his pockets, he breathed deeply of the sweet air and took in the scene. A group of young boys were kicking a soccer ball. Two mothers were taking an afternoon walk, pushing their babies in strollers. It could have been Central Park. Or even Lincoln Park. But the ancient towers and domes rising above the trees gave a singular majesty to the landscape. He was in Jerusalem.

It was a short walk to the Jaffa Gate and thence to the Muslim Quarter and the Via Dolorosa. The narrow stone passageways of the Old City, with their tiny market stalls, diverse sounds and fragrances, were jammed with tourists. He stopped often to check for an address, and when he did, a smiling shopkeeper, offering "surely the most exquisite purchase in all of Israel," would quickly approach him and tug at his sleeve.

Finally, Liam spotted Abu Hammad's shop, shoehorned between a jewelry store and rug shop. No name or number was over the door or stenciled on the milky window, nothing that would identify the business that was conducted inside, except for a small cardboard sign, sitting on the inside window ledge, that said ANTIQUITIES. The door was unlocked and Liam pushed it open.

"Hello?" he said as he slowly entered the shop. A tall brass urn sat like a center pole amid assorted pottery bowls, masks, maps, scrolls, copper bowls, hand-forged weapons, and books. Stacks of books. Shelves of books. Piles of books. The musty smell of old books permeated the store.

"This is like a medieval garage sale," Liam muttered.

It was hard to find a path through the room. Liam stopped to admire a large, flat, egg-shaped stone. He could barely make out the chiseled carvings that the ages had weathered away.

"It is part of a rolling stone, no doubt used to seal the entrance to a burial cave," said a deep voice in a thick Arabic accent.

Liam caught sight of the man's reflection in a framed mirror as he materialized from the clutter and shuffled forward. Abu Hammad was tall, maybe six feet two inches, but the years had bowed his back. He wore a gray tunic that hung down to his thighs. The loose, three-quarter sleeves rustled when he moved his arms. A knitted taqiyah covered the dome of his unruly, white hair. Decades of Middle Eastern sun had darkened his skin and carved deep folds in his forehead and the borders of his eyes. A rough goatee framed his wide mouth.

By contrast, Liam, in his jeans and Ulster Rugby shirt, was merely one of a million tourists who packed the stone passageways of the Old City.

"Maybe it sealed the cave Jesus was in before he ascended, no?" Abu Hammad laughed heartily. Then he flipped his hand. "Probably a piece of a burial stone from the third century. The inscription is interesting—'Rise with the morning dove, O learned one.' How do I help you, sir?"

"I come for conversation."

Abu Hammad squinted, as though that would help him more clearly see what Liam was all about. "I like the conversation where you want to buy something that I have and I want to sell it to you."

"Perhaps a small item before I go, but I would like to talk to you about Dr. Arif al-Zahani."

"Oh ho, now it comes to me." Abu Hammad smiled broadly. "You are here about the girl, Sophie."

"You know about her?"

He shrugged his big shoulders. "Hebron is a close community."

"But you are in Jerusalem."

"Business is better."

"I have been told that you know the doctor."

Abu Hammad pursed his lips and gave a nod. "Know him. Knew his father. Even knew his grandfather."

"I have been hired to see what can be done to return Sophie to her home."

Abu Hammad turned and walked to the back of his store. "Will you have a cup of tea?"

Liam followed, stopping to examine a copper plate.

"It's junk," Abu Hammad called out over his shoulder. "Eighteenth-century Persian." He dragged a wooden chair into a small sitting area. A worn, overstuffed chair, covered in crackled maroon leather, sat next to an antique sideboard. He set out a pot of hot water, two cups and infusers on a table, poured a cup for himself, then sat down in his stuffed chair.

"I do not think Arif intends to return the girl. He is fond of her."

"So is her father." Liam measured a small amount of tea into the infuser and poured himself a cup. "I have heard that maybe the doctor seeks to make a deal."

"I confess, sir, that you have heard more than I. From whom did you hear such things?"

Liam shrugged.

Abu Hammad shook his head. "Al-Zahani is a rigid man. Unforgiving. Bitter. He makes no compromises. It is in his bloodlines. He is just like his father and his grandfather. It is not like him to make a deal."

Abu Hammad stood, shuffled to the back wall, and beckoned Liam with his index finger. He pointed to a black-and-white photograph in a black frame. Three men in white keffiyehs stood with rifles in their hands. Liam studied the picture.

Abu Hammad tapped the figure on the right. "That is Hamid al-Zahani."

Liam nodded. "Arif's father. And the others?"

Abu Hammad tapped his finger on the figure to the left, turned, and went back to his chair.

"That's you? With the rifle?"

Abu Hammad picked up his tea. Age palsied his hand a bit. "In 1966."

Liam returned to his seat and took a sip.

"I was born in Haifa." Abu Hammad leaned back in his stuffed chair. "My family lived at the foot of the Carmel Mountains in the home of my ancestors. Arif's grandfather, Ibrahim, moved two doors away after Hamid al-Zahani was born.

"Arif was born there. He grew up swimming in the sea, playing on the streets of Haifa. Ibrahim was counsel to the mufti and spent most of his time in Jerusalem. I remember him bragging to us that von Ribbentrop had invited the mufti to Berlin to sit with the Führer and that he, Ibrahim, was going along as well. During the Second World War, he and the mufti stayed in Germany, but Ibrahim would come back every now and then. He taught his son and his grandson to hate—the British, the Americans, the Jews."

"But not you?"

Abu Hammad shook his head. "Ibrahim did not teach me. Besides, I was busy with other pursuits." He pointed at a small, oval picture frame. The silver was tarnished a bit, but one could see it had been cared for over the years. In the frame was a black-and-white photo of a young woman.

"Very lovely. She looks kind."

"She was that."

"Did your family stay in Haifa?" Liam asked, though he knew the answer.

The old man raised his eyebrows. "We left Haifa in 1948, as ordered by the Arab Command. We were told that the Syrian Army would soon overrun the city and expel all the Jews. Then we could come back. It was pure fantasy. But my family was nonviolent and we listened to others in the community. We left when they did."

"But there is a picture of you with a rifle."

"Well, yes, when I was young. The PLO was passing out Soviet rifles. So I took one." Abu Hammad shrugged. "I was not much of a soldier. I gave it back." He chuckled. "I confess that I am a man of peace. Perhaps just a coward, as Arif has called me."

"He called you a coward?"

"Many times. In May 1967, just before the war, his father was recruiting for the Jordanian Army. Hamid was commanding a division based in Hebron. They came to my house, Arif and Ibrahim, with enlistment papers. There would be great glory, they said. We would drive the Jews to the sea and rid Palestine of Jews forever. I declined. I stayed home with my Saja. I did not fight in '67. Arif tried to shame me into joining, but I refused."

"And Arif, did he join his father?"

Abu Hammad chuckled and shook his head. "He did not. He went to medical school. But Hamid, like his father, was a born fighter. It was as if he started battling the moment he came out of the womb. He was always in the middle of some skirmish. With guns and grenades. He met his maker in the Kidron Valley during the siege of Jerusalem in 1967. Arif blames many for his father's death: the weak Jordanians, the aggressive Israelis, and me."

"You?"

"People like me. I refused to fight. I did not stand on the hill and fire weapons alongside Hamid. To Arif, I will always be a coward."

"And his father's death, that would account for Arif's vendetta?"

The old man scratched the side of his cheek. "It doesn't take much to impassion a displaced Arab, one who thinks his land has been taken from him. Double so for Arif, who lost his father and his grandfather to Israeli gunfire. He has a vendetta, to use your word, against many. The British. The State of Israel, the UN, the US. Peaceful Arabs. And me."

"Because you didn't fight."

"Partly. Also because I'm a shopkeeper. I get my money in Israel. I am like a, uh, a collaborator. A traitor to the cause. Maybe I should live in a refugee camp in Jordan? Pretend that Israel does not exist? Take the meager welfare handouts from the UN? Wait for the great uprising? According to Arif, that would be honorable. Doing business with the Israelis is dishonorable. We have been on opposite sides of the philosophical fence for many, many years."

"But Arif does not live in a camp."

Abu Hammad chuckled. "The gentleman doctor? He lives in his father's fortified castle." He stood and stretched. "I am tired. I have talked too long."

Liam stood as well. "I thank you very much for sharing that information with me. I would like to know a little more about Sophie Sommers. Whether there are arrangements."

"I have heard no talk of plans to return the girl, or as you say, to make a deal. There are some in Hebron who would know. For you and for her father, I will inquire. Come back. Next time, buy something."

Upon returning to the King David, Liam found a note waiting for him: *We are going to Hebron tomorrow. Be ready at noon. Kayla.*

Liam reached for his cell phone and dialed Catherine.

"Hi, Cat. It's me."

"Hi, me. How's it going?"

"Okay, I guess. I met with a shopkeeper today who has contacts in Hebron, and I'm hoping he'll flush out a little information for us. We're going there tomorrow. How was court today?"

"Surprising. Kelsen showed up. It was just a routine status call, just the attorneys positioning themselves for an upcoming round of depositions. It was not the kind of thing that clients ever attend. But there was Victor Kelsen, brash as ever, barking at the courtroom, trying to get his case accelerated for trial. Judge Sherwin almost threw him in jail."

"Where does the lawsuit stand? Is there a trial date?"

"Preliminarily. January seventeenth. Of course, that'll be kicked back, it's far too early in the game. There are several cross-complaints and motions pending. At this stage, there's no evidence proving who was at fault or how the wire instructions were altered. Key witnesses are dead or missing. And no one knows where the money is. It's actually quite fascinating."

"Isn't there a presumption that Jenkins and Fairchild was responsible?"

"A presumption, but rebuttable. J and F never had possession of the money. It was under the control of the title company."

"But didn't J and F direct the title company to send the money to a false account?"

"The wire instructions bore three signatures: Sommers, Harrington, and Ellis. At this point, we don't even know if the signatures are valid."

"Oh, come on, Cat. Sommers had the motive and the means. He took off right after the money was wired."

"So did Harrington. So did Ellis. Eighty million dollars is a lot

206 : Ronald H. Balson

of motive. Anyway, those are the competing arguments. This case is just beginning."

"Cat, I miss you and I love you."

"I know. Me too."

FORTY-TWO

• • •

"CHILD, YOU'RE WEEPING." AL-ZAHANI stood next to Sophie's bed. She lay on her side, facing away from him, holding tightly to her bear. "Tell me what troubles you so." Sophie shook her head.

"Were the children mean to you? I will send Bashir to punch them all right in the nose."

Sophie smiled, shook her head again, and sniffled. "Jamila can't play with me anymore. She was my only friend."

"Why not? I thought you were good friends."

"We are, but her father won't let us play anymore. She told me at school."

"Did she say why?"

Sophie sadly shook her head.

Al-Zahani ran his hand smoothly over her hair. "I will speak to him. I'm sure it's just a misunderstanding. It will get straightened out. Don't be sad."

Despite his reassurance, she sobbed. "I miss my mommy and my daddy. I miss my friends. I want to go home. I don't belong here."

"Oh, Sophie, so many times I tell you, there is no one at your American home. It is empty. I proved it to you. You made the telephone calls. This is now your home. You do belong here. Of all people, I know it is sad to lose your home. Do you know when I was just a boy, about the same age as you, I lost my home?"

Sophie looked up. "You did?"

"My family's home in Haifa was taken from us by the Israelis.

We were forced to run off to Jordan. But now I have a new home and you have a new home. We are here for you now because your parents have left you. Your Jadda and I will make sure you are well loved always and grow up to be a beautiful, strong woman."

Sophie rolled over to face al-Zahani. Her eyes were red. "My mommy didn't leave me. She went to heaven."

"It is hard for me to speak of her with you. It makes me sad, just like you. Maybe someday."

"Why did she have to die?"

Al-Zahani hesitated. "It is because she had turned from her faith."

"Was Allah angry with her?"

"I do not know what is in the mind of Allah. But perhaps." He reached down and smoothed the covers. "It is time for sleep."

"Could you read me a story?"

"I'm sorry, but I don't have any children's books and I don't know many children's stories. I can tell you stories about the Prophet Mohammed. He too lost his father and his mother." Al-Zahani pulled back her covers and tucked her in. "What is your favorite book?"

"*If You Give a Mouse a Cookie.* That's my favorite."

"I will find it and buy it for you."

"It's very good and funny."

"I will send Bashir first thing in the morning. And we will find out what happens when you give a mouse a cookie," he said, which elicited a few giggles. "Now tonight, you go to sleep."

Al-Zahani kissed her on the forehead, turned out the lights, and left the room. In the sitting room, Lubannah was smiling. "Are you building your relationship, Arif?"

Al-Zahani looked serious. "What is the situation with Jamila? Sophie is upset. This was her only friend. We cannot allow a setback."

Lubannah lowered her head. "Hassan will no longer let Jamila associate with Sophie. He says that Sophie talks constantly of her life in America and the things that she does. She tells Jamila how wonderful it is. She praises America. Hassan says he cannot allow such ideas to be put into Jamila's head. He has ordered Basima to keep their daughter away from Sophie. Basima is sorry but there is nothing she can do."

Al-Zahani curled his lip. "Well, there is something I can do. I will talk with Hassan. He does not know Sophie. If he took the time to know her, he would see that she is worthy of his respect. She's not like other Americans. I will change his mind. You will see Jamila back here very soon; that I promise you. Do not worry."

Lubannah wrapped her arms around al-Zahani. "I like it when you're strong for our Sophie."

"She is so much like Alina." He kissed Lubannah on the forehead. "She has a will, that one. A curiosity. I see much in her future. In a few weeks, though, I may need you to take her to Amman until my business is finished."

"Why must we leave?"

"Because it is my wish. For your safety. And hers."

"I thought the years of such business were over."

"No more questions, please. I have to leave."

"Where are you going tonight, Arif? Again. Every night. Why do you go out so often?"

"I have many responsibilities. Why do you interrogate me?"

"When will you be home?"

"Do not wait up."

FORTY-THREE

• • •

O N H E R W A Y T O Hebron, barely thirty minutes south of the Old City, Kayla took a cutoff through the Rachel's Crossing Checkpoint and drove the Agency car into the crowded city of Bethlehem, where she made her way to the central area and the Church of the Nativity.

"The square is now a pedestrian mall, so we'll have to park a few blocks away." She maneuvered her way past several parked tour buses.

"Why are we stopping here?" Liam asked.

"I need to meet with someone. Just for a minute. And I thought you might like to see Bethlehem. It's a Palestinian town, although very touristy. It's friendly. Very different from Hebron. Westerners are commonplace here."

Kayla pulled into a parking space, locked the car, and fed the meter. "Called Beit Lechem, 'house of bread,' Bethlehem has always been a small, poor town," she said as they walked. "When Jesus was born, there were maybe four hundred residents. Compared to the larger West Bank cities, Bethlehem is still very small—twenty-two thousand today. The economy is almost entirely tourist driven. It was one of the areas handed over to the PA in 1995 after the Oslo Peace Accords."

"Zone A?"

Kayla nodded. "Correct. Zone A. Self-governed by the PA."

They walked to a small diner on a side street. Standing on the sidewalk, Kayla pointed to a white tower. "That's the Mosque of Omar, which sits at one end of Manger Square. Before modern times, Muslims and Christians would share the responsibility of bringing oil to light the lamps of the square." She peered in the window of the restaurant. "If you wouldn't mind, right now there's someone I need to see. Could you wait just a bit? Better yet, why don't you go on in and order some falafel. It's great here."

"I'll just hang out here."

Kayla entered the restaurant and a few minutes later emerged with a small man with a neatly trimmed black beard. He nodded to Liam.

"Liam, this is Kadin, a friend of mine. I need a few minutes with Kadin, if that's okay."

Kayla and Kadin walked to the corner, crossed the street, and disappeared into a small, gray building. Liam leaned on a parking meter and took in the scene. Bethlehem might be small, but the square was crowded. People watching was enjoyable. Many were obviously tourists in Western attire. Others were covered in traditional Arab dress.

A boy in shorts and woven sandals tugged at Liam's sleeve and offered to sell him a plastic manger scene. "Baby Jesus. Only twenty dollars," the boy said with a wide smile.

"Twenty dollars?"

"Okay. Five dollars."

Liam dug into his pocket and pulled out a ten.

"I take that too," the boy said, and Liam made the purchase.

Fifteen minutes later, Kayla returned alone. "Sorry for the delay." She pointed at the souvenir. "I see you've already improved Bethlehem's balance sheet."

"Cute kid. I couldn't resist."

The restaurant was small—fifteen tables tightly organized. Liam and Kayla sat at a table for two beside a brick wall. A busy waiter in a white apron put down paper place mats with graphics of the square, a basket of hot pitas, and a bowl of hummus. He set out cardboard menus and olive oil. Although Liam could not understand any of the multiple conversations, the milieu was a tasty slice of West Bank.

"Am I supposed to know why you met with Kadin?"

Kayla shook her head. "Just a friend I needed to talk to."

Liam looked around the restaurant and smiled.

"What do you find humorous?"

"A thought occurred to me," Liam said. "That this is Portillo's of the West Bank, minus the Italian beef."

"I'd hoped you would make that observation. Look around. What do you see?"

He shrugged. "Just ordinary folks having lunch at a local diner. What am I supposed to see?"

"Just what you said—ordinary folks. People who have jobs and businesses and go home to their kids at night. These people aren't terrorists, they're not dangerous. They just want to live their lives in peace. The man I met with, Kadin, is a sweet man with a beautiful family. He's a man that works for peace and longs for peace in this troubled land. People like Kadin deserve peace just the same as the ordinary folks on the other side of the separation wall. He deserves self-determination. Autonomy. Peaceful relations. He deserves a Palestinian state. But al-Zahani, the Sons of Canaan, Hamas, Islamic Jihad, and all the other extremists will do anything they can to prevent that from occurring."

"Why do you say that? Don't they also espouse the Palestinian cause?"

"No. Peaceful solution leading to two states is the Palestinian cause. Israel is already a state; Palestine wants to be one. And it won't get there if terrorists run their government. Guaranteed, secured borders, negotiated between responsible parties, is the only way the conflict can be resolved. It will never be resolved by terror."

"And you think the Sons of Canaan are planning an attack to thwart peace talks?"

"I'm not sure the present talks are significant to them, but it's clear the Islamist extremists don't want any talks to result in a two-state solution if one of the states is Israel. They are anti-solution. They foster hate. And to that end, they've been enormously successful. They've stoked the fires of racism on both sides of the fence. From an early age, the young Palestinians are carefully taught to believe Israeli Jews are their natural enemies.

"On the Israeli side, bombs, rockets, tunnels, kidnapping, and fiery rhetoric have demonized the Palestinians. Israelis are against a two-state solution because they fear extremists will infiltrate and control a Palestinian state. During the fifty-day war with Gaza, forty-five hundred rockets were launched and aimed at Israeli cities. Air raid sirens sounded many times each day. People lived in shelters. Children were traumatized. Israelis who were formerly liberal and sympathetic to the Palestinians became hardened right-wingers.

"Ben Gurion International Airport is less than ten miles from the West Bank. In the last skirmish, the FAA and the EU halted air traffic when a Hamas rocket landed in a field two miles away. What if Hamas, Hezbollah, or some other Islamist extremist group took over a fragile West Bank government? They've already threatened Ben Gurion many times over. What do you think the FAA would do if there were a hostile Palestinian state within easy striking distance of the airport?

"The sad fact is this—both sides are victims to the terrorists. As President Peres said, 'The Arabs are not Israel's enemy. The terrorists are the enemies of both of us.' And the consequence is further polarization of the two peoples, which, of course, serves the terrorists's goals."

"I understand," Liam said, constructing a large falafel sandwich on fresh-baked pita, with lettuce, tomatoes, onions, and tahini.

"Golda Meir once said, 'I fear the war with the Arabs will go on for years because of the indifference with which their leaders send their people off to die.' She also said, 'Peace will come when the Arabs love their children more than they hate us.'" Kayla gestured at the people eating their lunch. "These everyday folks, they don't want to die, they want quality of life. We have to counter the teaching of intolerance. It'll mean peace for both sides."

"Kayla, this falafel is calling my name. What do you say we stop talking and eat for a while?"

"Can I tell you something funny?"

"Now that would be a welcome change."

"Golda also said, 'Let me tell you the one thing I have against Moses. He took us forty years into the desert in order to bring us to the one place in the Middle East that has no oil!'"

Liam, with his mouth full of food, suppressed a chuckle, took his napkin, and wiped his face. "By the way, I think this is the best falafel I ever had."

"There's a restaurant in Jerusalem that serves falafel just as fresh and just as tasty. The falafel tastes the same on both sides of the wall. There's really no difference."

"Lord Almighty, Kayla, I get it. You're beating on a dead horse." She smiled proudly.

RESUMING THEIR DRIVE TO Hebron, just south of Bethlehem, Liam pointed to a hillside town. "What's up there?"

"That depends who you ask. Palestinians would say it's an illegal settlement. It's a town west of the Green line where Israeli citizens live. That one is Neve Daniel, formerly a farm belonging to the Cohen family going back almost a hundred years. There are one hundred and twenty or so Israeli towns that are located in the West Bank, with almost half a million Israeli citizens. Many live in large cities that have grown up over the past forty-five years, with schools, parks, hospitals, factories, and thriving businesses, many of which employ thousands of Palestinian workers."

"How did these people end up there? Why were Israeli cities built in the West Bank?"

"Towns expanded naturally. Families grow. Businesses form. Housing in Israel is expensive, especially in Jerusalem and Tel Aviv, so families move to areas where they can afford to buy—into new construction, subdivisions built on previously unoccupied and unused land. So now, in the disputed territories, there are five hundred thousand or more Israelis. The PA calls them 'settlers' or 'occupiers.' They want them all to leave. What would you do with those towns and cities?"

"Why would you have to do anything? Why can't they remain in a newly created State of Palestine? Arabs live in Israel, don't they?"

"They do, but numerous polls have shown that Israelis, even Arab Israelis, don't want to live in the proposed State of Palestine. And the Palestinian leadership doesn't want them there. Mahmoud Abbas said, 'In a final resolution, we would not see the presence of a single Israeli civilian or soldier on our land.' Palestinians don't want to live in Israel and vice versa.

"This afternoon we'll arrive in Kiryat Arba. Dead center of the

West Bank. A town of seventy-five hundred Israelis. Beautiful homes, shops, businesses. Intelligent use of the land. Almost fifty years of natural growth. Jews have been in Kiryat Arba for over thirty-seven hundred years. It's a settlement as old as the Bible. Are you going to tell those people to pack up and leave—they don't have a right to live there anymore?"

"So, what's the Kayla solution?"

"You're giving me too much credit. I'm not a Nobel Prize–winning statesman, and that's what it will take. But as long as radical terrorists and jihadists are able to influence the Palestinian populace, a peaceful, shared border is out of the question. We need for the Palestinians to renounce violence as a political tool. Men like Kadin are working for that, at great risk to himself and his family. I don't doubt for a minute that the world would get behind Palestine if it denounced extremism."

"Devon Avenue, that's what you need," Liam said matter-of-factly.

"Devon Avenue?"

"Starting at McCormick Boulevard, driving east on Devon, you'll pass an Orthodox Jewish community, then an Arab community, then a Croatian cultural center. Further east it's Pakistani. Further east it's Indian. Then Korean. All within three miles. A mélange of food stores, restaurants, clothing shops, bakeries. Just about the most interesting street in Chicago. And all the folks live right in the neighborhood and most attend neighborhood public schools. That's what you need out here. Devon Avenue."

Kayla nodded and smiled. "Maybe so. Do you have terrorists on Devon Avenue?"

"Point taken."

Kiryat Arba, the town on the hill, was quiet when they arrived, though Liam felt an eerie sense of tension in the air. Kayla parked the car in front of a three-story building, similar to many of the other structures lining the streets of Kiryat Arba: cream-colored Jerusalem stone, boxlike window openings cut into the façade, many covered with iron gratings. The city looked bright, new, and clean, but nervous. No children were playing unguarded on the streets.

The Agency apartment was efficiently furnished with functional pieces. Three bedrooms surrounded a sitting area with leather couches and black, cube end tables. Wooden stools were tucked under the kitchenette bar.

"There are two wireless connections here," Kayla said, handing Liam a note card. "You may use this one; the password is on the card. It's secure. I'll take the back bedroom."

FORTY-FOUR

• • •

I CONTACTED THE WILSON broad this afternoon."

The cell phone connection was patchy, but the caller's tough street dialect was clear enough.

"You saw her? Did you go into her house?"

"No, sir. I talked to her on the phone. She wouldn't open the door for me."

"And? Did she tell you where her brother was?"

"Nah."

"What did you say to her?"

"Just like you told me. I said I had a package addressed to John Sommers. It was an oil painting made from a photograph of Mr. and Mrs. Sommers and their kid. I told her that Mrs. Sommers had ordered it over a year ago from our Chicago office, but she never picked it up and we were trying to find Mr. Sommers to deliver it. We were told that she was the sister. Could she give me his address so I could deliver it? It's all prepaid. Very beautiful."

"Exactly. What did Wilson say?"

"She said she hadn't talked to her brother in years. As far as she knew, he lived in Chicago. I told her we went there but it didn't look like anybody was still living there, and then I talked to the neighbor who gave us her address. So could she give me a forwarding address for her brother so I could send it there? Then she told me she had no idea, don't bother her no more."

Silence. Then: "She's not telling the truth."

"We can make her talk. She's got kids. She'll give up Sommers if I start to talk about her kids. Want me to make the call?"

Silence. Then: "Not yet, Yuri. Maybe later. Right now I have another idea."

IN A SHOTGUN BUNGALOW on Chicago's northwest side, a young man sat in front of a wall of electronic equipment. His tussled hair was omnidirectional, over his ears and badly in need of a scissors. A plaid shirt was buttoned to the neck, and his wide leather belt gathered the waist of his rumpled khakis.

Behind him, in designer casual-wear, a man stood looking over the young man's shoulder at the computer screen. "Well, Marvin, is it something you can do or not?"

The young man nodded. "Should be," he answered, though everything he said was qualified with a cautionary negative. "Unless he uses a sophisticated scrambler."

"He's not sophisticated; he's just a paper pusher. I need to know where this man is when he goes online, when he leaves a message. Can you pinpoint his location?"

Marvin tilted back in his chair and shrugged boastfully. "It depends on how you define *pinpoint*. When he e-mails you, I can get his IP address. If he uses an Internet café, some public source, I can probably give you the location." Marvin smiled smugly. "I have my ways of getting it from the ISP. Of course, if the man has installed a few security features that I sell . . . most people don't know about them." He shrugged. "He'd have to hire somebody like me."

"Well, let's assume he hasn't hired someone like you, Marvin. How can you get this done? How can you tell us where he is when he posts?"

"It would be best if I were online at the time. When do think that will be?"

"I can prompt him. Stay by your computer. He'll post later today, I guarantee it."

SOMMERS STARED OUT OF the window of his second-story motel room. The kids across the street were kicking a soccer ball. Spaces between the parked cars served as goals. For a moment, just a snippet in time, Jack saw Sophie running toward the ball. All of her teammates, five-year-old girls in their oversize team T-shirts, were running, en masse, converging on the ball, kicking to beat the band. Jack stood on the sidelines with Alina and the other parents, cheering and laughing heartily.

The amped bass from the corner bar, booming thunder through the neighborhood, brought Jack back to the present. He checked his watch. In thirty minutes he was meeting Marcy at the Polynesian Room.

I'm standing here reminiscing about the three of us, Alina, and I'm about to go to dinner with Marcy Grant. And you know what? I can't get the vision of her open robe out of my head. Would you scold me for that? Is it appropriate for me to have these thoughts? Answer me, Alina. Would you approve? Is the timing all wrong? For me? For her? Don't answer, I know it is.

He grabbed his laptop and walked around the corner to the Internet café. One more disappointing check of his e-mail account before dinner. But to his absolute shock, a new message was posted: *Happy to say that the deal is almost done. I need your help in signing parental authorizations to bring Sophie back into the country. US immigration regulations. That's all that's left. Can you meet with me? If not, can I e-mail the forms to you?*

Sommers could barely contain his enthusiasm. His heart was beating like a hummingbird. He quickly typed, *Wonderful news! Of course you can e-mail forms. Just attach them and I'll scan and send them back right away. When are you going to get her? I need to arrange to have someone meet you and Sophie. Please give me all the details. I can't thank you enough.*

Sommers couldn't wait to tell Marcy. Standing on the sidewalk outside the Polynesian Room, he felt like jumping up and down. He checked out every taxi that approached. Finally, she arrived.

"You didn't have to wait on the curb," she said with a smile. "I would have come inside."

Sommers hugged her excitedly and swung her around. "It's happening, Marcy. Sophie's coming home. We didn't need to talk to Taggart after all. My original plan is going to work."

"That's fabulous! I can't believe it. When is she coming?"

"I just got the message on the e-mail account. They didn't give me a date. They said they needed my parental authorization."

Marcy's smile lost some of its exuberance. "They didn't ask you to show up personally, did they?"

"They asked me if I could meet them, but—"

"Oh, no, Jack. That's what Taggart warned me about. You're the third and final witness."

"It's not like that. They don't know where I am. For all they know, I could still be in Chicago. They gave me the option of signing the parental authorization and scanning it back to them. I don't have to meet with them personally."

"How are they going to deliver Sophie?"

"We haven't discussed the details, but I can have Deborah pick her up anywhere."

"I don't mean to burst your bubble, but I'm worried about this e-mail."

Jack put his arm around her. "You're a worrywart. It'll be fine. Sophie will be out here in no time. Let's go inside and celebrate."

Jack called the waiter over and ordered a pricey bottle of wine. He couldn't stop smiling. His batteries were fully charged. His enthusiasm was contagious, and Marcy felt elated as well.

"I can't wait to see Sophie," Marcy said. "She's such a special kid. I hope this ordeal hasn't been too rough on her. You know, it'll probably take a while for her to get readjusted."

"I think she'll do all right. She's strong. And she's solid emotionally. Alina was right—she's unusual in that way." Jack leaned forward and spoke reflectively. "You want to know something about her that I never realized until after Alina was gone? Sophie has this uncanny sense of empathy, not just uncanny for a little girl, but for anyone. She can sense your emotion—what you're experiencing. She can share in your joy or know when you're unsure of yourself and give you the benefit of the doubt. And you can draw strength from her. When I was at the end of the road, she was strong for me. We were strong for each other. Just like we had promised Alina. How many people can do that? And she's only six years old." He swallowed hard. "Alina always said she was remarkable, that she would change the world. I teased her about it, but Alina was right."

Marcy concurred with a nod.

Jack tilted his head. "You think I'm just a father blowing smoke?"

"Nope. Not at all. I know her. She's just like her mother."

He smiled, but after a moment sat back and shook his head. "This whole scenario, the kidnap, the rescue, it never had to happen. I failed her, Marcy. She trusted me and I let her down. I badly misjudged the al-Zahanis, and now Sophie's the one who's suffering, locked up on the other side of the world. What would become of her if she were forced to live under house arrest in Hebron? She deserved better than me. Alina told me to take care of her and I didn't do it."

"Stop, Jack. Why are you beating yourself up? We're here to celebrate. Remember? She's coming home. This is a night for gaiety."

"You're right." He lifted his glass. "Here's to Sophie's return."

They feasted on a three-pound lobster and banana flambé. When the plates had been cleared, Jack said, "Is there some place we can go? I want to celebrate. I want to dance."

"You dance?"

"Like Astaire."

"You dance like Fred Astaire?"

"No, I was thinking about Myron Astaire, his half cousin."

Marcy picked up her purse. "I think they have a club across the street at the Hyatt."

At the end of the long hotel lobby, behind the fountain, to the dismay of Jack and Marcy, a sign on the glass door read CLOSED FOR REMODELING.

"Doesn't that figure?" Marcy said. "I finally have someone who will actually take me dancing and the club is closed."

"Shhh. Listen." The driving sound of a thumping bass came from the other end of the lobby. They followed the music to a large ballroom, where the kiosk announced RECEPTION FOR THE FISHMAN/DONOVAN WEDDING. Jack looked at the signboard and shrugged. "Okay, which one do we know, the bride or the groom?"

"Definitely the bride," Marcy said, and they barged into the party.

The wooden dance floor in the middle of the room was packed—shoulder to shoulder. People laughing, spilling drinks, dancing exuberantly. From time to time, Jack and Marcy would sit one out, catch their breath, have a drink compliments of Fishman or Donovan, and then jump right back onto the floor. Toward the end of the evening, close to midnight, the band played its final number.

Marcy rested her head softly on Jack's chest; he clasped his arms around her waist and they swayed more than they danced.

The music ended, but not the moment, and they continued to sway to the silence. Their eyes met and Marcy whispered, "You're wondering if all this is okay, aren't you? The way you feel?"

Jack gave a slight nod. "Is it okay for either of us? Especially at this time?"

"Well, it's okay for me. It's more than okay. You have to decide for yourself if you can handle it, if you can move on with your life."

When the dance floor cleared, they may not have been the only ones locked in an embrace, but they were the only crashers. As they stood there, Jack was tapped on the shoulder.

"You guys are a cute couple," the woman said. "I'm Sue Fishman." She held out her hand. "Pat's sister."

"We're Jack and Marcy," Jack replied, taking her hand. "Mazel tov."

"On behalf of the Protestant Fishmans and the Catholic Donovans, I thank you. Do you guys know *anybody* at this wedding?"

"Just Sue Fishman, Pat's sister."

The young woman giggled. "There's an afterparty around the corner at Kiki's. Please come. There's a band."

Marcy looked at Jack. They both nodded. "Thanks so much. We'll be there."

They walked into the lobby and Marcy stopped. "Jack, we have to get a card."

"Where are we going to get a card at midnight?"

"Then at least an envelope. We have to give them a wedding gift. They allowed us to celebrate with them. We can probably get an envelope at the front desk."

Jack nodded. "There's something else I can do at the front desk."

Arm in arm, they walked across the lobby. "The Rubicon," Jack mumbled.

"What?"

"The Rubicon. I was thinking out loud."

"And what's that supposed to mean?"

"Nothing. It's a river in northern Italy."

"On such a wonderful, romantic evening, you're thinking of rivers in Italy? Really?"

"No, that's not it." Jack had a comfortable expression on his face. "Julius Caesar, in command of his army, crossed the Rubicon River into the state of Italy on his march toward Rome. It was a capital offense, an act of war. But from then on everything would change and nothing would be the same. The Rubicon's always been a symbol for the point of no return. Take a step this way and things change. Before tonight, I wouldn't let myself think about anything but Sophie. My personal life, my own future, was out of the question. You asked me if I could move on with my life. Now my butterfly is coming home, and, well . . ."

Marcy smiled, took his elbow, and walked toward the lobby desk.

"Here's the couple I was telling you about," Sue Fishman said when Jack and Marcy walked into Kiki's. Jack was handed two glasses of champagne. A four-piece band was covering popular songs, and Marcy soon had Jack back on the dance floor. After a couple of numbers, she whispered, "Do you really want to stay here?"

Jack smiled and shook his head. He reached into his pocket and took out his room key.

"Perfect. Let's go."

FORTY-FIVE

• • •

I T WAS MORNING AND Liam sat on the apartment couch fiddling with the TV remote. "What are you searching for?" Kayla asked from behind as she entered the room.

"Something I can understand," he said without looking up.

"*The Bachelorette?*"

"Do I look like someone who watches . . ." As he turned, he caught a look at Kayla. "Oh." Unlike her previous stylish outfits, she now wore a flowing, paneled skirt, long enough to cover the tops of her shoes, a knit top with sleeves to her wrists, and a plum-colored hijab, which flattered the oval of her face.

Liam stared for a moment. "Where are we going that you need to pretend to be a Muslim woman?"

She smiled. "Who says I'm not?"

Liam shook his head. "Every day I'm with you, I know you less."

"We're going into H1, the Palestinian sector. I'd like to go to the Breadstone Bakery, and I don't want to attract attention to myself."

Liam smiled and shook his head. "I got news for you. You will turn heads wherever you go, in whatever you wear."

"Why, thank you, Liam. That was sweet."

"Just stating the obvious. You're a beautiful woman." He looked down at his cotton shirt, worn over a black T-shirt, shirttails outside his jeans. "How am I supposed to dress?"

"Just the way you are. Jeans are fine."

Liam squinted in the bright sun as they left the building and started their walk toward Hebron. The desert wind blew an occasional puffy cloud across the sky. The Judean hills, with their scruff and untamed grasses, spread to the horizon on a palette of ecru, goldenrod, and brown. Rocky limestone outcroppings and ancient olive trees spotted the hills, all of which seemed to say, *We are inhospitable.* Yet Liam and Kayla strolled toward Hebron, one of the oldest and most densely populated cities in the world.

As they reached the outer edge of Kiryat Arba, Kayla pointed to the hills in front of them, blanketed with thousands of square, white stone edifices, tightly packed together. "Hebron. Pronounced *Ch*evron in Hebrew and called Al-Khalil in Arabic. It's a city of nearly two hundred thousand people, largest in the West Bank.

"King David founded the Kingdom of Israel and ruled here for seven of his forty-one years. For thirty-seven hundred years, Hebron's been important to Jews. In 1967, at the end of the bloody battle for the Temple Mount, Menachem Begin stood at the Western Wall and prayed. He said, 'And we shall yet come to Hebron—Kiryat Arba—and there we shall prostrate ourselves at the graves of the patriarchs of our people.' Hebron's that important to Jews, Liam. Ben Gurion considered Israel's right to Hebron to be indefeasible."

A stone path through a small park took them down a hill and onto a narrow, paved street. The blacktop, broken and cracked in many places, wound its way along the Hebron H1/H2 border. A soldier in an olive IDF uniform, his Tavor TAR-21 strapped across his back, leaned against the door of a shuttered building and nodded as they crossed the street from Kiryat Arba. "We are now in H2 Hebron," Kayla said. "In 1997, Yasser Arafat and Benjamin Netanyahu agreed to split the city into two sectors. They called it the Hebron Protocol. Israelis may not enter Palestinian Hebron without permission. To all intents and purposes, the IDF has withdrawn its soldiers from H1."

Another IDF soldier passed them on the street, nodded, and said hello to Kayla in Hebrew. Liam looked at her. "Time to fess up. You know these people. You were stationed here, weren't you? You're not just some historical resource analyst in the State Department."

"Don't jump to conclusions. I do work for the State Department."

"But not *just* for the State Department?"

She shrugged.

"And before?"

"I thought we were going to leave those doors closed."

"If you have some clandestine agenda planned here in Hebron, we need to open those doors. I have a right to know. Exactly what is your assignment? It's certainly not to be my chauffeur and school-marm."

"Schoolmarm? I think it was. You asked to be educated. To know your adversaries, as I recall. I've done a pretty damn good job in that regard. As to the second part, I got you here safe and sound, with no complaints about my driving."

"Don't patronize me, Kayla. I've served my time in this business and I have a right to know who I'm partnering with."

Kayla nodded. "Yes, you do. On the books, I'm a diplomatic attaché, assigned as a resource to assist you in your investigation."

"And off the books?"

"As Harry told you, I'm looking at al-Zahani. It's not an official operation yet, so maybe I'm a tiny bit rogue in what we're doing. But there's no question his group is planning something and we need to figure it out. Our first stop today will be at Avraham Avinu. There's someone I'd like you to meet."

As they walked past a newly constructed apartment building, Kayla asked Liam, "Why did you leave the service?"

He shrugged. "My assignment in Ireland was over. I had no interest in an office or administrative job, and frankly, I was tired of working for the government. Unless we accept a senior staff post on some foreign desk, people like you and me, we have no future in this business. Working for myself seemed like a good idea."

"And has it been?"

"Pretty much. Why do you want to start at the bakery?"

"You'll know in a minute."

They opened the door to a domed building housing a tiny synagogue and entered the sanctuary through one of three stone archways. Walnut railings framed a bimah in the center of the room. An open book sat on a pulpit. A carved wooden ark, the *aron kodesh,* stood along the wall facing the Temple Mount in Jerusalem. A decorative *ner tamid,* the eternal light, hung above the ark. A large chandelier lit the center of the dome.

"Enchanting," Liam said, looking around the sanctuary. "And cozy. Is this where we're meeting your contact?"

She nodded. "This is the Avraham Avinu Synagogue. The original was built in 1540. In the years after the 1948 war, during the time that Jordan occupied the city, the Jewish section was torn apart and demolished. They converted this area into a trash dump and a public toilet. Right where we're standing, they placed a goat and donkey pen. As soon as Israel liberated the area in 1967, the synagogue restoration began."

A man who had been sitting quietly on a chair in the dark of a corner rose to greet them. "Quite right. Kayla knows her history."

"Aaron, this is Liam Taggart, the investigator. Liam, meet Aaron Weinberg, a treasure in this community."

"We are grateful for your service," Aaron said as he clasped Liam's hand. To Kayla, he said, "We have not seen Fakhir at the bakery yet today, so it may be a good day to try for the placement."

She nodded. "And the evil doctor?"

"Nothing unusual. No change in his routine."

"Have we learned anything further about the group?"

He shook his head. "That is why we hope you can successfully place the device." He handed a small plastic square to Kayla.

"I think we'll head to the market now," Kayla said.

"I'll walk partway with you," Aaron said. Then he asked Liam, "Have you been to Israel before?"

"No. This is my first time."

Walking from the synagogue, Liam noticed a colorful mosaic on the side of the stone wall. He stopped to examine it, furrowed his forehead, and looked at Aaron. "That's a disturbing piece of artwork."

Aaron nodded. "Tell me why you think so."

"Well, it's an orange baby buggy, but it has giant red flames of fire coming out of where the baby would sleep. And there's a line of Hebrew words that I don't understand."

"It's a memorial, Liam. To a ten-month-old girl, Shalhevet Pass, who was murdered right here where you stand. Just a baby." He pointed at the horizon. "Do you see the security tower on the crown of that Hebron hill? It used to be the site of a tall building in the Palestinian neighborhood of Abu Sneineh. From there, a sniper shot the little baby through the head. Her father, who was pushing the buggy, was hit by two bullets himself. The shooter's building was subsequently torn down by the IDF."

Aaron brushed away a leaf from the memorial. "As if that weren't disturbing enough, when they caught the sniper, he confessed that he was aiming at the baby."

"Thank God they caught him."

"Well, the Palestinians were the first to arrest him, but then they let him go. It took Israeli security to find him and take him into custody."

Kayla reached down, lifted a handful of arid, rust-colored sand and held it out for Liam to see. "This dry dirt, these pebbles, these astringent stones of Hebron, from which you would think nothing can grow? Well, you'd be wrong. Hebron spawns some the world's worst terrorists. They erupt from the soils here, Liam. So many of them. Full of rage and hate. They sprout out of the ground like weeds and find nourishment in the stones here. They don't want peace in this land and they never will accept it. That sniping occurred during the Al-Aqsa Intifada." She dropped the stones, brushed her hands together.

"There are schools throughout the Palestinian territories that are named in honor of suicide bombers," Aaron added. "Even kindergartens, in tribute to terrorists."

Liam shook his head. "And they call this the Holy Land."

"The baby's father, his name was Yitzhak Pass. He was a young man, a student here," said Aaron. "You can't imagine his despair. The whole country wept with them. But then Yitzhak joined a group that planned an act of retribution. Violence begets violence, Liam. And, regrettably, it hasn't been all one-sided."

"That's true," Kayla said. "Except on this side of the fence, people do not gather in the streets to cheer violence and shoot guns into the air. Here, we put them in jail. Yitzhak Pass was arrested in possession of explosives and was sentenced to two years for plotting."

"Israel jailed the baby's father?"

Kayla nodded. "Terrorism is terrorism. No exceptions. Let's move on."

A quarter mile farther and a huge stone fortress came into view—an ancient structure whose thirty-foot walls were built of large, rectangular blocks of oatmeal-colored limestone. A guard-house with armed police sat at the top of wide steps that swooped upward from a small plaza below.

Liam looked to Kayla and tilted his head in the direction of the structure.

"The Cave of the Patriarchs," she said. "Ma'arat HaMachpelah, the land that Abraham bought from Ephron to bury his wife. Genesis tells the story in exquisite detail. This place has been a sacred site for thousands of years, a place of religious pilgrimage, long before there was any significance to Jerusalem."

Kayla stopped and stared. Her throat caught and she turned her head to dab her eyes. "Would you mind?" she said to Liam and Aaron. "May I have a moment, please?"

She walked a short distance to where the grass met the walk-way, bowed her head, and appeared to be lost in prayer.

"What is this all about?" Liam asked Aaron.

"She's saying kaddish," Aaron said quietly. "A prayer spoken by mourners. Really, a series of prayers, praising and sanctifying the name of God and praying for peace."

"For whom does she say kaddish?"

"It's not for me to say. She'll tell you in her time if she wants you to know."

When she returned, her eyes were red and her lips were quivering. It was clear to Liam that she had confronted a difficult memory. "Are you all right?"

She tried to speak, but just shook her head. He put his arm around her shoulders. She put her head on his chest and wept.

As they walked slowly from the site, Aaron picked up the conversation. "Three thousand seven hundred years ago, so the story goes, Abraham, the wandering shepherd, was seated outside his tent, right in this very area. Three strangers approached. Abraham offered them shelter and a meal, but the calf he selected for dinner broke loose and ran into one of the caves. Abraham went searching. There was a fire in the mouth of a cave, placed there by angels so that no man could enter. But when Abraham approached, the fire died and Abraham went in. There he smelled a sweet and lovely fragrance. As he walked further into the cave, he came upon Adam and Eve in their eternal rest. Beyond them lay the entrance to the Garden of Eden, from whence the lovely fragrance emanated. But Abraham could not enter because man had been expelled from paradise. When Abraham returned to his tent, the strangers were gone. It is that cave, that very cave, Machpelah, which Abraham purchased for the burial of his beloved wife, Sarah.

"The structure you see was built by King Herod two thousand years ago to surround and protect Machpelah, and it has remained generally intact throughout the ages. Saladin, the first sultan of Egypt and Syria, who conquered this land in the twelfth century, added the turrets. A mosque was constructed inside. Access to the caves themselves has been closed for five hundred years. There are now cenotaphs—empty tombs for the patriarchs and matriarchs, decorated and sitting in small chapels—which can be visited within the structure."

"So, Abraham actually purchased this land?" Liam said. "He got a deed?"

Kayla nodded. "I see where you're going. My teachings have not fallen on deaf ears. Yes, as it is written, he purchased the land, the fields, the caves, and all the trees within its borders, to bury his wife and so that he might be buried there as well. It was all done in a well-documented real estate transaction for four hundred shekels, a fair market price for the property, in the presence of all the Hittites."

"And so the father of the Jews becomes the first Jewish landowner in Hebron."

"In all of Israel, as far as we know," Aaron said. "He insisted on a deed. Ephron wanted to make a gift of the property, but Abraham was shrewd. He knew he could only pass it on to his heirs if it was purchased and deeded. You could certainly say that the concept of a Jewish homeland began with that real estate purchase. But remember, Muslims consider Abraham to be a prophet and an ancestor of Muhammad."

Kayla put her hand gently on Liam's arm. "Thank you for your understanding back at the steps."

They walked on a little farther until they reached the Israeli checkpoint at the H1 border. "This is as far as I can go," Aaron said. Liam shook his hand and bid him good-bye.

Once Liam and Kayla had cleared the checkpoint and began their walk into the center of Hebron, Liam said, "You were at that wedding, weren't you. At the cave of Machpelah? Where the terrorist shooting occurred?"

Kayla shut her eyes. "Yes, I was."

"And back at the checkpoint, one of the IDF guards knew you, didn't he?"

"Not IDF. Magav, Israeli Border Police. They provide the security here."

"An old friend?"

Kayla nodded and they walked on.

The market area of central Hebron, Bab al-Zawiyah, was bustling with daytime shoppers. Just off the square, a fluttering canvas awning over a shop proclaimed in Arabic script it was the Breadstone Bakery.

Liam stopped Kayla before they could enter the bakery. "Tell me why we're here. It's not because we might pick up a little gossip. It's not because the group met here in the past. And it's certainly not to buy a doughnut. Why are we really here?"

Kayla moved close to Liam and opened her hand to reveal the small, black plastic listening device that Aaron had handed to her. "I'm going to plant this in a back room. Let's enter separately."

Breadstone's interior walls were lined with glass cases displaying the morning's products. The customers, mainly women, were snatching up hot rolls, sweets, and pitas. Liam pretended to be interested in the pastries, while Kayla conversed with a young man behind a display case. She asked for a sample wheat pita, which she held to her nose. She took a small bite out of the edge, tilted her head back and forth in a "so-so" gesture and said a few words to the clerk, who snapped a few words back at her. She turned and ambled back to where Liam was standing, stopping to look into the bakery racks.

"I told him the pita was tasty, but a bit dry and cold, so I couldn't tell how old it was," she said quietly. "I ordered twelve hot pitas, right out of the oven, and I didn't want him taking the cold pitas and putting them in a microwave. You saw him. He said he didn't sell old pitas, that I should take them out of the oven myself, and I said, 'Fine.' The oven is in the back room, which is what I had hoped for." She looked around at the busy bakery. "I need a distraction. When I go into the back, see if you can grab the attention of the shopkeepers and keep them busy. I just need a couple minutes."

Kayla followed the clerk into the back. Liam elbowed his way up to the case and pointed at a pastry. "Excuse me. Excuse me," he said loudly. "I'd like a sweet roll. Understand? Sweet? Roll? Do you have to take a number here? I didn't see any numbers. Where is your number machine?" A clerk came over and spread his hands in a questioning gesture.

"I want something sweet and gooey. That one. No, no, not that one. That one. Yep. Yep. Nope. More to the left. That one. Nope, the other one." The salesclerk uttered a phrase under his breath, shook his head, rolled his eyes, and called for the other clerk to come from the back room to help him.

"I speak English," said the second clerk. "What you want?"

"I want a gooey, cinnamon sweet roll and a cup of coffee."

"No cinnamon. No coffee." The clerk reached into the case. "Here, take this, you like it."

Liam furrowed his forehead. "What's in it?"

"Almond. It's good. Here, take it."

Liam fumbled with some money in his pocket.

"No charge. No charge. Good-bye."

Liam saw Kayla come out of the back room with a paper bag and leave through the front door. He took a bite of his sweet roll. "Mmmmm." He held it up for all to see. "Man, this is pretty good. Not too bad at all." He nodded to the women in the store, holding out the sweet roll. "You all should try this. It's almond. Very tasty."

The clerk closed his eyes. "Okay. Okay. Go now. Go."

"Have a nice day," Liam said loudly to the clerk and the women in the store, bowing, smiling, and backing out the door to meet Kayla on the sidewalk.

"Nice work, Liam. The clerk took me into the back where the baking ovens were. The pita oven is a noisy, belted thing. I waited by the oven taking my pitas as they dropped onto the tray. The clerk stood right beside me until you started your commotion. As you know, he rushed into the store to quiet you down. Behind the ovens there's a large office. It's also a sitting room with chairs and a couch.

I managed to attach the bug to the underside of the couch. I believe that's where the group held its meetings."

"Why is that important? You told me they met here in the past but they don't meet here anymore."

"I have reason to believe they might meet here again. Now, let's have a look at al-Zahani's residence."

"What about Fakhir, the baker? I want to talk to him, see if he'll let on whether there's a deal in place."

"He's not coming in today. His son told me he only comes in a couple times a week. He'll be back on Thursday. We can come back then. Right now I'd like you to see al-Zahani's layout from street level, and then we'll head back to Jerusalem. Maybe it's time for you to pay another visit to Abu Hammad."

They exited the taxi three blocks from al-Zahani's home and approached the walled residence from the west, walking slowly on the opposite side of the street.

"The compound is huge," Liam said. "He must have three acres."

"Four point two to be exact." Kayla pointed. "The black iron gate in the front is controlled mechanically. On satellite we've seen what appear to be multiple security guards. Sometimes they patrol the perimeter."

"Why the hell does a doctor need multiple security guards?"

"I doubt it has anything to do with Sophie. It's all about what's going on behind those walls. The devil's workshop of the Sons of Canaan."

Liam shaded his eyes and stared at the property. "What's on the other side of those walls? How many structures?"

"Three. A large home, easily four thousand square feet. A small building, probably a utility garage. And a rectangular, one-story structure, maybe three thousand square feet. That's where the mysteries lie, and we don't have a clue what's going on inside."

Just then, a large man in a tan sport coat, holding the hand of a little girl, turned the corner and headed for the front gate. In his free hand, he carried a small, pink backpack. Sophie skipped along, trying to keep up with his stride. Their conversation was animated. Sophie laughed. Suddenly, three guards materialized in front of the gate.

"That's Sophie." Liam immediately grabbed Kayla by the shoulders, turned her to the side, and wrapped his arms around her. "I don't want the guards to see our faces. Let them think we're lovers standing on the corner."

From the corner of his eye, appearing to be locked in a passionate embrace, Liam watched the guards take their stations and open the mechanized gate for Bashir and Sophie. When the two had entered, the guards closed the gate and resumed their patrol of the perimeter. One guard lit a cigarette, pointed at the kissing couple across the street, and chuckled and sniggered to his companions.

When they were out of sight, Liam released Kayla, who opened her eyes widely, took a deep breath, and smiled. Her face was flushed. She licked her lips. "That's quite a move you've got there, Irish. You got my heart beating. I'm impressed."

He took Kayla by the elbow and walked away from the property. "They must be coming home from school." He checked his watch: 3:15. "We should find that school. It might be a good location if we want to grab her."

Arm in arm, they walked a few blocks past al-Zahani's walls, tracing Bashir's route, and came upon a mosque with an extended school building. A fenced-in area held a little playground. Liam took a couple of pictures with his phone.

On the return to Kiryat Arba, they once again walked passed the Avraham Avinu Synagogue. Kayla pointed. "In August 1929, this was one of the locations of the Hebron Massacre."

"You didn't tell me about the Hebron Massacre."

"I told you, when we were back in Chicago, that 1929 was a violent year. Mufti Amin al-Husseini and Ibrahim were waging a heated campaign against Jewish immigration and those who had already settled here. They called them 'Zionist invaders.' They demanded that they all leave Palestine. In the heat of the summer, tensions heightened. Jews were randomly attacked leaving their schools.

"Then, in August 1929, there was an incident—three Jewish children and three Arabs were killed in Jerusalem. That was a starter's pistol shot for Amin and Ibrahim. They riled up their followers with wild street demonstrations. An Arab messenger raced to Hebron on his motorcycle and announced, 'I bring news from the mufti. The blood of thousands of Muslims is being shed like water in Jerusalem.' A crazed mob then took to the streets with knives, clubs, and axes. They stoned Jewish houses, ransacked the hospital, raped, murdered, mutilated, tortured." Kayla shook her head.

"Where were the police?"

"Because Hebron was such a peaceful town, there weren't many British police stationed here. Basically, the Jews and Arabs in Hebron got along pretty well before the riot. Anyway, here in this synagogue, many came to hide from the marauders. But, eventually the doors were breached and the people were slaughtered.

"Hebron's Chief Rabbi Slonim sheltered several of the Ashkenazi yeshiva students in his home, but they were soon surrounded. Many of the Arab rioters knew and respected Rabbi Slonim. They banged on his door and offered him a choice: hand over the Ashkenazi students and we'll let you, your family, and the Sephardic Jews live. 'I'm sorry,' the rabbi said, 'that, I cannot do.' Thereupon, Rabbi Slonim, his entire family, and all the Jews he was sheltering were slaughtered.

"All in all, sixty-seven Jews were murdered. Finally, British reinforcements came to Hebron and took the four hundred eighty-four survivors north to Jerusalem."

"Never quits in this region, does it?"

"It *will* quit, Liam. You have to believe it. When we rid this land of extremists like the al-Zahanis, it will quit. And the proof was here in Hebron. Before the Hebron Massacre, it was a peaceful town of Arabs and Jews living side by side. It can happen. The proof was here."

"But not anymore."

"Not yet."

FORTY-SIX

• • •

MARCY WAS BOOKED FOR a weekend photography
show at the Sheraton, so she and Jack loaded up his car
at her house and headed into Waikiki. Sommers's mood
was light. It had been that way since he received the e-mail four
days earlier. Jack had downloaded the parental-authorization
form, signed it, scanned it, and immediately returned it by e-mail.
Soon Deb would pick up Sophie, and if he managed to stay under
the radar, he'd figure out a way to get Sophie out to the islands.
After she was healthy and stabilized, he would get her back to
Deborah and turn himself in. He knew that sooner or later law
enforcement would catch up to him. He couldn't run forever. And
he didn't want to. Turning himself in and confessing was the right
thing to do.

He dropped Marcy at the hotel and drove to the Coral Reef,
parking his car on the street in front of the motel office. He was on
the way up to his room when Glenn stopped him.

"Say, Mr. Wilson, you had some visitors a couple days ago."

"Visitors?" Jack's face immediately flushed.

"Yeah, man. One said he was a cousin of yours. They showed
me your picture and asked if you was living here or if I seen you."

"A cousin? I don't have any cousins." Jack's adrenaline was
pumping. "What did you tell them?"

Glenn put his hand on Jack's shoulder. "Don't worry, man. Ol'
Glenn's got your back. Them fucking bill collectors'll say anything.
I know from experience. I told them I ain't never seen anybody
looked like that picture."

"Thanks, Glenn, you did the right thing. Why do you suppose they came here, to the Coral Reef? Did they tell you?"

Glenn shook his head. "Nah. They just said they was your cousins and they were pretty sure you was living here. But I seen them go into the Breakers across the street. So maybe they don't really know where you live."

"What did they look like? Did they show you any ID?"

"Well, they weren't cops. That I could tell you. They didn't show me any badges or ID cards, and they talked with some funny foreigner accent, like they was from Europe. Maybe Russia. And Mr. Wilson, they called you Mr. Summerfield, or something like that. They didn't even know your right name. But they did have your picture."

"Thanks a lot, Glenn. I owe you. If they come by again, just tell them you never heard of me."

"Don't have to worry a bit. I ain't helping out no bill collectors."

Jack went into his room and packed his suitcase, removing every trace of his tenancy. He threw the bag into the car and went back into the office.

"Glenn, here's the rent for the next two months." Jack laid $1,600 on the counter. "And here's an extra five hundred dollars for you. You never heard of me, right?"

Glenn smiled widely. "Heard of who?"

Sommers then drove back to the Sheraton, where he sat in the corner of the bar with a cocktail trying to settle his nerves. After Marcy's show, while they were loading her photographs into his trunk, she said, "What's wrong, Jack? You look like you've seen a ghost."

"Some guys came snooping around the Coral Reef and showed the manager my picture."

"I thought no one knows where you're staying."

"Don't know how they did it. No one knew. Not even my sister. Damn. The last e-mail message said they were close to bringing Sophie home. They needed my authorization. I sent it to them."

"Why do you think it's them? Maybe it's the police."

Jack shook his head. "Glenn said they didn't have any IDs and they spoke with a European accent. It's them all right."

"Glenn would know that? A European accent?"

"He said they sounded Russian. He said they were asking about me, even knew my name, except in Glenn's mind they said Summerfield."

"You sure you haven't told anybody where you are?"

"Nobody." Jack shook his head. "If they were truly speaking with a Russian accent, I got a pretty good idea who they are. But it doesn't make any sense. I just got an e-mail saying they were bringing Sophie home. Why would they be out looking for me?"

"Jack, you're scaring me. You're the third person, the only one left who knows about the theft. The only one who can tie them to the murders."

Sommers slipped into the driver's seat and started driving in the direction of the North Shore. "Do you think they could have traced my cell phone or my computer? What if that's how they caught up to me?" Sommers pulled off the highway.

"What are you doing?"

"If they can find the Coral Reef, why can't they find your house? What if they traced me through phone records? I used my cell phone at your house. There are phone calls between you and me. We have to think this through."

"Jack, you told me that you and your sister have safe cell phones. They were purchased by other people and no one knows the numbers."

"That's true. Maybe they found me through the Internet. They could have traced me when I went online to check for e-mail."

"That's paranoid. How would these guys have that kind of equipment? If that stuff even exists. I mean, maybe if you were in an Internet café and they could trace the connection . . ."

"That's it. I always went online from the coffee shop around the corner. That must be why they were searching through the neighborhood."

"Did you ever go online from my house? From my Internet connection?"

Sommers thought for a minute and shook his head. "No. Never. Not even on my phone."

"Then how would they know about me? We'll be safe at my house. I'll lock my doors."

"Lock your doors? Seriously? Whoever these people are, they're killers, not burglars. They killed two people and now they know where I am."

"I don't think they do. They were canvassing the neighborhood. They don't know anything about Eugene Wilson. They were asking about a guy named Summerfield. They don't know about me, or where I live. You didn't make contact from my house. You're a needle in a haystack. There's a million people out here."

"Maybe. But I sure can't go back to the Coral Reef. I'll have to stay somewhere else."

"You can stay at my house. Lay low for a while until they leave the island."

"Thanks for the offer, but I'm going to find another place to stay for a while. It might be best if we didn't see each other."

"I'm not afraid. They have no idea who I am."

He started the car. "We need to think this through."

FORTY-SEVEN

• • •

L IAM ENTERED ABU HAMMAD's antiquities store before noon. As before, there were no customers. "Jamal?" he
called.

The old man shuffled out from the back room. *"As-salaam
alaikum."*

"And peace be upon you."

Abu Hammad smiled, nodded, turned, and retreated to his back
room without an additional word. Liam followed and stood patiently by the wooden chair while Abu Hammad brewed his tea.
When both were seated, Abu Hammad spoke. "Of course, I do
not know everyone in Hebron, but I believe if an arrangement for a
ransom or a payoff was in place, certain people would know. Even
so, in discussing this matter, one must be cautious. One may only
broach the topic from a distance, like jackals circle their prey."
He shook his head. "But, so far I have learned nothing. People
speak of the doctor's love for the little child, not of an arrangement
to pay money. They dismiss the notion that he would agree to sell
her, even back to her father."

"Thank you, Jamal. I am grateful for your efforts. I suppose the
next question is, would he consider return of the child if he were
offered a great deal of money? Perhaps many millions? I could arrange it."

Abu Hammad leaned back and with his weathered fingers
stroked the whiskers in his goatee. He took a long, wheezy breath
through his nose and wagged his index finger up and down. "You
know, Liam, for many, many years, Hebron was just a simple town,

a market place for bedouins. There they could come and buy water bags, wine, cloth, shoes—provisions they would need. There they could sell their sheep and goats, or the milk and cheese they made. In many ways, Hebron is still a simple town. But Arif, he is different. He stands in his walled palace and looks down upon the peasants in the town. He is wealthy beyond the imagination of most Hebronites. Many millions would make a difference to almost everyone in this poor town. And surely in other towns as well." He shrugged his shoulders. "But maybe not to Arif."

"One never knows though, eh, Jamal? Who knows how he spends his money? Let me ask a more difficult question. How would I get word to Dr. al-Zahani that I would be interested in proposing such an arrangement? I'm sure there would be a generous payment to you as well."

"I want nothing from such commerce. Were it not for the little one, I would send you on your way. But I am troubled for Sophie. Myself, I have been the target of Arif's anger. I have seen the demon in him. And a man such as Arif could surely fill a child with hate."

"I'm sorry if I offended you, Jamal." Liam rose and reached into his back pocket. He handed Abu Hammad a business card. "I meant no harm in offering to pay you for your help. I'm only trying to reunite a daughter with her father. Here is my contact information. If you learn something you think I should know, I'd appreciate a call."

"I took no offense. I will help if I can because it is right, not because I seek to profit. You should know, there are many good, honest people on this side of the barrier, people who seek only the right to live in peace."

Liam nodded. "I am honored to know such a man."

FORTY-EIGHT

• • •

FAKHIR LED YOUNG DANI into the apartment's front room, where the Sons of Canaan were seated in a circle. One by one, the members of the group welcomed the sixteen-year-old and offered him tea and date-filled cakes. Dani was confused and scared.

"Sit please, Dani," Fa'iz said, pointing to an empty chair. "Join us." The old man's whiskered face wrinkled with a beneficent smile.

Dani nodded tentatively and took the empty seat beside al-Zahani, who patted him on the shoulder.

Fa'iz continued, "You probably wonder why you have been brought upstairs, when you usually guard the door for us, no?"

The boy nodded.

"Dani, we would like to invite you to have a very important role in our project."

"Very important," echoed Nizar.

"What do you know about jihad, Dani?"

The boy shrugged. "It's our continuing struggle in the cause of Allah."

Fa'iz smiled broadly and nodded. "And we understand our struggle to be for the cause of truth, don't we? A true jihadist is a warrior whose whole purpose is to establish the truth. You understand that, don't you, Dani?"

He nodded reflexively, unsure where all this was leading.

Fa'iz leaned back in his chair and folded his hands on his stomach. His ample beard covered his chest. "That is good. Do you know the meaning of *shahid*, son?"

Dani shook his head slowly.

Fa'iz spoke gently. "A *shahid* is one who sees the truth and witnesses it. He dedicates himself to the truth and is prepared to fight and give up his life for the cause of truth. That is why a *shahada*, a martyrdom, guarantees that a *shahid* shall know paradise and be exonerated from the torments of the grave."

"And let's not forget seventy-two dark-eyed virgins," added Nizar with a sly smile.

"Is that actually true?" Dani said, finally grasping the meaning of his presence.

Fa'iz nodded. "It is written. The *shahid* will be wed to the *houri* and will not know the torments of the grave."

Dani looked around the room. All eyes were focused on him, and all were smiling paternally.

"The concept of *shahada* is very similar to the concept of prophethood," continued Fa'iz. "Both martyrs and prophets are paradigms. They are examples. They are models for us all. Do you follow me, Dani?"

"I'm not sure. I . . . I don't think so."

"*Shahids* are the leaders who spearhead our struggle. They embody truth. Martyrs are elite models of the Divine Message. They ensure the success in our struggle for the cause of Allah. Dani, you can become such a *mujahid.*"

"You want me to blow myself up?" the boy said in a shaky voice.

"No, Dani."

"Whew," he said with a smile. "I thought . . ."

Fa'iz raised his finger. "We want you to join us in our holy struggle. Are you with us?"

"Sure," Dani said slowly.

"We have developed a weapon, a very potent weapon. Much more devastating than a bomb. But it needs to be tested."

Dani swallowed hard. "You want me to test this weapon?"

Fa'iz nodded deeply with a smile. "We will honor you with that opportunity."

"Is it dangerous?"

"Very. It will take the courage of a true martyr. That is why we look to you, Dani."

"Would I have to die?"

Everyone looked to al-Zahani, who nodded. "I'm afraid so. It's irreversible."

Dani moved around uncomfortably on his chair. "I don't know. I have a lot of things I have to do. My mom needs me. I—"

"Your family will be well taken care of," Fa'iz said warmly. "They will be given a home and a place of honor in Hebron. Your sisters will have money to attend school. Your memory will be cherished by all."

"And you will be given paradise," added Nizar.

"C-can I think about this?"

"Of course," Fa'iz said. "Think about it, but tell no one. Can we count on you to be silent?"

Dani nodded.

"Not even your mother," Fakhir said. "Our holy struggle depends on secrecy."

"And if I don't want to do this?"

Fa'iz spread his hands. "Then you can go back to watching the door like before."

The group stood. Nizar came up to Dani and put his hands on his shoulders. "Be a hero to our people. Your family will be honored forever. And you, Dani, well, seventy-two virgins is not so bad, eh?"

"Come back tomorrow, Dani," said Fa'iz. "Let us know your decision."

Dani turned to leave the room, but Nizar put his arm around him. "Let us all join hands."

The group stood in a circle, hand in hand, Dani between Nizar and Fa'iz, and chanted, "From the river to the sea. From the Golan to the Gulf. We will take Jerusalem brick by brick, stone by stone, until the land is once more ours."

"You are one of us, Dani," said Rami, and the boy beamed with pride. They patted his back as he left the room, albeit a little unsteady on his feet.

"Will he betray us?" asked Rami.

"I have no doubt he will discuss this all with his mother. We will have to dispose of her, no matter what his decision," Fa'iz said, retaking his seat. He then turned to al-Zahani. "Be prepared to run the test tomorrow when he returns."

"I am already prepared, but what if he decides not to volunteer?"

Fa'iz shook his head. "We will run the test with him regardless."

Everyone nodded. As they stood to leave, Rami said, "I have one more piece of good news. As you know, Ghanim applied for a job in the pharmacy department of Haifa's B'nai Zion Hospital. Well, yesterday his application was approved and he will start in June."

Fa'iz smiled. "Allah shines on us today. We will hit Tel Aviv and Haifa in July. Arif, you must step up production. Day and night."

"Understood."

FORTY-NINE

• • •

MOTHER NATURE DANGLED A taste of spring in the face of Chicagoans on a mid-March afternoon. But it was just a teaser. The thermometer climbed into the high fifties, and winter coats and scarves were set aside for cotton jackets. Though St. Paddy's Day had come and gone, the Chicago River still flowed with vestiges of kelly green. The fountain in Daley Plaza still bubbled green water, and the tops of downtown buildings still lit up like four-leaf clovers. Just a teaser, for the Northeast Hawk would soon return to Michigan Avenue and the snow would blow a few more times before winter would loosen its grip.

On North Clark Street, a mother held the door open while her son struggled on his crutches and entered the law offices of Catherine Lockhart. "We're here to see Attorney Lockhart," the woman said to the receptionist. "Please tell her that Darius and Violet McCord are here."

A moment later, Catherine came out to her lobby. "Very nice to meet you both. And, Darius, I confess, I don't know much about college basketball, but I was saddened to read about the assault and your tragic injury. Have they caught the assailants?"

"No, ma'am," Violet said. "That's why we're here. Darius has something he wants to tell you."

Catherine gestured toward the hallway. "Come on back to my office and we'll talk. Gladys, will you please get them both a soft drink."

"I'll just have water, thank you," Violet said.

Violet helped Darius settle into one of the two client chairs opposite Catherine's desk. Gladys brought in the drinks and closed the door on her way out.

"Again, Darius, it pains me to see you struggle with those crutches. When do the doctors think you'll be up and around?"

"I don't know," he said sheepishly. "Maybe a few months."

"Do the police have any leads? Any way to find out who did this?"

Violet leaned forward, putting her forearms on the desk. She was thin and tall, but still considerably shorter than her son. She appeared to be no older than her late thirties. "Miss Lockhart, what we tell you today, is it a secret?"

Catherine nodded her head. "Yes, it is. It's confidential and privileged. And call me Catherine."

"That means you can't tell no one if we don't want you to?"

"That's right."

"Are you the attorney in the case against Mr. Kelsen?"

Catherine nodded. "I'm defending a client that's being sued by Mr. Kelsen's company."

"So, you're against him, right? I been reading about it in the paper."

Catherine smiled. "I guess you could say I'm against him. It's his company."

Violet sat back in her chair. "Then you're the right person."

She unscrewed the cap on her water bottle, took a drink and a deep breath. "Miss Lockhart, I need to tell you about my son and me. We been down a long, hard road. You prob'ly don't know what families have to do to get their boys into Division One basketball."

"No, Violet, I don't."

"Well, it starts when they're babies. From the time Darius was just a squeaker, he had talent. I could see it. Everybody could. When he was old enough to hold a ball, he had to have a ball in his hands. It was like him and the ball was one. All the time bouncing a ball. Off the floor, off the walls." Violet smiled at her son.

"I wanted him to be a good ballplayer, as good as he could be. Everybody in our part of town dreams of their baby playin' pro ball, but I didn't have any idea what we were getting into." Tears came to her eyes. She wiped them with the back of her hand.

Catherine took out a box of tissues and set them on the desk.

"He was only eight years old and there was scouts on the Forty-Seventh Street playground talking this way and that. Eight years old and they come to watch Darius. When he got into the fourth grade, I got a call from Mr. Robinson. 'We want Darius to be on our AAU team, the Chicago Tigers,' he said. 'One of the best in the country.'"

"At nine years old?"

Violet nodded. "I didn't know anything about the AAU, but the other mothers told me, if Darius wants to be anybody at all, he's got to sign up. So we did. Before I know it, there was shoes, jerseys, strength equipment, all delivered to my apartment. They put us in touch with Father Paul over at Holy Resurrection so we could use the gym in the afternoon. Every day, all year, Miss Lockhart, except for the time he was practicing with the team, and then we still would go at night sometimes. Darius'd come home from school and go straight to the gym. Three hundred layups, four hundred free throws, three hundred spot-ups. I stood under the basket and fed him the ball. Then we'd go home and have our dinner at eight." She looked at her son. "He was ranked as the second-best ten-year-old in the country by *Youth Hoops Magazine.*"

"The second-best *ten-year-old?*"

"Yep. From time to time, this coach or that would come over to the church and work with Darius. It was all a business to them, but I could see they were teaching him and getting him ready for college and pro ball. Who's paying all these people? I don't know. And I guess I don't need to tell you about all the sneaky agents who ain't supposed to be talking to kids, wantin' me to sign their papers. AAU took us all over the country, Miss Lockhart."

"Catherine."

"Tournaments almost every week. New York, Washington, Dallas, LA. His baby brother, at first I could bring him 'cause he'd sit on my lap, but later he's too big and I don't have the money, and I have to stay at home or get people to watch him." Violet's eyes glassed over and her voice would occasionally seize up. "Terrell, he didn't get the attention he needed growing up. He needed attention too, but there was no more of me to go around." She took a few pieces of tissue and rocked a bit in her seat. "Now he's in and out of trouble."

Catherine waited while Violet composed herself. Darius sat with his head bowed. "By the time Darius was ready for high school, he had played hundreds of games and everybody wanted him. We had coaches from private high schools sitting in our front room from the time he was in seventh grade. Catholic schools offering full tuition. One of them even said they'd pick him up and drive him to school every day. High school up in Maryland would've moved us to an apartment in Baltimore. An academy in Florida showed us pictures of first-rounders and told us he could stay in the dorm. Major university lab school—he'd live right on the campus.

"Darius didn't want Catholic school, he didn't want no academy or lab school, he wanted to be with his friends and play in the Public League. You may have read about him when he was at Jefferson. He was a high school all-American and ranked number twenty-two in the country in his senior year. Number four point guard.

"Then there's certain days when the colleges can come visit you. Mercy me. You'd a thought we was the king and queen of England. Letters from people and places we never heard of. They all be your best friend."

"I get it."

"No, ma'am, you don't. You see, every last one of 'em is sitting in our front room, all sayin' that the years of practice and sacrifice is gonna finally pay off. Someday, Darius, you gonna play in the NBA, and we gonna get you there. Then you'll be able to take care of yourself, your baby brother, and your mama. This is your ticket out, they say.

"So we keep workin', Miss Lockhart, day in, day out. Keepin' up the basketball, keepin' up the grades so he can get into college and not sit a year. Twenty-three on his ACTs. Always a B average. He wants to go to St. Joe's 'cause it's right in town and I can come see him every game. Two years of St. Joe's. He didn't want to be no one-and-done. He stayed the extra year for Coach Washburn. Now comes the tournament. He's showing everyone he's the best. A first-rounder for sure. We made it."

Violet gave a quick pop to Darius's shoulder. "Tell her, Darius," she said sternly. "Tell her what you and Marcus Fields did."

Darius hung his head even farther and talked so softly he was almost inaudible. "We took money."

Violet looked crossly at her son. "Tell her what you did for that money."

"We shaved points." He looked up. "We never lost on purpose and we never threw a game. But we did shave points. We controlled the score."

Catherine leaned forward. "What does this have to do with Mr. Kelsen, Darius?"

"He's the one. He gave us the money. And I know we weren't the first. He's been hanging around St. Joe's for years."

After a pause in the room Violet popped Darius again. "You ain't done, Darius."

"Last week, we played Western Alabama in the tournament. We was supposed to keep the score under fourteen, but I scored too many points and Mr. Kelsen got real mad. He did this to me."

"Mr. Kelsen broke your leg?"

"It was the Russian dude. Hit me with a pipe in Mr. Kelsen's car."

"Miss Lockhart, Kelsen is in with those Russian gangsters," Violet said. "A man named Dmitri. Tell her, Darius."

Darius swallowed hard. "Mr. Kelsen plays the points with some Russians. The main dude is Dmitri, but I don't know his last name."

"And Dmitri broke your leg?" Catherine asked.

"Nah, that was Evgeniy. I seen him a few times when we was on the road. I ain't never seen Dmitri at a game."

"Did you tell this to the police?"

"We don't want to do that," Violet said. "Darius's leg is broke, but it's not a career-ending break. He'll be better in a few months. We probably have to skip the draft this year, so Darius'll be back at St. Joe's next year. Darius can't admit to no one he was taking money. Sports bribery's a federal crime. He'd be kicked out of school. No NBA team'd want him. It'd be the end of Darius's career."

"Then why are you telling me this?"

"Because Mr. Kelsen and his Russian friends been messin' up kids' lives. And they'll keep doin' it. And they won't think twice about bustin' up my boy again next year if he don't play along. And maybe they keep doin' it even when he's in the pros. You got a case against Mr. Kelsen. When does that case come up in court?"

Catherine spread her hands and smiled. "We're in the Cook County courts. Trial is at least a year away. But there's a status call next week."

"Will Mr. Kelsen be there for the status call?"

"You never know with Mr. Kelsen, but I don't think so. It's just intended for the lawyers."

"Somehow you gotta get the word to him that people be knowin' what he does. Then he'll have to let Darius alone, 'cause then if something happens to my boy, everybody will know it was him. Mr. Kelsen's only able to control people because he does it in se-cret. He won't commit a crime in a fishbowl."

"We're scheduled to do depositions starting next week. I sup-pose I could slide a comment in here or there, but if I do, I might be opening a door. One way or another, it could lead to people finding out about Darius and what you told me today. I can't guar-antee the information will remain confidential. And maybe it even would put Darius in danger."

"We'll take that chance. He's already in danger. And I don't think Mr. Kelsen's going to do anything if he knows other people are watching him."

"Really, Mrs. McCord, I think if you went to the police—"

"No, ma'am. Officially, Darius was mugged. We just need this Mr. Kelsen to leave Darius alone. You get the message to him some way, that you know all about him and Dmitri. He's gotta stop. Otherwise, he'll control my boy forever." Violet stood and helped Darius to his feet.

He looked at Catherine. "I'm sorry, Miss Lockhart, for what I did, I truly am."

FIFTY

...

WHAT IF HE DOESN'T show up today?" Rami said.

"He'll be here," answered Fa'iz from his seat in the corner. The old man leaned back on his futon, his hands folded on his belly. "Of that I am sure, but I don't know if he'll have the resolve to submit willingly."

"And if he doesn't?" Nizar said.

Fa'iz looked to al-Zahani, who nodded, reached into his bag, and extracted a syringe and a small bottle with opaque liquid. "It's a short-term sedative."

Dani returned to the apartment at noon and was warmly greeted by the group.

"Our warrior has arrived. Hail to the hero," Nizar said. "From the river to the sea, eh, Dani?"

Dani spoke directly to Fa'iz. "I don't think I can do what you ask. I'm not a suicide bomber."

"It's not a bomb, Dani. It's a very potent weapon, like nothing the world has seen, that will bring us great glory. Your family will be very proud."

"My mother doesn't want me to do this. Even though you'd buy her a house. She told me not to come back here, but I promised I would, so here I am. I'll help in other ways, but not by doing this. I'll guard the door for you, I'll run messages, but I'm not going to let you kill me. I'm not doing it."

Fa'iz rose from his chair. He put his arms around Dani in a strong hug and kissed him on the cheek. "We are all very proud of you. Allah will surely grant you entrance into Jannah."

From behind, al-Zahani inserted the needle into Dani's neck and quickly plunged the sedative. Dani's eyes widened. He tried to speak but his body went limp in Fa'iz's arms.

"We need to get him to the lab within the hour," al-Zahani said.

The group placed Dani onto a blanket and carried him outside, where he was laid in the backseat of Rami's car.

"You know old Abu Hammad?" Fakhir said to al-Zahani outside the car. "The shopkeeper in Jerusalem's Old City?"

Al-Zahani looked up with a stern face. "I know him and detest him. He's a coward and a traitor. I should have shot him for desertion when I had the chance. My father would be alive today if it wasn't for cowards like Abu Hammad."

"That may be, but I saw him last night and he told me a very interesting story. He said a private investigator hired by Sophie's father had been coming around his shop asking questions about you."

"What was he asking?"

"If you made a deal to ransom your granddaughter."

"Ransom? Where would he get such ideas?" Al-Zahani waved it off. "No matter. Sophie is safe. We're well protected."

"But listen, Arif, he says the father is willing to pay millions of dollars to get her back."

"Tell Abu Hammad to go back to his junkyard. I'm not interested in such nonsense. Sophie is not for sale. That's insulting, but typical of Abu Hammad."

"Wait," Fa'iz said. "Do not dismiss this talk so readily. How many millions of dollars did Abu Hammad say?"

Fakhir raised his eyebrows. "He said *many* millions."

Nizar laughed loudly. "Where is a young lawyer supposed to get many millions?"

"It's not impossible," al-Zahani said. "He has very wealthy friends. But this conversation is going nowhere. Sophie is not for sale."

"How do you know his wealthy friends can pay millions, Arif?" Fa'iz asked.

"I met one such man. A Russian. A business client and friend of Sommers. In fact, it was this man who flew Sophie, Lubannah, and me from Chicago last year. That's how we got here."

"Some friend." Nizar laughed. "Why would he let you steal Sommers's daughter if he was his friend?"

Al-Zahani shrugged. "I didn't ask. Sommers didn't let me *steal* the daughter. He gave her to me to *watch* while they went to Los Angeles. It was a bizarre situation and one doesn't look a gift horse in the mouth. This man came into the hotel restaurant in Chicago where Lubannah, Sophie, and I were eating our breakfast. He told us that he and Sommers had an emergency in Los Angeles and he was very worried. He said half a billion dollars was at stake and that Sommers was at the office at that very moment working on the deal. He asked me if Lubannah and I could watch Sophie for a couple weeks while he and Sommers went out of town. I told him that I had to get back to Hebron, I'm a doctor, and besides, I didn't want to violate the court order. Then he told me not to worry, they would take care of the court order. And if I wanted to, I could watch her at my home in Hebron, he'd fly us here and bring us back.

"He was a wealthy man who owned a jet plane. He was so confident, he left no doubt in my mind. Then it all came to me—that's the way to get custody of Sophie. I thought this man was an eccentric, crazy man, but if I could get Sophie on a plane to Hebron, I'd certainly never bring her back to Chicago.

"So I told him, 'Of course we will take care of Sophie. But you have to arrange for the flight and Sophie's passport.' He said it's all done. He had Sophie's passport. He insisted we leave right away so he could get back to his meeting, which was okay with me. The sooner we got out of Chicago, the better. So we packed our bags, got in his limousine, and rode to some small private airfield where he kept his plane. His men flew us to Nova Scotia, then to Kiev, and then to Amman. Two weeks came and went and he didn't call. I never heard from him again."

"So you think this man would now pay millions of dollars to get her back?"

Al-Zahani shrugged. "Maybe he's sorry for what he did. But what does it matter? Sophie is never going back to America and I'm not talking to anybody about a ransom."

Fa'iz held up a finger. "Not so fast. Millions of American dollars would be an immeasurable help in our struggle."

Al-Zahani straightened his back. "Not for sale, Fa'iz. Not for any amount of money, and I'll hear no more of this."

"Now the truth rises to the surface," Nizar said in a mocking tone. "The dedicated freedom fighter, the holier-than-thou doctor who does not think twice of sacrificing young Dani in the cause of our struggle, would not part with his precious little American Jew, even though it would mean millions of dollars."

Fa'iz smiled broadly and stroked his wiry beard. "Do not stress, Arif. I will never ask you to part with Sophie. But I have a plan. A plan to get the money and still keep the little one. Now let us get young Dani to the lab and finish the test."

FIFTY-ONE

. . .

THE BELL ON THE Coral Reef's office door rang and Glenn shuffled out to the counter. The two men had returned.

"I told you guys, I ain't never seen the man in the picture and I don't know any Summerfield."

"Sommers," said the larger of the two. "Sommers. Not Summerfield."

"Summers. Winters. Don't matter. I don't know him and wouldn't help no bill collectors if I did."

"We'd like to see your register."

"Go fuck yourself."

"Why you make this so difficult?" the shorter man said in a rough accent. "We want only to look at register, just see who check in and who check out. Then we leave you alone."

"I ain't showing you shit. I don't have to and I'm calling the cops if you don't get the fuck out of here."

The short man quickly pulled a .38 from his pocket. "I hate when people talk like that to me. Where is register?"

Glenn reached under the counter and pulled out the book. He set it on the desk, never taking his eyes off the gun.

The taller one scrolled through the entries with his finger, stopping midway down the page. He smiled at Glenn. "Mr. Wilson. Eugene Wilson. Room 212. Is this a picture of Mr. Wilson?"

Glenn shrugged. His eyes were fixed upon the .38 in the short man's hand.

"Why you make this so hard? You're either very brave or very stupid. How does he pay you? Does he use a credit card?"

"I don't take credit cards. He pays in cash."

"Does he have a car?"

Glenn shrugged. "I don't know."

The tall man reached out and grabbed Glenn's shirt at the throat. He pulled his face down to the counter. "We're trying to have a civil conversation. Don't you get it? Where is this motherfucker Wilson?"

"He moved out. I swear. His room's empty. You can check."

"What kind of car does he drive?"

"Blue Acura."

"Do you know the license number?"

Glenn shook his head. "He got no license. He just bought it."

The man released Glenn, who stood, his face flushed, his pants wet.

"I should shoot him," the short man said.

"Maybe, but I think this fat clerk has seen the light of day. You'll help us now, won't you?" The tall man took a pen off the counter and wrote a phone number on a slip of paper. "We'll be back soon. In the meantime, if you should hear from Wilson or Sommers, you call us, understand? If we find out you tipped him off—"

"Oh, fuck it," and the short man fired two rounds into Glenn's chest. "He said he moved out. If he is around here, this fuck would tip him off anyway. Let's get the hell out of here, Evgeniy. We'll find him ourselves."

"Wait. Maybe the cops can help us out." Evgeniy retrieved his slip of paper, put it in his pocket, and drew a circle in the register book around the name of Eugene Wilson. Then he laid the open book on the Glenn's arm. "They find this dead guy, they see the register, and they want to know why Wilson's name is circled. Maybe they lead us to him, maybe they arrest him. They got better resources than we do."

"And if they arrest him . . ."

"We can pay him a visit in the jail."

FIFTY-TWO

• • •

T HE SUN ROSE OVER the tops of the Old City towers and warmed the balcony on which Liam and Kayla were having breakfast. "So, what time are we heading back to Hebron today?"

Kayla shook her head. "Fakhir's son said he wouldn't be in for two more days. There's no reason to go before that."

Liam leaned forward and talked softly. "If you can get a van, and maybe one other guy, I can grab Sophie on her way home from school. I've been thinking about it. The street's wide-open. Five blocks from al-Zahani's. Only one man comes to walk her home. We'd have the element of surprise and we can get her back to Jerusalem before they know what's going on."

Kayla delicately poked her fork into a slice of melon. She did not look up or respond.

"Did you hear me? I can get her. This is a simple operation. I just need someone to detain the bodyguard. You've got friends in Hebron, friends with assault rifles who like to stop people and ask for IDs. Maybe take them in for questioning. We get Sophie, she goes home to her aunt, and the threat of paying millions to terrorists is over."

Kayla's eyes were focused on her plate of fruit. She pushed the slices around with her fork. Finally, she raised her face. "We can't do that. We have to let this play out."

"What?"

"It's too soon to break the operation."

Liam put his fork down. "I should have figured. Damn it, Kayla, we can rescue that girl."

She put her napkin on the table, walked to the railing, and pointed to the city. "Look, Liam, there's almost a million people out there. And somewhere in Hebron, there's a terrorist ring planning a horrible act. We don't know all the members or what they're planning. How and when will they strike? Is it already in place and are they just waiting for the okay? Where will the strike be? Sophie gives us a reason to get close to them. She opens a door into the organization. She gets us inside the walls. If we pick her up now, snatch her off the streets, we'll lose any chance at further dialogue. And they'll realize you weren't just some PI from Chicago."

"Just some PI?"

"They'll know the Agency's involved. We'll likely force the group further underground. We'll never learn who they are or what their plans are until it's too late."

"So, it's never been about the money or the girl. You're just using me to get close to the terrorists."

"Not true, it's also about the money and we do care about the girl. But don't you see? There's a jihadist cell planning a deadly operation and I can't let it go down. Look out there." She waved her arm across the horizon. "There are thousands and thousands of innocent people going about their daily business. Women, children, tourists, Muslims, Jews. Whatever al-Zahani's group is planning will endanger all their lives, and I don't know enough to stop it."

"How do you know, Kayla? How do you know this group is planning anything at all? How do you know they're not meeting to play checkers?"

"Because they've done it before. This very group of bastards has killed innocent people before." Kayla's voice caught in her throat. "And I need for them to pay for what they've done."

"You can't make this personal, Kayla."

Kayla clenched her fists. "Personal? Are you serious? Mass murderers killing innocent people indiscriminately are personal to me and should be to you as well. Terror for the sake of terror, in furtherance of a political agenda, is personal to me. Murder behind a pretense of holy war is personal to me and should be to anyone. And it isn't only what they're doing to their enemies, the so-called infidels or settlers, it's what they're doing to their own people, the millions of Palestinians who deserve better, like the folks we saw at lunch. It should make you incensed. Everyone should be outraged until there are no more terrorists."

She turned and faced Liam. "Israel is a speck of land. Take away the Negev Desert and it's half the size of Vermont. You could fit ninety Israels into Saudi Arabia alone. It's a jewel in the desert and they had no part in building it. Yet it sticks in their craw. These Islamist militants, these jihadists, they just can't let it be. And there won't be peace, Liam, because they don't want peace. They want this jewel. They want to loot it, demolish it, and eradicate it, until there is no more State of Israel. No more Jewish homeland. And what would be next for them? Peace? Not a chance. In this part of the world, civil war always follows so-called liberation. Look at Egypt. Look at Iraq. Look at Syria. Lebanon. Yemen. This entire region will be a battleground, and maybe that suits the Sons of Canaan just fine."

She grabbed Liam's arm. "I need you to play out your role as a private investigator trying to set up a ransom for the release of your client's daughter. Your cover is the perfect excuse to get close to al-Zahani. And not just al-Zahani, but whoever is the mastermind. It gets us inside the walls. But it serves your quest as well, because you'll get closer to Sommers. I believe your assignment was to recover the money?"

"As you may remember, thanks to you, my assignment was broadened."

Liam's cell phone buzzed in his pocket. He looked at the number and nodded.

"Mr. Taggart. This is Jamal Abu Hammad. I have some interesting artifacts from Hebron I'd like to show you."

"I can be there in half an hour." Liam looked at Kayla and raised his eyebrows. "Abu Hammad. He's learned something."

FIFTY-THREE

• • •

DANI AWOKE ON A hospital bed with an IV in his arm, hooked up to a patient monitor measuring his heart rate, respiration, oxygen, blood pressure, and temperature. He pulled at his blue hospital gown, tied in the back. A nurse sat beside the bed.

"Wh-where am I?"

"You're at the clinic." She smiled brightly. "Dr. al-Zahani said you fainted and he brought you here. You were very dehydrated so we're giving you liquids."

"I don't remember that. When can I go home?"

She smiled and smoothed his covers. "The doctor will be here soon."

A few minutes later, al-Zahani walked in. "Well, how's the patient doing?" he said to them both.

"I think he feels better," said the nurse.

"I'm fine. How did I get here? I need to go home."

Al-Zahani sat on the corner of the bed. "Dani, the best we can tell, you have a bad case of the flu. You fainted at the apartment and were quite dehydrated. Don't you remember?"

He shook his head. "I remember walking to the apartment, but that's all. My mother doesn't want me to . . ."

"We know that, son. It's quite all right. You told us before you fainted. You had a fever of one hundred and two, which we have managed to bring down. Has anyone else in your family been ill?"

Dani shook his head. "No, I don't think so. My mom said she didn't want me to . . ."

"We know. You already told us. It's fine." Al-Zahani patted Dani on the arm. "We'll give the honor to someone else. When you're better, you'll come back and guard the door. You can go home in a little while, after we finish hydrating you, but I want you to keep an eye on how you feel. If you start feeling bad again, I want you to call me right away. Okay?"

"Sure, Doctor. Thanks."

Just then, al-Zahani's cell phone buzzed.

"She's gone, Arif, Lubannah said in a hurried, hysterical voice. "Bashir went to her room to take her to madrassa and she wasn't there. We looked all over the house. She's gone. She's not here. Oh, I'm so worried."

"She's not gone, Lubannah. She's just hiding in the house somewhere."

"You're wrong, Arif. Her stuffed bear is also missing. She took it with her. She's run away, I tell you."

"Stop crying, woman. Put Bashir on the phone."

Al-Zahani could hear Lubannah's footsteps, her calls for Bashir, her intermittent sobs. "Oh, my little one, my little Sophie," she cried.

Al-Zahani shook his head.

"Yes, *Sayyid,*" Bashir said.

"Are the gates closed?"

"Yes, *Sayyid.*"

"Have they been closed all morning?"

"Since you left, sir."

"Has the wall fallen down?"

"No, of course not."

"Then she's still there. Find her, Bashir. Make certain she does not go into the laboratory. Post a guard at the lab door. Immediately. Then search the grounds."

"Yes, *Sayyid.*"

"I will be home later."

"Shall I call you when I find her?"

"No. Just put her in her room and lock the door. I'll deal with her when I get home."

"Madame al-Zahani has asked if you are coming directly home."

"Tell her no. I have important appointments all afternoon."

FIFTY-FOUR

· · ·

ABU HAMMAD HELD THE cup to his lips and inhaled
the vapors of the tea. "As I had promised you, I put out a
fishing line to see what I could catch. I let it be known that
I heard a man was willing to pay a royal sum for the little girl's return to her father. It did not take long for the comment to make its
way to Fakhir, the baker, which did not surprise me. I know him
to be one of Arif's close associates. Fakhir called on me last night.
Of course, I could only tell him what I had heard, a pure rumor,
you understand. Nothing more. Millions of dollars for the return
of a child. Who knows if such a thing is true? Fakhir laughed it
off. I, myself, pretended to laugh as well and retired for the night.

"Early this morning, Fakhir walks into my shop." Jamal pointed
his arthritic finger. "He sits right there. He says, 'I have also heard
rumors, Jamal, about five million dollars.' I say, 'Why do you tell
me this?' He shrugs. 'You say you heard rumors. I pass along further rumors, that's all,' he says. 'People say, if we are to believe the
rumors, if a father loves his daughter so much, he would come to
Hebron himself and bring five million dollars. Not merely make
rumors on the street. That is the only way a man like Arif would
even consider returning a little girl. And such a transfer should
never be a public event or involve strangers. No one could ever expect a man like Arif to hand his precious little granddaughter over
to anyone but the father himself. Alone. It would surely be too trau-
matic for the little one to have others involved. Pure rumors, you
understand, but that is what I have heard.'"

Liam stared quizzically. "You believe him?"

"Do I believe that Arif gave that message to Fakhir? Yes. Do I believe he intends to relinquish the girl? No."

"Al-Zahani insists that Sommers bring him the money alone? Does he expect Sommers to walk down the streets of Hebron with a wheelbarrow full of money?"

A deep laugh resonated from Abu Hammad's chest. "It is a question I raised myself. Fakhir responded that the details can always be worked out between reasonable men."

Liam stood to leave. "Sounds like Sommers would be headed to the gunfight at OK Corral."

Abu Hammad shook his head. "Is that a movie?"

"It is. An old cowboy movie with Burt Lancaster and Kirk Douglas."

Jamal smiled. "*Old* is a relative term in this store. But I will look for it on Amazon." Abu Hammad held the door for Liam. "It should go without much more discourse that Arif cannot be trusted."

"Understood."

Abu Hammad reached for Liam's hand, placed a small, dark coin in his palm, and closed Liam's fingers around it. "This is a Judean coin, almost as old as these hills."

Liam examined the beaten and misshapen disk, a chalice on one side and a tree on the other. "Thank you."

"May the branches of the olive signal peace for this troubled land and may we all drink sweet wine from the cup when it arrives. Godspeed, my friend." Jamal watched Liam leave, then closed and locked his shop door.

Back at the hotel, Liam explained his visit to Kayla. "Abu Hammad told me that al-Zahani wants five million dollars in exchange for Sophie."

"Wants? There was never a deal in place? Strange. Sommers embezzles the money two months ago, and there's still no deal? What was this whole embezzlement thing about if not to ransom Sophie?"

Liam shrugged. "Maybe Sommers was just a pawn."

"Evidently. But the money is somewhere, and Sommers either controls it or knows where it is. In any event, Abu Hammad has given us good news. The door is now open. What are the terms of the exchange? How and when are you supposed to deliver the money?"

"That's the tricky part. Al-Zahani will only make the exchange in Hebron directly with Sommers, who he says must come alone."

"With Sommers? Why does he care whether it's Sommers or someone else who hands over the money?"

"Well, he says it's because Sophie's so precious, he doesn't want to turn her over to anyone but her father."

"He loves her so much that he kidnaps her but will return her for five million dollars?"

"It's pretty obvious. He intends to kill Sommers and keep the money."

"No doubt. But now we have a problem. Without Sommers, we can't maintain the façade or play out the exchange. He'll know it's an Agency operation. He's not stupid. We need Sommers and we have no idea where he is."

Liam smiled smugly, a broad smile, and fluttered his eyelashes.

"You bastard." Kayla put her hands on her hips. "You know where he is. You've been holding out on me. How did you find him?"

Liam folded his arms across his chest. "Impressed, aren't you?"

"Well, yeah. Where is he?"

Liam wagged his index finger. "I found him. I call the shots."

"Agreed."

"I want this in blood. I'm the first one to make contact. I don't want to lose him. I have a job to do."

"Liam, I agree, you make the contact."

Liam nodded. "I'm pretty sure he's in Hawaii."

Kayla sighed. "So are a million other people."

"I know who he's staying with."

"And an address?"

"No, but I'm sure you spies can come up with her address."

"Then we need to return to the States and set up our trip to Hawaii. There's nothing more we can do here."

C AT, IT'S ME."

"Hi, me."

"We're coming home."

"Oh, that's fabulous. I've missed you. When do you get in?"

"I'm not sure exactly, sometime tomorrow. We leave Israel late this evening. Unfortunately, I'm coming back empty-handed. No Sophie. No money."

"Oh, I'm sorry you weren't more successful."

"Well, not so fast. We made a little headway."

"The last thing you told me was that you were going to meet with the shopkeeper. Was he able to find out anything more?"

"Quite a bit, actually. I'll tell you about it when I get home. So, how would you like to go to Hawaii?"

"Is that a trick question? When?"

"Right after I get back. I'm going to track down Sommers."

"But, Liam, I have Kelsen's deposition set for this week and I can't change it. Can't we go in two weeks?"

"No, honey, I'm sorry. I have to go right away."

"Then I'm afraid you'll have to go alone."

"Well, not exactly."

"Oh, I get it. Miss State Department gets to go to Hawaii with my fiancé."

"It's her operation, Cat. Of course she's going. Postpone the deposition and you can come with us. Lawyers change deposition dates all the time."

"I said I can't change the date," she snapped. "It's set by court order. You know what, just forget about it. Go with Miss State Department."

"She's not with the State Department. I'm not sure exactly who she's with, but she's definitely an intelligence agent. She's a spy."

"Well, that makes me much more comfortable. I suppose she's not married either, is she?"

"No, Cat, she's not married. If you're so damn worried, then postpone the deposition and come with us."

"Aren't you listening to me? I can't postpone it. It's set in stone. And who says I'm damn worried?"

"This jealousy is very unlike you."

"Really? What's like me?"

"Look, I'll be back in Chicago tomorrow. We can talk more about it then if you want."

"I don't think there's anything to talk about."

Liam paused. "All right, I'll see you tomorrow. I love you."

"See you tomorrow."

Liam hung up, took a deep breath, and walked into the lobby where Kayla was standing by their luggage. Kayla noticed he was shaking his head. "Problems?"

He shrugged. "I don't really understand women."

"Catherine?"

He nodded.

"How long have the two of you been together?"

"Oh, a long time if you go back to when we hung out in high school. But, as a couple, just about a year."

"You dated in high school?"

"No. I never had the nerve to ask her out. She was too pretty, too popular. We were just friends. Best friends, really. I was afraid to spoil that relationship by asking her out and screwing it up. Years later, we got together while working on a case."

"But now you think there're problems in your relationship?"

"I didn't think so until recently. We've had a couple of awkward conversations. Now she seems real upset about my going to Hawaii."

"Is she worried about you traveling without her? Globe-trotting with the femme fatale?"

"Is that what you are, the femme fatale?"

She smiled.

Liam shook his head again. "I don't know. Once she told me she wanted to go to Hawaii on her honeymoon."

"Are the two of you getting married?"

"I always assumed so. She brought it up the other night but I totally dropped the ball. Now she doesn't want to talk about it. I told her I'd be happy to discuss it."

"You'd discuss it? Did you ever ask her to marry you?"

"You mean, like, right out? 'Will you marry me?'"

Kayla smiled. "That's usually the way it's done."

"Not in those words. I've asked her if she wanted to talk about it."

"Very romantic." Kayla picked up her bag.

"Thanks for your incisive analysis. I told you I don't understand women."

Kayla smiled and bit her bottom lip. "Is it so hard for you to understand that your girlfriend might be jealous? I experienced a few of those Irish moves outside of al-Zahani's house, and I have to admit, there's some style there. Maybe she wants to protect her property. I'd be jealous too."

Just then, the Agency car pulled up and they loaded their luggage for the ride to the airport.

FIFTY-FIVE

· · ·

AL-ZAHANI UNLOCKED THE DOOR to Sophie's bedroom. She was sitting on her bed, rocking back and forth, clutching her bear tightly to her chest.

He sat on the edge of the bed. "Where did you go today?"

"Outside."

"Why did you hide?"

Sophie pressed her lips and looked away.

"Answer me, Sophie!"

"I want to go home," she snapped.

"You are home. This, this is your home. Are you so foolish you think you can walk across an ocean? Do you think your Jadda and I will not find you wherever you go?"

"I want my daddy, I want my home," she said defiantly.

He put out his hands and cupped her face tightly. "Listen to me. He is gone from your life. You will never see him again. Your mother, your father, they are not here for you anymore. Ever. Stop this useless pining."

"He is *not* gone," Sophie yelled. "He will find me, and when he does, you'll be sorry."

Al-Zahani slapped her on the cheek. "You will not disobey me again. You will not disrespect me or your Jadda."

The door opened and Lubannah, responding to the cries, walked a few tentative steps into the room.

"Leave us, woman," al-Zahani snapped.

Lubannah stood at the doorway. "Arif, please . . ."

"I said leave us! Now go. I will handle this."

Lubannah hung her head and left the room, shutting the door behind her.

"You will suffer punishment for what you have done, Sophie. There will be no dinner today. If you run again, I will tie you to your bed." Al-Zahani stood and looked down at her with a stern face. "Do not disobey again."

FIFTY-SIX

• • •

I TAKE IT FROM your expression that there were no further e-mails." Marcy sat behind the wheel of Jack's car outside a strip-mall Starbucks in the west Oahu town of Waipahu.

Sommers slid onto the passenger seat with his laptop. Jack had taken a room in a motel in Kaneohe since the day he learned that Glenn had visitors. Jack and Marcy were now being careful how they met up and where they went.

"Nothing. Not a word in days. Every day we drive to a different town, to a different Wi-Fi spot. Every day I get my hopes up. Now I've come to believe you were right. They gave me false information to lure me into the open."

Marcy looked at him sympathetically. "I'm sorry."

"I gotta go back to Chicago and confront these guys. I know who's involved and all the details. I know where the grapes of wrath are stored. I can put them all behind bars. They can't afford to double-cross me."

Marcy grabbed his forearm. "Jack, that's foolish. You know everything about them and what they've done. That's exactly why you can't go back. It's just what they want you to do. No one else is left to put them behind bars. But I don't understand why you need them at all. You've got the money. Find a way to make your own deal."

Sommers shook his head. "It's not as simple as that. I need these guys. They have the contacts in the Middle East."

"Jack, if you go back to Chicago, you'll get arrested, or worse, you'll get killed." She leaned over and put her arm around his shoulder. "Please don't do something stupid, Jack."

"Marcy, I'm not going to fail Sophie again. If you have any sense, you'll bow out of this right now. Get out and cut your losses. I knew when I got into this scheme that I'd probably never get away with it. Divert the money, rescue Sophie, and live happily ever after in Hawaii? Pretty far-fetched. But there was an opportunity to save Sophie. Grab it or lose it. And I kept thinking, 'We must take the current when it serves.' The tide was right for me. It was my chance and I grabbed it. I had to. The guy gave me a plan when I had none."

"But, Jack . . ."

"It was my only shot at getting my daughter out of Palestine. But, in the end I was naïve and foolish. Now I gotta go back to Chicago. I might still be able to put this deal back together."

"If you go back there, you're more likely to lose your life than put a deal back together."

"You might be right, but I have no choice. In any event, it's time for you to get out of this mess. You know I'm fond of you, Marcy, but this is the wrong time and place."

"I hope you don't mean that."

Sommers nodded and hung his head. "It was wrong for me to let you get involved. I shouldn't have kept calling you. It was purely selfish on my part."

"Selfish because you need someone?"

"Don't say that. You're not just someone," he said quietly.

"Selfish because you can't go through this alone? Because maybe you have feelings?"

He nodded. "Maybe so. But it's the wrong time for the two of us."

"Well, maybe I don't agree." She smiled. "Why don't I contact Liam Taggart? He said he could help."

Sommers shook his head. "He didn't have a solution. What can he do?"

"I don't know, he said he was going to be on the ground in Israel. It can't hurt to find out what he has in mind. Tell Deborah to text him and I'll meet him in LA."

"I can't allow you to go back to LA."

"You can't allow me? Don't I have a say in this? If I want to go to LA, I'll go to LA. There has to be some way this all works out. I'm going to help us find that way."

"No. You don't have a say in this. I was, and I still am, willing to sacrifice myself. I'm not willing to sacrifice you."

"Jack, I'm going to LA. And you can't talk me out of it."

"You're crazy, you know that? You may be even crazier than I am." He shifted around in the car seat. "Damn you, Marcy."

The two sat silently in the car staring at each other. Finally, Jack said, "You're a good friend and I'm lucky to have you on my side. The only thing I can figure is that the Fates must have been looking down and seen this poor sap sitting in a ratty motel room in Honolulu burying his troubles in a bottle of Scotch. 'Boy, has life fucked him over,' the Fates must have said. 'It must be time to give this guy a break.' So they dangled this travel brochure in my face with a picture of McDuffy's-by-the-Sea. 'Why don't you drive out there for dinner?' they said. And those same Fates probably made you thirsty and whispered in your ear, 'Hey, Marcy, how about a beer at McDuffy's?' That's the only explanation for why you and I are in this car at this time." He leaned over and kissed her on the cheek. "Nothing else makes any sense to me."

"That was no kiss. Don't you give me a peck on the cheek." She cupped his face and kissed him hard. "I'll accept that theory. The Fates put us together. Now we're going to get Sophie back. And it's permissible for me to think about a future, if I want to."

"There's no future, Marcy."

"Yes, there is."

As they drove north, Jack said, "Okay, this is the deal. Whatever we do, I insist you cannot cross the line. You can go to LA, but you cannot do anything illegal. I will not let you implicate yourself criminally or become an accomplice or an accessory after the fact. Deal?"

She nodded. "Deal."

"At some point, Marcy, you just may have to cooperate and turn me in."

"That's never going to happen. I'm a Bonnie riding with my Clyde."

"I won't let you do that. You're not going down with my ship. The moment they start closing in, we separate. Promise me."

"No, I won't. Because then I'd be admitting to that possibility. There has to be a way that everything works out. I just believe it.

You're going to get Sophie back, you're going to return the money, and there won't be any charges."

"Even you don't believe that."

"Jack, I won't concede that there's a dead end. I don't know how, I just know it's going to work out. Why else would the Fates have made me thirsty?"

FIFTY-SEVEN

• • •

A BLUE-AND-WHITE TOUR BUS approached the highway checkpoint from the east. The painted logos on the side of the bus read HOLY LAND TOURS. The driver smiled as he presented his credentials to the guards. The passengers were each examined, and once the security screenings were completed, the tour bus drove on to Jerusalem and then to the Central Bus Station.

One by one the passengers alighted, each thanking the driver and the armed security guards for the wonderful, educational tour of Hebron and the Tomb of the Patriarchs. The driver expressed his deep appreciation for the gratuities from several of his passengers. Once the security personnel and the tourists had disembarked and the bus was emptied, the driver headed west to an industrial part of Jerusalem.

He pulled into an open loading dock of a one-story warehouse. The sign on the front façade read GLOBAL FISHERIES—COLD STORAGE. Once the bus was in, the overhead door was closed. Three men opened the bus's luggage compartment and unscrewed the metal floor panels. From beneath the floor, six boxes were carefully removed and carried into a refrigerated storage room. "MEDITERRANEAN MEDICAL SUPPLY COMPANY" was stenciled on the side of each of the boxes. In the storage room they were placed on a pallet alongside other similar boxes.

The driver returned to the bus, replaced the metal floor panels, and backed out of the Global Fisheries loading area. His job completed, the driver returned the bus to the yard where it would not be needed until next Tuesday's run to Hebron.

* * *

HPD CAPTAIN GRANT OKOYE handed a slip of paper to Communications Sergeant Donna Miwa. "I need an alert to go out to all eight divisions. We're looking for a guy named Eugene Wilson. DMV records show he purchased a 2008 blue Acura, license number 175 889. We want him picked up for questioning."

"What did he do, Captain?"

"I don't know that he did anything. The detectives who were investigating the Coral Reef homicide found a motel register on the chest of the dead clerk. Wilson's name was circled on the register. The deceased had his arms around the book when he got shot. There's a good chance that Wilson's name was circled for a reason. My gut tells me he must know something. I want to bring him in."

"Yes, sir. I'll put the alert out. It'll be on the screens within ten minutes."

Fifteen minutes later, two civilians, in shorts and tank tops, sitting in a black Cadillac, saw the alert on their laptop. "Thank you, Marvin," said the shorter one.

JUST AS AL-ZAHANI WAS finishing dinner, his cell phone rang. It was Fakhir.

"Arif, Dani's mother is trying to reach you. He's very sick."

"Tell her I will meet him at the clinic."

"She says he can't get out of bed."

"Then I will go to their home."

Dani and his family lived in a three-story walk-up in the center of the city. A dry cleaner's occupied the first floor, filling the hallways with tetrachloroethylene fumes. Al-Zahani covered his nose with a handkerchief as he climbed the stairs to Dani's apartment. *These people will probably die from the carcinogens in the air anyway,* he thought. Dani's mother, barefoot and in a robe, answered the door.

"Oh, thank you, thank you, Doctor, for coming here. Dani is so sick. There is blood in his stool. You can help him though, right? You can cure him? Give him medicines?"

Al-Zahani followed her into the bedroom. The stench of vomit and urine, rancid and sour, was overpowering. Dani was lying faceup on his bed, sweating profusely from a high fever and barely cognizant of his surroundings. Al-Zahani examined him carefully, stretching the boy's eyelids to peer deeply into his eyes. He wiped his burning forehead with a cloth. Dani narrowed his eyes and tried to focus. In a rasping, broken whisper, barely audible to the doctor, he said, "You did this to me, didn't you? You fucker. You did this." Finally, the doctor reached into his bag and withdrew a syringe and a bottle of morphine. He gave Dani a strong dose.

"That will help him sleep," al-Zahani said to the worried mother, wiping his hands with sanitizer. "I will have an ambulance bring him to the clinic in the morning."

As the doctor walked away from the apartment building, his cell phone buzzed again.

"Arif, Fa'iz would like to see you."

"Now? It's midnight."

"He says we are to gather at his home."

As al-Zahani pulled up to the curb outside Fa'iz's one-story stone residence, he noticed Fakhir's car and Nizar's car were parked there as well. A quiet, young woman showed him into a sitting room, where Fa'iz reclined on a pillowed couch. Nizar and Fakhir stood to either side.

"How is young Dani?" Fa'iz said.

"He will die tomorrow," al-Zahani said.

"Peace be with him."

"Why are we meeting here tonight?"

"The apartment building where we have been meeting has been closed by the health department," Fakhir said. "They say they found rats and infestation."

"It's probably true."

"It's the IDF. They know we meet," Fakhir said.

"Nonsense. The IDF doesn't condemn buildings," said Nizar with disgust.

"No matter," Fa'iz said. "We cannot meet there anymore. We must meet again in the back room of the bakery."

"My bakery? No way," Fakhir said. "The IDF—"

"The IDF, the IDF," screamed Nizar. "Why do you keep saying that? The IDF does not operate in Hebron. They know nothing. We need to meet and you have the room. I know the elegant doctor does not want us in his pristine palace," he said with a sneer.

"Enough," said Fa'iz. "We will meet at the bakery. What is the status of our shipments?"

"Three busloads have passed through," Nizar said smugly. "Aziz is doing his job. His bus is indistinguishable from the Hebrew tour bus. Aziz unloads the containers at the cold-storage center and waits until another day to bring more tourists to see the tomb. Then he returns with six other containers. Unlike the good doctor, he is right on schedule."

Fa'iz smiled and stroked his mottled beard. "Good. Very good. We will use that warehouse for our Tel Aviv and Haifa operations as well. How many of these IV units do we now have in Jerusalem?"

"Eighteen hundred and forty 1000 ml bags," Arif answered. "Most are common saline solutions, but we have also provided a number of 2.5 percent dextrose-added solutions to make sure we can satisfy the medical demands. All of the bags bear the identical imprints of Sexton International, the American health-care company that supplies Mediterranean Medical Supply, the distribution center in Jerusalem. I defy any nurse or technician to tell the difference."

"And the rest, Arif? Are we making more?"

"Of course. Forty a day. I am working on a process to increase to sixty a day. By the summer, we will have many thousands. But for our immediate needs, we will surely be ready by April sixteenth."

Fa'iz rubbed his hands together and smiled wide. "This is such good news."

"Ahmed, have you talked to Sami? Are we confident he knows his responsibility?"

"He knows. Every morning he makes his delivery run. Mediterranean gives him a printout of his route, so many units to deliver to this hospital, so many to that. He knows on April sixteenth to make the switch at the Global Fisheries. Then he will deliver Arif's bags. He'll do fine."

Fa'iz stood and reached for the hands of Fakhir and al-Zahani. He shook them hard. "From the river to the sea, my friends, from the Golan to the gulf."

"Before we leave," Fakhir said, "I have passed the ransom information on to Abu Hammad. I told him that Arif would return the girl for five million dollars."

"Did you tell him to come alone to Hebron?"

"Of course."

Fa'iz looked at al-Zahani. "Well, if he is foolish enough to come here, then it's a simple matter to dispose of him and fill our coffers with his money."

CALL FOR YOU, CAPTAIN."
"This is Okoye."

"Captain, this is Trooper Colin Watanabe. I saw your APB for Eugene Wilson. I stopped this guy Wilson a few weeks ago for speeding on Highway 99, heading for the North Shore. Blue Acura. License 175 889. I remember the guy. Straw hat. Real nervous. I gave him a warning. I'll keep an eye out for him, but you might want to alert the patrols in Hale'iwa and Waialua."

Okoye ordered his communications sergeant to amend the APB for Wilson, last seen on the North Shore, blue Acura, license 175 889. The alert was soon seen on the patrol car computer screens. And on the laptop in the black Cadillac.

FIFTY-EIGHT

• • •

MARCY HANDED THE KEYS to Jack outside the Harbor CharHouse. "You'll have to drive us home. One too many martinis for me."

Jack grinned. The ride along the North Shore that night was peaceful. It mirrored their mood. They had each other. They had a plan to contact Liam. Their luck was sure to change.

They didn't notice the sedan parked on the street near Marcy's house when they pulled into her driveway. Jack opened the passenger door for Marcy, put his arm around her shoulder, and walked with her to the front door. As they unlocked the door, they heard sounds of car doors opening and shutting. They turned and saw two figures walking toward the house. Quickly, they entered the house and locked the door.

"Did you get a look at them?" whispered Marcy.

"Not really, it's dark. A big guy got out of the driver's side."

Sommers took his phone from his pocket.

"What are you doing?"

"I'm calling 911."

"Are you crazy? You can't talk to the police. Get out of here. Go out the back door and head down to the beach."

"And leave you here? No way. I'll stall them, you go out the back door."

The doorbell rang.

"C'mon, Jack, the two of us, we can make it to the beach."

The doorbell rang again. "It doesn't matter, they found me. Run,

Marcy. Get the hell out of here." He started to press the numbers on his phone.

She slowly pulled back the draperies, just enough to get a glimpse of the front porch. "Wait. It's a man and a woman," she whispered. "Don't call yet."

"A woman can fire a gun."

"Glenn said it was two *men*." Marcy flipped on the porch lights. "It's Taggart. It's Liam Taggart."

She turned the dead bolt and swung the door open. Liam and Kayla entered the hallway. Sommers stood in the middle of the room and made no effort to move.

Marcy backed up and sat on the arm of her couch. "How did you find us?"

"Does it matter?" Liam said.

"Well, yeah, it does. Did you follow me from LA?"

Liam shook his head. "You opened your purse when you paid the bill. I saw your ID."

"You looked in my purse? You goddamn snoop."

Liam smiled and tilted his head. "I'm a private investigator. I snoop for a living."

"That doesn't mean you can look in a woman's purse. Didn't your mother teach you any manners? You violated my privacy."

"I deeply apologize. Can we move off this subject?" Gesturing toward Sommers, Liam said, "I assume this is Jack."

"Maybe," Marcy said. And are you going to introduce the person that came in with you?"

"Sorry. This is Kayla Cummings. She's a spy. We just want to talk."

"I'm not saying anything," Jack said.

"Jack, would you relax," said Marcy. "One's a private investigator and the other's a spy. They found us and they didn't bring the cops. So they've come out here for a reason and I'd like to know what it is."

"Thank you, Marcy," Liam said, still standing by the door. "May we come in?"

"I'm sorry. Now I'm the one who has no manners. Please." She gestured to the couch. "Would either of you like a soft drink or a glass of water?"

"Water for me, thank you," said Liam.

"I'll have a glass as well," Kayla said.

Marcy started for the kitchen, then stopped. "Or a beer, if you'd like."

"Now you're talking," Liam said.

"I'll stick with the water," Kayla said.

Marcy returned to the living room with a tray. She placed the drinks on the table. "Three beers and a glass of water for the spy."

Kayla pursed her lips and scolded Liam with her eyes.

With all four sitting around the coffee table, Marcy said, "To tell the truth, Mr. Taggart, I was planning on contacting Deborah to meet with you again. But now that you've discovered where we live, you go first. What do you want?"

Liam took a sip of beer, pointed his index finger at Marcy. "I like this girl, Jack. She's got spunk. She's a tough little firecracker."

"No kidding," Jack said.

Liam took another drink. "I saw Sophie."

Sommers leaned forward. "You did? Where did you see her? Did you talk to her?"

Liam shook his head. "Didn't talk to her. She's in Hebron and she appears to be fine. We saw her from a distance. She didn't know we were there."

Sommers looked at Kayla. "You went too?"

Kayla nodded. "I work for the State Department. We have a mutual interest in Arif al-Zahani."

"Why didn't you bring her back?"

Liam answered, "It's not that simple. Can we start at the beginning and have this conversation on a more organized platform?"

Jack nodded. "If you didn't go to retrieve Sophie, can you tell me why you went to Hebron?"

"We were under the impression that there was an arrangement to pay a ransom to al-Zahani for Sophie's return," Kayla said. "The US cannot allow eighty-eight million dollars, or any sum, to be paid to suspected terrorists."

"He's a terrorist?"

"We think so," Kayla said. "We think his group is planning something."

"Well," Jack said, "I also believed there was an arrangement to pay a ransom, but I'm beginning to doubt the deal was ever made."

"So are we," Liam said.

"You wasted your time coming all the way out here. I don't have any money here. You can have me arrested, but that's not going to get Kelsen his money."

"We can talk about that later. I think there's a play here and you might want to consider it."

"All I want is Sophie, and I'm not interested in talking to anyone about anything until Sophie is returned."

Marcy reached out and touched his arm. "Jack, why don't we listen to what he has to say instead of digging our heels in?"

Liam nodded and pointed his finger at Marcy again. "This girl's got common sense, Jack. You'd be smart to listen to her."

Sommers sat back in his chair. "Okay, I'm listening."

"First, I'm going to advise you that your country wants your help. That ought to tell you that there might be something in it for you. It could be a little dangerous, but it might be a way to rescue Sophie and do yourself some good."

"I don't care if it's dangerous. I'd do anything."

"I know you would. Why don't you begin by telling me how this whole embezzlement scheme began?"

Jack took a sip of his beer, set the bottle down, and drew a deep breath. "That Sunday, when Sophie didn't come home on time, I knew in the pit of my stomach they had snatched her. I immediately called the police and the FBI. I told them to alert the airports, the train stations. We put out an Amber Alert." Jack shook his head. "I don't know how they got out of the country. The FBI monitored all the flights.

"I was sure he took her back to Hebron, but as you already know, he's got quite a fortress. It's not like I could go knock on his door and take my daughter. And it's not like I could call the Hebron police and show them my court order. So I went the political route. I tried everything. Every US agency, every foreign agency. Everything. Do you understand? There was nothing I could do. I had hit a stone wall.

"Then, maybe a couple of weeks later, Dennis Harrington calls and tells me to meet him at the Rockit Bar and Grill up near

Wrigley Field. We were both working on the sale of his company, so I figured it had to do with a problem in the paperwork. He's the CFO of Kelsen Manufacturing, and my law firm was representing Kelsen. They were selling out to Leland Industries. The net profit payable to Kelsen was over ninety million dollars.

"We sat in a booth in the corner of the bar, and Harrington starts by telling me how sorry he feels that Sophie was kidnapped."

"How did he know?"

"Shit, everyone knew. There was an Amber Alert. It was on the damn TV. So, Harrington says, 'Why don't you go get her or offer the guy money to return her?' I told him that al-Zahani was very wealthy and well protected, and besides, I didn't have that kind of money.

"So we talk some more and Harrington says, 'Kelsen's such an asshole. He's been on my case for twenty years and I'm glad he's selling his company.' Then he leans over and he says quietly, 'If you help me get back at him, I can help you with your daughter.'

"It's obvious to me that Harrington wants to run some kind of scheme on Kelsen, and I'm also certain there's no way this middle-aged accountant can help me do anything to get Sophie out of Hebron. I tell him his problems with Kelsen are his business and I don't see that he's in any position to help me. He looks at his watch and says, 'Not so fast. You want your daughter, don't you? I know a guy. He's real important. He can make things happen. He's the kind of guy who can get Sophie back for you.'

"'I'm listening,' I said.

"'Give me a few minutes,' he says, and he gets up to make a phone call.

"Ten minutes later, a man walks into the bar. My first impression is, this guy is made of money. He's dressed in a camel cashmere coat, white silk scarf. He smiles, hands his coat to his driver, and slides into our booth. He's got a diamond ring on his little finger, a Patek Philippe watch, a tailored suit with a silk pocket square, and a thick Russian accent. We're in a neighborhood bar and he looks like he's sitting down for a five-hundred-dollar dinner on Michigan Avenue. He sits right next to me and orders a vodka martini, straight up.

"'I'm very sorry to hear this thing about your daughter,' he says.

'I myself have a child and I don't know what I'd do if someone tried to take him from me.' I say, 'Thank you for your concern.'"

"Did this man give you his name?" Liam asked.

"He did not, but when he left, I heard his driver call him Dmitri."

Liam turned to Kayla. "Does that mean anything to you?"

Kayla shook her head. "No."

"What else did Dmitri say to you?" asked Liam.

"Nothing to begin with. He just drank his vodka and made small talk. Then he moved the conversation to the Middle East. He told me he had just returned from Dubai. He had business interests all throughout the Middle East: Jordan, Saudi Arabia, Qatar.

"He told me it was important for his business to have discreet relationships with highly placed officials throughout the Middle East. As a result, he could get things done in Arab countries. 'Especially,' he says, 'in the lands of the Palestinians. Dennis has told me of your sad story, and I can help you. I can get your daughter back for you.'

"I said, 'How are you going to do that?'

"He smiled. He smugly tipped his head from side to side. 'It can be done.'

"'What do you want from me?' I said.

"He didn't answer directly, but he said, 'Getting your little Sophie back will be no problem for me.' He shrugged, like it was as simple as ordering a pizza. 'I can be a very good friend to you. I will talk to this al-Zahani and he will make agreement. That is what I do. I make agreements. I'm a fair man. When I propose a business transaction, it's fair. People never turn me down. Especially not some pip-squeak like this Palestinian doctor.' Then he breaks into this sardonic laugh. *Ha. Ha. Ha.*' But it isn't a laugh, it's a warning. 'And even if this al-Zahani is foolish enough to turn me down, I am certain the Palestine authorities will help me. I'm big supporter.'

"I say, 'That is very good of you. I don't know why you would offer to do this. What can I do in return?'

"He smiled and said, 'I do this partly because it is wrong to kidnap a man's child and partly because I myself need a favor.' Now the sweat starts running off my brow. I don't know what he's going to ask me to do, but I've already crossed the line. Short of murdering someone, there isn't much I wouldn't do to get Sophie back.

"'All you have to do is sign a paper,' he says. 'Nothing more.'"

"And the paper is the escrow instruction for wiring the eighty-eight million dollars?" Liam said.

"Correct."

"So, now you're in a fix," Liam said. "You do what he asks and maybe you get Sophie in return, or you refuse . . ."

"No. You can't refuse, that's not an option. Remember, no one turns him down, ha ha ha. At that point I had no choice. But, truth be told, I'd have agreed anyway if there was even a spark of hope to get Sophie. He said that Harrington would get in touch with me in a day or two with the details of the plan. With that, he raised his hand and his driver came over with his coat and the two left the bar."

"One question," Liam said. "How did you know the other man was his driver?"

"He had keys in his hand. I just assumed."

Liam nodded. "What happened next?"

"The next day, I got a call from Harrington and we set a meeting for my office. It was natural because we were busy working on the sale of his company and he was in our office a lot. It was on a Thursday. He laid out the plan to divert the Exchange loan pay-off to Panama, but he said that Dmitri wanted me to go to Panama and set up the account.

"'Me? Why me?' I said.

"'Because Dmitri thinks it will be better,' said Harrington. 'He thinks Kelsen will notice if I am gone for two days.' With that, he hands me a round-trip ticket to Panama City. I set up the account at the First Republic Bank in the name of Capital Investment Funds, Inc., spent the night at the Hilton, and came back the next day.

"I knew that I couldn't stay in Chicago after we diverted the funds, and my plans started taking shape on that long flight from Panama. If I had any chance of not getting caught right away, I would have to leave before the escrow was scheduled to pay out and the theft was discovered. I knew I'd have to move far away and tell no one where I was going, not even my sister. The funny thing is, I trusted Dmitri. I didn't fear him because I wasn't going to double-cross him. In retrospect, I was a fool, but I really believed that Dmitri would honor his promise. You know, honor among thieves.

"The farthest place I knew where I could go without using a passport was Hawaii. I'd been here three times with Alina. So I start to formulate a plan to move Sophie out to the islands. Deb would find a way to bring her out. We could stay together for a little while until I was sure Sophie was emotionally strong enough for me to leave. If I got caught, Deb would raise her. I cashed in my retirement, set up my own separate Panama accounts, and did everything so I could leave Chicago as soon as the money was wired. I thought there was a good chance for us to hide out as long as we needed to. Stupid, huh?"

Liam shrugged and nodded. "Yeah."

Jack continued. "I wanted to meet with Dmitri again, but he insisted we communicate only through Harrington. In fact, I never saw Dmitri again. I told Harrington that I needed a way to communicate with Dmitri, and we set up this private e-mail account. We'd leave messages for each other in the draft message folder. Dmitri said it might take him a month or two to get Sophie, but there would be no problem, and he'd give me updates by e-mail. The deal was closed, the money was wired to the phony account, and I left town.

"Now we know he never intended to do anything, just to trick me into stealing the money." Jack pursed his lips. "He couldn't do the heist without me, and Sophie's kidnapping provided the perfect opportunity. Guys like this rich Russian, they just seem to stumble onto dumb-ass luck. He just happened to find Jack Sommers, a guy whose daughter had been kidnapped, who was so desperate he'd do anything. And who just happened to be in control of eighty-eight million dollars."

Liam and Kayla looked at each other and nodded. "It might not have been dumb-ass luck," Liam said.

"You mean Dmitri set up the kidnapping?" Marcy said. "He's the kidnapper?"

Liam shook his head. "Al-Zahani is the kidnapper. But I think you're right, Dmitri was the guy who set it up."

"What an evil son of a bitch," Marcy snapped. "Kidnap a man's daughter to force him to steal money."

"I didn't have to do it, Marcy," Sommers said quietly. "I knew right from wrong. I jumped right into his scheme and then set up my escape. There was no reason on earth to trust this guy, but he said what I wanted to hear. And I wanted to believe him. And he knew it."

"Don't be too hard on yourself," Liam said, "I'd have done the same thing."

"Seriously?"

Liam nodded. "If it was my kid? Yeah."

"Thanks for that," Jack said, "but in the end, I was a fool. I still don't have Sophie. I lost everything I had in Chicago—my career, my reputation, my honor—and now I'm probably going to spend the next twenty years in prison. The only good that came out of any of this was reconnecting with Marcy."

Marcy walked over, put her arm around Jack, and kissed him on the cheek.

"Still, the two of you came all the way out here for nothing," Jack added, "because I don't have the money."

"Al-Zahani doesn't know that," Kayla said.

Liam smiled. "You are so right."

Sommers furrowed his brow. "I don't get it."

"Jesus, Jack, even I get it, and I'm not a spy," said Marcy. "He might be willing to return her for the money he thinks we have, am I right?"

"He's already offered. Five million dollars," Kayla said.

"And he believes I have that money?" Sommers said.

"We've told him that you do."

"All right, I'm dense," Sommers said. "A few minutes ago, you said the US cannot allow money to be paid to terrorists."

"Right," Liam said.

"But you want to make a deal to pay him five million dollars out of the money that we don't have."

"Right again," Kayla said.

"Look, I don't care how you do it, I just want Sophie out of that man's house. My sister has agreed to raise her. She's a good woman."

"There's no doubt of that," Liam said. "I met her. But I also mentioned to you earlier that there may be a play here for you. Al-Zahani has not only demanded five million dollars, he's insisting that he will only make the exchange with you. In person. In Hebron. We need this charade to go down."

"I'll do whatever you ask."

"We have to be honest with you," Kayla said. "The operation will be dangerous. Al-Zahani is part of a terrorist ring. I know for a fact that they have planned and carried out assassinations in the past. There is no reason to believe that al-Zahani intends to play this straight, and there is every reason to believe that he intends to keep Sophie and the money."

"And kill me, I understand."

"Wait, Jack," Marcy said. "You need to think about this." She squeezed his arm. "You're not an intelligence agent. You're not a soldier. You're a lawyer. You could easily wind up dead. Let *them* do this deal. Let Liam go into Hebron disguised as Jack Sommers."

Jack shook his head. "Arif knows me. It wouldn't work. I've got to do it myself."

Marcy got up and walked quickly over to Liam. Her hands were on her hips. "You said there's a 'play here.' Those were your words. What's the play? What can you do for Jack if he risks his life to catch this terrorist? What's in it for him?"

"Sophie's in it, Marcy," Jack said. "It's all about Sophie."

"Don't kid yourself," she said, focusing on Liam. "What's in it for Jack?"

Liam smiled. "I do like this girl, Jack. You've got a winner here." He turned to Kayla. "We can pitch the prosecutor, can't we? I'm sure there's a deal to be made. You can do that, right, Kayla?"

Kayla nodded. "I'll make the calls and see what can be done. I can't promise anything, but there's a good chance we can do something for you."

Marcy stood behind Sommers and held on to his shoulders. "I want Jack exonerated. Jack, don't agree to do anything until they promise to give you immunity. They need you."

Sommers patted her hand. "I can't do that, Marcy." He stood. "I'm in. Whatever you need. I'll go to Hebron, with or without a deal."

Just then, red, white, and blue lights strobed through the windows and bounced off the walls. There was a hard knock on the door. "Police. Open the door."

Liam held his hand out like a stop sign. "I'll handle this. Stay back." He opened the door for two uniformed HPD officers. They had their badges in their hands and walked into the room.

"I'm Sergeant Hanley. We're looking for Eugene Wilson. Are you Wilson?"

"No," Liam said. "What's the charge?"

"Where's Wilson? I need to see all of your IDs," Hanley said.

"I'm Wilson," Jack said, walking forward.

"You need to come with us, sir."

Kayla stepped forward and took out her wallet. "Hold on, Officer. He's in federal custody."

Hanley examined her State Department ID. "You're not a federal marshal. Do you have anything else? An arrest warrant, something showing that you have the present right to take him into custody?"

"Nothing written," she said. "We can make a call, but it's the middle of the night back in Washington."

Hanley looked at his partner and shrugged. "I'm sorry, ma'am, but unless you have something to show that you're federal law enforcement and have a right to take custody of this man, I got my orders to take him downtown for questioning in the death of Glenn Hawkins."

"He's dead?" Sommers's jaw dropped.

"Shot through the heart."

"This man is a central figure in a federal operation, Sergeant," Kayla said sternly. "I need to take him back to Chicago."

Hanley finished cuffing Jack and turned to lead him out the door. "You can pick him up later, if he's not charged."

"Are you taking him to Wahiawa?" Marcy asked.

"No, ma'am, he's going downtown. Pick him up at 801 Beretania."

Liam, Marcy, and Kayla walked outside and watched as Sommers was placed in the backseat of the HPD cruiser. A steady rain began to fall. A few houses down, a black Cadillac was parked along the curb. Its lights were off. As the cruiser pulled away from Marcy's home, the Cadillac started up and followed behind.

"Did you see that?" Liam said.

"See what?" Kayla said.

"The Cadillac. It's trailing the cruiser. Two guys in the front seat."

"Shit. We need to get downtown."

"I'm coming with you," Marcy said.

"No. You better stay here," Kayla said. "We'll call you when he's out."

"You can't stop me from going. I have my own car. The police department is open to the public and I'm the public. I'm going whether you like it or not."

Kayla looked at Liam and shrugged. "Okay. Let's go."

FIFTY-NINE

• • •

AN AMBULANCE PICKED DANI up at 11:00 A.M. He was placed on a stretcher and taken directly to the clinic. His condition had worsened significantly overnight and he was laid on the hospital bed, unconscious. Al-Zahani arrived shortly after noon. He checked Dani's vitals, said a short prayer, and administered a lethal dose of morphine. The official cause of death was listed as influenza.

THE RIDE FROM THE North Shore to Honolulu Police Department headquarters on South Beretania Street, from one side of the island to the other, took about forty-five minutes. The rain on the interstate grew stronger. At long last, a golden glow, coming from the lights of downtown Honolulu, appeared through the fog. It was almost midnight as Kayla pulled into a slot on the first level of the parking garage. In the heavy rain, Marcy's umbrella was barely large enough for three to share. As they turned the corner, Liam tapped Kayla's arm. "There. On the street ahead. It's the same black Cadillac."

"The motor's running," she said. "They're waiting for Sommers to leave the building."

Inside the station, Liam asked the desk sergeant for Richard Hanley. "He's in an interview," he was told.

"Would you tell him that Liam Taggart, one of the people he spoke to earlier this evening in Hale'iwa, thinks that the sergeant may have been followed? The car I saw trailing him is sitting outside. Tell him it has something to do with the case he's investigating, and the guys in the car are dangerous."

A few minutes later, Hanley came into the waiting area. His shirtsleeves were rolled up. He had a pencil tucked onto his right ear. "Mr. Sommers is not going to be released tonight," he said to the group. "I don't think that he was involved in the murder, but we've got other issues here, not the least of which is that he's pretending to be his dead brother-in-law to skip out on an Illinois warrant. So you guys can go on home."

"You were followed when you left Marcy Grant's house tonight," Liam said. "The car, a black Cadillac, is sitting across the street. There are two men in it. I would not be surprised if they are armed and waiting for Mr. Sommers to walk out the door. I would also not be surprised if they had something to do with the motel murder."

"What makes you think that?"

"Sergeant," Kayla said, "the Illinois warrants you mentioned were issued in connection with an embezzlement. Two other men who were involved in the crime have been murdered. The clerk at the Honolulu motel where Sommers was living was murdered. We have good reason to believe that Sommers is the next target."

"Do you have prints from the motel?" Liam said.

Hanley nodded.

"Then it might be a good idea for you to take a look at the men in the car. You might find that their prints match. You got anyone here who speaks Russian?"

"Russian?"

"It might come in handy with these guys."

Hanley gathered four officers and told them to check out the black Cadillac. They left the building with weapons drawn.

Kayla said, "Sergeant, I've placed a call to the Justice Department in Washington. As I told you, Mr. Sommers is critical to a federal operation. *My* operation. I've asked for a judicial order granting me custody of Mr. Sommers for transport back to Chicago. In the meantime, he must be kept under protective custody."

"Oh, he's under custody all right. He isn't going anywhere."

"I don't want him in general population."

"Look, Ms. Cummings, until I get an order—"

Hanley's response was interrupted by the sound of gunfire on the street. He pulled out his service revolver and headed for the door with Liam close behind. One officer lay in the street. The Cadillac was gone.

"They opened fire," an officer said to Hanley. "We approached from both sides. A guy popped out the passenger door with an automatic weapon. He sprayed the street and the Caddy took off. I called in the plates. Adam's down."

By this time, several officers and paramedics had gathered. Sirens wailed from the south.

"Sergeant," Kayla said. "Do you think you might keep Sommers in a secure area tonight?"

He nodded.

SIXTY

• • •

LUBANNAH ENTERED THE LIBRARY where al-Zahani sat reading his paper. "Arif, the little one is so upset tonight. Jamila will not play with her."

"I spoke to Hassan. I could not change his mind. He is a small-minded, bigoted man. To him, she is an American Jew, and they are all evil. He will not see the good in Sophie. He won't give her a chance. He says Sophie will corrupt his daughter with blasphemous talk. I told him that is nonsense, that she is of our blood, but he is filled with hate of America. Nothing more can be done."

"I am very sorry, Arif. Playing with Jamila was the one thing that brightened Sophie's day. It was the only thing that brought her out of her shell. Now she just sobs and looks out the window."

"She'll have to get over Jamila. We'll find her another playmate."

Lubannah looked sternly at al-Zahani. "That's not the only reason she's upset tonight and you know it."

Al-Zahani shrugged.

"She's upset because it's bedtime and she can't find her stuffed animal, her Sweetness."

Al-Zahani nodded and kept reading.

She raised her voice. "Arif. Do you know where it is?"

"Where what is?"

"The bear. Sophie's little bear. Have you seen it?"

"Why is that important? The madrassa, her studies, those are important. Teaching her the history of our people, helping her to take her rightful place, that's important. And where are you in all

this, Lubannah? What are you doing to educate her? Are you helping her to become what she can be—a leader in our struggle? Or
will she be just another silly woman buying produce at the mar-
kets? Are you teaching her, Lubannah, or are you leaving it all to
me? That stuffed animal is a crutch; it's an anchor to her past. I told
you we should have thrown it out when we first got here. I'll hear
no more of this bear."

"You took it, didn't you? Despite my wishes, you took the
bear from her."

Arif stood. "And what if I did?"

"How dare you," Lubannah yelled with her hands on her hips.

Arif shook his head in disgust, stood, and flipped the back of
his hand in a gesture of dismissal. "Woman, don't ever raise your
voice to me. Pay attention to your duties. The house should be
cleaner. It shames me."

He checked his cell phone, turned, and walked toward the door.
"I'm going out. I have important business tonight. Don't wait up."

THE GROUP OF TEN had resumed its meetings in the back
of the Breadstone Bakery. To soothe Fakhir's anxiety, each of
the participants arrived at different times, from different directions.
No one parked in front of the store.

"We are now eight days away from our first mission of glory,"
Fa'iz said proudly. "Does anything remain undone? Are we still
processing bags?"

"We are," al-Zahani answered. "Forty a day, and we will keep
on doing so until next week. We have nearly two thousand, all
safely stored in our Jerusalem warehouse."

"I think we should shut down," Fakhir said. "We have enough.
How much more impact will an additional three hundred bags
make? What if Aziz is detained? What if Arif's laboratory is discovered? We have been fortunate so far, why chance it?"

Fa'iz leaned back on the couch, his hands crossed on his abdomen. "Perhaps we should consider Fakhir's suggestion."

"Fakhir is a coward," Nizar said. "He's afraid of his shadow.
How many times have we heard him scream, 'The IDF'? He just
doesn't want us to meet in his bakery anymore."

"Nizar is quick to call names," al-Zahani said, "but here I agree with him. I'm in the middle of production. I can stop, but three hundred more victims, three hundred more wailing, mortified families begging Israel to concede the land and stop the occupation? That has great value. Twenty-three hundred dead enemies will certainly be regarded as the most glorious jihadist victory since the Twin Towers. And right in the heart of our enemy. Do not fear the discovery of my lab. I have wired it for destruction. If necessary, I can instantly firebomb the building and obliterate all remnants of our operation."

"But we are close to the deadline, and is two thousand so different from twenty-three hundred that we should risk discovery?" Rami said. "Why chance an unforeseen accident exposing the plan? I can go along with Fakhir."

"And you, Ahmed?" Fa'iz said.

He nodded. "Fakhir is wise. We are well positioned at this time. Arif can use the surplus bags for Tel Aviv."

"I, too, believe we should shut down," Fa'iz said. "Let us just concentrate on Sami's deliveries. We'll meet again on Monday." He reached for their hands. "From the river to the sea, from the Golan to the Gulf."

I N A WHITE MINIVAN, parked on a corner near the bakery, two members of a specialized unit had listened to the discussion. Through a concealed aperture, pictures of the group were taken as they left the bakery.

"Bags of what?" one of the men said. "Two thousand bags safely in a warehouse in Jerusalem? Sammy's deliveries? IEDs come to mind, but in a bag?"

"Chemicals?"

"I've never heard of chemical weapons dispersed from a bag," the other said. "Could be anthrax."

"Eight days. Isn't that Yom Ha'atzmaut? Whatever it is, it's pegged to happen on Independence Day."

"Well, our job is to collect the info and send it on. Let's get it off to Tel Aviv and let them figure it out."

SIXTY-ONE

. . .

I T WAS SHORTLY AFTER 10:00 A.M. when Liam and Kayla
walked into the chambers of the Honorable Nathan B. Kim on
the second floor of the Prince Kuhio Federal Building. They
were accompanied by Michael Green, the first assistant US Attorney for the District of Hawaii.

"Good morning, Your Honor," Green said. "I'm here to present
this petition for habeas corpus seeking the release of a prisoner
named John Sommers, presently held by the State of Hawaii at the
HPD jail on Beretania. With me this morning is Kayla Cummings
from the Department of State. Special Agent Harry Foster is available by telephone. Both of them are prepared to provide testimony
that Sommers is an essential participant in a classified US operation
in the Middle East."

Judge Kim read through the petition and set it down on his
desk. "Your petition states that he is being held because of an outstanding warrant from Illinois. What are the pending charges?"

"Embezzlement. Theft. Possible implication in two homicides."

"Let me hear from the Department of State," Judge Kim said.

Kayla stepped forward. "Mr. Sommers has a child who has been
kidnapped by her grandfather and taken to the city of Hebron,
which is located in the Palestinian territories. The grandfather is a
suspected terrorist and is thought to be involved in an impending
jihadist operation. Sommers was induced to participate in an embezzlement scheme in a misguided effort to rescue his daughter.
The State Department intends to use Sommers and a feigned

ransom as a way of getting into the jihadist base to foil the operation. And we hope to rescue his daughter as well. It's very dangerous, but Sommers has agreed to do it."

"How much money is he alleged to have embezzled?"

"Eighty-eight million dollars."

Judge Kim gave a low whistle. "And you say there are two homicides he's involved with?"

"There's no evidence he even knew about the homicides," Liam said.

Kayla nodded. "It appears that Sommers was manipulated and induced to participate in an intricate fraud to misappropriate eighty-eight million dollars from an escrow account. We think that the mastermind of this scheme, a man named Dmitri, arranged for the kidnapping. He then promised Sommers he'd secure his daughter's return if Sommers would divert the escrow proceeds. Two of the other participants have been killed and we believe that Sommers is the next target. We're very concerned about his safety."

"And there is no way of penetrating the terrorist ring without Sommers?"

"No, sir."

"Well, as to this habeas petition, we're not dealing with an unlawful detention. There is a warrant outstanding, I can't just release him. But I can remand him to the custody of the Department of State to be returned to the State of Illinois when the operation is concluded."

"That'll work," she said.

"What does the State of Illinois have to say about all this?"

"Mr. Foster has met with the Cook County State's Attorney, who does not raise an objection to the release. Although there are no promises, Illinois has agreed to consider Mr. Sommers's cooperation when the overseas operation is concluded," Kayla said. "But as of today, there are no leniency agreements in place."

The judge picked up his telephone and asked his clerk to send in the court reporter. "We need to make a proper record before I sign this order. Let's get Mr. Foster on the phone. Each of you will supply the sworn testimony, Ms. Cummings."

One hour after they had entered the federal building, Kayla and

Liam walked out into the warmth of the morning sun. The morning mist that had covered the island when they arrived at the courthouse had burned away.

Marcy, who had been sitting on a bench in front of the building, jumped to her feet. "Did you get it?"

"Sure did," Kayla answered. "A signed court order demanding that Jack be immediately released into my custody."

They quickly covered the five blocks to the police station, where they asked for Sergeant Hanley.

"Doesn't come in till tonight," the desk sergeant said.

Kayla produced the court order and placed it on the counter. "This is an order to take immediate custody of John Sommers. He was brought in last night."

The sergeant nodded and took the order back into a windowed office. Several minutes passed. Finally, a man in a blue suit, open collar, and loosened tie shuffled out of the back office and walked over with the order in his hand. "I'm Captain Nelson. We don't have a John Sommers here. In fact, all the guys who came in last night were sent over to bond court this morning, except for one."

"Who's the one?" Liam said.

"Eugene Wilson."

"That's John Sommers. Eugene Wilson is John Sommers."

"Well, he was booked as Eugene Wilson and he was sent over to Oahu Correctional this morning awaiting extradition. There's note that he has an Illinois warrant outstanding under an alias. There'll be no bond for him."

"I have an order placing him in my custody," Kayla said. "Will you please go get him? Send a car?"

Nelson shook his head. "He's in DOC custody. You'll have to take your order over to the warden. There's nothing I can do for you."

"Could you at least make a call? Have him brought to the front office? I'm worried about his safety."

"Warden Jennings is a tough guy. He won't listen to me. Just go on up there. Show him your order."

"Where's the prison?"

"Up on Kamehameha, not too far. Don't worry though, Sommers isn't going anywhere. He'll still be there."

"Captain, this man is crucial to a State Department operation," Kayla said, showing him her ID. "There are people who don't want him to cooperate with us, people who want him dead. He has to be protected. You've got to go get him."

"I'm sorry, ma'am. That's way above my pay grade. I don't tell wardens what to do."

"A federal judge does," Kayla said.

"Yes, he does. So go get a federal marshal or take that order up there yourself, it's just a few blocks away."

"One more thing," Liam said. "What happened to the officer who got shot last night?"

"He'll be okay. He was shot in the leg."

"Did they catch the guys who shot him?"

The captain shook his head. "Nope. Not yet. They ditched their car up at the Convention Center. The security cameras showed them splitting up and running off in different directions. But they were driving a rental car and paid for it with a credit card. We got a few leads. We'll catch 'em." He smiled.

"Liam, they'll try to get to Sommers at the jail. He could be dead before we get there," Kayla said.

"Captain," Liam said, "the guys who shot your officer last night were waiting for Sommers to leave the building. For all I know, they may have people on the inside of the prison who'll take care of business for them. Can you help me get him segregated?"

"I'll call, but Warden Jennings runs things his way. He doesn't like interference."

OUR FLIGHT TO OSAKA leaves in thirty minutes. We've already checked in," the tall man said into his cell phone.

"That's good. Good. From there you can make it safely to Moscow. Are you sure everything is taken care of?"

"Without a doubt. Yuri knows his assignment. He will not let you down. He was arrested three days ago, and, of course, he did not try to make bond. At visiting hour this morning, he told us he would take care of the matter in the yard or at midday meal. There are always fights."

"I will provide a lawyer for Yuri. He will bond out, he's only charged with theft. He will soon join us. Your loyalty will be rewarded, Evgeniy, I will see you later this month in Moscow." The line went dead.

Evgeniy put the cell phone in his pocket and tugged at the sleeve of his companion. "Come along, Gregor, our flight is boarding. We're going home. Dmitri is proud of us."

SIXTY-TWO

• • •

SINCE ARRIVING AT THE prison in the early-morning
hours, Sommers had settled into the corner of his cell, cross-
legged on the floor. The cell had six beds and six mattresses,
but a 350-pound Samoan had taken three of the mattresses for
himself. Sommers, discreetly choosing not to argue the point,
took his place in the corner, pondering all of the possibilities and
praying that Liam and Kayla would somehow find a way to get him
released. At 8:30 A.M., the doors on his cellblock clanged open and
the prisoners were allowed to mingle on the block. The noise, the
level of shouting, the clanging on the bars, was both insufferable and
terrifying. Sommers remained in his cell, sitting in the corner, with
Sophie haunting his thoughts.

At 11:50, his wing was assembled and led to the dining hall for
lunch. Most of the men at his table were loud, boisterous, and even
lighthearted, the incongruity of which Sommers found unsettling.
As he sat with his lunch tray, Sommers felt eyes on him. A tall,
muscular man with buzz-cut, widow's-peaked hair, and a crescent
scar on his right cheek, sitting two tables away, was staring at him.
Sommers kept averting his eyes, but from time to time he'd take a
quick check. There was no doubt. The man continued to glare.
Sommers felt vulnerable and longed for the seclusion of his cell.

A heavy man to his right, with tattoos covering both of his hairy
arms, pointed at the plate of SPAM and greens that sat before
Sommers. "You gonna eat that?" he said in a low voice. Sommers
shook his head and pushed the plate to the side, leaving only his

juice and the crackers that came with his meal. The man with the scar never took his eyes off him.

A bell rang and the lunch crowd stood in unison. They made a quick turn toward the aisle and shuffled forward. The man with the scar was gone.

Liam, Kayla, and Marcy arrived at the prison just after noon. The warden, a hefty man, in his midfifties, was in his office and about to leave for a meeting with the lieutenant governor. "How can I help you, miss?"

Kayla handed the order to the warden. "We're here to take custody of John Sommers, also known as Eugene Wilson."

Warden Jennings spent a long time studying the paper, making twisting movements with his lips. "All in good time. Eugene Wilson was brought in early this morning. He may still be in processing."

Warden Jennings sat behind a broad desk of polished koa. Flags of the United States and the State of Hawaii were perched in stands on either side. A framed picture of Jennings and the governor, in their Bermuda shorts on the first tee of Waialae Country Club, sat on the corner of his desk. He picked up his phone, said a few words, listened, nodded, shrugged his shoulders, and ended with "I'll let them know." He looked across his desk. "His wing's at lunch. He'll be back in his cell in about forty minutes."

"Will you have him brought up here immediately, please?" Kayla said. "There is good reason to believe he could be attacked in a group setting. It might be a mistake to let him go to lunch."

The warden shook his head. "Listen, young lady, I have a prison to run here. And we're pretty careful about mistakes. I don't like your insinuations. Besides, it's easier for us to bring him from his cell than to have one of my guards take him from a lunch table."

"There'll be a lot of unhappy people in Washington if anything happens to John Sommers," Liam said.

The warden leaned over his desk. "Are you threatening me, Mr. Taggart? Was that a threat? I don't answer to people in Washington. I answer to the people of the state of Hawaii and the governor who appointed me." The warden sat back in his chair and smiled. "When Mr. Sommers finishes his lunch and he's marched back to his cell, and if there's a guard available that can be spared from his duties, I will consider having him brought up front."

The warden stood and hitched up his trousers. He took his suit jacket from the hook behind the door and slipped it on, checking his appearance in his mirror. "Now, if you ladies and gentleman will wait on the chairs outside by Ms. Figgens, I have to leave for an important policy meeting with Lieutenant Governor Duncans. I'll take care of this matter when I return."

As they walked through the office doorway, a buzzer alarm sounded. The warden quickly grabbed a phone. He listened and looked sheepishly at Liam. "There's been an incident in the lunch hall. Your man's been injured. Apparently, he was involved in a fight. They're taking him to the infirmary."

"Son of a bitch," Liam said.

"Just one minute, son. Who the fuck do you think—"

Before he could finish, Kayla dialed Judge Kim on her cellphone. She spoke a few words and handed the phone to Jennings.

"Yes, sir, I understand," said the warden saccharinely. "Of course, Your Honor, we're taking all immediate steps to comply with your order. This young lady has only been here a few minutes and we are already in the process of having the prisoner rushed to my office. But, unfortunately, before I could act, there was an incident. Mr. Sommers got himself involved in an altercation and he was stabbed by an unknown assailant. We're taking him to the infirmary."

"The hell you are," Kayla interrupted. "He's in my custody. You get an ambulance here. Now! He's going to a hospital."

"Well, Your Honor," Jennings said smugly into the phone, "it seems like my responsibilities are concluded. The young lady says she's going to take custody of Mr. Sommers and have him brought to a hospital. I want you to know that we are terminating our protective custody of this man. He is no longer in the care of the Department of Corrections."

Five minutes later, paramedics arrived and were directed into the facility where Sommers lay bleeding. They wheeled him out on a stretcher and into the EMS van. Bandages on his back and left side were turning red. Oxygen and fluids were being administered. Jack gazed weakly at Marcy, who frantically scrambled up into the van to sit beside him. She grabbed Sommers's hand and squeezed. "Hang on, Jack. Be strong. There's a lot for us to do."

"Sophie," Jack said softly. "You must . . ." He swallowed. "You must . . ."

"I'll get her, Jack. Whatever I need to do. You can count on it."

Sommers was rushed to the Queen's Medical Center and wheeled into the emergency room. When Liam and Kayla arrived, Marcy told them that a surgical team was already at work. Hours went by. They paced the waiting room, intermittently strolling by the receptionist to ask if she had any news. They stared blankly at the little TV hanging from the ceiling. They fed money into the vending machines. They fidgeted.

Finally, a young doctor came out and the group scrambled to encircle him. "He's hanging in there. Good thing you got him here quickly. He wouldn't have lasted much longer. Of course, his condition is critical. His vital signs are not yet stable, but I would not say his indicators are necessarily unfavorable."

"Doctor," Marcy said and shrugged, "what does that mean?"

"His injuries were very serious and he required a lot of repair. We're hopeful, but he's not out of the woods yet. In some ways, he was very lucky. He was stabbed with a narrow knife. There are three entry points. Two on his back and one on his side. Although they caused damage, none of his vital organs was beyond repair. How well they'll heal remains to be seen. If he stabilizes, as I hope he will, he'll need rest, medications, fluids. He'll probably be here for quite a while."

"What's quite a while?" Kayla asked.

"Oh, it could be weeks. There's organ damage, muscle damage. Walking without assistance will be out of the question for at least four weeks. Given his injuries, I expect a considerable rehab period."

"I don't think we have that much time," Kayla said. "I may have to move him."

The doctor shook his head. "I don't know what you have in mind, but he can't be moved."

"No, Doctor, the question is, how *soon* can he be moved?" she said firmly.

"You mean if he survives?"

"What's wrong with you?" Marcy snapped at Kayla. "We're talking about Jack's life. Don't you care anything about his life?"

"His life and many, many more, Marcy. He may be our only hope of diverting a catastrophe."

"You can't move this man," the doctor said. "And that's final. Who's his next of kin?"

"He has a sister in Louisville," Marcy said.

"As of right now, this court order makes me his next of kin," Kayla said. "I'll decide when and if he should be moved."

"You bitch," Marcy said.

"Calm down, Marcy. I want him alive as much as you do. Doctor, I want him to get the very best care this hospital can provide. The United States government will stand for all expenses. I want the best specialists on the island. I want you to treat this man as though he were the president of the United States. Are we clear?"

"Clear."

S O H O W L O N G *ARE* you going to be in Hawaii? With the demure Miss Cummings, I might add," Catherine said.

"Demure? You should have seen her today. She was as cuddly as a porcupine. If Sommers survives, we're going to stay here until she can move him, which I would guess will be several days. So, can I get you to fly out?"

"If Sommers survives?"

"That's what the doctor said. Stop changing the subject. Will you come out? We have some unfinished business. Can I buy you a ticket?"

"I don't know. I'm very busy. I'm really putting in some heavy hours. Let me think about it. Does Sommers know who tried to kill him?"

"No. He was standing at the lunch table when a guy came up from behind and stuck a shiv in his ribs. That's the last he remembers. HPD says the assailant's name was Yuri Porushkin, a Russian citizen here on an expired visa. He was arrested a couple of days before Sommers on a charge of breaking into a jewelry-store display case at the Westin and grabbing a handful of watches. At eight in the evening in a busy hotel."

"Sounds like he wanted to get arrested."

"That's what I think. But I want you to come out here after the deposition."

"Liam, the only thing on my mind right now is Victor Kelsen's depo tomorrow. If you think you'll be there for a while, I'll think about it. But no promises."

"I think if Kayla had her way, she'd bring him to Hebron tomorrow, but the doctors won't let her move him. I'm sure we'll be here for some time."

"Liam, did you say the assailant was a Russian named Yuri Porushkin?"

"Yes."

"They're sure he's a Russian?"

"That's what they said, on an expired visa. It seems like the Russians are all over this. Sommers told us that he and Harrington made the deal to steal Kelsen's money at a bar in Wrigleyville with a Russian named Dmitri. Dmitri has contacts in the Middle East and was supposed to set up the ransom—Sophie's release in exchange for some of the embezzled money. And the motel clerk, before he caught a bullet in the chest, said that the men who came looking for Sommers spoke with a Russian accent."

"Liam, Kelsen's connected to Dmitri."

"How do you know that?"

"I can't tell you. But Kelsen, Dmitri, and a man named Evgeniy have been involved in fixing sporting events. Kelsen's in bed with the Russians. They've been working together."

"But Dmitri stole Kelsen's money."

"He doesn't seem like a very good partner, does he?"

"Do we know anything more about this Dmitri character, like where he lives and where he banks?"

"No, only the first name."

"I wonder if Kelsen suspects Dmitri's behind the embezzlement."

"I doubt it. He's certain Sommers stole the money. You should see him in court. He has to be restrained by his lawyers. He has so much rage. I doubt that he has any notion that Dmitri has his money."

"We need more information on Dmitri. What if you were to

bring up Dmitri's name a couple of times at Kelsen's deposition tomorrow? Just throw it out there? See what happens."

"Hmm. That's a great idea."

"I get 'em now and then."

"That's why we make such a good couple. We're so damn diabolical. Love you, Liam."

"Do you really think we make a good couple?"

"What? Of course I do. Why did you say that?"

"No reason. Love you too."

SIXTY-THREE

...

VICTOR KELSEN AND HIS attorney arrived at Jenkins & Fairchild's office promptly at 2:00 P.M. and took their seats around the conference table. A court reporter, her steno machine between her knees, her laptop on the desk, and her microphone in the middle of the table, sat poised to take down all of the questions, answers, and lawyers's posturing. Catherine sat at the end of the table, a legal pad and a stack of documents before her. Walter Jenkins sat to her right, his well-manicured hands folded on the table. Kelsen raised his right hand and swore to tell the truth.

"Mr. Kelsen," Catherine said, "would you please say your full name for the record?"

"Victor Wallace Kelsen."

"Are you an officer of Kelsen Manufacturing, Inc.?"

"I'm the president."

"Are you also a shareholder?"

"One hundred percent."

"What is the business of Kelsen Manufacturing?"

"You mean what was the business? We sold it."

"Very well, what was the business before you sold it?"

"We manufactured and sold packaging materials. Why does any of that matter? Where's my money?"

"Who was Dennis Harrington?"

"Kelsen Manufacturing's CFO."

"Was he involved in the sale of your company?"

Kelsen looked at his lawyer and made a face as if to say, *Is she kidding?*

"Mr. Kelsen," Catherine said, "he can't answer the questions for you. You have to answer them yourself."

"Yeah, he was involved. Of course he was involved. Maybe too involved, because he got himself killed."

"What were his responsibilities with regard to the sale of your company?"

"He was working directly with Walter Jenkins, or whoever Jenkins assigned to do the paperwork. How the hell do I know? He did what had to be done. That's why I paid him."

"And as far as you know, did Mr. Harrington review and approve all the paperwork?"

"Yeah."

"All of the loan documents?"

"Right."

"All of the financials?"

"Right."

"Because that's what you were paying him to do."

"Exactly."

"Including reviewing and approving all of the escrow paperwork?"

"Oh, I see where you're going. Mr. Sommers reviewed them too. Kelsen Manufacturing was paying exorbitant legal fees to this man over there"—Kelsen pointed a stiff finger in Jenkins's direction—"to protect us so we wouldn't be cheated out of our money." Kelsen stood up. "You were supposed to protect me, you pompous fuck. Look at him in his fancy suit. Fancy paneled office. Offers me a cigar. Goody-two-shoes asshole."

"Really, Mr. Russell," Catherine said calmly, "do you think you might control your client and remind him of the decorum of a deposition, and that these outbursts are on the record?"

Kelsen's attorney gave a small tug on Kelsen's jacket. "Sit down, Vic. There'll be plenty of time for emotion later."

"That's not good enough," Catherine said. "Mr. Kelsen, we're not in a courtroom, but according to the rules, the examination and cross-examination in a deposition are to proceed as they would at trial. For example, the same rules of perjury apply. Everything you say today is being memorialized in the stenographic record, including your abusive tirade of a moment ago. If you refuse to conduct yourself in a civil manner, I will have the court reporter transcribe this proceeding and present it to the judge with a request that you be held in contempt. Are we clear?"

Kelsen turned his head and looked out the window.

"Are we clear, Mr. Kelsen?"

He flicked his head nonchalantly. "Yeah."

"Fine. Do you claim that someone stole your company's money?"

"What are you, crazy? You know they did. Eighty-eight million. I was supposed to have a profit of ninety-six million dollars, but I only ended up with eight million dollars. Jenkins let some slimy lawyer steal the money that was supposed to pay off Exchange Bank. I had to make that payment myself out of my net profits."

"What slimy lawyer stole your money?"

"Sommers did, or he let someone else, I don't know."

"Do you have evidence that Sommers took the money?" said Catherine.

"No, but I don't have to. It was Jenkins's job to protect me."

"Was it Jenkins and Fairchild's job to protect you from yourself?"

"What are you talking about?"

"Who was Mr. Harrington's boss?"

"I was."

"I understand that Mr. Harrington went missing right after the closing and you couldn't find him, is that right?"

"Yeah. Him *and* Sommers. Both of 'em."

"Did Mr. Harrington take any of that money?"

"How the hell do I know?"

"Exactly my point. You don't know whether Mr. Harrington, Mr. Ellis, Mr. Sommers, or some other person managed to misdirect the wired funds, do you?"

"It doesn't matter. I hired Walter Jenkins. Jenkins was supposed to protect me. From all enemies, foreign and domestic."

"Interesting you should use that phrase. Speaking of foreign enemies, do you know a man named Dmitri?"

Catherine noticed that Kelsen's body twitched and he blinked hard. "Dmitri who?"

"That's what I'm asking. Do you know a man named Dmitri?"

"I know a lot of people. What's his last name?"

"How many Dmitris do you know?"

He turned to his lawyer. "Can I get a glass of water here?"

A silver pitcher sat on a tray in the middle of the table. Catherine gestured toward it. "Help yourself."

Kelsen poured a glass of water. His hand shook slightly. He took a sip and placed it down. "I don't know any Dmitri. Dmitri who? Does he go by another name, maybe?"

"I wouldn't know. Just so the record is clear, under oath, subject to penalties for perjury, you are stating that you are not acquainted with any person named Dmitri, correct?"

"Dmitri who? Dmitri who? I don't know. I meet a lot of people, maybe once I met someone named Dmitri."

"I understand, Mr. Kelsen, that you are quite the basketball fan. Is that right?"

"Does this have something to do with the money that was stolen from me? Was it stolen by a basketball player?" Kelsen laughed nervously and looked at his lawyer, who shrugged.

"I guess that all depends on your definition of *player*, doesn't it?" Catherine said.

"What does that mean?"

"Well, some might refer to people who gamble on basketball games as players."

"What are you insinuating?"

"Why, nothing at all. I just asked if you were a basketball fan. I had heard that you attend all the St. Joseph games."

"I'm not answering any stupid questions about basketball. I sued Jenkins for the money that was stolen. Ask your questions about that. You're irrelevant, immaterial, and unconstitutional."

"Did you and Dmitri bet on basketball games?"

Kelsen's face turned deep red. He screamed at his lawyer, "Russell, are you going to do something, or are you going to let her throw shit at me all afternoon?"

"Ms. Lockhart, your questions are abusive and harassing. This deposition is being conducted in bad faith, in a manner designed to embarrass and oppress the deponent. Betting on basketball? Really? Unless you confine your questions to the issues at hand, we will seek a protective order."

"This is my deposition, Mr. Russell, and I will decide which questions to ask."

"How does betting on basketball have anything to do with this case?"

"I don't see the need to educate you on my theories, Mr. Russell, but I'm sure you realize that in fraud and embezzlement cases, the claimant's financial condition is material. Accordingly, his gambling activities may very well lead to relevant information."

"You gonna let her tell you what to do?" Kelsen said to his lawyer.

"She has a point, Vic. We have to let her ask a few questions in that area. The rules don't permit me to instruct you not to answer a question on the basis of relevance." Then Russell turned to Catherine and spoke brusquely. "But we will not countenance abuse and harassment."

Catherine tapped her pencil. "Let's get back to basketball. Did you go to the St. Joe games with Dmitri?"

"No. I don't know any Dmitri, but maybe I met one once, but I don't go to games with any Dmitris."

"Are you acquainted with Darius McCord?"

Kelsen swallowed audibly. "He plays for the Deacons."

"Well, not since his injury. Have you ever met Darius McCord?"

"Probably at some booster event, I'm not sure."

"Are you acquainted with a man named Evgeniy?"

Kelsen shook his head. He reached for his glass of water but tipped it over. Catherine placed a stack of napkins on the table.

"Let's get back to Evgeniy, Mr. Kelsen. Do you know him?"

"Russell, do something, will you?" he snapped at his lawyer.

Russell shrugged. "Just answer the question, Vic. Tell her if you know a man named Evgeniy."

"I don't know any Evgeniys, I don't know any Dmitris, I don't know Darius McCord, except maybe from the basketball luncheons. I'm not answering any more of your bullshit questions."

Kelsen stood, grabbed his coat and headed for the door, but stopped before his lawyer. "Why didn't you object, Russell? That's your fucking job. Irrelevant and immaterial. Abusive and harassing. What a dogshit lawyer you are. File a petition to protect me." Kelsen stormed out of the office.

When he reached the street, Kelsen pulled out his phone. His fingers shook so badly he could barely dial. "Hello, Dmitri, Dmitri? Dammit, answer the phone. Call me back, we got serious problems. They're asking me about the games." He paused. "Fuck it, I'll see you later."

SIXTY-FOUR

• • •

MARCY SAT WITH HER stack of magazines in Room 8 of Queen's ICU. Bundles of tubes and wires hooked unconscious Jack Sommers to a panel of monitors. Doctors thought it best that he stay sedated for the first few days in order to manage the pain and reduce movement. Nevertheless, Marcy kept vigil, leaving his bedside only to grab a sandwich or to use the ladies' room.

From time to time, she'd rub his arm, wipe his brow, or hold his hand. Even though he slept soundly, she would talk to him: "It's going to be okay. You're going to pull through this. You're a fighter, the bravest man I know."

She stared at the monitors as if they were TV screens. Green heartbeats popping up and down. Sommers's breathing was slow and deep. She squeezed his hand. "Well, I sure got myself mixed up in a fine mess. Falling for my best friend's husband, who just happens to be a guy wanted by the police and the Russian mob. I can't say you didn't warn me. You said, 'Marcy get out now.' But did Marcy listen? Nope. I should have trusted my instincts and said, 'Good-bye, Jack or Eugene or whoever you're calling yourself today.' But you knew I couldn't do that, didn't you? You knew I was just as committed to rescuing Sophie as you were. But I didn't have to fall in love. That was my own doing. I should never have had that second bottle of Grenache. I think that was *my* Rubicon. Way before the Fishman wedding. Down goes Marcy."

She stood to stretch her legs and walked to the other side of the bed. "Is it totally naïve to believe that when this is over the government will clear you? Liam said there's a play for you. If the government wants your help, they're going to have to pay for it. They cut people deals all the time—immunity, pardon, clemency, whatever the hell they call it."

She wiped his brow and kissed his cheek. "So, maybe it's not so crazy to think we'll be together—you, me, Sophie. We could get a house, maybe out on the North Shore, one with a big backyard. And, of course, a piano. Maybe Sophie could have a brother. What do you think?" She kissed him again. "Liam and Kayla, I have faith in them. It's going to work out, Jack, we're going to get Sophie and we're going to make a life together." She looked at his sleeping face and smiled. "You don't have to say yes right now."

Early in the afternoon, Liam stopped in to visit Sommers. Marcy set her magazine on the table and greeted him with a hug.

"How's he doing?"

"I don't know," she said with a catch in her throat. A tear rolled down her cheek. "They're giving him a lot of drugs." She pointed to the patient monitor. "But his heartbeat is steady and his breathing is good."

Liam smiled and nodded.

"He's still listed as critical, but the doctor said he thought he was stabilizing. That's a good sign, right?"

Liam put his arm around her. "I'm sure it is. Has he been conscious at all today?"

Marcy shook her head. "They don't want him to be conscious. You know, the pain. They said maybe in a few days. Is that policeman still sitting in the hallway?"

Liam nodded. "As far as we know, the two men in the Cadillac are still at large. They tried once, they could try again."

"Where's Kayla?"

"Haven't seen her yet today. She was headed to the federal building for a meeting. Why don't you go home for a while, Marcy? Or at least take a walk. I'll stay with Jack."

Marcy smiled. "Thanks, but I'm fine. I picked up a turkey sandwich and I'm just sitting here reading. It's okay, really."

* * *

IT WAS NEARLY SUNSET when Kayla strolled into the Beach Bar at the Moana Surfrider and found Liam sitting at the far end of the veranda, where the brick pavers met the sand. He watched her approach on confident steps. The combination of the evening breeze and the diaphanous fabric caused her pastel blue sundress to hug her shapely legs and accent the contour of her stride.

"I just came from the hospital."

Liam pulled a chair over for her. "I was there earlier. Any change in his condition?"

She shook her head, and her shoulder-length black hair danced and tousled in the gusts of the evening trade winds. "No, he's pretty much the same. I spoke with his doctors. They're going to take him off sedation tomorrow."

"Tomorrow? I thought they said a few days."

Kayla leaned forward and spoke in a whispered voice. "Liam, we need him *now*. We've received disturbing news from Hebron. Whatever al-Zahani's group is planning, it's set to occur on Yom Ha'atzmaut. Nine days away. That's Israel's Independence Day, and several celebrations are scheduled. We can't let it happen."

"How do you know that?"

"The bug I placed at the bakery."

"What else do you know?"

She shook her head. "Pieces of information. Not enough to provide any clear answers. Something about two thousand bags that have been delivered to a warehouse in Jerusalem. Bags of what— we don't know. The location of the warehouse—we don't know. Initially we thought the bags would contain component parts to be assembled somewhere for a WMD. Or a bunch of IEDs. But the conspirators talked about each bag having a single victim. Three hundred extra bags would mean three hundred dead enemies, they said. And they talked about using surplus bags for a future operation in Tel Aviv."

"So you think each bag contains a single weapon?"

She nodded. "There are more bags being manufactured by al-Zahani—he said he can make forty a day—and I'm certain that it's all being done in that outbuilding in his compound."

"Do we have any intelligence that al-Zahani is a munitions expert?"

"No. He's spent his entire professional life in a white coat. Medical school, laboratories. Hospitals. But that doesn't mean he can't be supervising munitions construction."

"What about chemicals?"

"Could be, but why describe them as bags? Toxic chemicals would be dispersed from cylinders, warheads, spray tanks. And a chemical dispersion in the air or the water wouldn't focus on a single victim. The conspirators said, 'Three hundred more bags means three hundred more victims.'"

"What about biological? He's a doctor and a lab scientist. What if he's growing germs?"

"Well, we thought about that, but we've dismissed it. There are insurmountable challenges for a small Palestinian group like the Sons of Canaan to use biological weaponry. An effective dispersal mechanism, storage, a delivery medium. It'd have to be introduced through the food chain. Water supply. Even atmospheric. You don't disperse germs from a bag. All of the toxins we know about that are suitable for such a small operation would be largely ineffective. They certainly would not be thought of in terms of one bag, one victim."

"Yet, al-Zahani said he could produce forty a day?"

"Right. Forty bags. I have to get into al-Zahani's compound. I know the answers lie in that one-story building."

"Why doesn't the IDF just go in there? They can certainly manage to get through the walls of a Hebron residence. I mean, we're not talking about breaching the Kremlin."

Kayla shook her head. "He's rigged the building to explode. He said on the recording that he could instantly firebomb the building if he was attacked. And we know he's got a sophisticated security system. If an Israeli police force or Israeli soldiers were to attempt an entry by force, if they tripped the alarm, he'd detonate the building. Then we'd never know what he was producing. But it's worse than that. Two thousand devices are already sitting in a Jerusalem warehouse. The breach would only prompt the terrorists to move up the attack. We need al-Zahani alive. He knows all the players and how it's all going down." She shook her head again. "We need to get into the compound peacefully. Pretextually. For that, we need Sommers. Awake and walking. It's the only way."

"What did his doctor say?"

"What do you think? He said it's too risky to get him up. He said no traveling. What did you expect?"

"You told him to take Sommers off sedation, didn't you?"

Kayla nodded. "I had to."

"What if he doesn't make it?"

"Then you and I will have to find a way inside." Kayla stared at Liam's tumbler of Scotch. "Aren't you going to offer to buy a girl a drink?"

Liam smiled. "I'll do better than that. I'll buy her some dinner."

Liam called the server over and they ordered the catch of the day and a bottle of sauvignon blanc. A glass of wine or two, a few laughs, and some small talk later, and Kayla asked, "Did you get Catherine to come out here?"

Liam shook his head. "She said she might, but I don't think she will."

Kayla raised her eyebrows. "Jealousy, or is it something else?"

"I don't know, things aren't going as well as they should right now. Maybe it's the lawsuit. Maybe it's jealousy. Maybe she's got something on her mind. But there's no doubt she's backpedaling from where we've been. You know, acting a little standoffish? I must have pissed her off somehow."

"Then why don't you just bring her out here? The enchantment of the islands. They say it works magic on broken romances."

"To tell the truth, I think if she came out here, it'd be uncomfortable."

Kayla took a sip of wine and stared at Liam with raised eyebrows, as if to say, *Because . . . ?*

Liam squirmed a little. "You know, it's just the sense I get. Lately, when I've tried to talk seriously with her, she's backed away."

"And now you're worried about her level of commitment?"

"Well, I never was before, but maybe I am now. It's just a feeling I get. I could be wrong. Yesterday she told me we made such a good couple."

"What's wrong with that? You don't believe her?"

"No, I do think we make a good couple. But then I asked her if she really thought so and she sounded shocked and pissed and said, 'Of course.'"

Kayla scrunched her face. "Wait. She said you two made a good couple and you asked her if she *meant it*? And *you're* questioning *her* commitment?"

"I guess that was a dumb thing to say, but it just popped out. There shouldn't be any question in my mind, but there is."

"Maybe in her mind it's your commitment that's in question."

Liam poured another glass of wine for each of them. "Why? I give her no cause to doubt me. What basis does she have to feel insecure?"

"I can think of a few. You came out to Hawaii, her dream destination, with another woman, one that she sees as a rival—"

"A rival? You? Seriously?"

"Oh, thanks very much."

"I didn't mean it that way. You certainly could be anyone's rival. A smart, beautiful woman like you. It's just that I don't think . . ." He paused. "Do you really think that's it?"

"Follow me. You told me she that she had been betrayed, I think you used the word *blindsided*, by her ex-husband and his multiple affairs."

"And criminal activities."

Kayla nodded. "Now she's involved with you, an old, dear friend, one who couldn't pull the trigger when she was younger. The one man she really wanted to marry when she was young turned out to be too insecure to even ask her out."

"Now wait . . ."

"No, you wait. You've been sweethearts since high school, that's more than twenty years. And now you've been together for over a year and you still haven't popped the question. And maybe you never will. And why do you suppose that is?"

He shrugged and shook his head. "It's only been a year or so. Is that too long? I didn't want to rush her. I just never thought she was in a hurry."

"And when she put it to you directly, about the 'tide in the affairs of men'—God, what could be more direct—you told me you totally dropped the ball. So in her mind, maybe you never will marry her. Maybe it's your commitment that needs to be questioned here."

"Mine? I don't think so."

"Do you still have your apartment?"

"I do, but I stay with her most of the time. Why are you putting me through a paper shredder? I've asked her a couple of times if she wanted to have a discussion about our future."

"Oh, you romantic devil! Why didn't you offer to prepare a memorandum? You know, you could exchange deal points." Kayla smiled impishly and took a sip of wine. "Here's a clue: I don't think she's looking for discussions."

Liam nodded. "I know you're right. She told me when the time is right she wants it done with pomp and circumstance. So you think I should be more direct?"

Kayla shook her head. "No. What I think is, you need to do some self-evaluation. You need to decide if you want to marry her, and if you do, you should go out, buy her a ring, and do it right. Or quit complaining."

Liam tightened his lips and nodded pensively. He pretended to hold a microphone to his mouth and said, "Folks, we're visiting tonight with Kayla Cummings, international spy and adviser to the lovelorn."

Kayla winked. "Go buy the ring. If she turns you down, who knows, it might not be the end of the world. I might make a play for you." She smiled.

Liam reached for the check, but Kayla stopped him. "This one's on me. I've given you a hard time. I'd like you to join Harry and me for a videoconference tomorrow. I'll pick you up at three thirty."

"Okay."

"A.M."

"Three thirty in the morning?"

"Right. Israel is twelve hours ahead and we need you to call Jamal Abu Hammad." She signed the check, leaned over, gave Liam a kiss on the cheek, and turned to leave. "Good night, Irish."

Liam watched her as she walked away, her shapely silhouette sashaying in the moonlight. He took a deep breath, signaled for the server, and ordered another drink.

* * *

ATELLITE IMAGES OVER THE past month do not show any
trucks entering or leaving al-Zahani's residence," Harry said by
videoconference.

Kayla sat beside Liam and stared at grainy satellite shots of the
compound on the computer screen. "What about loading bags into
the trunk of al-Zahani's car? Or someone else's car? Maybe they
transported the bags piecemeal," she said.

"If he loaded anything into his Mercedes, we didn't catch it,"
Harry responded. "But again, anything transported to Jerusalem
in the trunk of a car would be discovered at the checkpoint."

"What about the workers? Could they take them out piece by
piece and drive them to a central location?"

Harry pursed his lips and nodded. "Well, there's a parking area
to the west of his building where the workers park their vehicles.
If they've been transporting these *bags* one at a time out of the compound, they've been pretty smart because we haven't caught it."

"So, if he's manufactured something in his building and
transported it to a central location to be stored in a Jerusalem
warehouse . . ."

"We have no idea how he did it or where it is."

"Or what it is?"

"Or what it is."

"Then we have to assume they slipped the weapons passed us."

Harry nodded. "That's the obvious conclusion. Two thousand
of them are sitting in a warehouse."

Kayla turned to Liam and put a hand on his shoulder. "It's up
to you, Irish. The answers are inside the walls. The ransom exchange
is our best chance of getting inside without risking the demolition
of the laboratory. We need to set up the exchange as soon as possible. It's four thirty P.M. in Jerusalem. Do you have Abu Hammad's
number?"

Liam fished the paper from his wallet. He reached over the desk
for the landline phone, but Kayla put her hand over the handset.
"His caller ID needs to show your cell phone."

Liam dialed Jamal's number but the call went to voice mail. "Jamal, this is Liam Taggart. I'm sitting with Jack Sommers and he
has a briefcase full of money for Dr. al-Zahani. I know it's an

imposition, but you are my only contact with the doctor. Can I ask you to put me in touch with him, or one of his friends, to arrange the exchange? Please call me back. Thank you for your help."

"So, now we wait," Kayla said.

Harry nodded. "Keep me in the loop."

Liam stood to leave and his phone buzzed. The text message said, *Booked a morning flight to Honolulu. Meet me at the airport at 3:15 P.M. Love you, Cat*. He showed the message to Kayla.

She smiled. "Don't screw this one up, Irish. I need a partner with his head on straight."

SIXTY-FIVE

• • •

T HE HOLY LAND TOURS bus pulled into the parking lot
at the Tomb of the Patriarchs as it did twice each week.
Twenty-three passengers alighted, cameras hanging from
their shoulders, guidebooks in their hands. One by one, they lined
up to go through the metal detectors and into the shrine.

Aziz smiled at each of the tourists, informing them that the bus
would depart in two hours. When the last one headed up the steps,
Aziz checked his phone and saw the following text message: *Cancel the pickup. Meet me at the corner of the plaza.*

Aziz locked his bus and made his way toward a man sitting on
a bench.

"We're not shipping any more IV bags, Aziz," al-Zahani said.

"Why not? Everything is working smoothly. I get through
the checkpoint each week without a problem."

"I know. Allah has favored us, but it is the collective decision of
the group to cease the transport of any more bags. They have decided to be extracautious. There'll be no pickup today. We will start
again in a few months."

Aziz smiled broadly. "I saw Sami yesterday. The Israelis, they
do not suspect he's one of us. They call him Sammy or Shmuel.
Mediterranean Medical Supply trusts him completely. He runs his
delivery route every day without any suspicion. On the sixteenth,
he will load his truck with Mediterranean's IV bags, bring them to
the warehouse, swap them out for ours, and complete his delivery
to the hospitals, just as we have planned. Our bags will be unloaded
and put into use before anyone discovers the difference."

"Is Sami sure he will be assigned to deliver IV bags that day?"

"Of course, Arif. They deliver IV sets to hospitals every day."

"But are we sure Sami will be assigned to deliver the IVs and not some other driver?"

Aziz smiled widely, showing a gap between his two front teeth. "It is all worked out, my friend. Mediterranean has three delivery trucks, two of which will unfortunately encounter mechanical difficulties. Do not concern yourself with the deliveries. Your responsibility was the manufacture of the poison. You have done well."

"Thank you."

"The poison," Aziz asked with a sly grin, "will it cause a panic?"

"Oh, yes, it will."

"And they will not discover the source immediately?"

"No, my friend, it has a slow incubation period. That's the beauty. I myself have designed this organism. For a few days, the victim is totally unaware of the toxin. Most will have left the hospital and returned home before there are any signs. Then they'll think they have the flu. After a few days, when the victim becomes very ill, it's too late, the bacteria have done their work. No antidote, no antibiotic, can reverse the internal damage. And it's unlikely the hospitals will ever discover that the toxins were contained in the IVs. They will have already disposed of the empty bags."

"Arif, you are a genius."

SOPHIE SKIPPED ALONG THE sidewalk, Bashir close behind. He smiled warmly at her. "You are so much like your mother. Full of boundless joy."

"Did you know my mother?"

"Oh, child, I walked with her as I walk with you. When I shut my eyes, it is as though I have picked up little Alina from her madrassa. She skipped along just like you."

"Did you love her?"

"Very, very much. I would have done anything to keep her from harm."

Sophie looked down and kicked a stone on the sidewalk. "Why did she have to die?"

Bashir shook his head, but smiled. "She was so sweet that Allah must have wanted her close to him, to keep him company and make him smile."

"Jaddi says she died because she had turned from Allah. He says she turned away from her faith."

"Well, that is your jaddi. Myself, I do not believe it is true. Your mother was pure in heart and could never have offended Allah. She was sweet and loving." He touched the tip of Sophie's nose. "Just like you."

"My mother used to call me her little butterfly." Sophie looked up at Bashir. "Do you like butterflies?"

He looked down and nodded. "Oh, of course. But I do not see many in our part of Hebron. Perhaps because there are not many gardens."

"I wish I was a butterfly."

"But you are such a pretty girl, why do you want to be a butterfly?"

"They can fly so high. They can go wherever they like. Walls cannot stop them."

They entered the home and al-Zahani greeted Sophie with a hug. "I have a chocolate for you."

She sat on her grandfather's lap and drank from a small cup. "I love Bashir. He is very kind."

Al-Zahani smiled. "Kind and strong and brave."

"Is he like a strong warrior?" Sophie took a sip of chocolate, leaving her with a brown mustache, which she wiped with the back of her hand.

"Exactly. Like a strong Canaanite warrior. Come with me, Sophie." He held her hand and led her to the wall of the library. He pointed to a black-and-white photo of a smiling man in a white pillbox hat. He picked up the child and held her high so that she could get a good look.

"That is my beloved grandfather, Ibrahim al-Zahani, the greatest warrior of them all. He is your great-great-grandfather. His magnificent blood runs through your veins. For many years, he led our people and fought against our enemies. He even defended our homes right here in Hebron."

"This home?"

"Well, not this very home, but our neighborhood. It was back in the summer of 1929. People were coming to our land from far-away countries. They wanted to settle here, even though it wasn't their land. They were moving into our cities, buying up our homes, threatening to change our way of life. Many of them were Jews and did not worship Allah, and many of these Jews had come from Europe. They called themselves Ashkenazis. The grand mufti of Jerusalem warned them, told them not to come, told them to leave, but they would not listen. One day there was a fight outside the mosque in Jerusalem, and three Arab boys were killed. Arab families were afraid for their lives.

"The mufti sent Grandfather Ibrahim to Hebron. 'Get the Ashkenazis out of Hebron,' he ordered Grandfather. 'Tell our people about the dangerous invaders. Protect our women and children.' Ibrahim gathered the bravest warriors in Hebron and took up arms, whatever they had. Some had guns, but others only had clubs or axes. No matter. The Jews were no match for us. Many tried to hide, but Ibrahim found them all. Finally, the British police came and took the Jews from Hebron to Jerusalem. There were no more Jews left in Hebron. Ibrahim had done his job. He had made his mufti proud. That was called the great Hebron liberation."

"Was Bashir one of those brave warriors?"

Al-Zahani laughed. "No, he was not even born yet. Neither was I."

Al-Zahani pointed to another black-and-white photograph, this one of a man with his arm around a boy. "Do you know who these people are, Sophie?"

She shook her head.

"Well, that is my father, Hamid, your great-grandfather. Can you guess who he's holding?"

Sophie pointed to Arif.

"Right! It's me!" He planted a kiss on the top of her head.

"Was your father brave too?"

"Oh, child, the bravest of them all. He fought the British. He fought the foreign settlers. He fought alongside our warriors in 1948, and after we won, he was put in charge of the army battalion stationed right here in Hebron. He was a respected leader in our town. He built this house for us."

SAVING SOPHIE : 329

"What happened to your father?"

"He was murdered by Israeli soldiers in 1967."

"Were you very sad when he died?"

"I am still very sad. But I have vowed to carry on the ideals of my father and grandfather. To this day, I honor their memories."

He turned and walked back to the sofa, where the cups of chocolate were placed. "Someday, Sophie, you will have the honor of carrying on the work of the al-Zahanis."

SIXTY-SIX

• • •

"MARCY?"

Curled up in the chair beside Jack's hospital bed, Marcy awoke quickly. She smiled. "Hi," she whispered in a sleepy voice. Reflexively, she scanned the patient monitor. His vitals were steady. "How are you feeling?"

"Groggy. A little achy. Just fine if I don't move. Have you been here the whole time?"

"Pretty much."

He smiled. "You just won't give up."

"No, I won't."

"Thank you."

She scooted her chair close to the bed and reached for his hand. "I want you to get better so we can go climbing mountains in our sandals."

Jack reacted with a short chuckle and grimaced from a sharp pain. "Where are Taggart and the State Department woman?"

"Oh, they're still around. I'm sure they'll come over today."

"What day is it?"

"April eighth."

"Wow. I've been asleep for three days."

The nurse came into the room with her monitoring equipment, and Marcy stepped out. When she returned, they had raised Jack's bed to a sitting position. He was sipping from a styrofoam cup. "The nurse told me that the doctor decided to take me off sedation. And he wants me to try to practice getting in and out of a wheelchair."

Marcy pursed her lips. "I know. That was Kayla's idea. I have to warn you, Kayla intends to fly you to Israel as soon as she can arrange it."

"That's good. I need to get to Sophie."

Marcy shook her head. "The doctor doesn't think so and neither do I. You had serious injuries and you lost a lot of blood. Don't go yet. Just tell them you need a little more time."

"I can't. If I don't cooperate, I won't get any consideration from the court."

"That's right," Kayla said, walking into the room, carrying a large purse and a newspaper. "I'm glad you understand."

Liam followed her in.

"I'm fine, thank you for asking," Jack said.

"Sorry," she said. "How are you feeling?"

"Shitty."

Kayla looked at his chart. "You're improving."

"Since when are you a doctor?" Jack said. "I hear you want me to go to Hebron right away."

"I'm afraid I do."

"When?"

Kayla pulled up a chair. "Soon. We're waiting to hear that the arrangements have been made to exchange the money. It could be as soon as tomorrow."

"That's ridiculous," Marcy said. "Are you trying to kill him?"

"Don't, Marcy. I need to go when they want me to."

"But you can't even get out of bed."

Jack shrugged. "The doctors told me they want me to sit in a wheelchair."

"If you're going, I'm going with you," Marcy said.

Kayla shook her head. "She can't go with us, Jack. It's a dangerous mission."

"He needs my help."

"Talk to her," Kayla said to Jack. "She doesn't belong over there."

"She's right, Marcy. I need to do this myself."

"I can help with Sophie. I'm her aunt Marcy." Tears rolled out of her eyes and her jaw quivered. "Jack, look at you. You can barely sit up. Don't shut me out of this, please."

He shrugged. "Can she go part of the way, Kayla, as long as she stays out of danger? I'm not exactly marathon ready. Are *you* going to nursemaid me?"

Kayla paced by the foot of the bed. "It's a bad idea. It's a dangerous intelligence op. There's just no room for you, Marcy. I'm sorry."

Liam held up a hand. "Maybe we can work this out. Why don't we let Marcy go part of the way, maybe to Tel Aviv. What harm can that do?"

Kayla thought for a moment and walked to the bedside. "All right, here's the deal. If you'll make the effort, do whatever you can to get yourself ready, even if we have to leave in a day or two, I'll let Marcy go as far as Tel Aviv. Not all the way to Hebron."

"Deal." Jack held Marcy's hand. "Now, if you two wouldn't mind giving us a few minutes alone, there's nothing that needs to be done right now."

"Sure." Kayla handed the Honolulu newspaper to Jack. "There's something I want you to see first." The newspaper was folded back to a story on page twelve entitled, "Suspect Killed in Prison Rumble."

While Sommers read the story, Kayla said, "We thought it better to run a story that you died in a knife fight. They haven't caught up with the two men in the Cadillac. The man who stabbed you, a Russian national on an expired student visa, isn't talking. His lawyer and two other inmates swear that he acted in self-defense. So, officially, Eugene Wilson is dead."

"Well, that's the second time he's died." Jack put the paper down. "It's freaky to read your own obituary."

Kayla nodded. "I didn't want either of you to be surprised. I'll leave you two alone."

Kayla and Liam left and shut the door behind them. In the hallway, Kayla said, "Thanks for your help in there. And I think you're right. Marcy will be a calming influence until we have to go into Hebron."

"You're welcome."

"So, Catherine's coming in this afternoon? Are you going shopping?"

"You're being a little pushy, aren't you?"

Kayla smiled. "I just don't want to get to Hebron and have my partner all worried about his love life."

"God, you are a tough woman."

She shrugged.

When Kayla and Liam had left, Jack beckoned Marcy to sit down. "I know what you've been thinking, that everything is going to work out for the two of us, but the odds are stacked against us. Kayla's right about the dangers. The Palestinians don't want to exchange Sophie, they just want to see if they can make a quick score. They'll try to kill me and take the money. I've already been stabbed in the back by a Russian, probably Dmitri's man. And even if the exchange all worked out and I came back alive, it's likely I'll spend the next ten or twenty years in prison. I want us to be together as much as you do, but we need to look at the realities."

"Gosh, Jack, I never considered any of that."

"What's wrong with you that you're planning a future, a house and children, with a man who has no future?"

Marcy stood with her hands on her hips. "You sneak. You eavesdropped on me. You were pretending to be asleep."

"Pretending?"

She smiled and pointed her finger. "Well, I'm just not going to accept a dead end. I'm going with you and I'm bringing you and Sophie back, and somehow this will work out."

CATHERINE'S PLANE WAS DELAYED for over four hours. She finally landed at Honolulu International at 7:30 P.M., thirteen hours after she took off from Chicago. Her watch, still on central daylight time, read 11:30 P.M. The reunion with Liam at the baggage carousel was joyous and emotional. "I feel like it's been a year since we've seen each other," she said, with her arms around his neck.

"I'm so glad you decided to fly out. Why did you change your mind?"

"I heard something in your voice that I didn't like. I just figured we had some talking to do."

"Did Kayla call you?"

"What? What's Kayla got to do with this?"

"Nothing. Just . . . never mind."

"Is there something going on here, Liam?"

"No. Absolutely not. Kayla picked up on the fact that there was some tension between us, that's all. Please don't stress out about Kayla. She is strictly business. Okay?"

She nodded. "Okay."

"I'm sorry if I worried you on the phone. Are you hungry?"

"Starving! I refuse to buy that airplane food."

"There's a great outdoor grill at our hotel." Liam gave her a squeeze, grabbed her suitcase, and led her out the door. "It's so good to see you."

Liam and Catherine sat at the Moana Surfrider's grill studying the dinner menus. Behind them, waves broke loudly on the shore, and above them birds squawked in the palm trees. Ambient noise, loud enough to strain conversation. To Catherine Liam seemed to be more nervous than usual.

"Is something wrong?" Catherine said.

Liam shook his head, but he was obviously about to say something. He leaned forward and cleared his throat.

"You okay?" Catherine said.

He reached across the table and covered Catherine's hand gently with his own. He looked into her eyes, took a deep breath and cleared his throat again. "Catherine, you know I love you and there's no other person in my life. I have something I want to ask you."

Just then, a familiar voice interrupted them. "Hello there, you two."

Catherine responded flatly, "Hello, Kayla."

"May I?" She pulled a chair over to join them. "So, you got a text from Abu Hammad?"

Liam sighed and nodded. He passed his phone across the table to Kayla, who read the message: *I have spoken to Arif. I have his terms. Please call me at 10 A.M., my time.*

Kayla looked at her watch. "That's in forty-five minutes." She motioned to the waiter and ordered a glass of chardonnay. "I saw Sommers again. He looks pretty good. They want him to try sitting in a wheelchair."

Liam shook his head. "So you can roll him down the streets of Hebron? Is that your version of dead man walking?"

"Very funny. The doctor says he can fly out there, take his wheelchair with him, he'll be fine."

"Fine? He can barely move."

"I need your help here, Liam."

"And if he's not ready? I would think the last thing you want is a relapse."

Kayla looked at her watch and spoke quietly. "Today is the eighth. Yom Ha'atzmaut, the target date, is little more than a week away. We can't waste a minute. It takes almost a full day to travel. The exchange must be scheduled at the earliest possible time. We have to push Sommers's recovery."

"And if he can't make it?"

Kayla bit her lip and took a healthy drink of wine. "He has to make it."

At ten o'clock, Liam placed the call from his hotel room.

"Hello, my friend," Abu Hammad said. "How are things in Chicago?"

"Cold and windy, as usual. And in Jerusalem?"

"My shop is very comfortable."

"I'm surprised you spoke directly to Arif."

"I am also surprised. I was speaking with Fakhir, but when it came down to the details of exchanging money, Arif called me."

"I thought the two of you didn't speak."

"We did not. We still do not. The conversation was mechanical, devoid of cordiality. Nevertheless, he communicated his terms and hung up."

"I see. I apologize for putting you in such an awkward position."

"You did not put me. I put myself."

"I thank you for that."

"His terms are simple. The father, John Sommers, is to come alone to a bakery in Hebron. On April twenty-fifth. He is to bring five million dollars in U.S. currency or the equivalent amount in euros. Nonconsecutive bills. Following delivery and examination of the money, the child will be brought to the bakery and Sommers may leave with her."

"One moment, please, Jamal." Liam put the call on mute and explained the terms to Kayla.

"No way. It has to be before the sixteenth. Try for the twelfth. And not at the bakery. A straight exchange at al-Zahani's. In his home. We need to get inside those walls."

Liam nodded. "Jamal, my friend, we need to modify those terms a little. Would it be possible for you to communicate our desires back to Arif?"

"I can talk to Fakhir. He will tell Arif to call me. What changes would you have to his terms?"

"First, Mr. Sommers has had an unfortunate accident. He has been seriously injured and is recovering from surgery. He cannot walk. He's in a wheelchair and requires assistance. I will accompany him along with his nurse. As to the exchange, he wants a direct swap—money for Sophie. Same place. Simultaneously. No Sophie, no money. And he does not want it at a public location, both for Sophie's well-being and his own. Mr. Sommers will meet al-Zahani at the doctor's home, where he will take possession of the child and her things.

"And, Jamal, please tell him, this is most important: I'm going to pack the briefcase for Mr. Sommers. It'll have five million dollars in it, but it will also have an explosive device. If some guy grabs the case and tries to open it without the correct combination, the case will explode and the contents will be destroyed, not to mention the guy who tries to open it. It's not that I don't trust the good doctor, but it may just discourage one of his friends from trying to finance an early retirement. Only Mr. Sommers can open the briefcase. Make sure Arif understands this.

"Finally, my friend, Mr. Sommers is most anxious to recover his daughter, the sooner the better. He has the money in his possession and would like to make the exchange in four days. We will make arrangements to be at Arif's home on April twelfth. Jamal, we are indebted to you for interceding on our behalf. I'm sure that Mr. Sommers will express great interest in Middle Eastern antiquities."

Abu Hammad laughed. "Antiquities, for certain. I do not seek profit from my assistance, but if Mr. Sommers should find his way to my shop, I will gladly show him a few precious items."

"You are a good friend, Jamal."

"I understand. I will make sure Arif receives your terms. Good-bye, my friend."

Liam hung up and nodded at Kayla.

"I need a moment with Liam," Kayla said to Catherine, and she took him out into the hallway.

"So now we wait again," Kayla said to Liam quietly. "What if Arif doesn't respond? I don't want the IDF storming the compound. Abu Hammad's got to get us in."

"Five million dollars? He'll respond. We'll get in, but I want to make sure we get out. How much support has the Agency devoted to this operation? Men and matériel?"

Kayla shrugged. "I don't know for certain. That's not under my control."

"Well, we need an operations expert to manage this *ruse de guerre*. You and I are not equipped."

"I'm sure we'll get all the help we need. Don't worry."

"Don't worry? Do you remember when we sat around Jenkins and Fairchild's conference table, weeks ago? 'We need you to make the exchange, Liam.' 'We want you to be the go-between.' Do you remember that?"

"Of course."

"Skillfully omitted from that conversation was the part where good ol' Liam was informed that there was an imminent terrorist strike and that good ol' Liam was expected to walk into a firing squad."

"I told you al-Zahani was a terrorist. I told you the beehive was active."

"And Harry told me it was theoretical, that he hadn't committed any assets to the project. Kayla, we cannot do this without proper support. We need to know where his guards are stationed and how they're armed. We'd need aerial surveillance, and not just satellite. Like a couple of those hummingbird drones. And backup. Lots of backup."

She nodded. "I'm sure it's all arranged."

"If we go into Hebron with Sommers, carrying a suitcase full of money, we're targets the moment that suitcase's opened. Assuming that al-Zahani buys the gambit and grants admittance to his compound, we'll need a unit to take out the guards on the outer perimeter. Once the guards are down, and while we're inside, we'll need a unit to break into his weapons plant and secure the workers and whatever he's manufacturing. As to persuading al-Zahani to give up the information about the terrorist operation, I leave that entirely up to you and your interrogators. But Sophie, Jack, and I will need safe transportation out of Hebron."

Kayla nodded. "I said it's done, Liam. This is not our first go-round. We'll talk about it later."

Liam started to go back into the room, but Kayla grabbed his arm and pulled him back. "So, did you ask her?"

"I was just about to, but someone showed up at our dinner."

"Sorry. Were you going to give her the ring?"

Liam grimaced. "I didn't get a chance to shop."

Kayla shook her head. "Liam, you can't just *ask* her. You have to give her a ring. You have to do it right. She'll want to remember this for the rest of her life."

Liam sighed. "I know you're right."

Kayla smiled and walked away. "See you tomorrow."

SIXTY-SEVEN

• • •

S O THAT'S WHERE YOU left it?" Catherine said. "You asked
her about support and she said, 'We'll talk about it later'? I
hope you said, 'Let me know how this all turns out.'"

"Not exactly."

"Well then, you can't go."

Liam smiled. "Thanks, Mom."

"I'm not kidding, Liam. It's one thing to ask you to poke around
and ask questions, and yet another to ask you to pretend you'll pay
the ransom money. But to ask you to jump into the middle of a military strike with inadequate backup, or no backup, that's insanity."

"Do you hear me arguing with you?"

"Good. Then you're not going."

Liam scrunched his face. "Well . . . I didn't say I wouldn't go.
Kayla's going to talk to Harry tomorrow, and she says we'll have
all the support we need."

"I don't trust her, Liam. You heard Harry say she's obsessed with
this doctor."

Liam nodded.

"And you also heard him say he's never seen any proof that the
man's a terrorist."

Liam nodded.

"Stop nodding! I don't want you to go."

"I get that."

Catherine put her arms around him. "Please don't do something
foolish. Don't be so damn macho. Let the CIA handle their own
problems."

"I'm not being macho. I'm the one who made the contacts and set this whole thing up. I'm the one who's supposed to go with Sommers to get his daughter. That's the plan we sold. How do I back out now? And what if Kayla's spot-on? What about those two thousand bags in Jerusalem? Two thousand screaming victims? She says the answers are all in the outbuilding. If we get the CIA's support, get into the building, and stop the attack, we'll save a lot of lives. Do you really want me to back out?"

"Yes. Of course I do. I don't want you anywhere near this operation." She hung her head. "But you're right. If you're able to help prevent an attack, *and if the CIA protects you*, then you should go."

He kissed her on the forehead and held her head on his chest. "That's my baby."

C ATHERINE TOSSED AND TURNED, waking Liam every few minutes.

"Can't sleep?"

"It's the time zone. I'm wide-awake and it's only three A.M. And there's quite a bit on my mind. I think I need to go for a walk."

Liam rubbed his eyes. "All right, I'll go with you."

"You don't have to."

"It's okay." Liam climbed out of the bed and put on his bathing suit. "Come on, we'll take a walk on the beach."

The grounds of the Moana Surfrider were still and quiet. Oil torches lit the path to the beachfront, where the full moon laid an undulating path of yellow paint on the surface of the sea. Liam and Catherine walked barefoot onto the cool sand and then ankle deep into the surf. Hand in hand, they sloshed along, making their way south in the direction of Diamond Head.

Catherine squeezed Liam's hand. "I know you wanted to talk to me at dinner. Is this a good time?"

"I do want to talk, but . . . but not right now. I'd like to wait a little bit."

Catherine, an obvious look of disappointment on her face, stood still. "That's why I came out here."

Liam put his hands on her shoulders and looked into her eyes. "I know. But it's just . . . I want it to be perfect, and I need to do something first. Look, can I promise you, the tide will not go out without us? You can depend on it. I have my reasons. Let me do this my way. Okay?"

She nodded and took his hand, and they continued their slosh through the surf.

"We *do* make a good couple, you know," Liam said.

Catherine nodded. "I know."

They eventually came upon a secluded, little alcove on the beach beneath a palm. Liam spread his T-shirt like a blanket, and there, on a warm Hawaiian night, they lay on the soft sand watching the moon make sparkles on the water.

K AYLA RETURNED TO THE hotel the next morning. She found Catherine and Liam at the breakfast buffet. "I need to borrow your boyfriend for a few minutes," she said to Catherine.

"There are lots of reasons that I should not like you," Catherine said. "Including the fact that you are sending him into a war zone. Please take care of him. He's got this goofy macho mentality that makes him do things he shouldn't do."

"I understand. He'll be well protected."

"Did you talk to Harry?" Liam asked Kayla as the two of them walked along the beach path behind the Moana Surfrider.

"We're all set."

"That's a little too general for me. How are we all set?"

"We'll have proper support, outside and in."

"The CIA's going to fully support this operation?"

Kayla stopped and turned to face him. "Not the CIA. The support will come from in-country assets. I'm not CIA, Liam."

"So, we've finally decided to be honest? Who the fuck are you?"

"Nice talk. I'm Shabak. Israel Security Agency. Arab Affairs Department. Counterterrorism. We'll get our support for this mission from the Israeli intelligence community. You can be assured of adequate manpower and matériel."

"And Harry? Is he Shabak?"

She shook her head. "No. Harry is CIA, but in a liaison role."

They walked a bit farther in silence, then Kayla said quietly,

"I never meant to deceive you, you knew I wasn't just a resource analyst."

"That's not the same as being honest."

Liam's phone buzzed. He took it out of his pocket, read the text message, and showed it to Kayla: *Arif agrees to your terms. He will see you in three days at his home. April 12 at noon.*

"Good work, Liam. You got us in. We'll leave tomorrow."

M IDAFTERNOON AND KAYLA AND Liam entered Sommers's hospital room to find the bed empty. The station nurse informed them that he and his young lady were taking a walk. They found him sitting in a wheelchair in the hallway just around the corner. His IV was still in place and attached to the hook on the wheelchair. Jack was out of breath.

"We didn't get very far," Marcy said.

"Keep up the good work, Jack, you're looking very good," Kayla said chipperly.

"You need to get your eyes checked," he said.

"How much have you done?"

He shook his head.

"More than he should," answered Marcy. "He had a hard time getting from the bed to the chair, and it's painful for him to sit. He had to have an injection of painkiller just to sit in the wheelchair. I'm pushing him because he doesn't have the strength in his arms to wheel himself. But he's got his mind set on going to Hebron. There's no talking him out of it."

"I won't try," Kayla said. "We want to leave tomorrow night."

"Oh, come on, Kayla. What the hell? He's not well enough to travel and you know it," Marcy said. "The doctor told us next week at the earliest. You're going to kill him."

"I'm sorry, but next week is too late. The exchange is set for Friday. It's all been arranged. We have a flight out tomorrow night."

"Hold on, Kayla," Liam said. "You can't kill the man. If he's not well enough, we'll have to go without him. As long as we're carrying the money, they won't care who's bringing it in. They think they're going to kill the messenger anyway."

"That's encouraging," Jack said. "Don't you think there's some possibility that Arif will go through with the exchange? That he'll keep his word? That he'll give us Sophie and we can leave?"

"No. None at all," Kayla said. "But if she's there, I intend to bring her back."

"What do you mean 'if she's there'? Do you think he'd send her away or hide her?"

"In a heartbeat. But he's been told that it has to be a straight-up exchange. She'll need to be present for him to get the money."

Sommers turned to Marcy. "I've got to go, Marcy. Sophie will need comforting, reassurance, and someone whose number one priority is her protection. This whole business can fly out of control, can't it, Liam?"

He nodded. "Yes, I'm afraid it can. For everyone involved."

"Then we'll go tomorrow."

SIXTY-EIGHT

•••

D MITRI POURED A GENEROUS portion of twenty-five-
year-old single-malt into a crystal tumbler with a single
block of ice and settled into his soft leather couch in his
multimedia room to watch the Elite Eight quarterfinal basketball
game with his twelve-year-old son.

Dmitri put his arm around his boy and anxiously awaited the
tip-off on his eighty-inch screen. "I think we're in for a hell of a
game tonight, Davit. Two teams ranked in the top five."

"It's only a shame that St. Joe's didn't get this far, isn't it,
Dad?"

"A shame indeed. But next year, Darius will return."

Dmitri's cell phone rang. He looked at the number and denied
the call. It rang again. And again. Finally, he answered it. "Yes,
Victor, how are you?"

"Shitty. Why won't you take my calls?"

"Oh. Have you been trying to reach me?"

"Don't fuck with me. I've called a hundred times."

"You worry too much, my friend."

"I want to come see you. We need to talk."

"No, not tonight. I am watching a game with my son. We talk
another time."

"Dmitri, I'm already on my way. I'm in my car. You can break
away from your game for a few minutes."

"Ach. So then come."

Fifteen minutes later, the doorbell rang and Dmitri's shapely
young wife showed Kelsen into the darkened multimedia room.

Dmitri, in his white, cable-knit sweater with the sleeves pushed up, motioned Kelsen forward. "Come in."

Kelsen walked slowly into the darkened room.

"Victor, welcome. Have a seat. We talk at the halftime. Inessa, bring Mr. Kelsen whatever he wants to drink."

Kelsen sat in silence during the first half of the telecast. His breaths were short. He barely touched his glass of beer. Dmitri and Davit, on the other hand, were loud and animated in support of their team. Halftime finally arrived and Dmitri said, "Davit, Mr. Kelsen and I have a little business to discuss. Would you excuse us for a few minutes, please?"

"They know about our gambling," Kelsen said when the boy had left the room.

"You're upset because the woman lawyer knows we gamble? The NCAA tournament is the biggest gambling event of the year. Every business office has a bracket."

Kelsen wagged his finger. "I'm not talking about a bracket, you asshole. She knows about you and me, and even Evgeniy. And she brought up Darius McCord."

Dmitri turned around sharply, his gold chain necklace swinging to the side. "First of all, never call me an asshole. Are we understandable?"

Kelsen nodded. "Sorry."

"Second, I told you it was foolish to injure Darius." Dmitri took a sip of his Scotch. "I only wanted you to scare him. You were a madman."

"But it was your guy, Evgeniy, who broke his leg, and she knows about Evgeniy. What's next, Dmitri? Does she ask me about the money? Does she want to know who sent Sommers to Panama? I walked out before she could do that, you know."

"She will know nothing unless you open your mouth. I have taken care, because I am a responsible man, of everyone who could put the finger on us. Evgeniy is back in Moscow. Harrington, Ellis, and now Sommers. All dead. Thank you very much."

"Sommers is dead?"

Dmitri raised his eyebrows and nodded. He reached for his iPad, downloaded a page from the Honolulu daily paper, and handed it to Kelsen.

"Killed by a convict in jail?"

"*Da*. My convict. Which is now costing thousands of dollars for lawyers. But Sommers is dead and no one is left who can testify against us. No one alive but you, Victor. *Ha ha ha*."

"Not funny, Dmitri."

"Depends on the audience."

"What do I do if she asks questions?"

"I thought you already gave your testimony."

"I walked out. My lawyer was a stiff and I got scared. I'm going to have to go back for another session."

Dmitri leaned toward Kelsen. "Well, don't say anything. You don't know anything. You can't remember anything. Money was stolen from you and no one can prove otherwise."

"I don't know, she makes me real nervous. She knows stuff. It's like she can look through me. Maybe you should take care of her."

"You're a fool. Even if I did, someone else would pick up the case. I can't kill all the lawyers in this town. Maybe I should kill *you*."

"I don't appreciate your Russian humor."

"Stop your anxiety. I want to hear no more of this. Everything is buttoned up. Nice and neat. Now go. The second half is starting."

Kelsen stood. He shook Dmitri's hand. "Okay, okay. Good job with Sommers, but I'm still worried. What if she asks me how I know Evgeniy? It's not exactly a common name in Chicago. There ain't that many Russians around here. She'll connect you two together." Kelsen paused. "I know, I know. Shut my mouth. I don't know nothing."

"Right."

Kelsen turned to leave. "I hope you didn't have Duke in this game. You'd've laid eight points."

"Good-bye, my friend."

When Kelsen left, Dmitri punched in a number on his cell phone. "Evgeniy. I need you to come back to Chicago. We have one more door to shut."

SIXTY-NINE

• • •

MARCY PUSHED JACK'S WHEELCHAIR up to a table outside Lappert's Ice Cream shop, in the main concourse of Honolulu International, beside Kayla and Catherine. Liam approached carrying a tray with an assortment of ice cream cones, set them on the table, and distributed them.

"I told you coconut macadamia-nut fudge," Catherine said. "What is this?"

"White-chocolate macadamia nut."

"How could you possibly confuse the two? They're nothing alike."

"Well, excuse me. You could've done the shopping."

"I wouldn't have made *that* mistake."

"Here, take mine."

"What is it?"

"Kauai Pie."

"Kauai Pie? Seriously? What the hell is Kauai Pie?"

"You're about to find out when you wipe it off your nose."

"Stop," Jack said. "You're making my side hurt."

"What time is your flight to Chicago?" Marcy said to Catherine.

"Five thirty." Catherine looked at Liam. "I wish you were coming home. I'm getting neurotic about this mission."

"He'll be fine," Kayla said. "We'll take good care of him."

"I'm not sure I like the way you phrased that."

Kayla smiled. "There's a planning meeting in Tel Aviv tomorrow. They'll lay out the details of the rescue. They know what they're doing. Jack, Marcy, Liam, and Sophie will all be home before you know it."

"You promised you'd talk to the prosecutor," Marcy said. "Jack's risking his life."

"I talked to him this morning. They're reviewing it. There will definitely be an offer for his role in this operation. Unfortunately, I think a walk will be out of the question. Clemency? A possibility. Reduction in sentence? For sure. But a total drop of the charges—I don't think there's a chance. They're mindful of Jack's cooperation, but there's still the matter of the eighty-eight million dollars. Even though Jack may not have personally kept the money, he was an active conspirator in a major financial theft. The court will have to respect the victim and the financial injury done to his company. Jack will have to spend some time in custody. How many years, well, that's up to the judge. Nevertheless, the prosecutors will meet with Jack and his attorney when he gets back to Chicago."

"Whether I get clemency or not," Jack said, "I have to go. We have no chance of getting Sophie if I don't show up. The disposition of my case is always secondary. Whatever happens to me, at least Sophie will be back in the U.S. and cared for by my family."

"Jack might die and you can't even promise him a deal." Marcy's voice cracked.

"I think we have to face facts," Jack said. "I committed a serious crime. A prosecutor might recommend a lighter sentence, but I knew what I was doing. I helped a man steal a lot of money from Mr. Kelsen, and I'm not going to return home a free man. I don't deserve to be a free man. That's why I keep telling you it's time to cut your losses."

Catherine stood. "My flight's boarding. I better go." She threw her arms around Liam and held him like a vise. "Please come back to me, you crazy Irishman. We have to finish our talk."

"I promise. Count on it."

"Don't you let anything happen to him," Catherine said to Kayla.

SEVENTY

• • •

THE INSTITUTE FOR INTELLIGENCE and Special Operations, known as the Mossad, a Hebrew word for "institute," has its principal office in a fortified campus, a block and a half from the sea in north Tel Aviv. In a second-floor conference room, midmorning sunlight beamed across a long, polished table where a laptop played a recorded conversation:

"Nizar is quick to call names, but here I agree with him. I'm in the middle of production. I can stop, but three hundred more victims, three hundred more wailing, mortified families begging Israel to concede the land and stop the occupation? That has great value. Twenty-three hundred dead enemies will certainly be regarded as the most glorious jihadist victory since the Twin Towers. And right in the heart of our enemy. Do not fear the discovery of my lab. I have wired it for destruction. If necessary, I can instantly firebomb the building and obliterate all remnants of our operation."

"It appears that Kayla has been right all along," Harry said to the group as the recording played on.

"And five Iyar is the date? Yom Ha'atzmaut?"

Harry nodded. "Makes sense, doesn't it?"

The rest of the group grunted their approval.

"What have we overheard since then?"

"Nothing. Bakery noises. Apparently there have been no further meetings at the Breadstone Bakery. That was the last recording of the group."

"So, what stops us from going into this maniacal doctor's factory and grabbing what he's got?" remarked Eliezer, an older man in an open-collar, white shirt, curls of gray hair poking out from beneath his woven kippah.

"You heard the tape. He'll blow the building if there's an assault. Besides, two thousand devices have already been delivered to an unspecified warehouse in Jerusalem. They're not at the factory anymore."

"All the more reason to strike immediately. Let him blow the building and all the terrorists with it. Who gives a shit?"

"And where are the two thousand bags? And what's in them?" Harry said. "Kayla feels that if she can enter the compound and distract the doctor, allowing us to quickly gain access to the outbuilding, we'll find out the details of the plot—the nature of the devices, when and where the attack will occur. She thinks a precipitous strike would prompt the group to destroy the factory and all evidence of the operation, or worse, move up the attack."

"This group, these are the so-called Sons of Canaan?" Eliezer said.

"Right."

"We should not wait," said a woman in an IDF colonel's uniform. "We should go in tonight. The devices may be in a warehouse, but it's possible the logistics are not yet in place. We gain an advantage in scrambling their plan."

Around the table were grunts of approval and nodding heads. "Good point, Yonit."

Harry interrupted, "Getting Kayla inside is our best chance of learning what we need to know to stop the attack. She and Sommers are due in a few hours. Why don't we give her the benefit of the doubt? We owe her that courtesy. It's her op. A few hours won't make any difference. The entire operation is scripted. Give her an audience."

"Agreed," Eliezer said. "That's only fair. We'll reconvene at three P.M. and listen to her."

DMITRI LOOKED AT THE caller ID on his cell phone and uttered a Russian expletive.

"Hello, Victor. What is it you want this time?"

"Don't brush me off, Dmitri. I'm the one taking the heat here. I've been served with another fucking subpoena. Apparently, when I walked out the last time, Lockhart got a court order for me to come back and finish my testimony. I have to go back tomorrow at two P.M."

"So, go back. Testify."

"She knows, damn it. I don't know how she knows, but I can feel it. Maybe Darius talked to her."

"She knows nothing. You're a gambler. You go to basketball games. Big deal. You go to her office, you shut your mouth. You tell her you don't know anything."

"And if she asks me about Panama?"

"You shut your mouth!" Dmitri screamed. "Are you hard of hearing? You don't know anything! Repeat after me: *I don't know!*"

"I'm nervous. Can't you do something?"

"Yeah. I can do something all right. Good-bye."

Kelsen stared at the phone in his shaking hand. He didn't like that last comment.

I THOUGHT YOU SAID that Sophie and I were going to Amman this week," Lubannah said.

"I changed my mind," answered al-Zahani. "I need her here."

"Need Sophie? Need her for what, Arif?"

"It's my concern."

"Arif, talk to me. Why do you need Sophie here?"

Al-Zahani started to walk away, thought better of it, and returned to Lubannah. "Sommers is coming here."

Tears formed and streamed down Lubannah's cheeks. "He's coming to take her."

Al-Zahani shook his head. "He will never take her from us. She will never go back to America. Do you understand me? She will never leave Palestine."

"Then why, why, Arif? Why is he coming? Why are you letting him come here to our home? Let me take Sophie to Amman."

Arif gently put his hands on Lubannah's shoulders and smiled. "You know, you have been a good wife to me. And I haven't always been patient with you. For that, I am sorry. He is coming because he thinks he is going to leave with Sophie. But I will not let that happen, and you must let me handle this my way."

"Handle what, Arif? What is there to handle? Why does he think he can take our Sophie? You told me that would never happen."

"He is bringing money. He is so foolish that he thinks we will accept money to part with Sophie."

"Then we will lock him out," she said firmly. "Bashir will not let him in the gates."

Arif shook his head, but smiled kindly at her. "No, I must tell him myself. I will let him see Sophie. You will walk her into the room and then out. He will see her and then he will leave. It will be good closure for Sophie."

"Arif, have you lost your mind? If Sophie sees him, she'll be hysterical. She won't leave the room."

"You must let me do this my way. I will ask her to step out of the room just for a moment, and when she returns, Sommers will be gone. She will be told that he left without her, and we will be done with her pining. We will never hear from him again."

Lubannah's face grew serious and her lips taut. "I see through your plan. Do not take me for a child, Arif. You intend to take his money and—"

"Stop! Do not conjure up diabolical scenarios. It is simply as I have stated. We will do it my way and there will be no further discussions."

With that, al-Zahani left the room.

KELSEN'S CHAUFFEUR ENTERED THE dining room where Kelsen was eating a late dinner. His hat was in his hand and he stood sheepishly in his black wool coat.

"I am sorry, Mr. Kelsen, but I thought you would like to know."

"Know what?"

"Evgeniy. I saw him drive by the house. I thought he was coming to pay you a visit, but he kept right on driving. I waved, but he did not wave back."

"Impossible. Evgeniy is in Europe."

"No, sir. He's here in Chicago. I saw him quite plainly."

Kelsen's face rapidly lost its color. He stammered. "Wh-who was with him?"

"No, by himself. He was alone. He slowed down and then drove on."

Kelsen stood quickly. "I need my coat."

"Where are we going, sir?"

He shook his head. "I won't need you tonight. Get me the keys to my wife's car. I have something to do myself."

Kelsen took his coat from his chauffeur, walked into his den, and closed the door. In a side cabinet, a key ring hung on a nail. He fished for a brass skeleton key and used it to unlock a desk drawer. Inside lay three handguns. He chose the Walther PPQ M2 and a 9mm magazine. He shoved the gun into his belt, locked the drawer, replaced the keys, and walked to the garage.

SEVENTY-ONE

• • •

CATHERINE PAID THE TAXI DRIVER who carried her heavy luggage up the stoop to her front door. She was tired after her ten-hour journey from Hawaii. She fumbled with her key, finally getting it into the lock. Suddenly, she felt a strong poke in her back and a voice said, "Don't say a fuckin' word, just open your door."

She turned the lock, opened the door, and was pushed forward into her foyer. The door slammed behind her and she turned to see Victor Kelsen pointing a black handgun in her face.

"How did you know?" he said.

"Know what?"

"Don't. Fuck. With. Me!" he screamed. "How did you know?"

"I'm not going to talk to anyone who holds a gun in my face."

Kelsen waved the gun in the direction of the living room. "Move." He directed her to sit on the couch, and he sat opposite her on a wingback chair.

"Now. Now talk. Tell me how you knew about me and Dmitri."

"Why does it matter?"

Kelsen nervously waved the gun around. "It matters to me!" he shouted. "We had it all worked out."

Catherine bit her bottom lip. "Son of a bitch. It was both of you. The two of you arranged for the kidnapping and stole the money. Committing multiple murders and embezzling millions? That's what you call having it all worked out?"

"It was perfect. Perfect, until *you* figured it out. How did you know?"

"Perfect?" She shook her head. "I have to tell you, before you do anything crazy tonight, there are others who know what I know. The FBI knows. Killing me won't help. It won't go away. It will only make it worse for you."

"It was Darius, wasn't it? He told you."

"It doesn't matter how I found out. It's over for you."

"I know that." Kelsen lowered the gun and his voice. "I didn't come here to kill you. I may be a lot of things, but I'm not a killer. I want you to get me a deal."

"I'm listening."

"I know everything. I know where the money is. I can be a witness against everyone involved. Dmitri. Evgeniy. Gregor. Yuri. All of them. I want witness protection and I want a deal. You know who to call. My lawyer is an idiot."

"They're after you, aren't they? You're the loose end. You're the next target."

He nodded. "He didn't say it, but I heard it in Dmitri's voice tonight. Evgeniy's returned to town. There can be no other reason."

"Is the money still in Panama?"

He shook his head. "Caymans."

Catherine sat silently for a moment, then pointed her finger. "The gun."

Kelsen slipped the magazine out and slid the gun across the table. Catherine took her cell phone out of her purse, searched for a number, and dialed.

"Hello?" a whispered voice answered.

"Tom, it's Catherine Lockhart. Sorry to wake you. I guess I have a habit of calling you in the middle of the night."

"Tell me that you don't have another Nazi SS guard," the assistant U.S. Attorney said.

She smiled. "I have Victor Kelsen sitting in my house. He has information about the embezzlement and the murders that he'd like to share with you. He wants to talk a deal. And he needs protection."

"I'll send a car over."

She hung up the phone. "You didn't need the money, Mr. Kelsen. Why did you do it?"

"Well, everyone needs money, but it's about leverage. Taxes

on eighty-eight million would take almost half of my money away. If it's stolen and no one knows I have it, there's no taxes. I split the stolen money with Dmitri, I get forty-four million dollars tax-free. Then I still have my lawsuit against Jenkins for another eighty-eight million dollars. Simple math. I'm forty-four million dollars ahead."

"And that was worth the lives of several men?"

"I never knew he'd kill anyone. That wasn't the plan. Ellis and Harrington were each supposed to get a million. Sommers, well, Dmitri was running a number on him."

"Whose idea was it to kidnap Sommers's daughter?"

"Totally Dmitri's. Brilliant, I must say. We knew Sommers was essential to the plan. We also knew he was too honest to take a pay-off. So Dmitri said, 'Everyone's got a soft spot somewhere. I'll find his.' And he did. He flew the grandparents and the daughter to Palestine and then told Sommers he could ransom her back. Fuckin' brilliant. Would've worked too, if it wasn't for you."

Catherine shook her head. "It would not have worked."

"It was Darius, wasn't it? All I did for that kid. That son of a bitch."

"You didn't give a damn about him or his career. All those years he and his mother sacrificed to get him to the top. You tantalized him with chump change and tried to ruin him."

"You think he's so innocent? He and his friends were the ones who came to *me*. I've been a Deacons booster for years. They found out I paid for points in the past and they wanted to cash in. Darius and Marcus came to me after a preseason dinner and told me they could keep the next game within the spread. They wanted five hundred dollars apiece." Kelsen shrugged. "Easy money."

Headlights illuminated the living room and there was a knock on the door. Catherine let the two agents in. On his way out, Kelsen said, "It would've worked."

"You're an asshole," she said.

SEVENTY-TWO

• • •

FAKHIR BRUSHED HIS HANDS on his apron and finished counting his money. It had been a lucrative day at the bakery. He was bushed. He ambled back to his sitting room and plopped down hard on his couch. He heard a sound, as though something small had dropped to the floor. He thought it was a coin. For the moment, he thought, *Let it be*. But then, a coin is a coin. He looked under the couch and on the floor beneath saw a small, black plastic square. He picked it up. It had no markings. Then it came to him. "The fucking IDF!" he said aloud. He called Fa'iz and demanded an immediate meeting of the group.

Al-Zahani received a text message calling for an emergency meeting at Fa'iz's house. As his gates opened and his Mercedes pulled out onto the street, a young man on a bicycle took a cell phone out of his pocket and made a call. A light blue Ford picked up al-Zahani's trail two blocks later. Numerous photos of the members of the Sons of Canaan entering Fa'iz's residence were taken and simultaneously e-mailed to Mossad headquarters.

"Why have you called us all here to your home, Fa'iz?" said Ahmed when the group had assembled.

"I'll let Fakhir explain."

With a shaking hand, Fakhir held up a plastic bag for all to see. It was filled with the remains of the small listening device he had smashed with a hammer. "You all laughed at me when I said the IDF knew about us. That they knew about the meetings in the bakery. Now you see, you are all fools. I was right."

"It is indeed a listening device," Rami concurred. "It's safe to assume that the IDF or the Shin Bet now know of our plans."

"What do they know?" Nizar said sharply. "That we meet? That we hate Israel and wish its demise. Does that make us unique?"

Fa'iz held up his index finger. "We've only met at the bakery once in the past few weeks. If the device was there for our last meeting, they know what we discussed. It was a very short session, as I recall. What did we say?"

Nizar responded, "We said we have two thousand bags. That they're in a warehouse in Jerusalem. I don't recall our being specific. Arif talked about his laboratory, that he can produce forty bags a day. Did we say what was in the bags?"

Al-Zahani shook his head. "That information was discussed at the apartment. We only said that we should forgo the extra three hundred bags, that there would be three hundred victims."

"And we said it was set for April sixteenth," Fakhir added.

"That's true. We revealed the date."

"So what?" Fa'iz said. "They lack the essential details to defeat the plan."

"I agree with Fa'iz," al-Zahani said. "If they knew the details, if they knew who the participants were, they would have picked us up by now. They would have already stormed Arif's compound. They would have seized the Jerusalem warehouse. Have they done any of that? No. The bags are still safely stored. Sami is still making his daily runs. We are all still here."

"Nevertheless, we should postpone our mission," Rami said. "They are alerted to the date. They will take extra precautions on the sixteenth."

"Reluctantly, I must agree," Fa'iz said quietly. "We'll have to reschedule after the summer."

Nizar stood defiantly. "Well, I do not agree. Where will they take extra precautions, Rami? Do they know of the hospitals? Today, they know nothing. Next month, they may learn more. Every day presents an opportunity for them to investigate, to spy, to overhear. For one of us to make a mistake. I say we act immediately. Tomorrow. Why wait? We are poised to strike and they are not ready."

Fa'iz stroked his beard. "Is this something we can do? Can we put it together that quickly?"

The members looked at one another and nodded their agreement. "Why not?"

"Then call Sami. We move tomorrow. The tenth."

Fakhir held up his hand. "Fa'iz, when the attack occurs, what becomes of all of us? One by one, we will be captured and jailed. Or worse. They know who we are. They have surely seen us come and go from my bakery."

Fa'iz folded his hands and leaned back. "Myself, I will stay here. You may all do what you think is best. You will find safe harbors in our neighboring countries, if that is what you wish."

"I will never leave Canaan," al-Zahani said. "It is in my blood. But why would any of you have to leave? I assure you, they will never prove a connection between us and the deaths that will take place in Jerusalem. I have told you, again and again, this is a foolproof plan. The bacteria spread undetected throughout the system for days. One by one, the victims will start to fall sick. Maybe after a while they will enter a hospital. Two thousand will die a horrible death. Then we will post a message online claiming responsibility, but *not* from the Sons of Canaan. From some random Gaza group. We will tell them that the deaths were caused by freedom fighters, but nobody will be able to tie them to our group. They are looking for us to act on the sixteenth, not the tenth. In fact, I predict we will repeat this very operation in Tel Aviv and Haifa later this summer."

Rami shook his head. "No, my friend. When so many die, the IDF will investigate. They'll find out the poison came from the IV bags. I doubt we'll ever be able to repeat. But we will have had a successful mission. I'm with Arif and Nizar. We go now."

Fa'iz nodded. "I agree. They are preparing for the sixteenth. The doctor's wisdom is hard to refute. Tell me, Arif, how are your plans coming along for the ransom? When is the forlorn father expected to bring his suitcase full of money?"

"In a couple of days."

"Do you need our assistance? Do you need help in disposing of the body?"

"I have more than enough manpower to deal with this lawyer and his companions."

"He has companions?"

"He hired a private investigator who negotiates for him. It is the private investigator who proposed the exchange and confirmed the details through Abu Hammad. He will accompany him, along with a nurse."

"He needs a nurse?"

Al-Zahani shrugged. "He is in a wheelchair. He was in an accident and cannot walk."

Fa'iz shook his head. "This is beset with too many coincidences, too much intrigue."

"What intrigue? I will bring them into my house and secure the money. Then my men will take them out and get rid of them."

"Why do you need to bring them into your house? Why don't we just grab the suitcase and shoot them all as soon as we see them?" Nizar asked.

"He's not that stupid. He says the briefcase is rigged to explode unless the correct combination is entered. Whether true or not, there is no harm in letting Sommers open the case. He will do it in my house because he has demanded to see the child."

"This is an IDF plot," Fakhir said nervously. "Another IDF plot."

"To do what, you fool?" Nizar said.

"To get into Arif's house and sniff out our plans. Maybe to get the child?"

"If they wanted the child, they'd take the child," al-Zahani said. "She goes to school every day. They could take her on the sidewalk. If they wanted to get into my house, they'd force their way in. I can't stop the IDF. But they won't because the Israeli government is too concerned about overstepping its bounds and creating a crisis in Hebron. No, this is just a desperate father, working alone, trying to retrieve his daughter. And he's willing to pay a small fortune. Nothing more."

"What if the father shows up with soldiers to arrest you? What becomes of you then, Arif?"

"What becomes of me? I have done nothing illegal. The child was placed in my custody by the father's agent and flown to Amman. He has not contacted me since. I will simply return the child to her father who has come to fetch her. And unfortunately, my laboratory will catch fire and burn to the ground. I have broken no laws. We will start again next year."

"And the money? Is ransom not a crime?"

"What ransom? He's making a donation to the schools of Hebron in appreciation for my caring for his daughter in his time of grief. If the IDF was interested in rescuing the child, they would have sent their soldiers long before this. No, Fakhir, this is Sommers alone, not the IDF."

"I agree, and think of what wondrous things we can do with all that money," Fa'iz said. "Arif, you will contact Sami and Aziz and tell them that the deliveries are to take place tomorrow. We are a go."

DMITRI PAUSED HIS VIDEO when Evgeniy walked into the room.

"I drove by his house earlier this evening," Evgeniy said. "I thought I might catch Kelsen at his home, but his stupid chauffeur saw me and waved at me."

"Did you stop?"

Evgeniy shook his head. "No. I saw him rush into the house, so I have to figure he tells Kelsen that he saw me."

Dmitri nodded and took a sip of vodka.

"I wait around the corner until I see the lights of a Lexus pull down the block. Sure enough, it's Kelsen. Driving himself. I follow him into the Lincoln Park neighborhood. He parks behind a taxicab. There are people on the street, I can do nothing. When the cab leaves, Kelsen walks up to a door where a woman is standing. A couple of words and the two of them go inside."

"Who was the woman?"

"No idea."

"That old weasel. He's getting action on the side."

"That's what I think too. So I figure, it better be good, because it's the last action he's ever gonna get. I turn off the lights and wait for him to come out."

"Good work."

"No, Dmitri. Not good. Half hour later a car pulls up, two men get out, knock on the door, and arrest Kelsen."

Dmitri looked at his cocktail glass and flung it at the wall. "I told you to get him right away. Now the government has him."

"We can get to him like we got to Sommers."

"You're a fool. No one will get near him. I'm sure he's spilled his guts. It's probably too late already. We need to get out of here. Call Ilya. Tell him to file his flight plan to Moscow immediately. He must be ready to leave first thing tomorrow morning."

Dmitri walked upstairs and into the bedroom, where his wife was reading a magazine. "Inessa, we need to leave. Tell Davit to pack his things, we are going to Moscow for a while."

"He has school. He can't just leave, he'll fail his classes. Besides, I have Pilates class tomorrow. I don't want to go. This is too sudden."

Dmitri clasped his hands around her face. "I am not making suggestions. I am telling you to pack. We leave tomorrow morning."

"You do what you want. I am staying here."

Dmitri leaned over until his lips were inches from her face. "Stay if you wish. I can find tits anywhere on earth. But I am taking my son. If you interfere in any way, I will slice you like a potato." He let her go and left the room.

SEVENTY-THREE

...

A BLUE TRUCK, ITS sides emblazoned with MEDITERRANEAN MEDICAL SUPPLY in English and Hebrew letters in bright yellow, pulled out of the company's distribution center. Instead of taking the direct route to the hospitals, Sami drove across town to a cold-storage facility in west Jerusalem. The weather was clear and traffic was light. He pulled his truck into Global Fisheries and the overhead door was closed.

Inside, Aziz and his men quickly switched the boxes of Sexton IV sets with al-Zahani's poisonous substitutes stored in the cold-storage room. The job completed, the blue delivery truck was once again on its way. Three hospitals and two clinics were scheduled to receive their deliveries, a total of twenty-six hundred IV sets, two thousand of which were secretly manufactured in the laboratories of Dr. Arif al-Zahani.

Sami was dressed in his standard uniform: a dark blue jumpsuit with a yellow canvas belt. The oval symbol of Mediterranean Medical Supply, grape leaves around the Rod of Asclepius, was sewn onto the left shirt pocket. As with all MMS uniforms, the employee's name was neatly embroidered in Hebrew script above the pocket. A plastic identification card hung on a cord around his neck.

Sami backed his delivery truck into the loading dock of Jerusalem Memorial Hospital and hopped out of the driver's seat with his clipboard. A handful of papers were bound to the board by a rubber band. He knocked on the reception door.

"Delivery, Jake," Sami said to the guard at the door. "Twenty-two boxes of IV sets."

The security guard looked at his daily manifest. "Right in here, Shmuel." He opened the delivery door and Sami wheeled the hand truck into the hospital's pharmacy department. The pharmacy staff greeted the familiar deliveryman and promptly unloaded the shipment.

"ER needs three hundred sets immediately," said one hospital worker.

"I'll take them right upstairs," an orderly replied.

Sami tipped his hat and was on his way. At the next stop, Sami handed the clipboard to the guard at the loading dock, who carefully studied the bill of lading. He shook his head. "The IV sets are correct, Sammy, but your order is short. We're also expecting PICC lines and infusion pumps."

"Two of our trucks are down today. We concentrated on filling the orders for IV sets. The rest of the order will come later today or tomorrow."

"No matter. Just bring the boxes in."

Sami nodded and wheeled the boxes into the hospital. The hospital staff placed al-Zahani's IV sets in the central pharmaceutical department, available for immediate use. Sami nodded to the staff and drove to the next hospital on his route.

The routine was repeated at each stop without incident. Every hospital accepted and placed the deliveries into current inventory. His mission completed, Sami returned the truck to Mediterranean, retrieved his car, and drove to his home.

Al-Zahani's cell phone buzzed. He read the text and smiled. Immediately he called Fa'iz. "The resting places have been achieved," he said, and hung up.

EVGENIY CARRIED THE LUGGAGE from Dmitri's front hall to the limo in the driveway. Dmitri and Davit hurried out the door and slid into the backseat. The sun had yet to rise, and the April morning had laid a covering of frost on the lawn. Evgeniy was about to shut the door when Inessa came running out of the house, her robe barely tied around her nightgown. She climbed into the back, fastened her seat belt, and said in an animated tone, "So, we're off to the mother country?"

The car quickly left the quiet suburb and headed south along I-294. There was little traffic in the predawn hours and nothing was said on the way. Davit fell asleep and leaned his head against his mother. Seventy minutes later, they pulled into Independence Executive Airport and into a private hangar. The motors of the Gulfstream were whining when they arrived. They quickly climbed the metal stairs and took their seats in the plane.

Dmitri nervously looked out the window. The airport was quiet. No other planes were on the runways. The cabin door closed and the plane moved slowly forward from the hangar and made its way to the apron, where it stopped. After it remained stationary for a few minutes, Dmitri took off his belt and hurried to the cockpit. "Why aren't we taking off? Why did you stop?"

"Sorry, sir, but we have not received clearance to take off," the pilot said.

"Call the tower. Find out what's holding us up."

"I have done that, sir. They've asked us to wait. Perhaps there is an incoming flight, or an emergency."

The plane sat for another ten minutes. Dmitri squirmed in his seat. Finally, he once again unbuckled his belt and scampered to the cockpit. "We need to go. Call them again," he ordered.

"Independence ground, Gulfstream November Romeo Five Four Echo on west apron, request clearance for departure, direction east."

"Negative, Gulfstream. Request is denied. Please hold your position at this time. There's a total ground stop."

The pilot looked at Dmitri and shrugged.

"Go anyway. Just go."

"I can't. I'll lose my license."

Dmitri pulled a gun from his pocket. "Go!"

"Independence ground, Gulfstream November Romeo Five Four Echo proceeding runway three right, departing east."

"Do not take off. Repeat. Do not proceed. You are to stay at the apron, Gulfstream. There is a ground stop."

Dmitri sat in the jump seat, his gun pointed at the pilot. "Go!"

The plane started moving forward, but stopped abruptly.

"What are you doing?" shouted Dmitri. "I said to go."

The pilot pointed out the window. Four police cars were directly in the plane's path and headed toward them, their lights flashing.

"Shit," said Dmitri.

SEVENTY-FOUR

• • •

KAYLA AND LIAM HELD the conference room doors open as Marcy guided Jack's wheelchair to the table. Finding it difficult to sit erect, he leaned to the side, wincing in obvious discomfort. His complexion was pasty and beads of sweat had formed on his forehead. The strain of the journey had taken its toll. The group joined Harry and the others, who rose to greet them.

An aerial photo of al-Zahani's compound was projected on a retractable screen. The photo clearly depicted the property surrounded by the perimeter wall. His outbuilding, his home, a garage, and three individuals walking through the yard were identifiable. Four guards were pictured standing outside the perimeter walls. A parking area with six old cars was located to the rear of the outbuilding.

"Welcome to Tel Aviv," Eliezer said. "Make yourselves comfortable. I hope your flight was not too strenuous."

"It's good to be back, sir, thank you," Kayla said as she took her seat.

"I thank you, as well," Jack said. "I'm looking forward to seeing my daughter and taking her home." His voice was shaky and his bearing unsteady.

Eliezer gestured to the table and introduced the notables in attendance: the Israeli defense minister, the public security minister, the Shin Bet chief, and the IDF chief of staff. When all were settled, he said, "We have less than three days to learn the details of the terrorist plot and stop the operation. As we understand it, the proposed exchange is set for noon tomorrow in the al-Zahani compound. Am I right, Kayla?"

"Yes, sir, that's correct."

"It's only fair to tell you, we've been discussing the urgency of the situation all morning. There is considerable support for a preemptive raid as early as tonight."

"You can't do that!" Jack said. "Sophie'd get caught in the crossfire."

"Indeed," Eliezer answered calmly. "I'm afraid that's an unfortunate possibility. Our young soldiers may also get caught in a crossfire and it's not something we take lightly, but we are carrying a heavy responsibility here. We must protect our citizens from terrorism."

"But a preemptive raid is only under discussion, right?" Kayla said. "You haven't made up your mind?"

"Out of deference to you," Eliezer said. "Harry tells us that you fear the group will destroy the building and the evidence of the plot?"

"They've said so. It's on the recording. They're prepared to firebomb the building."

"What is the current situation at the property?"

"The entire compound is full of security guards," Yonit said. "We've watched it day and night. There are always guards outside the walls, never fewer than three, sometimes as many as five. We believe we've spotted armed guards within the compound, some near the doors of the outbuilding where the devices are being assembled. That factory—or laboratory, whatever it is—is working twenty-four/seven. Three shifts of workers leave and enter the property at specified times of day. The front gate opens at seven A.M., three P.M., and eleven P.M. punctually. Workers come and go. Other than at shift change, the gate is locked and, we presume, fortified."

"That supports my opinion that the compound cannot be breached without considerable resistance," Kayla said. "Such an engagement would take time and allow al-Zahani to destroy the building."

"It wouldn't take that much time," said the IDF chief of staff confidently.

"How much time would it take for al-Zahani to trigger the bomb, not only destroying the laboratory but anyone near it, including our soldiers? Can you give me assurances, Moshe?" Eliezer said.

Moshe shook his head. "Of course not."

Eliezer turned to Kayla. "This man, he would destroy all of his employees as well and put his own home at risk?"

"I know from personal experience that al-Zahani is ruthless and cares nothing for human life that gets in the way of his agenda," Kayla said. "Collateral damage will not deter his mission."

"But he will open the gates for you and Mr. Sommers and let you walk into his house?"

"Correct. And we will distract the doctor long enough for you to gain access to the outbuilding."

Eliezer turned to his IDF chief. "And you can respond quickly with your soldiers?"

He nodded. "Certainly. But seconds are critical. Once in the home, Kayla may need to take affirmative measures to stop al-Zahani from triggering the explosives."

"Understood," Kayla said. "But I'm not so sure he'll be anxious to set off the bomb. He's an arrogant man. He probably thinks he's got a foolproof plan for taking the money and disposing of us. He'll be transfixed on the briefcase. Undoubtedly, he has no intention of turning over the child. And he won't be eager to destroy his building. He wants to continue with his operations later this summer."

"Al-Zahani's aware there are three of you?" Eliezer said.

"Liam set up the conditions for the exchange through Abu Hammad. Al-Zahani was informed that Jack was confined to a wheelchair and would be accompanied by a nurse. So he knows there will be three."

"What about this young lady?" Eliezer pointed to Marcy.

"She stays here."

"No, no. Let me go with Jack. I can go as his wife. I can push the wheelchair. You'll need someone to help with Sophie. She'll be frightened. She knows me."

"Out of the question," Kayla said. "We told him there would be three. You'll just get in the way. We made a deal, remember?"

"Do not let her go," Jack said, his breathing labored. "She stays here."

"Jack!"

"I'm sorry, Marcy, but Kayla's right. You wait for me. If anything happens to me, you must take Sophie to Deborah."

"Really, Marcy, it's better that you stay here in Tel Aviv," Kayla said. "The IDF will make sure Sophie gets to you."

"What do you mean, the IDF?" Jack said. "What about you?" He looked hard at Kayla, who shrugged. "You don't think you're going to make it back, do you?"

"Well, I certainly intend to, but I'm aware of the risks involved. I've got a job to do."

"You mean you've got a score to settle," Liam said.

"We need to move on here," Eliezer interjected. "I see no reason why Marcy cannot go to Kiryat Arba, where you'll stay tonight. It's apparent to me that she's a comforting presence for Jack." Eliezer smiled. "He needs care, and she can care for him until the mission begins. And she can assist in bringing the child home."

"I disagree, sir," Kayla said. "She should stay here. She's a civilian. The mission will be dangerous, even in Kiryat Arba."

"Excuse me," Liam said, raising his hand. "Civilian, right here."

"Quite right," Eliezer said. "I see three civilians at this table, all willing volunteers on this mission."

"Speaking of my own personal agenda," Liam said, with a quick nod to Kayla, "I booked a return flight to Chicago and I intend to be on it." Turning to Eliezer, he said, "I'd like to know what support we'll have, sir, and how you've scripted this op."

"You'll have full IDF support, of course." Eliezer gestured to the uniformed woman at the end of the table. "Colonel Yonit Gershon will be on the ground and running this operation. Yonit, if you please."

Yonit stood and walked to the screen. Her uniform—olive slacks and a short-sleeve shirt—was fitted snugly to her taut frame. Her dark hair was pulled back and tied. She reminded Liam of a panther: quick, powerful, perceptive, dangerous.

"We will have troops here, here, and here, just outside the view of the security cameras." Yonit pointed to the aerial photo. "We'll have transports around the corner, here and here. The four guards outside the walls will be taken down simultaneously the moment you've entered the home. Quickly thereafter, we'll secure the entire compound.

"They'll expect you to arrive in a vehicle, and since Jack is in a wheelchair, we have prepared and modified a handicap van, the type that is routinely available from rental agencies. In fact, it's waiting for you downstairs. You'll drive it to Kiryat Arba."

She changed the picture to a gray Chrysler van. "This is your vehicle. There's a wheelchair lift, as shown here." She advanced the slide to depict the van with the side door open. "We're making some assumptions here. We expect the guards to search the van, and each of you, before the gates are opened. When they're confident you have no weapons, they'll open the gate and allow you to proceed into the compound and up to the house."

"No weapons?" Liam said. "We're going in with no weapons? Even al-Zahani wouldn't think we're that dumb. I have a gun."

"We know, but you can't bring a gun. This has been arranged as a peaceful exchange. There's no way they're going to let you in with a gun. We've planted weapons in the van, and I'll get to that in a few minutes," Yonit continued. "The IDF will have substantial assets on the ground to back you up, but you'll be on your own once you're inside the home."

"Do we think al-Zahani will have guards inside?" Kayla said.

"Maybe."

"Extra guards? I don't think so," Liam answered. "He'll have that big guy we saw with Sophie, but al-Zahani's going to think he's safe within his house. We'll go inside to make the exchange. I figure he takes the money, then maneuvers us outside, where he plans to have his guards shoot us. He's not going to want to have a gunfight in his house, especially with the child present. What's the collective judgment here?"

"We can't discount another guard or two inside, but we agree, he probably won't want a gunfight in his house," Moshe answered.

"And once we walk out the door, the Light Brigade will be waiting in the yard to protect us, right?" Liam said.

"That's the plan."

"Too many things can go wrong with that plan. I want a gun. I want Kayla to have a gun."

"I told you, we have planted weapons in the van," Yonit said.

Liam shook his head. "They're going to search the van. I'm a PI, they'll expect me to have a gun. Who would go to a gunfight without a gun?"

"He's right, Yonit," Eliezer said. "He should go with his gun. They would expect that. They'll take it from him outside, and then maybe they won't look so carefully in the van. Even better."

"You guys are nuts. I'm not going in without a gun."

Yonit shook her head and spoke forcefully. "They won't let you in the house with your gun. But if you pay attention, we'll tell you where you can find a hidden gun."

"If I pay attention?"

"Your Irish charm is fading," Kayla said.

"Charm? He has charm?" Yonit said. "When you get to the house and once they finish searching you outside the gates, and they take your gun, we expect you will get back into the van and drive through the gates. That is the plan. There will be weapons in the van, which they will not have found. You can extract them and hide them in the pockets of your jacket."

"Why won't they find the weapons?"

"Because they are in a hidden chamber in the back of the center console that will not open for them."

"What if they search the vehicle and then instruct us to walk through the gates?" Liam said. "What if they insist on driving the van into the compound themselves? What if one of their guards gets into the van with us? What if they search us again after we get in the gates? In all those scenarios, how do we get weapons?"

"We don't think they'll search you twice, there would be no reason to do that."

"Why would they let us drive into the yard by ourselves?"

"Why not? There are only three seats in the van. Driver, passenger, wheelchair. Three chairs—three tushes. No room for anybody else. They won't want you to leave the van in the street. They'll direct you into the compound."

"Yonit, you're logical. Your plan is logical," Liam said. "But the terrorists may not be logical. What if one of them gets into the driver's seat? Now what?"

"Still okay," Eliezer said. "We've considered the possibility that the guards will take possession of the van and drive it into the yard and tell you and Kayla to walk. But Jack is locked into the wheelchair seat and somebody has to operate the power lift. This, they cannot do."

"Why not? They don't have disabled people in Hebron?"

"Did someone once accuse this man of having Irish charm?" Eliezer said.

"We've made the chairlift impossible to operate unless you know the sequence of the buttons," Yonit said. "There's a code. There are two controls in the van. The one in front of Jack's wheelchair is not functional. It will not work. He will ask for assistance. The guards will try to operate the master controls on the door panel, but they won't be able to move the chair without knowing the code. They'll still need you or Kayla to enter the code and operate the lift to get Jack out of the van. There's a chamber hidden into the back of the center console. Once the code is activated, the clasp on the back of the console will release and the weapons can be accessed."

"And they won't see us?"

"The position of your bodies should block their vision. Each of you will wear a jacket. There will be two small handguns hidden in the console." Yonit spread her hands and shrugged. "We have confidence that you can do it."

"So, let me get this straight," Liam said. "We get into the yard and Kayla and I get out of the van. The guards search the van, but the console's not open, so they don't see the guns. We hear Jack say that his controls are not working. He needs someone to push the buttons on the door. The guards go over to operate the controls on the door, but they don't know the code, so the chair doesn't move. So I offer to operate the lift. I put in the code, the chairlift is lowering, the back of the console opens, I take the guns, slip them in my jacket pockets, and no one can see me do it. Right?"

"Exactly."

"Are you kidding me? That's the plan?"

Eliezer shrugged. "Why not? It's perfect."

"Has anyone practiced this maneuver?"

"Not yet."

"Oh, Jesus."

"The van is downstairs. We can all go practice. I have high confidence in the plan."

"Oh, Jesus," Liam repeated.

"Obviously, if you have hesitation, you need not participate. Your involvement, while highly valuable, is not compulsory, as is ours," Eliezer said. "We are prepared for the alternative, which is launching the raid tonight."

"No, please don't," Jack said. "Someone has to protect Sophie. I need to get inside."

"*We* need to get inside," Kayla said, "with as little commotion as possible. We know that al-Zahani's laboratory continues to assemble IEDs, explosives, chemicals, whatever, at the rate of forty bags per day. The recorded conversation disclosed al-Zahani's intent to repeat the attack at some future date. So, he's stockpiling. If you storm the compound, he blows the building, we learn nothing of the plan, and we have no grounds to arrest al-Zahani. Then he's free to organize the next attack."

Eliezer and Yonit nodded.

"Although we know he's mined the building, he's not going to be eager to throw the switch," Kayla continued. "He's arrogant and ambitious, a fatal combination. If he doesn't have time or the inclination to detonate the building, we can seize the remaining devices, interrogate the workers, and learn what we need to know about the pending operation in Jerusalem. For that, we need to get inside, and Jack is our only ticket."

"I understand," Liam said. "I'm just pointing out the risks when everything doesn't go according to plan. Then what?"

"Improvisation, I'm afraid," Eliezer said. "You'll be mic'd and we'll be listening. When or if something goes wrong, you'll alert us and the IDF will move in. You may have to scramble to access the weapons and do your best."

Eliezer eyed each of the attendees at the table. "Are we all on board with this?" Each nodded approval. Eliezer stood. "Yonit will show you the van. You'll want to practice." He smiled.

As the group filed out, Eliezer stopped Liam. "I understand it was your idea to tell al-Zahani that the briefcase is armed to explode. Very clever. You know he would have certainly shot you all the moment you showed up." Eliezer nodded and slapped Liam on the back. "Clever indeed."

"We did it in Antrim in 1996. Same plot, different movie. So, where's the briefcase and the money?"

"Yonit has them. A little under four million euros in five-hundred-euro notes. Eight and a half kilos. The case is metal, rotary combination, and otherwise quite ordinary."

"You get that all into a metal case? Four million euros?"

"Approximately thirty inches of bills, stacked top to bottom. They fit quite nicely. All counterfeit, of course."

"Counterfeit? That's hardly the IDF stamp of confidence, is it? If he succeeds in opening the briefcase, getting his hands on the money and killing us all, well, at least we've managed to give him bogus money."

Eliezer shrugged and gave Liam a weak smile.

Outside, a standard handicap van sat in the parking area, a metal platform extending from the open door and resting on the pavement. "We've opted for a mechanized platform rather than just a ramp, for obvious reasons," said Yonit. "This is top-of-the-line. The wheelchair locks onto the movable platform. Two sets of controls, one in front of the wheelchair and one just inside the door behind the passenger seat, operate the motor. As you can see, there are three buttons on each control box. The top button, labeled RETRACT, engages the motor to raise the platform from street level. The middle button is a pause or stop button. The bottom button, labeled EXIT, slides the platform from its passenger position sideways to the doorway and then down to the street. The mechanisms are simple to operate, unless you have reprogrammed them, as we have done.

"The lift will not work at all without the code. Here, look. To engage the lift in either direction you must first double-press the pause button. That will prevent the guards from operating the lift. They'll push the bottom button, and when the chair fails to move, you'll offer your assistance. Standing in the doorway, blocking their vision, when you double-click the middle button and the platform engages, this panel behind the center console, above the air-conditioning vent, will release. There will be two loaded handguns inside. Leaning over to guide the wheelchair will place your hand in proximity of the guns. Your actions should not be visible to others."

Liam stepped on the runner. His frame blocked the door. He pressed the middle button twice and then the bottom button, the lift engaged, and the back of the center console opened. He saw the two small handguns inside.

Yonit smiled. "There, you have the weapons."

Liam managed the maneuver without detection from behind, placing the guns in the inner pockets of his jacket as the wheelchair was lowered to the street.

Liam nodded. "Very smooth." He ran the test again without a flaw.

"Then it's a go for tomorrow at noon," Eliezer said. "You'll reassemble in Kiryat Arba. Godspeed, ladies and gentlemen."

SEVENTY-FIVE

• • •

"L UBANNAH, WHEN SOPHIE COMES home from madrassa, I'm going to talk to her and I want you to talk to her with me."

"Does this concern her father and his visit?"

Al-Zahani nodded. "It does."

"I want no part of this."

"Lubannah, I appeal to your reason. Did I not arrange to take her from Chicago, that depraved and unholy land, and bring her here to Hebron, just so that you could be with her?"

She nodded.

"Have I not always had her best interests in my heart? Do I not raise her as my own daughter?"

"Yes, you do."

"Then stop questioning me. Cooperate with me and help us to take the next step; to sever all ties with her American past. To help her accept her life here."

"What is it you want me to do?"

"Just be supportive. Talk to her with me. And when Sommers comes, help me to calm her and comfort her on her loss. That's all."

"What loss?"

"Sommers will come, he will offer us money, we will allow him to see Sophie, that she is being raised properly, and he will leave. Sophie will be told the truth—that he has left her for good. She must make a break with her futile, incessant pining."

"I will talk to her. I will support you, but she is strong-willed, like her mother. She will not believe us. When Sommers comes, she will be uncontrollable."

"Leave it to me. I will handle it."

Bashir entered the house with Sophie. "The little one had a very good day. Her teacher told me so."

"Really?" al-Zahani said. "Tell me, Sophie."

"Teacher said my painting was the best in the class." She held up a watercolor on construction paper.

"Very, very good." Al-Zahani held it up, turned it from side to side, and smiled. "I see many trees. Where is it?"

"It's a park in Wisconsin where my daddy took me."

Al-Zahani shook his head and put the picture on a table. "Your Jadda and I would like to talk to you. Sit down, here." He patted the couch. "You know, your father has not talked to you in many, many months."

"But, that's because—"

"No, wait." He held his hand up and closed his eyes. "I have demonstrated to you that he left the city, left your house, and, most importantly, left you. He quit his job. And he went away by himself to be apart from everyone he knew. Including you, Sophie."

"I don't believe—"

"Wait, wait, child. No one knew where he went. You made the phone calls. His house was empty. He quit his job. But I knew how sad you have been about this. So I said, I have to find this man for my Sophie. I searched and searched. And I sent men all around the world to find your father. And you know what? I finally did it. I found him."

Sophie jumped off the couch. "You did?"

She threw her arms around him and hugged him. "Oh, thank you, Jaddi. Thank you."

He patted her on the head. "Do not thank me so much yet. Your father did not want to come here. He didn't want to see you, I am sorry to say."

Tears welled up in Sophie's eyes. "You're a liar. You're a big liar."

"Wait, wait. I knew you would say that. So, I made him promise to come here anyway. He is bringing some papers. The papers will say that he wants us to raise you here in Hebron. You will see for yourself. He will be carrying a satchel when he comes, and inside that satchel will be the papers."

"No, he won't. He will want to take me home. And I will go with him."

"Oh, my child, I despair deeply of your impending disappointment. I ask only that you not get your hopes too high for something that will not happen. He has told me he will not take you with him. He has moved on in his life. Please, child, do not take my word for it. See for yourself. He will come here tomorrow and in his hand he will have a case. When you see that case, you will know that I have told you the truth. Then, if you will leave us alone for a little bit so I can review the papers, I will let you go outside and talk to your father all you want. That is, if he will even stay long enough to talk to you. If I'm lying about what I've said and he wants to take you home, you can go with him. I will not stop you. But if I'm telling the truth, then you have to stop all this crying and pining about going back to Chicago."

Sophie looked at Lubannah. "Is this true?"

"It is true, my Sophie. It is all true."

"When is he coming?"

"Tomorrow at noon."

SEVENTY-SIX

• • •

MARCY, KAYLA, AND JACK took their places in the van, pulled away from Mossad headquarters, and followed Yonit's car toward Kiryat Arba. The hills looked peaceful in the moonlight, their tranquillity belying the havoc that was sure to await them beyond the next ridge. Yonit took the southern route past Yavne, Kiryat Gat, Beit Guvrin National Park, and into the West Bank through a southern checkpoint. She dropped Liam at a four-story building and drove off. Kayla pulled in seconds later and parked the van along the curb.

"Yonit will be here in the morning," Liam said. "She'll have the briefcase, our microphones, and Kayla's nurse's uniform. She assured me al-Zahani would take my gun from me at the front gate and that the hidden-gun trick would work perfectly. Not so comforting, I'm afraid. Oh, and she said to get a good night's sleep."

"Why don't we take a ride by the house in the morning?" Jack said. "Maybe I could catch Sophie on her way to school. We might be able to avoid the confrontation altogether."

"Jack, you're dreaming," Liam said quietly. "Do you think he's going to be careless with Sophie on the day he's expecting five million dollars?"

Kayla nodded. "She's never alone anyway. She's guarded to and from school. You know we could never do that."

"Let's be honest," Marcy said. "You wouldn't do it if you could. Sophie's your passport into the compound. If Sophie was walking down this street by herself, you wouldn't stop to pick her up. That's the sorry fact of the whole thing."

"Stop, Marcy," Jack said. "If it wasn't for Kayla, we'd never see Sophie again. This is the only way I can bring her home."

"He'd better get clemency or immunity or something for doing this," Marcy said. "He better not put his life on the line to stop a terrorist attack just to return to prison. You need to take care of him."

"I promise, I'll push as hard as I can," Kayla said.

A T MIDNIGHT THE APARTMENT was dark and quiet. Liam found a bottle of Jameson in the cabinet, poured a couple of inches into a glass, and sat alone on a stool at the kitchen counter, musing over the events that had brought him to this juncture. A call from Walter Jenkins, a meeting in a conference room, and a simple skip trace turns into a firestorm in Hebron. Life's road has funny turns.

He reached into his pocket and took out a picture he had ripped from a magazine before he left Honolulu. Solitaire wedding rings. There had been no time before they left, it all just happened so fast. It would have to wait until he got home.

"Buy me a drink?" Kayla said, sliding onto a stool beside him.

He filled another tumbler and placed it before her. They clinked their glasses.

"You know, there's no way this goes down easy," Liam said. "Jack's a sitting duck, no pun intended."

"As long as they think it's just a ransom exchange and that you're the muscle he brought from Chicago, we have the element of surprise. They won't be ready for the IDF."

"I like Yonit. Her fearless bearing, that inner strength, I can see why men would follow her into battle."

"And women."

He nodded and smiled sheepishly. "And women, of course. That's an unusual name: Yonit."

"In Hebrew it means 'dove.'"

"'Dove'? Oh, that's terrific. Just what we need."

They sat in silence for a few minutes.

Liam looked down, swirled the whiskey in his glass. "How do you see this playing out?"

"I hope it's pretty much as Eliezer and Yonit have said. We'll pull up to the gate, the guards will search us—"

"I'm not giving up my gun."

Kayla pursed her lips. "They won't let you go in with it."

"We'll see. I don't trust this hidden-gun trick in the van, and I'm sure not walking into a terrorist's house unarmed."

Kayla shrugged. "Well, you'll have to play it as you see it. You've been in situations before. Just don't lose sight of the mission. We need to get inside the house, to al-Zahani."

Liam took a sip of his drink. "You mean *you* need to get to al-Zahani."

Kayla looked hard at Liam and emptied her glass. Liam freshened it.

"This mission doesn't depend on ransoming Sophie," Liam said quietly. "A military squadron could neutralize the compound in a New York minute."

"*Neutralize*? As in 'destroy'? Of course. But what of the terrorist operation? What of the IEDs already in place in Jerusalem? The threat is legitimate, and we don't know the particulars. I'm positive the secrets are locked away in the outbuilding, and we can't allow it to be destroyed. If everything goes down as planned, that'll be the best of all worlds. We'll get al-Zahani and enough information to stop the attack."

"And our evil doctor? You don't want him neutralized, do you? That's too easy. This mission's about you and al-Zahani."

She took another drink. "I want him alive. He needs to be interrogated. He's a fountain of information. But you're right, it's more than that. It's personal."

"It has to do with the wedding, doesn't it?"

Kayla nodded and took a deep breath. "Yes, it does. His gang of terrorists, the Sons of Canaan, killed my husband, Brian Cummings. We'd been married barely three years. Two teenagers shot him out of the window of a car on the streets of Hebron. At Ma'arat HaMachpelah, the holiest of sites. They fired wildly at the wedding party and sped away. A wedding party, Liam. Just peaceful, happy celebrants, dancing their way to a marriage ceremony at a holy site. Not soldiers, politicians, combatants. Not policy makers or oppressors. They threatened no one, they harmed no one. Just a fucking wedding party. They all deserved to live long, happy lives. But they were cut down by brainwashed, misguided youths, driven to murder by hateful puppeteers."

"And al-Zahani?"

"The most wicked of them all. He was not only vicariously responsible for the death of my husband, he personally murdered my sister."

Liam said nothing. He sat in shocked silence, his hands wrapped around the tumbler. He stared at the counter, unable to meet her gaze. Finally, he lifted his head. Kayla's eyes were red but her face was steeled.

"Until Jack and I talked recently, I hadn't put the pieces together. I didn't know what al-Zahani had done. I didn't know the depths of his wickedness. I had no idea until I learned the details of Jack's story. Then it all came together." She pushed her glass over for a refill. "My sister, Naomi, was to be married that day."

"She was the bride?"

Kayla nodded. "She was standing right beside me. I was the maid of honor. I held her as she fell."

"Oh my Lord, I'm so sorry."

Kayla emptied her glass. "As she approached the ceremony on the happiest day of her life, she took a bullet. Critically. In her lower abdomen. She needed medical care immediately. They shouted for a doctor and were directed to al-Zahani's home by a security guard. Joshua, her husband-to-be, carried her unconscious body into al-Zahani's house. Reluctant at first, al-Zahani agreed to treat her. He stopped the bleeding and bound the wounds. He saved her life!"

Liam looked at her quizzically.

"He wouldn't accept any money, or even a thank-you. He directed Joshua to take her to an Israeli hospital, which we did."

Kayla reached over and grabbed Liam's forearms. He felt her fingernails dig into his flesh.

"Naomi lay at Jerusalem Memorial for three days, recovering nicely. We talked about my husband. She comforted me. We talked about the others, the ones who were laid to rest while she was in the hospital. I urged her to reset the wedding as soon as possible, for herself, for my husband, and for all those who wanted to rejoice with her."

Kayla paused, her lips quivered. She moistened them with her tongue. "And then . . . then the infection set in. At first she thought she had the flu. But then it got worse. The doctors attributed it to the Good Samaritan care she received after the shooting—closing the wound and being stitched in a nonsterile environment. A likely consequence, they said. They would treat it with antibiotics, they said. But they couldn't control the infection. It was a wildly aggressive bacterium. It had spread internally, attacking her organs. It ate her up from the inside out. She died six days later.

"Until I met Jack, I never realized what had really happened. He told me about his wife, Alina, who had come to Hebron when her mother had a heart attack, and returned to Chicago with an infection. Just the same. The doctors could not control it and she died. The way Jack described Alina, all the symptoms, he could have been talking about Naomi. And then I remembered the boy in the hospital, the one I told you about."

"The shooter."

"Right. IDF caught one of the shooters, a seventeen-year-old boy, who had been wounded in the leg, but not a serious wound. I made several visits to the hospital to question him. Most of the time, he was delirious, in a drugged-out state. I caught him a few times in half-lucid moments and he identified Nizar Mohammed, Fakhir Ali, Fa'iz Talib, and the Sons of Canaan."

"But not al-Zahani."

"Here's the thing—al-Zahani was his doctor."

"No doubt the reason he was drugged out and couldn't talk to you."

Kayla nodded. "After three days, the boy came down with an infection. The same as Naomi. The same as Alina. Horrible. Internal bleeding. He lasted nine days."

"He killed them all," Liam said.

"He killed them all. He poisoned them with virulent bacteria. He killed the boy to silence him. He killed my sister because she was an Israeli Jew who came to him for treatment. And he killed his own daughter, his very own daughter, because she had the temerity to fall in love outside his ordained parameters."

"I'm so sorry for you. I almost wish you'd never found out about the connection."

"So painful a death. The brutal way in which they suffered. That's his plan for the attack, you know. It has to be. He's not a munitions expert, he's a laboratory scientist."

"How could he possibly infect two thousand people with a superbug?"

"I don't know. That's why we have to get into that building. But I know one thing—the bugs are already in Jerusalem."

"Let me ask you something, be honest with me, do you know for a fact that al-Zahani has rigged the building to explode?"

Kayla shrugged. "For a fact? No."

"I knew it."

"You said 'for a fact.' I heard him say so on the recording. Do you want to take that chance? Personally, I think al-Zahani would go to great lengths not to destroy his laboratory. As I said before, he's arrogant and ambitious. He's like Dr. Frankenstein in there, growing genetically modified germs, superbugs, for use as weapons in his jihad. I doubt very much he plans to blow up the building. But a quick takeover before anyone can pull the trigger would remove any possibility that I'm wrong, and the best way to quickly secure the building is for us to get inside."

"The IDF could secure it quickly enough, you know that's true. They'd also stand a damn good chance of taking out al-Zahani and rescuing Sophie."

"I don't have that level of confidence. I don't want to rely on a damn good chance. Al-Zahani will blow up his lab and all his workers in a minute to save his operation. Human life means nothing to him. We're better off getting inside with the ransom exchange and preventing him from pushing the button. And besides, I want him alive. I want to take him into custody, interrogate him, and bring him to justice. Not just him, but everyone he's connected with, including Nizar Mohammed. And Fakhir Ali. And the godfather, Fa'iz Talib. And whatever group's been funding them. I want them all and I don't want any suicides. No martyrs. I don't want any Hebron elementary schools named after al-Zahani or the Sons of Canaan."

Liam nodded. "Assuming he buys this ransom charade, when do you think he'll make his move?"

"Outside, after the payoff. I agree that he won't want a gunfight in his home in front of his wife and granddaughter. He'll complete the transaction, get his money, and walk us outside where he thinks his security guards will be waiting."

"But the IDF will be there instead?"

"That's the plan. If they're not, I hope you have a gun and you're a damn good shot."

Liam swallowed the last bit of whiskey and set his glass down. "I keep thinking about what Mike Tyson said: 'Everyone has a plan until you punch them in the face.'"

SEVENTY-SEVEN

. . .

A ROOSTER CROWED LOUDLY and the sun broke brilliantly over the Judean hills. Shafts of sunlight knifed into the Kiryat Arba apartment. The windows were open and the morning breeze played a soft rattle on the blinds. Jack and Marcy were sitting on the living-room couch when Liam entered the room. Kayla was in the kitchen.

"Did anyone sleep?" Marcy asked.

Liam raised his hand.

"Yonit should be here any minute," Kayla said, staring into an empty refrigerator. "I hope she brings breakfast."

"I hope she brings you a Smith and Wesson .40 caliber with extra clips," Liam muttered.

Kayla answered a knock on the door. Yonit entered the apartment with two young men, smartly dressed in olive IDF uniforms, pants bloused into black boots, red berets, their arms full of paper bags and packages.

Yonit handed a nurse's folded white uniform—shirt jacket and trousers—to Kayla. "Size six?"

Kayla nodded and left the room to put it on.

Yonit laid a silver metal briefcase on the coffee table. "Here is your booby-trapped case. The combination on the left is one-two-three-four, and on the right four-three-two-one." She clicked it open. Inside were stacks of €500 bills, neatly bound. On top of the currency was a red rod, eight inches long, with wires protruding from each end.

"This is a replica of a small explosive, inoperative of course, consistent with our threat that the case was rigged. It may also serve as a visual deterrent if all else fails, maybe to buy you a few seconds of distraction."

"Why isn't it real?" Marcy said. "Couldn't Jack have a need for an explosive?"

"If things deteriorate to the stage where he'd need an explosive device . . . well, it would probably result in getting Jack killed or providing an extra weapon for al-Zahani. In the exchange, if Jack hands the case to al-Zahani, well, we prefer that weapons, if any, be in the hands of Kayla and Liam."

"If any? What does that mean?" Marcy said.

Yonit shrugged. "Just a figure of speech."

"It means she thinks that we will enter the house unarmed," Liam said. "She thinks they won't allow me to approach the house with my gun, and she's less than confident of my ability to grab the guns hidden in the van. Am I right, Colonel?"

Yonit turned and walked to the kitchenette. "Just a figure of speech."

"Did one of you bring breakfast?" Liam asked. "Or should we just take a five-hundred-euro bill to the corner deli for some bacon and eggs?"

"You wouldn't get any bacon." Yonit took a paper bag from one of the soldiers and set it on the counter. "Here's some fruit, juice, and breakfast rolls."

Yonit cleared the coffee table and unrolled a schematic of the compound. Liam and Kayla hovered over the drawing.

"We'll have sharpshooters here, here, and here, but we're hoping for a quick grab without the need to fire. There's typically one guard, maybe two, at the front gate. Others patrol the perimeter. We've allowed for the possibility that they may increase the number for your arrival.

"You know the routine at the gate, we've been over it before. We'll be watching and listening. If anything goes amiss, we'll move in. If it all follows the plan, we intend to neutralize the perimeter guards after they open the gates and let you in. We'll have troop transports here and here, around the corner and out of sight. They'll enter the compound after you've gone inside the home."

"What if the gate closes after we've driven inside?" Liam said. "I doubt they'd leave it open. What if you can't get in the gate?"

"The wall is only eight feet high. We can manage it." Yonit took a small button from a pouch. "This is your microphone," she said to Liam. "It replaces the button on your jeans." She smiled. "I need to put it on. You'll have to take your pants off."

"You're putting the mic on my pants?"

"When you arrive at the gate, we expect a thorough search. They'll pat you down, they may ask you to take off your shoes, they may ask you to take off your shirt, they may even wand you, but we don't think they'll ask you to take off your pants. But even if they do, the mic is pretty much undetectable. It's very sensitive, won't set off the wand, broadcasts half a mile, and will pick up everything in the room. Now, let me have your pants."

"I have to take off my pants?"

Yonit grinned. "Unless you want me working in that neighborhood with a sharp tool. Now, will you stop being such a baby?"

Liam stepped out of his pants, stood in his boxers, and frowned at the general chuckling in the room.

When Yonit had finished, Liam examined the brass button on his jeans and pulled them up. "Very cool. Looks good. Can't tell the mic from the original button. Is it working? Picking up the sound?"

One of the soldiers with earbuds nodded.

"It's on a dedicated frequency," Yonit said. "No one but the IDF will hear it. Bear in mind, it's not only for your protection, but ours as well. Should things break down inside, it's there for the safety of my soldiers. If you see al-Zahani move to trigger explosives in the outbuilding, you have to alert us. We don't know how he's got it wired, but if he gives you any reason to think he's going to blow the building, let us know. We'll be listening."

For the next two hours the group made small talk, fidgeted, reviewed the protocols, paced the room, stared out the windows, and watched the clock. The movement of the minute hand was imperceptible.

Liam had hesitated all morning, but finally took out his cell phone and made the call.

"Hey, Cat."

"Liam, are you all right?"

"I'm fine. We're about to head over to Hebron to pick up Sophie."

"Oh, hell, Liam, I wish you weren't going."

"I know. But, it'll be a simple little operation. I don't have to do much. The Israeli army's going to handle the heavy stuff."

"You are such a liar."

"No, really, Cat. I . . . I just called to . . . say hello."

"Liam . . ."

"Cat, I love you very much."

"I know. I love you more."

"Cat, I gotta go."

"Liam, wait."

"Can't. Gotta go."

"Call me. The moment you're done. I'm going to sit by the phone."

"Good-bye, sweetheart."

Marcy sat on the couch with Jack, her arm around his shoulders. She smoothed his hair. "Jack, what can I say?"

"Don't say anything. Arif's a bastard, but he loves Sophie. He will not harm her or put her into danger, no matter what happens. It's a good plan. When this is over, the IDF will bring her out. You must promise me that you'll take Sophie to Deborah."

"Jack, you'll take her—"

"No, Marcy. Promise me. No matter what happens to me, you must make sure she gets to Deb."

"Jack—"

"Promise me."

"I promise."

"Tell her . . . tell her that I never left her. Tell her that I never stopped loving her, not one second. Tell her—"

"Jack, stop. She knows."

He nodded and took a picture out of his wallet. "This picture of Alina, show it to her, give it to her, and remind her that her mother loved her very much."

Marcy bent over and hugged him tightly. Her lips quivered and tears ran down her cheeks. "Don't do anything stupid. Let Liam and Kayla handle it. Just go get Sophie and come back." Then Marcy stood up and threw her arms around Liam's neck. She tried to speak, her voice caught in her throat, and she put her head against his chest.

"We'll bring him back," Liam said gently. "Sophie too." He gently patted her head. "Don't worry, we'll be back."

Yonit looked at her watch. Eleven thirty. "It's time."

SEVENTY-EIGHT

• • •

L IAM GUIDED JACK OUT to the van, slid the door to the side, and paused. In the momentary interlude, he stood to take in the setting. To his right lay the rolling countryside, a palette of earthy colors, peaceful, pastoral, dry and thirsty. To his left sat tens of thousands of white stone buildings on the Hebron hills, all boxlike, all with dark windows that looked like hollow eyes. What was it Kayla had said, "a spawning ground for terrorists"?

He rolled the wheelchair onto the platform, pushed the controls, and engaged the lift to raise it into the van. As he did so, the hidden panel released and opened just enough to permit access to the two handguns. Liam checked to see that the guns were in place, shut the panel, and nodded to Yonit.

"Are we set?" she said.

He nodded.

"Okay, follow me."

Kayla slid into the driver's seat, smiled nervously at Liam, and started the van. She followed Yonit's blue BMW down the hill, through the checkpoint, and along the bumpy streets of the ancient city of Hebron.

Along the route, on the walls of shuttered buildings, graffiti proclaimed GO DANCE ON YOUR OWN STREETS, END THE SIEGE IN GAZA, and RECLAIM HEBRON. They drove slowly, inconspicuously, bypassing the marketplace and heading north. Soon Kayla recognized al-Zahani's neighborhood, and his walled compound came into view. They watched Yonit drive past the property and turn around the next corner. No soldiers were in sight. "Everyone ready?" Kayla said.

She slowed the van, took a deep breath, and turned into al-Zahani's driveway. Three men stood in front of two black metal gates, eight feet high and ten feet across. They watched the van approach, took a last drag on their cigarettes, and ground them out on the pavement. One guard, in a weathered, tan cargo jacket and checkered keffiyeh, grabbed his assault rifle, stepped away from the gate, and approached the driver's window.

"Come out of the truck," he said in Arabic.

"We're here to see Dr. al-Zahani," Kayla said. "We have an appointment. Please let us through."

"I said, come out of the truck," he said more forcefully.

Liam felt for the pistol tucked into his belt.

Kayla didn't miss a beat. "And I said, we're here to see the doctor. You don't give me orders. I don't know who you are."

The second guard walked to the passenger door and knocked hard with the butt of his rifle. Liam fingered his weapon. "I hope you're listening, Yonit," he said quietly.

"We work for Dr. al-Zahani," said the guard to Kayla.

"Then call for Dr. al-Zahani." Kayla pointed to the bronze keypad next to the gate. "He'll confirm our appointment. It's a business meeting."

"We know what it is. Do you take us for fools?"

"I don't take you for anything. You don't interest me at all. Unless you let us in, I'm going to drive away."

With that last comment, the three guards leveled their rifles at the windows of the van.

"You're not going anywhere. Get out of the truck. Now!"

Kayla sat back, folded her arms across her chest, and stuck out her chin.

"Are you crazy?" Jack said softly. "They're going to fire at us."

"I don't think so," Kayla said. "You have a briefcase on your lap with four million euros and they don't know the combination. Hang tight."

"Get out," they screamed, and hammered on the doors with their rifle butts.

Amid the confrontation, the mechanized gates parted and

slowly opened inward to reveal a man standing in the middle of the driveway. Dressed in cream cotton slacks, a beige, collared shirt worn outside his trousers, and tan suede loafers, he stood tall in the afternoon breeze.

"Al-Zahani," Jack said.

The doctor walked toward the van and waved his guards away with a flick of his hand. *"As-salaam alaikum,* welcome to Hebron," he said to Kayla through the open window. "I assume you are the nurse?"

"Wa-alaikum salaam. Yes, I am. This gentleman is Mr. Taggart, who has negotiated this meeting, and I'm sure you recognize Mr. Sommers."

"Hello, Jack," al-Zahani said in English. "I'm sorry to see you in a wheelchair. I wish you a speedy recovery."

Jack clenched his teeth. He nodded.

"May I ask that you all step out of the van, please?" al-Zahani said. "I'm sure you understand the need for caution these days. In this violent region, my home is a place of peace. There are no weapons of any sort inside, and we do not permit any weapons beyond this portal. So, if you've brought a weapon, would you please hand it to my security personnel to be returned to you when you leave."

Kayla stepped down out of the driver's seat and Liam jumped down from the passenger seat.

"As you know, Dr. al-Zahani, I'm a private investigator licensed to carry a gun," Liam said. "I don't go anywhere without it, and that goes double in the Palestinian territories. I have a gun and I don't intend to give it to your men."

"In that case, I'm afraid you will not be allowed into my home. You'll have to wait here."

"Jack's not going in without me."

"Then perhaps our meeting is over."

"Look," Liam said, "we did our part. We brought the money. You don't want us to leave with the money, do you?"

"Oh, of course not. That money is earmarked for the schools of Hebron. Five million dollars will go a long way to build new schools for our children, and it would be a shame for the children to lose out on that donation, but my home is a weapon-free zone and you must respect my wishes."

"So, unless I give you my gun, you'll tell us to drive away?"

"And wish you all a bon voyage." Al-Zahani smiled.

"Give him the gun, Liam," Kayla said.

"Kayla."

"Give him the gun."

Liam frowned at Kayla. He reached around, lifted his pistol from his belt, and handed it to the guard.

"And the nurse, who speaks such fine Arabic," al-Zahani said with a tinge of irony in his tone, "May I ask, which hospital employs you?"

"I'm in private practice."

"Yes, I'm sure you are. Do you have a weapon?"

"I do not."

Al-Zahani motioned for the third guard, who walked over with a metal-detector wand. "It's not that I don't trust you, but one can never be too careful."

The guard waved the wand over Kayla and then Liam. It did not beep.

Al-Zahani looked through the opened door into the backseat. "Do you have any weapons, Jack?"

"No."

"That's good enough for me." Then to Liam and Kayla, the doctor said, "Would you follow me please?" He turned and walked through the gates into the compound. Kayla started to head back to the driver's seat, but al-Zahani said, "Oh, don't bother, my men will bring the van into the yard."

Liam and Kayla followed al-Zahani on foot up the driveway and toward the front door. One hundred yards to his left, Liam spied the long, stone, one-story outbuilding. No guards were visible at the doorway. He stopped to wait for the van to catch up.

"Again, Mr. Taggart, my men will be happy to assist Jack from the van," al-Zahani said.

"The controls on this rental vehicle are tricky," Liam said. "It's better that I help Jack."

"I'm sure we can handle it."

The guard in the checkered keffiyeh stood by the van door waiting for Jack to engage the lift. Jack pushed the buttons on his control pad a few times and finally shouted. "Liam, my controls aren't working again. You'll have to use the buttons on the door panel."

Liam shrugged and looked at al-Zahani. "I told you."

"Yusef," the doctor said to the man in the checkered keffiyeh, "use the controls on the door panel."

Yusef tried several times unsuccessfully to engage the lift. He pulled hard on the lift mechanism and on the back of the passenger seat. He yanked. He pushed. He slammed his fist on the button pad and even kicked at the platform. Liam glanced nervously at Kayla. After several tries, the guard shrugged and opened his arms.

"As I told you," Liam said, and walked over to the van. He leaned forward into the passenger compartment, positioning his jacket and body to block the view of the interior, and double-clicked the middle button before the bottom button. The motor engaged and the lift moved slowly. Liam reached around to the console but the panel did not release. Liam quickly paused the lift mechanism. He backed it up and tried again. Again the platform slid toward the door, and again the hidden panel would not release. With the three guards now standing behind him, staring inquisitively, Liam tried a third time. Same result. He shook his head as he allowed the platform to slide the wheelchair to the door, out of the chassis, and down to the ground. "Yonit, we're going in naked," he said to his belt buckle.

Liam pushed the wheelchair forward and followed al-Zahani and Kayla into the house. Yusef handed his rifle to his companion and followed the group into the home. Jack held the briefcase tightly on his lap. The outside of al-Zahani's home, though large, was commonplace in every sense—white Jerusalem stone, two stories, recessed windows. But inside was a sultan's palace. The generous entry hall gleamed in subtle shades of white and caramel travertine. A grand staircase, covered in purple Persian runners, rose regally to the second floor.

Al-Zahani led them past the staircase, down the hall, and into a large library with twelve-foot ceilings. Several small Persian rugs lay on a floor of beige Italian marble. Two large palm plants punctuated the corners of a wall of windows that overlooked the gardens.

"Where's Sophie?" Jack said.

"She's here," al-Zahani said. "Happy and comfortable. I wish you would reconsider your insistence that she return to America.

Why don't you tell her it's okay to stay here? She is so well integrated into our community, it would be a shame to take her away."

"It didn't bother you when you kidnapped her out of Chicago where she was so well integrated in her community, did it?"

The doctor shook his head. "I can see that this discussion will lead us nowhere. Just as before, you care more for yourself than your daughter. Still, I wish you would at least consider an accommodation. We would be open to allowing you to visit here anytime you wish. You are obviously a man of means. Travel expenses would not seem to be an obstruction. I would even share the expenses with you. Tell Sophie you would like her to live here."

"Look, I brought the money, where's my daughter?"

"As soon as I see the money. Open the case."

"Hold on, Jack," Liam said. "*Simultaneously* was the agreement. No Sophie, no money."

Al-Zahani shook his head again. "True to your character, Jack, you chose an ill-mannered investigator. Very well." The doctor turned to the doorway and called out, "Bashir, would you please bring Sophie to the library."

Jack sat in his wheelchair in the middle of the room, the briefcase on his lap. Kayla stood to his side and slightly behind him. Liam positioned himself a few steps in front, as a buffer between Jack and al-Zahani. Yusef stood by the doctor's side, a constant grin upon his face. From the opposite corner, Bashir walked into the room, hand in hand with Sophie. Lubannah trailed behind.

"Daddy," Sophie shrieked, and tried to run to him, but Bashir held her close. He bent down and gently said, "Wait, child. Wait, as your Jaddi has asked. You will have your time."

Al-Zahani wagged a finger. "Remember, Sophie, what we talked about before? We made an agreement. If he chooses and cooperates, your father will meet with you in a few minutes outside. But now, child, I ask you, do you see his briefcase? Do you remember what I told you?"

"Sweetheart," Jack interrupted, "I love you so much. I'm here to take you home."

"I told you!" Sophie shrieked, and wriggled to get loose from the strong grip. "Let me go, Bashir."

Bashir looked to al-Zahani, who slowly shook his head. Turning his attention to Jack and rolling his fingers in a beckoning gesture, al-Zahani said, "And now, the case."

Jack focused on the combination lock. His hands shook. First one side, then the other. The clasp clicked and the case opened. The money lay bundled beneath the false explosive device. Kayla placed the case on a table.

"Why, Jack, it is mousetrapped after all."

"*Booby-trapped,* Doc," Liam said. "The term is *booby-trapped.* Now we'll take Sophie and be on our way."

"No," Lubannah cried. "You cannot take our Sophie. You promised me, Arif." She came up from behind and put her arms around the child.

"Be at ease, Lubannah," al-Zahani said, "no one will take Sophie. That, I do promise you. She will never leave Canaan."

"You said I could go home with my daddy. You *said,*" cried Sophie. She beat her fists and broke loose from Lubannah, but al-Zahani reached out and grabbed her arm with a strong grip.

Jack rose from his wheelchair, took a step forward. His leg buckled, and he stumbled. He grimaced from the pain and leaned against his chair. "Let her go, Arif. I've done my part."

"Why don't you understand?" Lubannah pleaded. "She's safe here. She'll be raised in a loving home with loving grandparents."

"Loving grandparents?" Kayla said. "Do you know what a murderous monster you're married to? Do you know how many people he's killed and how many more he plans to kill?"

Jack steadied himself and started to walk toward al-Zahani, but Bashir leveled a semiautomatic weapon and shook his head.

"Take them outside, Bashir," al-Zahani said. "I have the money. See that they bother us no more. Yusef, go with them."

"There's an automatic weapon in here, Yonit," Liam said loudly. "In the library. Two guards."

"Lubannah," Kayla continued, "did he tell you how he killed Alina? Did he tell you he injected her with virulent, deadly bacteria that ate up her organs and caused her to die a beastly, painful death? The same thing that he did to my sister?"

"What?" Jack said. "*You* did that? *You* made her sick? You killed Alina?"

"Arif?" Lubannah said. "Arif, what she said . . ."

"Ask him what he's doing out in that laboratory," Kayla said. "Go on, ask him. Have you ever been out there, Lubannah? It's a madman's laboratory. He's making more poison to kill more people. Just like the poison he gave to Alina."

"Shut her up, Bashir," snapped al-Zahani, trying to hold on to Sophie. "Take them all outside. Now!" But Bashir didn't move.

Lubannah pulled hard on al-Zahani's shirt. "Arif? You told me she got an infection and the American doctors didn't know how to treat her."

"She already had that infection when she came home," Jack said. "She got that infection here. By the time she got home, it had already caused irreparable damage."

"Arif. You could not do that to our daughter. Tell them."

Jack glared at al-Zahani. "It's all so clear. The doctors couldn't treat Alina because they had never seen that strain before. It's a biological weapon, and you gave it to her, didn't you? You poisoned her because she wouldn't stay here and be your perfect little—"

"Shut up!" al-Zahani snapped, shaking Sophie by her arm. "Bashir, do your job. Take them outside, now! Yusef, get them out of here."

Bashir held his hand out to stop Yusef. He stood before al-Zahani and gave him a hard look. "*Sayyid,* when you treated Alina for her allergies—"

"Why are you just standing there?" al-Zahani said in a frenetic voice. "How dare you question me. Shoot them or give me the gun."

Bashir was steadfast. "You gave Alina medicine. She told me. An injection for her allergies right before she left Hebron." He lowered his gun and took a step back.

"Kill them, damn you!" al-Zahani shouted. "Yusef, take them outside." But Bashir shook his head and blocked the path.

"Daddy," screamed Sophie, struggling to free herself from al-Zahani's grip. She kicked at his legs, she swung her fist. "Daddy!"

"Arif!" Lubannah yelled. "Tell me she's lying." She reached for him.

With his free hand, al-Zahani backhanded his wife and she fell hard to the marble floor. "You stupid woman, Alina left us long before I gave her the injection."

The sounds of shouts and gunshots were heard from the outside.

Through the windows al-Zahani saw uniformed soldiers running through the courtyard.

"It's all over, Doc," Liam said. "That's the IDF. You and your plans are finished. Let her go."

Al-Zahani backed up to the bookshelves, his left hand tightly gripping Sophie's arm. He looked around the room at the individuals closing in on him. He looked outside at the dozens of soldiers in the yard.

"It's time, Yonit," Liam said loudly.

Al-Zahani's face broke into a demonic smile. "Nothing is over. It's just beginning. You're all too late, you see. The damage is done. Canaan is avenged."

Al-Zahani reached behind him, onto one of the shelves, and grabbed his black medical bag. He quickly extracted a hypodermic syringe and held the needle up. "Get back now, all of you. This child will stay with me. She is a daughter of Canaan. She will never leave her homeland. I am going to walk to my car with Sophie. Do not interfere, or I will inject the child. My granddaughter and I will leave together or we will die together." He started walking slowly toward the door, his left hand gripped tightly around Sophie's arm, his right hand holding the syringe. Yusef trailed behind him. Sophie screamed, "Daddy!"

"Yonit. Stand down," Liam said, quickly stepping in front of al-Zahani and blocking his path to the door. "Hold up, Doc. You don't want to do this. You're not going to hurt Sophie. You know you love her and she loves you. Just let her go and this will all be over."

"Do not doubt my resolve. This child is now a soldier in our struggle, and she will be deployed in any way that furthers the cause. My work is critical. I must be allowed to continue my work. I'm going to my car. Move out of my way."

"I can't do that, Doc. Even if you could make it out the door, you wouldn't get very far."

"Then we'll both die and our blood will mingle with our forefathers in the sands of Canaan. Tell them, Sophie. Say proudly, I am a daughter of Canaan!"

"I won't. I'm not. Let me go." Sophie twisted, kicked, and pulled at al-Zahani.

"You son of a bitch," Jack said, and lunged at him, but al-Zahani quickly stepped to the side as Jack fell to the floor. At that moment, al-Zahani's focus distracted, Kayla saw her chance. She lashed out, grabbed al-Zahani's right wrist, and pulled it to the side. Off-balance and struggling, al-Zahani could not restrain Sophie. She broke loose and ran to Jack, who covered her with his body.

Yusef pulled a knife from his belt and with a fiendish sneer dashed toward Kayla. Liam flew at him, intercepted him, and tackled him at the knees. Yusef hit the marble floor hard, and the knife slid toward the windows. Yusef scrambled to his feet, glanced at the knife, but turned and darted out the front door.

Al-Zahani continued to struggle to free himself from Kayla's grip. He slammed her with his elbow but her hold was tight. Suddenly, his eyes grew wide and he stiffened his back. His breath seized in his throat. Bashir, standing behind, twisted the knife up, then sideways, and pulled it from the doctor's back. Al-Zahani's facial muscles tensed, he tipped forward, then back. As he fell, he windmilled his right arm around, stabbed the syringe into the side of Kayla's neck, and pulled it down hard, opening a gash. She pushed him to the side and he stumbled and collapsed on the floor facedown. Kayla clawed at the wound and looked at her fingers. A tiny droplet of viscous white liquid was visible in the midst of her blood.

Liam grabbed Kayla by the shoulders. "Your neck. That's a bad cut. Did he inject that crap into you?"

"No. Maybe. Maybe a little. Doesn't matter. I'm fine. We have to go the outbuilding. We have to find out what he meant by 'the damage is done.'"

Liam grabbed a cotton doily from the table and held it tight against her wound. "I don't like this cut. Keep the pressure on," he said.

They dashed out the door to where Yonit stood in the yard. She was holding an IV bag, embossed with the logo of Sexton International. "This is what they were making. The woman over there told us that two thousand of these bags, all with the Sexton logo, have been shipped out."

"IV bags!" Kayla said. "They plan to infect patients intravenously. That's what's in the Jerusalem warehouse. Send the word out to every hospital and clinic in Israel. Tell them not to use Sexton IV sets. Tell them to make immediate arrangements to obtain sets from alternative sources. Do not use Sexton." Yonit dispatched her lieutenant to make the call.

In the library, Jack sat on the floor, his back against the wall, Sophie on his lap. Sophie's face was buried in Jack's chest as he wrapped his arms tightly around her. She shook and cried. Jack smoothed her hair, kissed her on the forehead, and rocked from side to side, their tears commingling.

"I'm so sorry, Sophie," he said between kisses. "I tried so hard to get to you. I'm so sorry I failed you, sweetheart."

"I just want to go home."

Jack nodded and carefully got to his feet. Sophie looked back at her grandmother, sitting on the couch, her face in her hands. "I have to say goodbye to Jadda."

Jack walked her over to Lubannah. "Oh, my child, I'm so sad all this has happened," Lubannah said as she embraced Sophie. "Jaddi was very troubled. He didn't know what he was doing. The jihadists made him think like that. But he did love you very much. He told me so. Now it's time you go home and be happy with your father."

Jack turned to al-Zahani, prostrate and lifeless on the floor. He walked slowly to where al-Zahani lay and stared at the body. A line from *Julius Caesar* played out in his mind and he repeated it aloud: "'When could they say till now, that talked of Rome, that her wide walls encompassed but one man?' And like Caesar, Arif, your ambition devoured you. 'Ambition's debt is paid.'"

Jack reached down and lifted his daughter. "Oh, my little butterfly, I missed you so much."

She looked at her grandfather. "He was going to hurt me."

"No, I don't think he was. Your grandmother was right. He was very troubled, but he loved you very much and he would not have hurt you."

"Jaddi told me you had gone away without me. But I knew he was lying. I knew you'd never leave me."

Bashir quietly approached the two, bowed, and held out the little stuffed bear. "Here is your Sweetness." He kissed Sophie on the top of her head. "Good-bye, my little joyous one, so pure of heart. May Allah favor you in all your life's journeys."

In the yard, Yusef and the other handcuffed prisoners were filing into the IDF vans. A perimeter had been established around the laboratory. Jack walked on unsteady legs from the house into the yard, Sophie beside him. He walked directly to Kayla. "The syringe is empty," he said, holding it for her to see.

Kayla pawed at her neck. She looked at the blood-soaked cloth.

"Kayla, listen to me," Jack said. "The doctors told me they would've had a better chance to save Alina if they'd caught the infection early. The problem was she waited too long to get treatment. You need to get to the hospital right away."

"He's right," Liam said. "These soldiers will take you there."

"I'll be okay. I think it's just a simple cut. He winged me. Most of the solution probably went on my clothes."

"Well, we need to get you to the hospital right now, even if it's just a cut. There's a lot of blood," Liam said.

Kayla shook her head. "This operation's not done. I want Nizar Mohammed. I want Fakhir Ali, and most of all, I want that bastard Fa'iz Talib. Alive. My husband and sister demand their justice, and I won't leave without finishing the job."

Yonit flipped her car keys to Liam. "We'll pick up Fakhir and Nizar," she said. "You go get Fa'iz."

Kayla looked at Liam. "C'mon, Irish, back me up."

He nodded. "Okay. You're the boss. Let's go."

"You might need this." Yonit handed Liam a gun. "Sorry about the guns in the van. It looks like al-Zahani's guards jammed the mechanism."

"Didn't you hear us?" Liam asked. "What happened to the cavalry?"

She smiled. "We were listening, but we were kind of busy. Besides, we had confidence in you. And then, when you told us to stand down, we figured you had it under control."

A uniformed officer pushed the wheelchair over to Jack and Sophie. "May I give the two of you a ride back to Tel Aviv? It would be my honor, sir."

SEVENTY-NINE

• • •

L IAM SCREECHED TO A stop in front of Fa'iz's home and
banged on the door. A maidservant met them and immediately backtracked when she saw the gun in Liam's hand.

"Where is Fa'iz?" Kayla said.

The maidservant slowly pointed to the right.

"Ask her how many more servants are inside," Liam said.

"She says no others."

They found Fa'iz lying on an overstuffed futon when they entered his room. He stroked his wiry beard. "As they say, money
is the root of all evil. We should never have considered the ransom.
So, you have come for me. I am informed of the disturbance at the
home of Dr. al-Zahani." In his right hand he held a fourteen-inch
scimitar.

"Get up, you murdering asshole. Drop the knife and put your
hands behind your back," Liam said.

He shook his head. "You're too late," he said. "For many things.
Too late to stop me from my *shahada*." He pulled his tunic up and
ran the scimitar along the inside of his leg, slicing his femoral ar-
tery. Blood instantly began to pool from beneath his gown and inch
across the floor.

"I will die a martyr and I will know paradise," he said thinly.
"You come too late to stop our jihad, as well. The bags were delivered to hospitals all over Jerusalem and are now in use. Hundreds,
maybe thousands, are already infected. I have declared to the world
the triumphant news that the Sons of Canaan are to be given
credit for their glorious deeds."

"Look at my face," Kayla snapped, taking the gun from Liam's hand. "Because this is the last thing you will see before you die. A face that curses you. Curses you for Naomi, curses you for Brian, curses you for all the innocent people of this land who have their lives tarnished by shit like you. Carry this face into your eternal damnation. You're not a martyr. Your legacy is shame. The likes of you will never stop the promise of peace. You're not even a speed bump."

"Let's go," Liam said, taking Kayla by the elbow. "This guy is history."

Kayla took a step toward the door, stopped, turned, and pumped three rounds into Talib's chest. "Now he is."

Liam pointed to her neck. "You're still bleeding. Pretty badly. We need to get you to the hospital."

Backing the car away from the curb, he said, "How do I get to Tel Aviv?"

"This is Yonit's car. We have to bring it back to her."

"I'm taking you to the hospital."

"I'll be fine. I just need a few stitches."

"How do we get to Tel Aviv?"

Kayla pointed the way out of town. Her eyes were losing their focus. She blinked several times. Her breathing was shallow. Liam headed west through the town and into the barren West Bank hills. They rode in silence for a while. He looked at Kayla, who seemed to be slipping in and out of consciousness.

"Kayla, talk to me."

"I'm not feeling so hot, Liam."

"Stay with me, damn it. Stay alert. I need you to guide me. We'll be there soon."

"You know . . . he didn't just wing me," Kayla finally said with a catch in her throat. "He didn't miss. I felt the hypodermic needle. I felt him push the plunger. I felt the liquid enter my neck. I knew what had happened and I knew there would be no reversing it."

"Let's not start the eulogies. When this is all over, I'm taking you for the best steak dinner in Israel. You're going to be okay."

"No, I'm not. I have that poison in me. Just like my sister." She turned her face toward Liam. "I'm scared, Liam, it's a horrible death. She suffered so badly."

Liam looked straight ahead. "I said you're going to be okay." He slammed hard on the accelerator.

"But I'm not sorry. It was worth it. We did it, didn't we? We stopped the attack and rid the world of the Sons of Canaan. We saved a lot of lives today, Liam."

"*You* did, Kayla."

She started to cry and hid her face in her hands. Liam pulled over onto the shoulder and put his arm around her. "Oh, Christ, look at that wound." He took off his shirt, ripped it into strips, and tried to clean the cut and stop the bleeding. "What's Yonit's number?"

With a shaking hand, Kayla handed her phone to Liam.

"Kayla, listen to me. I'm going to get you to the hospital. We'll be there soon. You heard Jack. The doctors told him they could have saved Alina if they got to her right away. They're going to get to you right away. Stay with me now. Keep the pressure on that cloth."

"It won't matter. They tried to save Naomi. They tried everything. I've got those bugs in me now. I know they're crawling though my veins. I saw my sister waste away. It was horrible."

Liam pushed the numbers on the cell phone and then spoke to Yonit. "I'm on the highway to Tel Aviv, but Kayla's in bad shape. We need help here. She needs a hospital and I don't know where the hell I'm going."

"Where are you?"

"Highway 35 heading west."

"Keep on going and leave the phone on. We'll come to you."

Kayla slumped to the side. "Liam, I'm not feeling too good. I'm real dizzy."

"You're going to be okay. I promise."

Kayla swallowed hard. "Will you stay with me, Liam? Till the end? I have no one else."

"I'm right beside you, Kayla." Liam wove in and out of traffic.

"Promise me, please, you won't leave me until the end."

"I won't leave you, Kayla. I promise. I'll be right by your side, but I'm telling you, you're going to be all right."

"I'm so glad to have met you, Liam. So glad." And she closed her eyes.

"Kayla, don't you die on me, goddamnit." Liam gunned the

BMW. In his rearview mirror he saw the flashing lights of an IDF paramedic van. He pulled to the side, and Kayla was transferred from the car to the ambulance. Liam followed, and the flashing lights and sirens took them north toward Tel Aviv.

FAKHIR WAS STANDING BEHIND the glass counter arranging sweet rolls when he saw two jeeps and a van pull up. "The IDF," he mumbled. He grabbed the cash out of his register and darted for the back door. The sweat on his palm made it hard to turn the doorknob. He pushed it open and stopped suddenly.

"Going somewhere, Fakhir?" Yonit said.

"I'm going home."

"I don't think so. Not now. Not ever."

"I have done nothing. The IDF has no right to stop me. This is H1 territory. Let me by."

"Al-Zahani's dead."

"Unfortunate for al-Zahani, but it has nothing to do with me. I'm just a simple baker."

"Not any longer." Yonit cuffed him and walked him around to the street. "Who was in charge of delivering the bags?"

"I will tell you nothing. You'll get no information from me."

She pushed him forward to the paramedic van, where two guards roughly shoved him onto a gurney and strapped him down. A paramedic opened the cabinet and extracted a plastic tube, a clamp, and a needle.

"Tell me the name of the person who delivered the IVs," Yonit said.

"What IVs? I don't know what you're talking about."

Yonit smiled and held up a Sexton IV bag. She turned to the paramedic. "He looks dehydrated to me. I think he needs IV therapy."

The paramedic took the bag from Yonit and set it on the hook. Fakhir tilted his head to watch in horror. Sweat poured off his forehead. Large wet circles grew in the armpits of his shirt. He struggled against the straps. The paramedic took the needle and catheter out of the kit and tapped the veins on Fakhir's wrist.

"No, no, wait. Wait. I will tell you. Don't do that, please. I have a wife and children."

"Who delivered the IVs?"

"I think his name is Samuel, but I'm not sure of his address. Somewhere in East Jerusalem."

"Not good enough." She nodded to the paramedic, who swabbed Fakhir's wrist with alcohol and inserted the needle into his vein.

"I want his address and I want to know how and where he made the deliveries."

Fakhir's eyes were fixed on the paramedic. He began to cry. "Oh, stop. Please don't connect that bag. Please. Sami works for the Mediterranean company. Mediterranean Medical. That's his job. He's a delivery driver to Jerusalem hospitals. Please don't give me that solution. It has a horrible disease in it. I don't want to die. You can't do this. It's inhuman."

"Where did he deliver the bags?"

"He took them to the hospitals on his route. The company will know which ones. I don't know, on my mother's grave, I don't know."

"When were the deliveries?"

"Yesterday, the day before."

"I want the names and addresses of everyone involved in your godless plot. I want to know where they are right now." She gave him a pen and paper. Fakhir was crying convulsively. His hand shook so badly, he could barely hold the pen.

THE CENTRAL INTERCOM OF Jerusalem Memorial broadcast an emergency message. All Sexton IVs were immediately to be taken out of use. Any patients receiving IV treatment with any Sexton product within the past two days were to be identified and contacted. In the moments after Mediterranean Medical Supply called each of the hospitals on Sami's route, the Sexton IV bags were segregated. Substitute IV sets were rushed from other hospitals. Calls went out to alternative medical supply companies in several countries.

OKAY, MR. KELSEN, WE'RE going on the record." Assistant US Attorney Thomas Tryon sat opposite Victor Kelsen and his lawyer in the small government conference room. A ten-page statement lay on the table in front of Kelsen. A video camera was recording the event. "Please identify yourself."

Kelsen nodded. "My name is Victor Wallace Kelsen."

"The purpose of this meeting is to place your signed statement into the record, is that right, Mr. Kelsen?"

"Yeah, and to make a deal for a reduced sentence."

"As we've explained to you, the Justice Department can only make recommendations to the court. The judge will determine your sentence after you plead guilty and your presentence investigation is finished."

Kelsen looked at his lawyer. "But we've made a deal for twelve years, with a chance I could get out in ten, right, Marty?" The lawyer nodded.

"That will be our office's recommendation," Tryon said. "But as we've explained to you at least three times, there are no guarantees on your sentence. The judge can disregard the recommendation. Please affirm you understand that."

"Yeah, yeah, I understand. No guarantees. And you'll put me in some minimum-security prison under a false identity so that those fucking Russians won't know where to find me. Right? I mean, that's the deal."

Tryon nodded and patted the statement. "Again, that will be our recommendation. You need to sign and identify your statement."

"And my wife. Can you put her in witness protection somewhere?"

"We'll see." Tryon tapped the paper. "Please read and sign your statement."

Kelsen read the ten-page statement into the record.

"Have you fully and accurately supplied the information about Dmitri Borsinov and his involvement in the scheme to kidnap the Sommers child and embezzle the escrow money?"

Kelsen nodded. "It was all his idea."

"But you willingly participated?"

Kelsen nodded. "Yeah. I shoulda never let him into the basketball payoffs. That was my big mistake. Wish I never met him or his goon Evgeniy."

"Have you fully and accurately set forth the details of your sports bribery scheme?"

"Yeah, it's all there. All eleven years."

"Finally, you understand it is your obligation to testify in accordance with this statement at the trials of Borsinov, Karisov, and Porushkin. If you refuse to testify or testify falsely, this plea agreement will be voided and you will additionally be prosecuted for perjury. You understand all that?"

Kelsen nodded.

"Do you affirm that the statement you just read is true and correct?"

He nodded. "Yeah."

"And made voluntarily with no threats or coercion."

"Yeah, yeah, yeah."

"Sign your statement."

Kelsen flipped to the last page and signed his name.

"Okay. This recording is completed. Take him away."

TWO DAYS LATER, ON a blistering-hot afternoon, just east of Eilat, at the Yitzhak Rabin Border Crossing, several travelers stood patiently in line with their passports. One such man in traditional white desert garb—an ankle-length *thobe* and a full, white keffiyeh held in place by a golden, braided *igal*—anxiously awaited his turn to present his documents and enter Jordan.

A woman's voice caught his attention from behind. "Hebron no longer suits you, Nizar?"

He spun around to see a woman and two men in IDF uniforms. Yonit beckoned him with her index finger. "This way, please."

Nizar bolted out of line and ran toward the sea. He was quickly apprehended but appeared to be choking. He collapsed and died in the arms of an IDF soldier.

EIGHTY

· · ·

LIAM STARED AT HIS buzzing phone. The text message read, *Please call me.*

"Hey, Cat, what's up?" Liam said.

"It's been four days since the rescue and I just wanted to know when you're coming home. I'm missing you."

"I miss you too."

"I'm not sleeping well since that incident with Kelsen. I wake up. I leave the light on. I need you to come home."

"I know. I'm sorry, but I can't leave Israel just yet."

"Why not?"

"Because I made a promise."

"A promise? What does that mean? I thought the operation was finished. When are you coming home?" Liam heard the tension in her voice.

"I'm not sure. I'm not sure when I can leave."

"What do you mean you're not sure? What's going on Liam?"

"I made a promise."

"It's Kayla, isn't it? That's why you can't leave?"

"Yes."

"Damn you, Liam!" The line went dead.

He called her, he redialed her, but she wouldn't pick up. Finally, he texted, *I think Kayla's dying.*

A few minutes later his phone rang. "I'm sorry," Catherine said softly. "I thought . . ."

"My fault, I should have explained. You remember, I told you that Kayla suffered a bad injury at the compound and al-Zahani managed to inject that poison into her. What I haven't told you is that the doctors have been unable to stop the disease. Even though we took her straight to the hospital, it didn't matter. They'd never seen anything like it, and they didn't know how to treat it. Now they tell me they're trying a new antibiotic, but so far she's real sick. She can't eat, she's lost a lot of weight. Cat, she looks terrible." He paused. "She doesn't have any family, she doesn't have anyone. I promised her I would stay."

"I'm so sorry, Liam. You should stay. Shame on me."

"Listen, Cat, I miss you a lot. There's a United flight out of Newark at ten fifty tonight. What do you say?"

"You want me to come to Israel? Just drop everything?"

"Yes, I do. More than anything."

"I don't know . . ."

"Please?"

Pause. "I'll try. I have an appointment at the US Attorney's Office later this morning. I'll see what I can do."

L IAM CHECKED THE ARRIVAL board for the hundredth time. Catherine's flight was delayed yet again. Rain in Newark. Damn the rain. Does anyone ever get out of Newark on time? He sat at a table in the arrival hall, drinking his fourth cup of coffee, watching as passengers wheeled their luggage through the customs doors to meet their friends and family. He fidgeted. This was to be a big moment—he hoped.

Finally, Catherine walked into the lobby. Liam smiled broadly, rushed up, and hugged her tightly, lifting her off the floor.

"My goodness, Liam."

Liam looked around the busy hall, turning his head in every direction, surveying the crowded terminal in consternation.

"Is something wrong? What are you looking for?"

"Nothing." He took her by the elbow and led her to an area near the coffee shop. He took a deep breath. "Excuse me," he said nervously to a couple standing nearby, "I need a little room here."

The couple backed up. Liam dropped to his knee and held out the open jewelry box. "Oh my God," Catherine said, "are you crazy?"

"Cat, I'm sorry the setting isn't more romantic, but I can't chance another interruption."

"Oh my God."

The crowd of passengers began to form a circle. "I want to see this," a woman said as she yanked at her husband's sleeve and pulled him over to the front of the gathering.

"Cat, there's only you. All my life, there's only you. It's high tide, sweetheart. Will you marry me?"

"Oh, yes, I will. You bet I will." She wrapped her arms around him, and the welcome hall of Ben Gurion International Airport broke into cheers and applause.

EIGHTY-ONE

• • •

A S THE SUN RISES over the spires of Jerusalem's Old City, a man in a black suit, the fringes of his white tallit showing beneath his jacket's hem, like a slip beneath a skirt, walks through Jerusalem's Jewish Quarter to say his morning prayers at the Kotel, the Western Wall. He walks spritely, proudly, with his two young sons. Hundreds of others are already praying there. No matter the time of day, prayers are offered to God at the wall of Herod's Citadel. Above, on the Mountain of the House of God, is the Dome of the Rock and al-Aqsa Mosque. Beneath the Dome lies the Foundation Stone, the holiest site of the Jewish religion, upon which the Ark of the Covenant was placed in the First Temple.

Directly to the west, in the Christian Quarter of the Old City, Catholic mass, served in Latin, is beginning in the Church of the Holy Sepulcher. The church stands directly upon the Hill of Calvary, where Jesus Christ was crucified, anointed, and laid to rest in the limestone cave donated by Joseph of Arimathea. The small aedicule in the center of the rotunda embraces the tomb. A line has already begun to form, and worshippers wait their turn to pray in the aedicule. The Church is Christendom's most holy site, a place of pilgrimage, the site of the Resurrection.

In the Muslim Quarter, a man passes through a guarded gate and walks up the ramp to the Haram al-Sharif, the Noble Sanctuary, on the Temple Mount. The Dome of the Rock, the golden shrine completed in the year 691 to cover the Foundation Stone and the place where David and Solomon had planned their temple, is open for him to enter and pray. Across the square is the silver-domed al-Aqsa Mosque, Islam's third-holiest site, where the Prophet Mohammed was transported from Mecca during his Night Journey, and from where he ascended to heaven. From a small room inside the mosque, a man chants the *adhan* into a microphone and the Arabic call to prayer is heard throughout the Old City.

Throughout the narrow walkways of the four quarters, shopkeepers begin to unlock their doors and unfold their awnings. They sweep the stone sidewalks and lay out displays of their colorful wares. Even old Abu Hammad will soon shuffle up to his door, open his antiquities store, and wait to have a cup of tea with a curious visitor. Jerusalem is waking up, coming alive. The streets will soon be filled with tourists, shoppers, worshippers, pilgrims. Another glorious day begins in this troubled land. Safe and secure from the threats of yesterday. On guard for today.

Fifty-five kilometers to the west, on the sixth floor of Tel Aviv Medical Center, a group has gathered.

"Another hospital room, another enclave," Marcy says, pouring a glass of water into a tumbler. Jack sits by the foot of the hospital bed near Sophie, who is perched at a little desk with a coloring book, Sweetness on her lap. A McDonald's hamburger and shake sit on the corner of the desk.

"Thank you," Kayla says, accepting the water with both hands. She lays propped up on her bed, hooked up to patient monitors, with antibiotics dripping into her veins.

Suddenly the door opens and Catherine and Liam enter the room. Marcy smiles. "How was your flight?"

"Long and tiring, but well worth it. Liam told me he's not leaving until Kayla gets better, so here I am, Catherine the world traveler. I can't leave my man alone with a gorgeous spy."

Kayla looks at Liam. "Did you do it?" she whispers.

He nods. He blushes.

"Let me see the ring," Kayla says with a broad smile.

Catherine holds out her hand. Kayla and Marcy examine the diamond closely and give their enthusiastic approvals.

"Mazel tov," Kayla says. "Tell me. Did he do it with pomp and circumstance?"

"Oh, did he ever," Catherine answers. "He got down on his knee in the middle of the airport. Everyone was watching."

"Way to go, Irish," Kayla says with a wink.

Catherine stares at the video monitors. "So, how's our gorgeous spy doing?"

"Not feeling so gorgeous right now. They're working on me," she says with a shrug. Her complexion has lost a shade or two. "They tell me it's a real nasty bug, but they think this new antibiotic is doing the trick. I'll have to stay here for a while until my blood work comes back clean, but they're optimistic."

"You're looking much better today," Liam says.

Kayla nods. "I'm feeling better. I think the medicine's working. I even had some breakfast."

"You're an amazing woman," Catherine says. "You saved a lot of lives and rescued a very sweet little girl."

Kayla smiles and reaches out for Catherine's hand. "Thanks, but I had a lot of help. Sadly, there were fatalities. The IDF didn't recover all the bags in time. Some patients received the IV solution before the hospitals were alerted. News reports warning of possible infections were broadcast on every channel, in every paper, but some folks are remote and won't hear. They probably won't know to get treatment. Some are bedouins who have returned to their simple lives in the desert. They weren't even targets of the terrorists."

"And the Sons of Canaan?"

"Like Canaan, they are no more," Kayla says. "Seven of them were taken alive and they will spend their lives in prison. Nizar Mohammed took his own life at the Jordanian border crossing. Ironically, he poisoned himself. Fakhir Ali gave Yonit all the details of the operation—everyone involved, every location. He even provided the address of the cold-storage warehouse, where we discovered the boxes of Sexton IVs that were switched out for the poison.

"The IDF destroyed Al-Zahani's laboratory and all vestiges of the deadly bacteria. Israel incinerated thousands of IV sets. In the hospital storage rooms, it was impossible to tell the originals from the fakes, so they had to destroy them all. Several nations shipped replacements. Now, tell us the news from Chicago. A little birdie told me you have good news."

"A little birdie from the State Department?" Catherine looks at

Jack and then at Sophie, who smiles and continues coloring pictures on her papers, many of which have been taped to the walls of the hospital room. "Jack, I met with the U.S. Attorney right before I left Chicago. It was through your cooperation that a point-shaving ring was busted, murderers were arrested, embezzled money was recovered, and an international kidnapping was resolved. A major coup for the Chicago office.

"Kelsen, Dmitri, and Evgeniy are all in custody thanks to you. Kelsen and Dmitri face a number of federal charges stemming from the embezzlement and sports bribery. Dmitri and Evgeniy are additionally charged with three counts of murder. Yuri Porushkin is charged with attempted murder and will await trial in Hawaii. The escrow money has been recovered and placed in a government account pending forfeiture proceedings. But most significantly, because of Kelsen's involvement, there is no longer a victim of the embezzlement, nor any reason for a court to vindicate the interests of Kelsen Manufacturing. The lawsuit against Jenkins and Fairchild has been dropped. Walter is so happy, he paid for my airline ticket.

"All of Kelsen's and Dmitri's assets were seized as fruits of a criminal enterprise. The government took their cars, their money, their homes, even Dmitri's wife's jewelry. Everything. Boy, is she pissed. If she could, she'd personally administer the death penalty.

"And then the strangest thing—I don't know how this happened." Catherine winks at Kayla. "But the Israeli government has made a strong request through diplomatic channels. Jack is credited with helping to foil a major terrorist attack. I dare say, he's an international hero. I understand the president himself wants to thank you, Jack. All in all, you will not be prosecuted."

Jack turns his head to blot a tear. "Sophie and I thank you all so much. You saved our lives."

"The gratitude is all ours," Kayla says.

"Are we going to our home in Chicago soon?" Sophie asks.

"Maybe for a while," Jack responds. "Would you like to go to Hawaii? Maybe even live there someday?" He glances at Marcy.

Sophie's eyes widen. "Is that where they do the hula-hula dance?"

"You better believe it," Marcy says.

"Then I would." Sophie smiles and says, "Can Jamila come and play at our house in Hawaii?"

"Who is Jamila?" Jack asks.

"She's my very best friend in Hebron."

The room is silent for a moment.

"The answer is yes, Sophie," Liam interjects. "Definitely yes. I have come to believe, on good authority, that it will happen someday. Jamila will come to your house and you will go to hers. Not today, maybe not tomorrow, but someday, maybe when your generation is in charge. And you know why it will happen? Because there are more people like Kayla than there are bad people. And because, sooner or later, good people who deserve peace will stop listening to bad people."

Jack put his arm around Sophie. "He's right. Good people like you and your mother, who have the courage to accept people and love them for who they are, no matter what they're told by others. Racism will never win out. It's flawed in every sense because love is much stronger than hate."

Kayla smiles proudly.

"It seems you are surrounded by your disciples," Liam says to her.

"My last supper?" Kayla looks at her tray of Jell-O and fruit juice. "Not so fast, Irish. You're not getting out of it so easy. I intend to collect on that steak dinner."

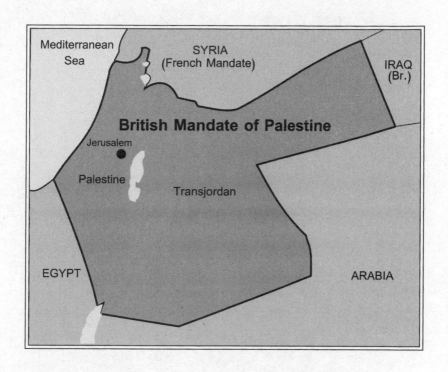

Mediterranean Sea

SYRIA
(French Mandate)

IRAQ
(Br.)

British Mandate of Palestine

Jerusalem

Palestine

Transjordan

EGYPT

ARABIA

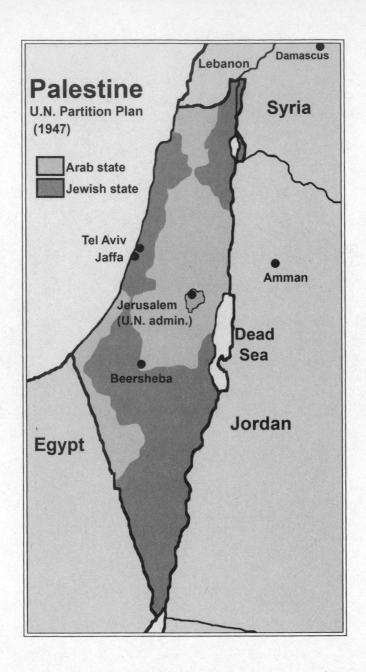

Palestine
U.N. Partition Plan
(1947)

Arab state
Jewish state

Lebanon
Damascus
Syria
Tel Aviv
Jaffa
Amman
Jerusalem
(U.N. admin.)
Dead
Sea
Beersheba
Jordan
Egypt

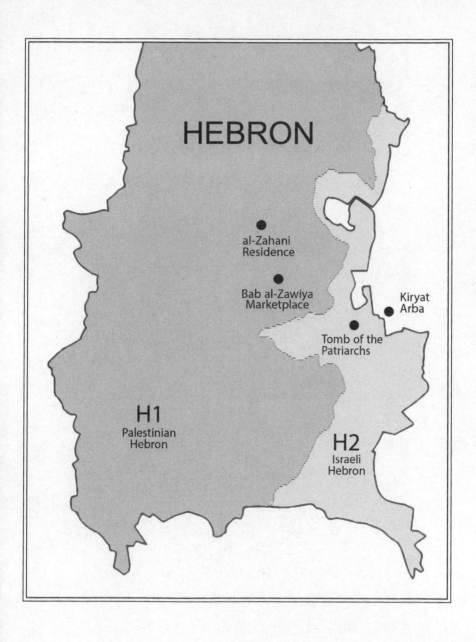

HEBRON

al-Zahani
Residence

Bab al-Zawiya
Marketplace

Kiryat
Arba

Tomb of the
Patriarchs

H1
Palestinian
Hebron

H2
Israeli
Hebron

Acknowledgments

Although *Saving Sophie* is a work of fiction, I have endeavored to portray the surrounding settings and historical events as accurately as possible. The history of Israel and the Middle East, from the Ottoman Empire to the present, is complex and rich, and I have capsulized it in the briefest of manners and only insofar as is necessary to paint the background for the novel. To that end, I have been aided by my good friend, historian, and law partner, David Pogrund. Because of his guidance and the wealth of materials available, I am comfortable that the environment in which the characters play their roles is authentic.

Of course, the al-Zahani family is entirely fictional and not based upon any particular person or family in Hebron or anywhere else. Similarly, the principal characters in the Israeli intelligence community are imaginary. However, the events concerning the Grand Mufti Haj Amin al-Husseini are accurate and may be confirmed through numerous sources, including available pictures of al-Husseini with Hitler, various Nazi officials, and reviewing his Bosnian troops.

I have described Hebron and Kiryat Arba as I saw them. I am indebted to Don Rabinovitz, Yerachmiel Weiss, and their families for taking me into their homes and communities and imparting not only a historical foundation, but a feeling for the people who call this dangerous part of the world their home. They are kind, courageous, and generous.

I am grateful to Michael Turkenich, a licensed Israeli guide and expert on Israel's history and culture. Mike, a former IDF paratrooper, conveyed the religious and historical significance of numerous sites and made them come alive. He holds an advanced degree in Christian studies, and his perspective into the mix of Jewish, Muslim, and Christian influences was an invaluable contribution to the fabric of the story.

I am indebted as well to my good friend Michael Jay Green, Hawaii's finest trial lawyer, for introducing me to the Honolulu legal community, in which I was privileged on a few occasions to ply my trade as an attorney. Nevertheless, the judges and attorneys in Chicago and Hawaii, as portrayed in the book, are fictional and not based on actual persons.

I am grateful to my editors, Jennifer Weis, Hilary Rubin Teeman, Stephen Boldt, and the staff at St. Martin's Press for their assistance and wise guidance. I am also grateful to my agent and good friend, Maura Teitelbaum. Thanks, as well, to my close friend Rabbi Victor Weissberg, who took the time to review the manuscript and offer his always-cogent suggestions. Thanks to my readers for their suggestions, among them, Rabbi Sidney Helbraun, Kathy Huck, Katie Lang Lawrence, Kathleen Smith, and Richard Templer. A big thank-you and hug to my son David, a fine editor in his own right, and my son Matt, who prepared the maps, and to each of them for their contributions to the raw manuscript.

And as always, my deepest gratitude to my wife, Monica, for her continuing support and encouragement.

Reading
Group
Gold

SAVING SOPHIE

by Ronald H. Balson

About the Author

- A Conversation with Ronald H. Balson

Behind the Novel

- A Selection of Photographs

Keep on Reading

- Recommended Reading
- Reading Group Questions

A Reading Group Gold Selection

Also available as an audiobook
from Macmillan Audio

For more reading group suggestions
visit www.readinggroupgold.com.

 ST. MARTIN'S GRIFFIN

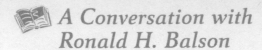
A Conversation with Ronald H. Balson

Could you tell us a little bit about your background, and when you decided that you wanted to lead a literary life?

I can't say there was a date or a time or an event where I made a decision to lead a "literary life." I just added writing books to my nonliterary life. Through the years, writing has always been a central focus for me: I was an editor of my high school and college newspapers. I've been a litigation attorney for over forty years and, of course, in that capacity I've written countless briefs, memoranda, appeals, and arguments. When you get right down to it, it's all really storytelling. I always thought that writing a novel was on my horizon, but I never got around to it, or I never got my mind wrapped around a story that impelled me to get around to it. Finally, opportunity knocked hard nine years ago when my practice took me to Poland on a telecommunications case. Traveling around that country, encountering the remnants and scars of World War II, I was inspired to write a book about a family in wartime Poland, which ultimately became *Once We Were Brothers*. Getting back to "leading a literary life," I concede it's been a shift. I still practice law and go about my routines, except now I get to travel all around the country (world, even) and talk to people who want to engage me in discussions about my books. I confess: It's fun.

Is there a book that most influenced your life? Or inspired you to become a writer?

As I said, I've always been drawn to writing, so I am constantly in awe of authors whose clever imagery and artful deployment of language far exceeds my own, writers such as John Steinbeck and Truman Capote and Ernest Hemingway. And Joan Didion, whose self-description sits on my printer and reads, "I am a writer. Imagining what people would say or do comes to me as naturally as breathing." A statement

> *"Through the years, writing has always been a central focus for me."*

to which I aspire in the humblest of ways. Relative to becoming an author of historical fiction, the captivating wartime novels of Leon Uris and Herman Wouk certainly inspired me. They are craftsmen, whose wonderful characters consumed their readers and thrust them into the World War II milieu. I aspire to their brilliance in the feeblest of ways. Scott Turow, a fellow member of the Illinois bar, is the master of legal dramas, and is a prime example of how to infuse a contemporary legal thriller with intelligent writing.

What was the inspiration for Saving Sophie?

It has so many subplots; I'd have to say that the creative ideas sprung from different sources. A few years ago I was involved in a complex escrow closing in which the funds to purchase the business were almost sent to the wrong bank. It occurred to me that a good mystery could be based on that misdirection. And I once spent six weeks trying a case in Honolulu (which is a far less exotic experience than you might think), where I became familiar with the Hawaiian legal environment. As to the central conflict, the Israeli–Palestinian struggle, my time in Israel and my involvement in several organizations motivated me to set *Saving Sophie* in the middle of that complex conundrum. It seemed to me to be a good opportunity to foment discussions about an impossible situation.

Your last book, Once We Were Brothers, *dealt with a different aspect of the Jewish experience, the atrocities of wartime Poland. Can you talk about how you approached this subject matter of the Israeli conflict?*

The Jewish experience in wartime Poland was dehumanization, slavery, and extermination. Those few that survived the camps were universally staunch Zionists. They wanted to go to Israel. Israel was their rebirth. I think it was a natural transition for me as well to go from submergence in Holocaust research and writing to stories of the Jewish experience in Israel, starting with the country's formation to the present. When you mention the Israeli conflict—and we tend to think of it in present-day terms: the claims of the Palestinians, the West Bank, the settlements, the Green Line, the peace process—we have to keep it in proper perspective. This present-day struggle has been active since the days of the British Mandate, and I think it can be better understood from its historical perspective. That's why I spent considerable time laying the groundwork in *Saving Sophie*.

Do you scrupulously adhere to historical fact in your novels, or do you take liberties if the story can benefit from the change? To what extent did you stick to the facts in writing Saving Sophie?

Scrupulous as possible. I try to present my historical environment as authentically as I can within the confines of a fictional piece. Obviously, the al-Zahani family is entirely a product of my imagination, so they could not have been involved with the Grand Mufti of Jerusalem, Mussolini, or any other figure. But the scenarios that played out around them are accurate. Thus the narrative about the Mufti Amin al-Husseini training and reviewing Bosnian troops for Hitler, for example, is factual. He wasn't accompanied by grandfather Ibrahim, but he was a real figure and just as evil as I described him. The Hebron Massacre of 1929 is, regrettably, factual. The events which occurred during the British Mandate, the creation of the state of Israel, and the Arab–Israeli wars are all well documented. The descriptions of the geographic locales in which the characters play out their roles are based upon my personal observations and described as keenly as I am capable.

Can you take readers into the process of writing this novel? What challenges did you face in terms of plotting and structure, for example?

I do not write from an outline and I don't always know at the beginning what will happen at the end (although I have a pretty good idea). My principle goal is to create strong characters with believable identities. They become real for me, and I can and do communicate with them every day. When I toss them into a devilish situation, I hope they will respond in a way that is true to their character. It may not be the way you or I would respond, but if I've done my job, their personalities will emerge in the crisis. Liam's courageous decision to place himself in the crossfires of the Hebron operation, even though he wasn't an operative or a soldier and had no skin in the game, as they say, and against Catherine's wishes, is the only way his character should respond. Making sense of the Israeli–Palestinian conflict is a challenge that is, to all intents and purposes, insurmountable. I did not try to do that. I just set my story in the midst of embattled passions and let my characters and my readers think what they will.

Do you have a favorite scene from Saving Sophie—*an incident or even dialogue that's especially meaningful to you?*

I have many favorite scenes, some funny, some intense, some reflective. I especially like the scene between Kayla and Liam the night before the al-Zahani exchange. It's a moment of honesty—their guards are down. Secrets are shared. Nothing is hidden. Both are full of doubts, yet neither is hesitant about the assignment. On the humor side, I like the short scene at the airport ice cream shop before the group leaves Honolulu. It's a touch of humor, but bittersweet because it is a point of embarkation and impending danger. I like the scenes in the shop of Jamal Abu Hammad. I wrote those scenes before I shared a cup of tea in a similar antiquities shop in the Via Delarosa with an Arab shop owner who I posited was the real Abu Hammad. I searched to find such a man in the Muslim Quarter to prove to myself that my descriptions of Abu Hammad and his shop were authentic and his personality was believable. And they were. It was indeed a pleasant afternoon.

Is there any material that you wrote that never made it to the final draft? Can you tell us about it?

Oh, yes. Definitely yes. My original manuscript had substantially more historical data—dozens of pages about the history of Israel and the West Bank, pages about Lawrence of Arabia and the Ottoman War, pages about the turmoil during the British occupation, pages about the prelude to the Six Day War and much more detail about the 1948 and 1967 wars. It was all left on the cutting room floor. In truth, it turned out to be too much detail and a distraction from the story. But I'm a historian at heart and I err on the side of inclusion.

Are you currently working on another book?

I'm very proud of my third novel, currently named *Karolina's Twins*. I'm back to the Holocaust. *Karolina's Twins* is inspired by the true story of a beautiful, courageous woman who I met during the *Once We Were Brothers* book tour. She grew up in a small town in western Poland. As a young teen, she hid in her attic when the Nazis broke into her home and grabbed her family. She survived on her own in the ghetto of Nazi-occupied Chrzanow, was sent to the Gross-Rosen slave labor camp, and ultimately escaped from the Auschwitz death march. In the novel, now seventy years later, she hires Catherine Lockhart and Liam Taggart to fulfill her promise to find two little girls lost during the war. *Karolina's Twins* is in its final polishing stage and should be published in 2016.

The following photographs were taken by the author during his visits to the region. Captions are his own.

Palestinian Hebron

The Abraham Avinu Synagogue in H2 Hebron, where Liam and Kayla meet their Mossad contact.

The Hebron Memorial for Shalhevet Pass, the baby murdered by a sniper during the Intifada.

The Tomb of the Patriarchs, where the bride is murdered.

*This is a scene which I found quite disturbing
but emblematic of life in violent Hebron. It depicts a
family outing to the Ma'arat HaMachpelah, the Tomb
of the Patriarchs—the mother, father, and three young
children out for the day visiting a holy shrine—and
conspicuously strapped on the father's back is his
TAR-21 automatic assault weapon, carried much
as you or I might take along an umbrella.*

Jerusalem

The antiquities shopkeeper and me
at his shop in the Via Dolorosa.
(Photo taken by my wife.)

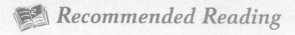 ## Recommended Reading

For more information about the subject matter and related themes addressed in *Saving Sophie*, the author suggests the following books for further reading.

The Prime Ministers
Yehuda Avner

My Promised Land
Ari Shavit

A History of the Israeli-Palestinian Conflict
Mark Tessler

Battleground
Samuel Katz

Myths and Facts: A Guide to the Arab-Israeli Conflict
Mitchell G. Bard

History of the Jews
Paul Johnson

Hebron Jews: Memory and Conflict in the Land of Israel
Jerold S. Auerbach

Reading Group Questions

1. How did Jack confront the conflict between his legal and moral principles and his desperate need to rescue his daughter? Was Jack too quick to trust people? Was that his character flaw?

2. Having washed his hands of Alina, why was al-Zahani so possessive of Sophie, the child of the union he despised?

3. Do you fault Jack for overruling the judge and giving the al-Zahanis liberal visitation? Would you have done the same?

4. What do you think would have become of Sophie had she not been rescued?

5. How did Arif al-Zahani perceive and process Sophie's exclusion from Jamila's playgroup?

6. What do you think drove Liam and Catherine to suspect a lack of commitment? Do you think there was a moment of indecisiveness?

7. Given the history of the region and how many times the land has changed hands, what is your feeling about al-Zahani and his group's claims for exclusive possession of the country as "Sons of Canaan"?

8. Do you think at the critical moment that al-Zahani was prepared to sacrifice Sophie?

9. How does the prospect of fame and wealth of a professional basketball career create a surreal world of impossible expectations for young athletes? Are you critical of Violet McCord?

10. What would you do with a child who shows gifted talents? Does the lure of success encourage parental exploitation?